"From its delicious title to an intriguing plot involving spies and secret codes in 19th-century England, *The Debutante's Code* kicks off Erica Vetsch's new Thorndike & Swann Regency Mysteries with action, humor, and the promise of romance."
—Julie Klassen, author of *Shadows of Swanford Abbey*

"Intrigue abounds in this thrilling tale of a debutante turned spy. Amidst the whirl of stolen art pieces and murder, heroine Juliette Thorndike takes on a dangerous role to break a code before the villains discover it . . . and before the swoon-worthy Officer Daniel Swann figures out she's involved. Author Erica Vetsch once again pens a winner in *The Debutante's Code* . . . a must-read for Regency and mystery lovers!"
—Michelle Griep, Christy Award–winning author of *Once Upon a Dickens Christmas*

"Erica Vetsch has done it again, bringing the reader an exciting Regency historical romance, but this time with the twist of a delicious mystery. *The Debutante's Code* is completely entertaining, with the promise of more delights to come in the rest of the Thorndike & Swann series."
—Jan Drexler, award-winning author of *Softly Blows the Bugle*

"A mystery within a mystery within a mystery. Inventive!"
—Regina Scott, award-winning author

"A compelling, enchanting work of art filled with wit, danger, and clever plot twists, *The Debutante's Code* kept me turning pages well into the night. A cast of richly sculpted characters, an expertly woven tapestry of mystery and intrigue, and beautifully drawn spiritual truths set against the glittering backdrop of Regency England combine to make Erica Vetsch's latest creation a true masterpiece."
—Amanda Wen, author of *Roots of Wood and Stone*

"I am a big Regency romance fan, and I love what Erica Vetsch brings to this genre. The suspense on top of the lords and ladies is just excellent fun. And this one, *The Debutante's Code*, is the best so far. Absolutely impossible to put down once I started."
—Mary Connealy, best-selling author of *The Accidental Guardian* and the High Sierra Sweethearts series

"Erica Vetsch delivers a fast-paced and utterly riveting read set against the elegance and intrigue of Regency high society, destined to captivate longtime fans and capture the hearts of new readers. I'm eagerly antici-pating Lady Juliette Thorndike and Daniel Swann's next adventure."
—Amanda Barratt, author of *My Dearest Dietrich* and *The White Rose Resists*

"*The Debutante's Code* is a delightful and fast-paced visit to the under-cover world of espionage in Regency England. Vetsch offers all that we love about her writing in this twisting story: historical details, compel-ling characters, and an intriguing plot. This is the first in a fascinat-ing new series, and I did not want it to end! I'm thrilled to know we will continue this journey with Lady Juliette Thorndike and Detective Daniel Swann in the next installment."
—Gabrielle Meyer, author of *When the Day Comes*

"The Sanditon and Bridgerton–loving crowd will fall hard for this delight-ful heroine and dashing hero and the ease with which they appropriate the London *ton* on their pursuit of growing attraction and twisting and turning adventure. I look forward to many more installments in this exciting new series. Erica Vetsch is at the top of her game!"
—Rachel McMillan, author of *The London Restoration* and *The Mozart Code*

The
Debutante's
Code

THORNDIKE & SWANN

REGENCY MYSTERIES

The

Debutante's Code

ERICA VETSCH

KREGEL
PUBLICATIONS

Published by Kregel Publications, a division of Kregel Inc., 2450 Oak Industrial Dr. NE, Grand Rapids, MI 49505.

Published in association with the Books & Such Literary Management, 52 Mission Circle, Suite 122, PMB 170, Santa Rosa, CA 95409-5370, www.booksandsuch.com.

Library of Congress Cataloging-in-Publication Data
Names: Vetsch, Erica, author.
Title: The debutante's code / Erica Vetsch.
Description: Grand Rapids, MI : Kregel Publications, [2021] | Series: Thorndike & Swann regency mysteries ; vol 1
Identifiers: LCCN 2021005530 (print) | LCCN 2021005531 (ebook) | ISBN 9780825447136 (paperback) | ISBN 9780825477607 (epub) | ISBN 9780825469138 (kindle edition)
Subjects: GSAFD: Mystery fiction.
Classification: LCC PS3622.E886 D43 2021 (print) | LCC PS3622.E886 (ebook) | DDC 813/.6--dc23
LC record available at https://lccn.loc.gov/2021005530
LC ebook record available at https://lccn.loc.gov/2021005531

ISBN 978-0-8254-4713-6, print
ISBN 978-0-8254-7760-7, epub

Printed in the United States of America
21 22 23 24 25 26 27 28 29 30 / 5 4 3 2 1

For my friend Mary Connealy.
Even though we're both in the word business,
I find words inadequate to express what our
friendship means to me. Thank you for everything.

And to Peter, as always,
with much love.

Chapter 1

"IF YOU LEAN OUT ANY farther, you'll wind up in the drink. Which, I suppose, would be a fitting end to this disaster of a trip." Lady Juliette Thorndike ducked her chin and turned away from the fresh breeze, the deck rocking gently under her feet. Her heart pounded beneath her woolen cloak as she reached the end of one journey and anticipated embarking on a wholly new one.

"I just want to be there. The last twenty yards is taking longer than the entire voyage." As always when in high emotion, Agatha Montgomery, Juliette's best friend, used her adept skills in hyperbole. She leaned over the taffrail of the *Adventuress* as the ship eased into its berth, and her wide green eyes bounced from the wharf to the cranes to the warehouses. "I cannot believe we made it. I never want to endure a journey like this again."

Nor did Juliette. Their trip from Switzerland to London had been fraught with delays and discomforts, putting them a fortnight behind their expected arrival date.

But now they were moments from stepping on their native heath. Her beloved England. She was finally home. Searching the quayside, she hoped to see a familiar face, but though people thronged the wharf, all were strangers. Not that she was completely *au fait* with the family she hoped would meet her, having been away from home for so long. She had completed her schooling and would within the hour be back in the embrace of her parents, ready to begin her new life.

Men shouted, flinging ropes across the narrowing expanse of water, and with a jolting bump, the *Adventuress* docked. Juliette inhaled the scents of tar, hemp, wet wood, and smoke. The rigging creaked, and waves lapped against the pilings. Cold mist hung in the air, remnants of last night's fog, no doubt. But the sun, weak as it was on this last day of January, hovered overhead as if determined to burn off the dampness.

"Ladies, the gangway will be fixed soon, and your belongings will be the first off, as I promised." The captain, a desiccated stick of a man with so many creases on his sea-weathered face it was difficult to make out his features, paused on his way forward. "If you'll remain here out of the way, we'll see you off right smart." He touched his hat brim and sketched a small bow. .

The *Adventuress* was a cargo ship, ill equipped for passengers, but the captain had made an exception for them in Genoa when they'd discovered their original vessel had sailed without them. The first mate had vacated his tiny cabin—albeit with poor grace—to accommodate the girls. Juliette had joked that the berth was so small, they had to go out into the corridor to change their minds.

"You do think someone will be here to greet us, don't you? Even though we're late and on the wrong ship?" Agatha's brow puckered. She'd voiced the same concern throughout the journey.

"If no one is there to meet us, we'll get ourselves home. We're grown women now and certainly capable of getting from one side of London to the other." Juliette raised her chin. "If we can live in a foreign country for years and travel alone from Switzerland to England, we can navigate the last short stretch." Weariness dragged at her heart. It seemed she had been on her own for such a long time. She longed to be in the care of someone else for a while, to have her parents there to look after her, to help guide her in decision-making, to give her the feeling of home and comfort she had missed since the moment she'd left Heild House, their country estate in Worcestershire, for school seven long years ago.

"But we're not *supposed* to be traveling on our own. That's the problem. Our chaperone abandoning us partway to the port was a near disaster. What my father will say, I'm sure I don't know. He paid good money for an escort, and look what happened." Agatha's mouth tightened, as it often did when speaking of her father. From her description he was a man of moods and given to expressing them boldly. His rare letters to his daughter over the years had been terse and more often than not dictated to his secretary at one of the mills he owned.

"He cannot blame either of us, and if he's thinking at all, he should applaud our independence and bravery. Frau Hecht was not a good choice of chaperone, and I'm sure our parents will communicate their displeasure to the academy." Frau Hecht and the three men hired to take the girls to the port city of Genoa and aboard the correct ship had been in league with one another. They had taken their fees and money for traveling expenses and then abandoned their charges in the city of Turin, forcing the girls to find their own way from there.

"Ladies." The first mate, who always spoke as if clenching a mouthful of nails in his teeth, stuck out his arm, stiff as a spar, pointing to the gangway. There had been quite a set-to when the captain had agreed to take them on as passengers, led by the first mate. Something about women on a ship being bad luck? Tosh and twaddle. Juliette would be glad to see the back of him.

Holding her skirt with one hand and anchoring her hat with the other, Juliette made her way down the wooden slope that had no rails, her mouth in her throat until her feet touched the rimed cobbles of the wharf.

The sense of peace she had anticipated didn't come. Instead, the anxiety that had dogged her every mile of the journey remained. There were still so many questions, so much to do until she could feel settled at home. Her parents had expected her to arrive a fortnight ago. They couldn't know of all the troubles that had waylaid the girls. Had her parents come to the dock day after day hoping for her arrival, or had they dispatched someone to look for her?

Agatha bumped into Juliette's back. "Your pardon. The stones are slippery." She righted her bonnet. Lean and coltish, Agatha stood six inches taller than Juliette, and she constantly hunched her shoulders, keeping her head bowed in an effort to disguise her height. "Do you see anyone we know?"

Stevedores, teamsters, and sailors abounded. Bales, barrels, and bundles blocked anyone from walking in a straight path. "No."

"What should we do?" Agatha clutched Juliette's arm.

What indeed? Juliette had talked a good yarn about getting themselves across London, but how did one go about it? "We can inquire at the shipping office, I suppose. To see if our families have sent word or instructions."

Which only left the small issue of finding the headquarters for the ship they had been scheduled to travel upon but which had left them behind when they didn't arrive on time.

Before she could take a step, a long hand snaked out of the jostling crowd and latched onto her wrist. Startled, she jerked back, bundling into Agatha, who shrieked. Heads swiveled and bodies jostled, and Juliette whacked down on the clutching hand with an instinctive chop.

"Stop it, child." A man eeled between a pair of brawny stevedores, shaking his limp hand and scowling. "Don't you know your own uncle?"

She froze. "Uncle Bertie?" A flash of recognition from somewhere in her memory gave her pause. Of him laughing with her father, their profiles so similar.

"None other. How fortuitous to find you in this crush. I had business at the docks today." He smoothed the many capes on his cloak. Stepping back, he assessed the growing pile of baggage being offloaded from the *Adventuress*. "I assume these are your belongings? I'll have to see about hiring a luggage wagon. This will never fit in my coach."

"Of course." He had been at the docks for some other purpose? "Did Mother and Father come?"

"No, not today. Come along. I've wrung every bit of charm out of the dockyards over the past few days. I'm bored with the place." He flipped his hand and shrugged. "So much work going on all the time. I find it tedious. No, I must tell you about your parents, but . . ." His gaze flicked to Agatha, who hovered behind Juliette, and he raised his brows. "A friend?"

He spoke like the dilettante Juliette had suspected he'd become, from reading her parents' letters.

"Perhaps an introduction is in order, Juliette?" Agatha tried to sound polished, but her voice cracked.

"I'm sorry. Agatha, this is my uncle, Sir Bertrand Thorndike, my father's younger brother. Uncle Bertie, this is Miss Agatha Montgomery. We can take her to her home, can we not? To Belgravia?"

"Yes, yes, child. But hurry along. It's infernally cold, and this damp is wilting my cravat." He touched the brim of his tall hat to Agatha, offered his arm to her, and then the other to Juliette. "The coach is just beyond this warehouse. I couldn't get any closer, what with so many ships arriving today and all the bustle."

"Were Mother and Father very worried when we didn't arrive when expected?" Juliette held tight to his firm upper arm. Had he always been so fit? Her childhood memories of Uncle Bertie were of him coming and going and laughing. He gusted in at the family estate like a nor'easter, plied her with sweets, had once gifted her a puppy that proved to be endless trouble, only to sweep out again on adventures of his own. He never stayed longer than a few days, and no one seemed to know when he'd pop up again.

She knew he'd served in the army and was considered most eligible. He had been knighted by the Prince Regent some years ago, and he had an income from the family estate. His clothes were always fashionable and meticulous, and his manners precise. Beyond that, she didn't know what he did to fill his time or what interested him. He was a bit of a cipher.

"We'll get into all that later." He moved swiftly, and the crowds parted before him. "There's no time now. Things will be compressed because of the tardiness of your arrival. The house is in a bit of a dither. Your debut at court is tomorrow. If you hadn't shown up in time, it would have been embarrassing to have to inform the Queen you wouldn't be attending." A touch of censure brushed his voice.

A prickle of apprehension flickered across Juliette's skin. Court tomorrow. Making her curtsy before the Queen. Embarking upon her Season as a debutante. In less than twenty-four hours.

A footman opened the carriage door, and Uncle Bertie handed first Juliette and then Agatha inside. He swung aboard, graceful and lithe, and settled against the squabs opposite the girls. With the head of his cane, he tapped on the ceiling, and the coach lurched into motion.

Juliette grabbed the windowsill to steady herself. "After so many days at sea, it seems strange to be on land. I feel as if I don't know whether I'm coming or going."

"What did happen to delay you? We were beginning to worry."

Again she had that sense that she had inconvenienced him. She shook her head and raised her hands, palms up. "If there was a possibility of something going wrong, it seemed to, from the moment we set out from the school. Terrible weather, a flood that took out a bridge, forcing us to add two days to our journey as we went downstream to the next crossing. A lame horse. And then the chaperone the school hired absconded before we arrived in Genoa. By the time we arrived at the port, our ship was gone, and we had to find another transport. Captain Prussel was finally persuaded, with a liberal application of pounds sterling, to accommodate us, though his ship was not equipped for passengers."

Uncle Bertie stared out the window, extreme ennui smoothing his features. Did he not care about their troubles? Or did he think her story an exaggeration?

"When you didn't arrive on the correct ship, I had to make enquiries into what vessels were expected from Italy. I watched as ship after ship came in, and I wasn't alone. There was talk up and down the wharf that the *Adventuress* was nearly a week overdue. Were you delayed leaving Genoa, or was there trouble once you put to sea?" He flicked a bit of lint off his sleeve and shot his cuffs.

"There was a flap at the port. I thought it was something to do with the loading of cargo, but it was more sinister. The local magistrates, or whatever they call them in Italy, searched the *Adventuress*, made all of us vouch for our identities—though how they could verify who the crewmembers were, I don't know—and delayed us further. The captain finally told us someone had been killed in the town, and they thought the culprit could be attempting to flee aboard ship. We never did hear more details, because the moment the authorities allowed us to set sail, Captain Prussel weighed anchor."

Bertie's brows rose, and his dark eyes swiveled her way. "A murder? That's most unsavory. Hardly something your parents would want you involved with, even tangentially. I would suggest you not mention it in polite company."

"We can hardly be blamed or considered to be 'involved' with a murder. We were innocent bystanders. The authorities searched the ship, found nothing, and went on to the next. Once we finally put to sea, I thought it would be a quick trip around Gibraltar and then home, but we managed to encounter both a storm which blew us off course and a lack of breeze with which to fill the sails, one on the heels of the other." Puffing out a breath, she collapsed against the buttoned upholstery. "I feel I've aged a decade in the last month. I don't know what I would have done without Agatha for company. I'd most likely still be stranded in Turin, awaiting rescue."

Agatha fidgeted with the strings on her reticule. "I hardly contributed to our onward movements. That was all you and your determination to get home. I was the one you had to encourage and convince that we could go on." She turned her attention to Bertie. "Sir Bertrand, have you heard from my father? Was he very upset at our tardiness?"

Bertie spread his hands. "I understand he's most eager to see you, Miss Montgomery. The preparations for your dual debut were running apace the last I heard." He shrugged. "I know nothing about debutantes and entertaining, at least not from the perspective of a host though I've much practice being a guest. This process has been both exhausting and revelatory. I can only hope God spares me the need to ever bring a daughter out in society. Perhaps, if I should marry, He would bless me with only sons."

The carriage bundled along, and Juliette wanted to press her nose against the glass to catch glimpses of everything as they flashed by. London. England. At last she was home.

Though she wouldn't really be home until she was in her parents' arms. Every minute she had been away she had longed for them, and every delay on the journey home had chafed her homesick heart.

Seven years was far too long. When she had been sent away to school in Lucerne, she had never envisioned it would be such a stretch before she could come home. Her parents had decided that with the war raging in the Peninsula, she was far safer in the mountain stronghold of Switzerland than traveling home for the summer months. But with Napoleon finally defeated and exiled, and her last term completed, she was free.

They deposited Agatha at her father's Mayfair townhouse, and she hurried up the steps, stopping at the top to turn back and wave at Juliette. "I'll see you tomorrow." Her eyes looked enormous, and her lips trembled. The black lacquered door opened, and she hurried inside.

Bertie pinched the bridge of his nose as the carriage took off again for the short ride to Belgrave Square and the Thorndike residence. "Juliette, I have to tell you something, and I don't want histrionics of any kind. It's something you will not like, and I wish it was not my responsibility to tell you, but there it is. Tristan and Melisande charged me with the duty, and I will not shirk it."

Juliette frowned. "I am not given to histrionics, Uncle Bertie." Did he think her some spoiled miss who fainted onto the nearest couch at the hint of anything unpleasant? On the heels of her umbrage, her mind raced at notions of what her parents might have asked Bertie to say to her.

"You may be when I tell you that your parents are not in London. They were called away to the estate on urgent business." He dropped his hand and regarded her with his dark eyes. "They left yesterday and are uncertain as to the date of their return."

His pronouncement was a blow to her chest. "Not in London? But . . ." What urgent business could possibly be more important than being home when their daughter arrived after such a long time away? "Are we going on to Pensax then? What about the audience with the Queen?"

"You are to stay here, under my care, until they return. You will make your debut, attend the parties your mother has accepted invitations for on your behalf, and await their return."

He looked as frustrated with the situation as she felt.

"What has happened at Heild that would trump their being here?"

Bertie shrugged. "Something to do with the house? Or the fields? Or perhaps the staff? I don't know. All of that responsibility belongs to Tristan. He gets the title, he gets the hard work."

She turned away from his disinterested expression to look out the window, struggling with the same sense of abandonment she'd wrestled with for the last seven years. Here she had been anticipating a joyous reunion, eager to deepen her relationship with the parents she knew so little of, while they had seen nothing amiss in leaving on the eve of her presentation, a mere forty-eight hours before her debut ball, with no notion of when they would return?

It was almost as if her parents didn't want her.

***

The butler opened the door as Juliette came up the steps. She forced a smile. She'd known Mr. Pultney since she was a little girl. He had been her father's valet for years and then received promotion to butler while Juliette was away at school. With silver-tinged temples, blue eyes that missed nothing, and a friendly-but-not-too-friendly-for-a-butler way about him, he had been a favorite with Juliette.

He bowed. "Welcome home, Lady Juliette. May I take your wraps?"

Bertie closed the door and unhooked the closure on his cape. "Have our guests arrived, Pultney?"

"Yes, Sir Bertrand. Their Graces are in the drawing room." The butler took their cloaks. "I have served them tea, but shall I bring a new pot for you and Lady Juliette?" He phrased his intentions as a question, as he was wont to do, and Bertie nodded.

Juliette paused in untying her bonnet ribbons. "Guests?" Though she was perishing for a cup of tea, the last thing she wanted was to greet guests. Her world had been in upheaval for weeks, and now, when she should be welcomed into the bosom of her family, they had absconded to the countryside without a backward glance. She needed time to assess this change and come to terms with it.

"I'm afraid so. Your mother's departure has put us on the spot, as it were, and I called in reinforcements." Bertie checked his reflection in the mirror beside the door and smoothed his hair where his hat had mussed it. "Come along. I don't want to keep them waiting any longer. I'm only glad you arrived when you did, because otherwise they would have visited for nothing."

Juliette followed him into the drawing room, noting at first that the entire space had been redecorated. A trivial thought, but it gave her a heart pang. Did the décor reflect her mother's taste and preferences? If her parents had bothered to be here, she could ask.

A tall, handsome man rose from his chair, a half smile on his pleasant features. He wore his hair long, clubbed back in a queue at the nape of his neck, and the style, though out of fashion, suited him.

An older woman in a lace cap, with gray curls clustered about her temples, remained seated opposite him. Her sharp eyes took in Juliette, and Juliette stopped, aware of her travel garments and less-than-fresh appearance. The older woman was clad in black from her cap to her slippers. Was this a fashion decision like the man's hair, or was she in deep mourning?

Bertie nudged Juliette ahead. "Good afternoon, Your Grace. May I present my niece, Lady Juliette Thorndike? Juliette, this is His Grace, the Duke of Haverly, and the duke's mother, Her Grace, the dowager duchess."

A duke. In the drawing room. Her debut season was certainly setting off with a bang. She curtsied. "Your Grace. It's a pleasure to meet you."

"You've informed her?" the duke asked Bertie. He bent to set his empty teacup on a tray, next to a plate with two remaining biscuits on it.

"I have. She now knows that her parents have been called away to the country unexpectedly to deal with a situation at their estate."

Something in Bertie's tone caught Juliette's attention, and she witnessed a long look between him and the duke. Puzzled by an undercurrent she couldn't fathom, she twisted the gold and garnet ring on her right hand. A gift from her parents on her thirteenth birthday, the ring never came off her finger. Family legend had it that the gold had come from a Roman mine in Wales and that the ring itself was more than a thousand years old. It had passed down through her mother's family for generations, and Juliette prized it, not only because it had been a gift but because it anchored her, gave her a feeling of family and permanence, of tradition and the desire to carry those traditions forward.

"Yes, yes, we know all that." The dowager harrumphed, setting her own cup down. "We must get to the germane issue. Lady Juliette . . . Oh, do stop hovering there and sit down properly." She flapped her hand.

Juliette plopped into the nearest chair in a most unladylike manner. *Compose yourself, girl.* She arranged her skirts and folded her hands in her lap, keeping her back straight, trying to remember the countless deportment lessons she'd had. *Get this visit completed so you can run to your room and begin to sort yourself out.*

Bertie took a seat, leaning back, as if completely comfortable in spite of the dowager's curt tone.

Pultney entered with a tray and set it before Lady Juliette. Tea, a plate of tiny cakes, and some biscuits. Fresh cups for everyone. The butler took the used tray with him, unobtrusive and professional, just as Juliette remembered him to be.

She picked up the teapot and raised her brows in the dowager's direction. The dowager and the duke both shook their heads, but

Bertie nodded. She handed him a steaming, fragrant cup and poured for herself. The hot tea warmed her, and she realized how chilled she had been aboard the ship, in the carriage, and from the inside when Bertie had told her of her parents' priorities.

"Now, in your mother's absence, Lady Juliette, I will be serving as your chaperone and your sponsor tomorrow at court." The dowager nodded, as if completely satisfied with her ability and qualifications for the office, and as if Juliette could have no quibble herself. "I understand your court gown is ready and that you've had some instruction in the proper etiquette for one of the Queen's drawing room sessions?"

"Yes, Your Grace." The words came out tightly around the constriction in her throat. This was all wrong. This should be her mother giving gentle guidance and with happy anticipation. The dowager looked as if she were a sergeant addressing a raw recruit.

"Very good. We will get along very well if you only do exactly as I say. Good manners, little speaking, and a well-presented appearance will take you far this Season. You are pleasant featured, and your pedigree is impeccable. Yes, I can definitely work with this." She gave Juliette a raking look from toes to hairline, as if totting up her debits and credits. "Once I've brought you out at court, we can move on to the debut ball. I understand it is to be at the Montgomery house and held in conjunction with the debut of . . ." She looked to the duke and beckoned him to fill in the missing name.

"Miss Agatha Montgomery." The duke had resumed his seat, and most casually he'd crossed his legs. His booted foot swung ever so slightly, the white tassel on the front of his Hessian sliding in rhythm. He appeared to take his mother's forceful manner in stride.

"That's right. I'm to take her under my wing, as it were, too. When we leave here, we'll stop by her home for the introductions and for me to assess the situation."

Poor Agatha. Barely home a minute and a dragon comes breathing fire through the door.

"Your help is most appreciated." Bertie inclined his head. "I don't know the first thing about bringing out a debutante, and Melisande's departure left us as sixes and sevens. Thank you for answering my distress signal."

"I'm looking forward to the experience. My daughter, the Countess of Rothwell, managed to do me out of the experience of her debut season by marrying without the honor of being 'brought out.' This will, I'm sure, be a pleasure. I'm glad you thought to ask me to fill in. It shows good judgment on your part." A cat with cream on its whiskers couldn't look more satisfied.

"The debut ball is being handled by Montgomery's staff for the most part, I believe, and Tristan and Melisande engaged someone to be Lady Juliette's first dance partner. After the debut, you'll have to coordinate with my brother's secretary as to which invitations were accepted and where you will be needed."

"Of course. We'll liaise." The dowager sounded supremely confident.

Juliette felt too unnecessary for her own liking. It had been one thing when it was her mother accepting invitations on her behalf and planning the beginning of Juliette's debut season, but when it was her uncle and a stranger discussing and organizing her activities without even consulting her, her hackles rose.

The duke turned his attention her way and rose. "I believe we should make our departure, Mother. Lady Juliette has traveled a long way and must be tired. We've other calls to make, and I promised Charlotte I would be home in time to visit the nursery and help with the teatime rituals with the boys."

"Of course. We shall see you, Lady Juliette, at St. James's Palace on the morrow. Whatever you do, do not be late. I'll meet you in the anteroom and give you final instructions before you are presented." The dowager rose to her feet, and Juliette and Bertie did as well.

Pultney met them at the door, and a footman stood nearby with the duke's and dowager's garments. With a practiced swirl, the duke donned his cloak, and as he tugged on his gloves, he frowned at Bertie. "I can't say I'm happy with the way you've decided to approach this challenge, but for now, I will go along with it. I still think you're underestimating her."

Juliette's interest was momentarily piqued, but she was too tired and dispirited to inquire as to whether they were speaking of her.

The dowager, ignoring her son, allowed Pultney to settle her fur-lined cape on her rounded shoulders. "As I said, Lady Juliette, if you will follow my instructions to the letter, you will be a triumph this Season. I know it's only temporary, until your mother returns, but we'll make a good fist of it. You are surely disappointed that obligation has called your parents away, but my dear, that's what being a member of the nobility means. You must do your duty when duty calls, no matter the sacrifice." She put on her gloves and raised the hood on her cape to cover her lace cap. The black of her attire suited her, highlighting the silver in her hair and the faded blue of her eyes.

Duty. It was a lesson often covered in the curriculum at the academy. Duty to one's parents, duty to one's class, duty to one's lineage. Obey your elders. Marry well. Carry on the name of the family you would marry into.

What about duty to one's children? What about making them feel loved and secure and an important part of your life? Or is it the right and just thing to shuttle your children out of your way so that they cannot even recall the timbre of your voice?

Was she wrong to want more? To desire a rich, meaningful relationship with her parents, beyond letters?

It seemed for now she would have to continue to hope that eventually their reunion would be all she envisioned.

Montgomery Residence in Belgravia, London
February 2, 1816

"If I make a cake of myself during the debut dance, I will absolutely perish with embarrassment. Please bury me in the family plot, and have lots of flowers." Agatha put her hand to her forehead.

"Aren't you being a teensy bit dramatic?" Juliette asked. "You should audition for a role in a theater production." The buzz of voices drifted up the staircase from the grand foyer of the Montgomery townhouse, guests who awaited the arrival of the debutants before the party could truly begin.

Agatha shook her head, eyes round and face paler than usual as she stared fixedly at the far wall. "Do you not realize we are standing on the precipice of the rest of our lives?" Agatha fidgeted with the ribbon at her rounded neckline. "Everything will change forever over the next few weeks, and we'll never be the same. Everything hinges on what happens tonight."

"Surely not *everything*?" Juliette kept her tone light, though she felt as if she were garbed in lead sheets rather than a gossamer debut gown. Nothing was going according to her plans. There had been no word from her parents, not even a note apologizing for their absence. "We're meant to enjoy ourselves at our debut. You look as if you're headed to the gallows." *If someone slammed a door right now, you'd go straight up into the air.*

Juliette rested a hand on her friend's delicate shoulder.

Agatha jerked at the contact, her wide gaze clashing with Juliette's. "What?"

"Never mind. Are we going to stay up here all night, or should we think about going downstairs? The dowager will be after us if we don't appear soon."

"The dowager." Agatha groaned. "She took one look at me and I know her first thought was that I've the figure of a flagpole, and I'm nearly as tall. She couldn't stop staring at my red hair as if it was a puzzle she'd have to solve."

"Did she actually say anything rude?" Juliette's outrage gathered.

"No, but she didn't say anything flattering either. Between her and my father, it's as if neither knows exactly what to do with me." Unhappiness painted Agatha's face. "But then, that's been the case with my father since my mother died. He wants to be kind, but he has no notion of how to go about it."

"Then they're both lacking in common sense and imagination."

Juliette looped her arm through Agatha's. If she focused on her friend's distress, she could quell her own. "You look lovely, just as you always do. We're going downstairs, and we're going to make a wonderful first impression on our guests. They'll be so enamored of us, they won't be able to talk about anything else for the rest of the night."

"I wish our journey hadn't been delayed. And that your parents could be here. This all feels so rushed." Agatha paused. "I really am sorry they had to leave so quickly."

Juliette nodded, swallowing against the lump that wanted to lodge in her throat. "They have no timetable for their return, so it's best not to delay or back out of the invitations we've sent and accepted. To quote Shakespeare, 'If it were done when 'tis done, then 'twere well it were done quickly.'" After all, if her parents didn't care to be at her debut, then she shouldn't care that they weren't there, right?

"Wasn't that in reference to regicide?" Agatha sent her a skeptical look. "Our debut ball might be fraught with nerves and portent, but I don't think it's that bad."

Juliette nodded. "Quite right. Therefore, we should march downstairs and captivate with our wit and charm and stop dithering here on the landing like lost sheep."

Descending the stairs, her enthusiasm hovered near the floor. They were supposed to meet the dowager and Mr. Montgomery to be introduced to the guests and receive their well-wishes. To smile and greet people and pretend an excitement she now no longer felt. But she would do it because of . . . duty.

Agatha bit her lip. "I'm just glad our presentations to the Queen are over. You don't know how many nightmares I had of falling on my face when I made my curtsy or tripping over my train and landing on my"—she lowered her voice—"posterior . . . as I backed away." She reached the last stair but continued to clutch the newel post as if she would float into the sky if she lost contact with the ornate wooden sphere.

Mr. Montgomery, a towering man even beside his tall daughter, strode over. "There you are, my girl. 'Bout time you stopped primping upstairs and made your appearance. We can't start the party without you, you know. Why is it that women are always late for the very thing they've been anticipating most?"

To soften his chiding, he patted her shoulder, but with enough force to make her lurch forward.

"Lady Juliette. You look most fetching. The pair of you will be turning heads and stirring up the young bucks here tonight, eh?" His voice boomed in the atrium, bouncing off the marble floor and ricocheting off the high ceiling. Guests who were still arriving paused to catch a glimpse of the debutantes.

"Thank you, Mr. Montgomery. I am sorry we're behind our time. It's my fault. Agatha was helping me with my hair." Juliette touched the white bandeau holding her brown curls. "Have you seen my uncle Bertie?" She stood on tiptoe, looking over the crowd that was growing by the minute.

Mr. Montgomery frowned. "I fear he has been a bit in his cups already this evening. My butler was dealing with him, but I suggested he find Sir Bertrand's carriage and return him to his home."

Agatha touched Juliette's arm, her brows pinched and her eyes clouded. "Oh no."

"He's drunk?" At her debut ball? Before the ball even began? Heat raced into her cheeks.

"I am sorry, my dear, but lately your uncle has been hitting the liquor cabinet quite strongly. It's a shame, really, on what was supposed to be your special night. I tried to get him out of the house quietly, but he made a bit of a scene on the front steps, and I'm afraid several of our guests saw it." Mr. Montgomery's moustache twitched, his mouth set at an annoyed angle. "Has he always been like this?"

Juliette had no idea. Uncle Bertie had always been such fun, so dashing, first in his military uniform and then, according to her parents' letters, practically rivaling Beau Brummell in popularity and sartorial elegance. He'd been one of the most sought-after bachelors in the city, despite the fact that as a second son, he had no title beyond his knighthood. But she had been a child the last time she'd spent any time with him, and her parents would have hidden a drinking problem from her at such a tender age.

"Let's find your chaperone, shall we? It's high time you two ladies were introduced properly into society." Mr. Montgomery offered his arms. "Wouldn't surprise me a bit if I wasn't entertaining offers for you, Agatha darling, by morning, and you, Lady Juliette, will no doubt be deluged in tomorrow's post with posies, poems, chocolates, and invitations to trot along Rotten Row in some swain's carriage."

Juliette had no desire for such things herself, at least not yet, but she hoped it was true where Agatha was concerned. Her friend fretted about being ignored, or worse singled out for petty amusement, because of her height, her red hair, her angular features. But her greatest fear was that someone would marry her for her considerable inheritance rather than for herself.

Juliette only prayed that the young men of the *ton* would realize what a beautiful heart Agatha had, generous, loyal, sweet. And she had luminous skin, bright eyes, and a quick smile. Perhaps not conventionally pretty, but lovely all the same if anyone cared to look.

Somehow, Juliette had always felt rather plain and nondescript in comparison to her vibrant friend, who, when not overcome by anxiety, was vivacious and good fun. But Juliette's West Wales heritage gave her brown eyes and brown hair and skin that tended to tan in even the slightest bit of sunshine. Juliette had never been teased for her looks, but she'd never been praised either. Her complexion was a trial and a blessing. She loved riding and boating and archery and most every outdoor activity, and she never sunburned. Current fashion said a woman's complexion should be pale with just a hint of rose at the cheeks. Some women even went so far as to take tiny amounts of arsenic in order to keep their skin milk-white, which seemed ludicrous, not to mention dangerous.

Frankly it had only been in the last year or so that her features had homogenized into something more pleasant and adult looking than her awkward, adolescent self, and she had gained more confidence in social situations. Pray that held true for this evening.

Mr. Montgomery led them through the throng toward the ball-room, which took up most of the back of the house on the first floor. A small orchestra played a lively tune, and guests mingled and talked above the music. Greenery decorated the tables, and tall vases of flow-ers must have cost the earth and depleted greenhouses across the city.

"I see the dowager is beckoning. Are you girls ready?" Mr. Mont-gomery waved to the black-clad woman. "It's time to meet your fate." He grinned.

Mouth dry, Juliette nodded. She had looked forward to this day, the day of her debut, but more than being introduced into society, she had longed to be reunited with her parents. With them not here, and her uncle sent home in disgrace, the evening felt as flat as the dance floor. Yet she must pretend to enjoy herself, for the sake of her guests and the Montgomerys.

"You look very nice, girls." The dowager raised her lorgnette and studied them. "Very appropriate." Her appraisal halted on Juliette's ring. "Debutantes are not to wear jewelry. Give it to me for safekeep-ing." She let the lorgnette drop on the ribbon pinned to her collar and held out her hand.

Juliette covered the ring she wore atop her white gloves. "No, thank you. I will keep it. It was a gift from my parents, and I never take it off."

"But it is not the done thing, child. I do know best." The dowager flapped her hand again.

"Oh, let the girl keep her token. It's a little thing, and no use strain-ing at a gnat, and all that. Let's line up, shall we?" Mr. Montgomery ushered them into a row, but the dowager humphed.

"I'm certain your mother would not want you wearing that at your debut," she said from the side of her mouth, which was a feat, consid-ering how pinched it was.

"I have no idea what my mother would want, since she isn't here." Juliette offered her hand to the guests Mr. Montgomery presented to her. The niggle of resentment she'd carried from the moment Bertie gave her the news poked at her heart.

When the guests had finally filed through the line with plentiful well-wishes and myriad names and faces, Mr. Montgomery signaled the musicians. The orchestra played a short tattoo to get everyone's attention. Conversations ceased, and heads turned as the bluff, burly man made his way to the center of the dance floor as guests moved to the perimeter.

"Ladies and Gentlemen, welcome. We're delighted to have you here on such an auspicious occasion." His voice commanded attention, as did his mane of auburn hair. "It is with great pleasure that I present to you my daughter, Miss Agatha Montgomery."

He held out his hand, and Agatha gulped. She seemed frozen in place, and Juliette gave her a little shove to get her started toward him.

Agatha only tripped once and then remembered to lift her hem. With coltish grace she finally crossed the open space and took her father's hand.

Juliette joined in the applause as red suffused Agatha's cheeks, clashing with her hair.

Then it was her turn. Without her father there to present her, and with Uncle Bertie gone, the duty fell to Mr. Montgomery.

"And it is my honor to also present Lady Juliette Thorndike."

Juliette kept her composure, nodding to the guests, smiling, even as she reached for Agatha's hand.

The music began, and two men approached. Thankfully, one was well over six feet tall, and he bowed before Agatha and offered his hand.

Juliette's partner was shorter, darker, and had a calm, sophisticated look about him. He had to be somewhere in his mid-thirties. He seemed confident.

"Lady Juliette." Her partner bowed.

"Sir." Juliette curtsied, bending her knees deeply, as she had been taught.

Within moments the dancers chosen to perform the new and intricate quadrille had joined them on the dance floor. Thanks to her many hours of instruction with the dancing master at school, and her private lessons in deportment and ballet, Juliette was at home with the complicated steps. Dancing at a ball was much to be preferred to practicing in the schoolroom, she discovered.

"My name is Mr. John Selby. It's a pleasure to meet you, Lady Juliette. I am honored to partner you at your first dance." He held her fingertips lightly as they turned a circle. His eyes never left her face, and he smiled down at her.

He was very polished. Light on his feet. Though too old for her to be sure, he was a pleasant partner for her first dance. He had been chosen by her parents for this first outing, and she wondered where they had met. Was he the son of a friend? Was he a business associate?

Why couldn't they be here so she could ask them?

"Mr. Selby." She inclined her head.

He didn't speak again during the quadrille, for which Juliette was grateful. She couldn't abide a chatty partner, especially when the conversation must be conducted through several separations and rejoinings as they followed the dance patterns. The quadrille was still new in England, but the dancers acquitted themselves well through the many phases.

The music finally came to an end, and the couples bowed and curtsied to one another while the spectators applauded politely. Mr. Selby offered Juliette his arm.

"That was most entertaining, Lady Juliette. I hope you enjoyed it as well. You are most accomplished, and I am thankful that I sought tutoring in these new steps. I shall have to thank your father for requesting I partner you for your debut dance."

They threaded their way through the crowd, and Juliette searched for Agatha. She had made it through the quadrille without tripping on her hem or forgetting any of the patterns, so perhaps now she could relax and enjoy the party. What was the name of the young man who had partnered her? Had she enjoyed herself? Juliette checked her thoughts. Agatha was a grown woman now, and she didn't need Juliette's mothering . . . though the habit of so many years would be difficult to break.

"Ah, Selby, well done." Mr. Montgomery stood beside the dowager, a glass in his hand, looking pleased. "Juliette, enjoying yourself?"

"Yes, thank you."

"Selby here took good care of you, I see. Did you know he's an art and antiquities dealer? Buys and sells paintings and sculptures, brings them over from the Continent."

Juliette's brows rose. An art dealer? Juliette loved art, especially paintings. Her classes in art history had been among her favorites at school.

"He's procured several pieces for me, one in particular, which is the reason he's here tonight." Mr. Montgomery coughed. "That and to partner you for your debut dance, of course."

A stir near the door turned heads. An entourage entered, at its center a lean man in military dress. He stood so stiffly, Juliette wondered if he had a stair rod up his back. Thirtyish, with an air about him that said he wasn't British. Surely he was from the Continent, of the breed of men to which Juliette had become accustomed during her time in Switzerland.

"Ah, he's here. I must go greet him." Mr. Montgomery handed his glass to a passing footman.

The newcomer's eyes surveyed the room, and the lamplight shone off his precisely parted blond hair. A red sash crossed his chest, and medals winked on his tunic.

"Who is that?" a woman near Juliette asked.

"Duke Heinrich von Lowe. He's from somewhere in Brandenburg, I believe," a man next to the woman said. "A war hero as well. Fought bravely at Leipzig and was present when Paris fell. There was a column about him in the paper last week."

"What brings him to London?" a woman with quizzing glasses raised asked.

People leaned in to listen while they watched Mr. Montgomery approach the duke with his hand outstretched.

When they greeted one another, the partygoers hummed with speculation and opinions.

"He's part of a delegation sent on behalf of his country. Official business with the Home Secretary or something of that nature. Probably to do with setting new boundaries in Europe now that Old Boney is defeated."

"I heard he was sent by his family to find a wife from the British aristocracy."

"I was told he came to observe our textile and grist mills so he could take our advancements back to his country."

The rumors swirled around them. Which one was true? Or were any of them? Juliette twisted the garnet ring, merely to have something to do with her hands. Imagine having such an important person as a foreign duke at your debut.

Mr. Selby turned from staring at von Lowe. "Your Grace." He bowed to the dowager. "Thank you for the honor of sharing Lady Juliette's first dance. I do hope you will pass along my best wishes to your son. If the Duke of Haverly is ever in the market for new artwork, I hope he will think of me and my little gallery. I've just taken delivery of some very unique pieces. I delivered many of them to their owners today, I was that excited, but there are a few I bought on speculation, and perhaps there would be one or two things that might interest him?"

The dowager's brow darkened. "I do not pretend to speak for my son. Marcus, if he wants to delve into the art world, has his own contacts, I am sure. It is unseemly for you to be 'hawking your wares,' as it were, to me or any other lady at this function."

Mr. Selby winced, and Juliette bit her lip. It had been forward of him to pitch his business to the dowager, but she had certainly given him a setdown.

"I beg your pardon, Your Grace. Lady Juliette?" He bowed and all but scurried away.

"I don't know what your parents were thinking, asking that man to partner you in your first dance. I'm certain I could have engaged someone more of your class. Really, a common tradesman? I've heard your parents have eclectic taste when it comes to friends and acquaintances, but you can take liberality of mind too far." The dowager sniffed. "I've already taken requests from several young men to partner you tonight that would be far more acceptable."

She knew her parents had a wide range of friends, and her father had always maintained that entertaining poets and artists and businessmen made for a lively dinner party and a broadening of the mind. Juliette had so been looking forward to evenings such as he had described in his letters.

"Juliette, this is Viscount Swayford. Swayford, Lady Juliette Thorndike." The dowager waved her hand toward Juliette. "Enjoy yourselves. I shall locate myself with the other chaperones, and I will expect you to return her to me after your dance."

Juliette partook of every dance in the first set. She caught glimpses of Agatha in the crush and was happy to see her engaged for every dance as well. Keeping her smile in place, Juliette was ever aware of the watching eyes, especially the dowager's.

At the end of the first set, Juliette perched on the edge of the settee beside the dowager, keeping her posture straight and her hands still in her lap. The dowager gave her an approving nod. "Someone is causing quite a stir, isn't he?" The dowager fingered her pearl choker. Across the way, several guests clustered around the German duke. He stood several inches taller than the rest, and while those around laughed and talked, he remained quiet. Did he speak English? Or was he just bored with the entire event?

"The bits of gossip I've heard tonight have centered on no other topic," Juliette said. "You'd think it was the Prince Regent himself." The duke hadn't taken to the dance floor yet, but that hadn't stopped people from whispering and speculating about him all the same.

"I heard he's looking for a bride." The dowager's eyes flicked from the duke to Juliette. "Have your parents begun any negotiations in that direction? Not with the duke per se, but with someone in mind?"

"Not that I am aware." And not, she hoped, at all. She intended to take this first Season to enjoy herself and to get to know her parents, not to shop for a suitable husband. There was plenty of time for all that later.

Agatha and a young gentleman approached—a gentleman impeccably dressed, perhaps twenty-two or three? Color rode Agatha's cheeks, but she had a smile on her lips and stars in her eyes. "Your Grace, Juliette, may I present Lord Alonzo Darby, Viscount Coatsworth."

She nudged Juliette and leaned in to whisper, "I haven't tripped even once."

"Well done." Juliette squeezed her hand.

"Viscount Coatsworth, so nice you could attend tonight's party." The dowager offered her hand, and the viscount kissed the air above her knuckles. "How is your grandfather?"

"He's been a bit poorly recently. He's still of a sharp mind, though he rues the ravages of age." The viscount tucked his thumb under his lapel and raised his eyes to take in the mirrored walls, the frescoed ceiling, and the many chandeliers. "He is allowing me to take some of his burden finally, seconding responsibility for some of his vast holdings to my care."

Juliette paused. Something in the viscount's voice rubbed against her skin. His tone was condescending and more than a bit patronizing. And boastful. Was his family so wealthy? Vast holdings?

Agatha hung on his every word, keeping her hand through his elbow. Coatsworth didn't seem to mind.

"I've known your grandfather for more years than either of us would like to lay claim to. He pursued me once upon a time, but I was already spoken for. I'm sorry to hear he is ailing, but I suppose it comes to all of us eventually. I was laid low not long ago. I took a tumble down the stairs. It was such a blessing to have my family around to tend me as I recovered. I'm sure you are a comfort to the earl."

Before Coatsworth could answer, Mr. Montgomery's voice from the doorway drew their attention. "Ladies and Gentlemen, I know it is unusual, but as those who know me will say, I'm not much for conventions. I am thrilled that on the night of my daughter's debut, you all could be here to help us celebrate. And I have another reason to celebrate."

Heads turned.

"Before we go in to supper, I would ask you to please join me upstairs in the gallery. The new painting I purchased was delivered today." He nodded toward his left, and Juliette spied Mr. Selby smiling broadly. "I would like you all to be present at the uncrating."

Agatha rolled her eyes. "This is just like him. He's forever collecting new paintings, and each one is 'The best he's ever had.' Why can't he let this evening be about our debut and not his artwork? The few letters he bothered to write to me while I was away were always more about his newest painting than about himself or wondering about me."

"This won't take long, I'm sure." Juliette tried to placate her. "He's proud of you, and he's proud of his collection."

"But can't he be proud of them separately, if only for tonight?"

Viscount Coatsworth bowed to the dowager, took Agatha's elbow, and led her toward her father.

Juliette and the dowager joined the stream leaving the ballroom and following Mr. Montgomery up the stairs to the long gallery. Skylights, dark now, would bathe the room in light during the day, but for this evening, wall sconces and standing candelabra illuminated the walls. Servants stood nearby with pitchers of water on the floor behind them, discreetly hidden but available if necessary. With so many people and so many candles, Mr. Montgomery wasn't taking any chances of a fire.

Halfway down the wide hall, a wooden crate stenciled with arrows and the word "Fragile" stood alone before a blank space on the wall. Mr. Montgomery and Mr. Selby stopped there, allowing the crowd to pass and create a semicircle several people deep around them.

A footman stood ready with a pry bar.

Mr. Montgomery held up his hands, and the murmurs and whispers ceased. His eyes sparkled, and he rubbed his hands together, letting his anticipation build.

"I have long coveted having a Lotto in my collection, and this, *Messer Marsilio Cassotti and his Wife Faustina*, is one of my favorites of his work. Mr. Selby went to great lengths to procure it for me—at considerable expense, if I may say." He sent a rueful nod in the direction of the art dealer. "It will be the centerpiece of my collection."

With a wide gesture, he invited the footman to open the crate.

Juliette had to stand on tiptoe to look over the shoulder of the man in front of her. Candlelight flickered and reflected in Mr. Montgomery's eyes. She was happy for him, fulfilling a desire such as this.

"The portrait, as you will see, is of a young couple at their marriage, with the groom putting a ring on the bride's finger. Behind and between them, a cherub rises with outstretched wings, putting a yoke of leaves across their shoulders to symbolize their union."

The wood of the crate gave a final creak, and tufts of curled wood shavings burgeoned from the container.

"Here, let me." Mr. Montgomery stepped forward, eagerly swiping away the packing material. He paused. Scrabbling, he dug deeper.

"What is the meaning of this, Selby?" His voice filled the room, and even the candles seemed to stop flickering.

"I beg your pardon, Mr. Montgomery?" The art dealer moved closer, peering into the narrow crate.

"It's not here. What have you done with it?" Mr. Montgomery looked close to grabbing Mr. Selby by the lapels and possibly hurling him over the banister.

"Sir, I assure you, the painting was in that crate when I delivered it. I boxed it myself this morning and brought it straight away." Selby puffed out his chest. "Has the painting been sitting here in the hallway all evening?"

The footman who had opened the crate stood with pry bar in hand. "The top was tight closed, sir. Undisturbed until I opened it."

A murmur went through the onlookers.

"It's been stolen!" Mr. Montgomery's voice must have been audible in the street three floors below.

Agatha clutched Juliette's shoulder. "We are never going to forget our debut ball."

"If I had even one other officer available, I wouldn't be forced to send you."

Daniel Swann stood before his supervisor's desk, hands clasped behind his back, flexing his fingers around the handle of his truncheon. He prayed his face would not betray his true feelings of once more being doubted, slighted, and maligned by Sir Michael Biddle.

"Do not make a hash of this investigation. I'm of two minds about sending you in the first place, but I've no choice. Piggott and Fyfe are out on other cases. Beck is in Sussex with Tolliver, or I would give him the case. Perhaps I should go along myself to see that you do things properly."

Daniel had been employed at Bow Street for more than two years. Surely by now he'd earned the right to go out on a case without another officer to act as his baby nurse. He was no longer a wet-behind-the-ears probationer prone to making errors or leaping to investigatory conclusions. Having Sir Michael at a crime scene countermanding or second-guessing his every move would be intolerable. When would the man trust him? Hadn't he proven himself to this point?

"If it wasn't for pressure from the Home Office, I never would have hired you. You've done all right recently, but this case might be beyond you. It needs a good, hard man to investigate crime, and I am not yet convinced you have what it takes. But there you are—you have powerful friends who have saddled me with you, and I must bow, since they hold the purse strings." Sir Michael shifted one stack of paper and then another on his crowded desk, scowling hard enough to curdle milk. It was an oft-repeated opinion of the Bow Street supervisor, one Daniel was heartily sick of hearing.

It wasn't Daniel's fault he'd been put forward for the position and that as a result Sir Michael had not been able to hire his own nephew instead.

He held in his sigh. It would do no good to protest. The man in charge of his life until he reached twenty-five had launched Daniel in the career of his choosing, and that it had trampled Sir Michael's plans hadn't come into the equation. Daniel had tried to explain it once, but his attempt had only irritated the guv and strained their already tenuous relationship.

"What am I to investigate, Sir Michael?" The man was prone to losing the plot when he launched into a tirade, and if Daniel didn't keep him focused, it would take ages to get the details and be on his way.

"A theft."

He forced his shoulders not to slump. Theft. Would Sir Michael ever deem Daniel capable of a more difficult assignment? Theft hardly raised the heart rate. He'd been sent out on one petty theft case after another, always as a second to another constable. Catching pickpockets in Covent Garden or Vauxhall didn't exactly cover an investigator in glory.

"What was taken, and from where?" A lady's purse, probably. Or if he was lucky, maybe some footman had absconded with the family silver, and Daniel could mount a chase to apprehend him.

Sir Michael handed over a slip of paper. "A painting. From a house on Eaton Square. Another reason to send you, I suppose, since it involves art. A chance to use that fancy degree of yours." He sneered. "The hardworking men of Bow Street will no doubt be glad you can finally employ some of that book knowledge you lord over them."

Daniel's brows rose. Perhaps this might be interesting after all. Would he be called upon to finally use some of what he had learned at university? Thus far it hadn't seemed to do him much good. He ignored the jibe about lording his degree over his coworkers. He never mentioned it. That it was common knowledge in the detectives' room was thanks to Sir Michael himself announcing it the day Daniel had been hired and presented to his new coworkers.

The theft of a painting in Eaton Square. His mind picked up the pace.

Eaton Square was lined with townhouses full of wealthy people and expensive objects. "A housebreaking?" He checked the clock behind Sir Michael: 11:00 p.m. An odd time for a theft to be reported, surely. Property thieves often worked in the dead of night, and most thefts, if properly carried out, were not reported until the morning, when the owners discovered they'd been burgled.

"I don't know the details. If I did, I wouldn't need to send you. Now, stop dithering and get over there. And remember, you'll be dealing with aristocrats. Be polite and show them the deference they deserve." Sir Michael sent him a penetrating look. "Though starting life as a guttersnipe and household servant should no doubt give you the perspective you'll need."

Heat pooled in Daniel's collarbones and climbed his neck. With tensed muscles, and pressing his tongue hard against the back of his clamped teeth, Daniel took the paper, gave a short nod, and turned on his heel. His unconventional upbringing had long been a sore spot with Sir Michael. He didn't need it thrown into his face yet again.

Daniel entered the common room. Stale coffee, old cigar smoke, paper, and ink. He inhaled the familiar scents. Each inspector had his own territory in the office, arranged by seniority. Being the newest hire, Daniel's desk was a battered affair with one drawer that had a tendency to stick in damp weather, and it sat farthest from the fire. He made his way through the dimly lit room and retrieved his hat and coat from the peg beside his workspace. Once in the hallway, he held the paper up to the wall lamp and tried to decipher Sir Michael's deplorable handwriting.

"Eaton Square. Mr. Montgomery. Stolen painting," Daniel muttered as he shoved one arm into his greatcoat and transferred the slip to his other hand to finish donning the heavy garment. "Not exactly forthcoming with details." With a shrug he adjusted the many capes at the shoulders. His clothes were another cause for comment in the office, but what should he do? Throw his wardrobe in the ashbin and buy something secondhand? His fine clothes would wear out soon enough, and he would eventually purchase attire more suited to his station in life.

Thankfully, the clerks' rooms were empty at this time of night, or he would be forced to run the gamut of their curious stares and not-quite-disguised whispers. They took their cues from Sir Michael, distrusting or disdaining by turns. He had given up on earning their trust anytime soon and ignored their gossip as best he could.

Clattering down the stairs, tucking the paper into his pocket, he ran his fingers through his thick, curly hair. He really should see his barber soon, though longer, less fashionable hair was an asset when he wanted to blend in with the masses on his undercover jobs. As he exited the offices, he popped his top hat on his head and dug his gloves out of his pockets.

Bow Street was awash with carriages and hackneys, the drivers waiting patiently for their employers and fares to leave the Royal Opera House opposite the police station. Most drivers sat inside the carriages, trying to stay warm. Daniel felt for them. He'd spent plenty of time waiting in the cold himself. Sir Michael often gave him the jobs that required tedious amounts of surveillance.

He jogged up the street to the corner, wishing Bow Street kept its own conveyances for official business. They had a Black Maria for transporting prisoners, but for everything else, they hired out, which took time and money. And the keeping of meticulous accounts, since Sir Michael would not approve the reimbursement of any expenses unless there was prodigious documentation.

Halfway down Long Acre Street toward Drury Lane, a hackney sat idle, its driver hunched on the seat. Daniel hurried toward it. He could usually count on Cadogan to be sitting outside the Dragon and Child pub, waiting for a late fare.

"Evening, Mr. Swann. Where to?" Cadogan asked. The wiry cabman leaned over from his perch atop the carriage and spit into the gutter. His bright eyes reflected the light of the carriage lamps, his habitual insouciance on display in his cheeky grin.

"Eaton Square. Hurry." Daniel leapt aboard and settled into the padded seat, laying his truncheon on the bench beside him. His breath puffed in the cold January night air. The coach lurched, and the hooves of the mismatched mares, Sprite and Lola, which Cadogan doted on like a father, rang on the hard streets.

Daniel's mind bowled along like the carriage. An art theft on Eaton Square. His first solo case. A thrill feathered across his chest, and he fisted his hands. He went over the procedures in his mind, the questions he would ask, the way he would detail and document the crime scene.

The hackney made good time, traveling up the Mall toward Buckingham, swinging to the south, and entering Belgravia. When they arrived at Eaton Square, his heart sank to see that the townhouse he wanted appeared to be the center of a social event. Light blazed from every window, and carriages clogged the street.

The hackney slowed, and Daniel opened the door, half hanging out as Cadogan drew the horses to a halt. "Far as I can go, guv."

"Thank you." Daniel swung to the ground, straightening his coat.

"You want me to wait for you?"

It would cost more, but in the end he opted for the convenience of having ready transportation over the expense. "Yes, stay handy. I don't know how long I'll be."

Daniel threaded through the carriages and drivers and mounted the stairs. As he raised his truncheon to rap, the door opened.

Heat and light hit him in the face, along with the smell of perfume, roasted meat, and flowers.

Also voices. Lots of voices.

"Detective Swann, Bow Street," he informed the footman.

"Very good, sir. May I take your hat and coat?" The man spoke as if he had plums stuffed in his cheeks. His face showed no surprise, as if policemen showed up at the door during every party.

Daniel had no more than handed over the garments when a loud voice from the balcony boomed through the foyer.

"Is that the detectives? It's beyond time they arrived." A burly man hurried down the stairs, his face florid.

Daniel appraised the man as he raised his truncheon, the badge of his office. "Daniel Swann, Bow Street. I will be looking into the problem, sir." He raised his brows, silently asking for an introduction.

"Garfield Montgomery. And this is not a problem—it's a catastrophe. Where are the others?" He looked over Daniel's shoulder, as if waiting for the rest of the sworn officers to turn up.

"There are no other detectives assigned to the case at the moment." Daniel dug into his pocket for his notebook and pencil. As much as his truncheon with the leather grip and the brass knob was the overt expression of his trade, his real tools were his notes. Every crime he'd ever solved had come down to the information he'd obtained and the conclusions he'd drawn from them.

"This is a fine state of affairs. I call for aid, and they send me one man? Do you have any idea how much that painting is worth? Of course you don't. You don't know anything. How could you? Young pup." His scowl could start a fire.

Daniel was painfully aware of all the eyes and ears taking in this initial encounter.

"I suppose I'll have to make the best of it," Mr. Montgomery seethed, "but rest assured, tomorrow I will take my complaints to the Home Office. It's disgraceful." He turned and marched up the stairs, clearly expecting Daniel to follow.

The crowd on the steps parted, and Daniel's heart sank. In a house packed with people, how was he supposed to sort out this case? It could have been anyone, and he always operated from the assertion that everyone was a suspect until they weren't. "Mr. Montgomery, sir, could you please instruct your guests not to leave the premises?"

"What? I'm not going to inconvenience my guests." He tossed this back over his shoulder as he reached the landing. "Are you implying that someone from the party would do this? Preposterous. None of my friends would steal from me, and everyone was in the ballroom anyway. This is my daughter's come-out ball, and it's been disrupted enough as it is. I won't keep my guests hostage here while you float ridiculous accusations." He strode with force down the hall.

Daniel walked quickly in his wake, but he refused to be so undig-nified as to trot. *He's had a shock. You're not seeing him at his best. Stay calm, and don't let him dictate the investigation.*

At least the man had thought to keep the guests out of this area. Other than a pair of footmen who stood between the lamp stands illuminating the gallery, the hall was clear.

Daniel took in the empty space on the wall, the crate and pile of shavings, and the fact that there were eight doors that he could see opening off this one hallway.

More than one hundred people in the house, multiple ways to get in and out, and he was the lone investigator responsible for containing the crime scene and interviewing potential witnesses? Madness.

Unease coiled down his spine and prickled across his skin. If he didn't solve this case, he would never hear the end of it, and Sir Michael might find it reason enough to terminate his employment.

He couldn't let that happen. He'd be twenty-five in a matter of weeks. After that he was on his own. No more allowance, no more help finding employment, no more powerful support, however anonymous, behind him.

Time to take charge of the case. "You." He pointed to a footman. "Go out and find at least two night watchmen, preferably three or four. Post one at the front door and tell him he is not to let anyone leave. Have the others wait for me at the foot of the stairs." He would put them to good use. "And send up my driver. He's at the end of the street. Hackney with a mismatched team."

The footman looked to his employer, received a curt nod, and hurried downstairs, his embroidered coattails flapping.

"What do you want them for?" Montgomery asked. "And I told you I would not inconvenience my guests. They are free to leave when they choose."

"Sir, I wish the watchmen for reinforcements, and I will not inconvenience your guests beyond what is reasonable. I assume, since this is a private party, you have a guest list?"

"Of course I have a guest list. Do you think I just flung open the door tonight and shouted for anyone passing by to stop in? I told you, none of my friends would steal from me."

Time for some diplomacy. "Sir, it's possible that someone saw something, witnessed something unusual. I'd like to ask about everyone's movements. Perhaps someone saw something that they did not, at the time, connect with the theft, but upon reflection could prove useful."

How could he possibly track the movements of so many people over several hours?

"My secretary has a list in the office." He made a dismissive gesture.

"I'd also like your entire staff assembled."

"My staff? Of course." Montgomery paused, though clearly more at ease with the idea it might have been one of his servants who was the thief. "Do you want the temporary workers I hired for tonight's event too?"

"Yes, but please divide them into temporary and permanent help. In separate rooms, if you will."

With a nod, the second footman hurried away on the errand.

With those measures in place, Daniel asked, "Please tell me what happened."

Mr. Montgomery walked him through what was supposed to have been a triumphant unveiling.

"And the crate was empty. This is a shocking embarrassment. I paid a king's ransom for that piece." He removed a square of linen from his pocket and scrubbed his forehead. His bluster and outrage were turning to shock. "A Lorenzo Lotto. I first saw it in a gallery in Spain years ago. A wedding portrait of Cassotti and his wife. My dealer, who is here tonight as my guest, negotiated the sale. Mr. Selby of Turner and Rathbone."

A Lotto? Daniel had studied Lotto at university, but only briefly. His mind did a quick canter around what he knew of the Italian portraitist. Born in the fifteenth century. Known for his bold use of shadows, deeply saturated colors, the range of expressions in his subjects.

He glanced at Mr. Montgomery and judged that he would not appreciate a discourse on the topic. Daniel examined the crate. "The nails were undisturbed until the footman opened the lid?"

"That's right. It looked exactly as it had when it arrived from the gallery this afternoon."

"And you're certain the painting was in the crate at that time?" Perhaps the crime hadn't occurred here at all. Perhaps it had happened before the crate left the art dealer's.

"I helped carry it up the stairs." Montgomery held out his hand. "I know. I have servants for that sort of work, but I was excited. The crate was heavy when we brought it up." He toed the wooden box, watching it teeter. "Not like it is now."

Squatting, Daniel tipped the box on its side, easing it to the floor. The bottom of the crate stayed where it was, detached from the sides, sending a cascade of wood shavings onto the carpet. "That's how it was done, sir. The thief removed the bottom, took the painting, and sat the crate upright to disguise the method." And a neat job it was, too. The thief had been meticulous in his methods to leave no trace of shavings behind.

Montgomery's jaw set, and his big hands fisted against his thighs. "I'll have whoever did this strung up by his thumbs."

"You wanted me, guv?" Cadogan stood in the hall, twisting his hat in his hands. His nose and cheeks were cherry red from the cold.

"Yes." Daniel straightened and drew the jarvey aside for a private conversation. "I want you to chat up the drivers outside. Find out when they arrived, who they brought, what they saw during the evening. Who came and who went and if anyone noticed anything unusual."

The hackney driver's eyes widened. "Me, sir?"

"Yes, and work quickly. Take notes. You can write, can you not? The guests will want to leave soon."

"I can scribble words when I have to." Cadogan clapped his hat on his head and jogged down the stairs two at a time.

What Sir Michael would say to Daniel enlisting civilians to do police work, he couldn't imagine, but he needed help, and Cadogan was a smart man who would meld quickly with the other drivers.

"I'll begin with the guests so they may be on their way quickly." Daniel tucked his pencil inside his notebook and snapped the pages shut. He cast one last glance at the artwork to either side of the empty space where the Lotto should hang.

Why had the thief taken that painting rather than the far more expensive Bellini? *Portrait of a Condottiere* would surely fetch a higher price than the Lotto.

He almost chuckled. When he had entered Oxford to read art history and literature, he never imagined he would become a police constable, much less ever need to draw upon his university studies in his new career.

As they reached the ground floor, Daniel sensed a change in the atmosphere. The guests no longer stood in little clusters, whispering and enjoying the spectacle of the theft. Frowns, pursed lips, and hot eyes formed a phalanx.

"I say, Montgomery, this man says we aren't allowed to leave." A pale older man with hair combed over the top of his head from one ear to the other, and sporting a rotund middle, barged forward. "I'm sorry about the theft and all, but I'd like to go home." He scowled at the night watchman in his dark-blue cape and postilion hat.

One man moved forward half a step. "What is the meaning of keeping us here? I'm sorry the wretched painting was stolen, but surely that isn't our affair."

"And you are, sir?" Daniel asked.

"You will address me as Viscount Coatsworth."

"I apologize for detaining you, but there is no help for it. If you will be patient, I will get to you as quickly as I can."

"You mistake your position." He drew himself up to his full height.

Daniel estimated the viscount to be a bit younger than himself. He had sharp features, with a sneer to his lips that marred what might be considered an agreeable face.

"We are not cattle to be herded hither and yon, and we will not be dictated to by a mere constable. I am taking my leave, and I am certain the rest of the guests will follow suit."

"Lord Coatsworth, if you attempt to leave without permission, that man will be forced to stop you." Daniel pointed to the burly night watchman at the door. "This will undoubtedly cause unpleasantness for your host and the other guests, particularly the ladies. I'm sure you don't want to be the cause of such a scene." He nodded to the slender red-haired young woman in the white dress who hovered near the viscount's elbow.

With a scowl, the viscount pivoted, linked his arm through the young woman's, and marched out of the foyer into the crowded drawing room.

A wraith of a man appeared at Daniel's elbow. "The guest list, sir." He held out several pages of precise writing. "Is there anything else you need? Any way I may be of service to you?"

Briefly perusing the list and surveying the mood of the guests, Daniel shrugged. There was no help for it. He didn't have enough men to question everyone, and Sir Michael would have his head on a charger if he inconvenienced the aristocracy or in any way intimated that the theft could have been perpetrated by a member of the peerage.

"You." He pointed to the night watchman at the door. "You and . . ." He turned to the skeletal man. "You are?"

"Mifflin, sir. Mr. Montgomery's secretary."

"The two of you stand here. Mark the guests' names against the list. Get an accurate account of who was here, then allow them to leave."

Daniel made his way downstairs to the servants' dining room. He questioned the servants, who all claimed to know nothing. Two of the house staff were unaccounted for, a maid and a footman, and for a moment he thought he might be on to something. But after a thorough search of the house in case the painting had been stashed somewhere for later retrieval, the couple were discovered in a clinch in a storage room upstairs.

Of the painting, nothing was to be found.

Daniel trotted down the staircase to the echo of Mr. Montgomery's stern tones dressing down the amorous staffers. It was the only humorous moment of the evening.

Thus far Daniel had nothing to go on. Midnight had come and gone.

The only small consolation was finding a single wood shaving beneath a skylight. But he couldn't see how a thief could have gotten the painting up through the skylight without help. Was he looking for a pair of thieves?

A small number of guests remained in a parlor when he went in search of the secretary.

One caught his eye. Dressed in white, she must be a debutante. Nineteen or twenty perhaps? She had softly curling hair held by a white band of fabric, and she wore no jewels as befitted a debutante . . . except for a ring on her right hand. She twisted the ring as she listened to something an older woman said. Did the ring signify a romantic attachment? A token from a suitor?

Her nose titled up slightly at the tip, and her chin came to a gently rounded point. A white fan dangled from her white-gloved wrist. Delicate of features and form. But intelligent of eye, too. She didn't seem distressed by the evening's events. If anything, she seemed slightly bemused.

He pushed away his momentary fascination. She may have caught his eye, but she was no different from others of her class.

Some spoiled aristocrat who had no notion of what it meant to go hungry or to put in a full day's work following someone else's orders. Pretty but ornamental, without any real use but to look nice, to marry well, and to carry on some silk stocking's family line.

Montgomery stormed into the room behind Daniel and went to the woman seated beside the debutante. "Your Grace, I do apologize for the uproar. I hope it hasn't cast too much of a blight upon the evening." He stretched his hands out to the black-clad woman.

"It's most irregular. I hope they apprehend the thief quickly. A servant no doubt, taking advantage of the festivities? It's infuriating, but I'm sorry to say, not a unique occurrence." She used his help to rise to her feet. "Lady Juliette, I will take my leave. You've acquitted yourself well tonight, in spite of the upsets. I'll be in touch about our next event."

The younger woman bobbed a curtsy. "Good evening, Your Grace, and thank you for everything."

The secretary checked her off the guest list and handed it to Daniel. "That was the Dowager Duchess of Haverly. Some guests left before the police arrived, but only a few. I've noted those in the margin. Lady Juliette Thorndike is a guest of Miss Agatha Montgomery's and will be staying the night."

"Thank you. Most helpful." He read through the list, noting that Mr. Selby, the art dealer, had left first. Daniel pocketed the list. He would call on the gallery tomorrow first thing. Daniel surveyed the lavish drawing room. Lady Juliette had gone to stand by the tall redhead, also clad in white. That must be Agatha Montgomery, daughter of the house.

They made a pretty picture standing before the fireplace in their finery.

He shook his head to clear it. He wasn't here to be distracted by debutantes.

"Mr. Montgomery, I shall continue my inquiries and call back in the morning. If you would be so kind as to assemble the relevant documents regarding the purchase and provenance of the painting, I would be most obliged." He bowed to the ladies present and prepared to take his leave.

"Useless. What could Sir Michael have been thinking, sending a single raw recruit to handle an important case? It's disrespectful to me, I say." Mr. Montgomery's loud voice followed Daniel out of the room. "He will be hearing from me on the morrow, I assure you."

Daniel had to refrain from snatching his cloak and hat from the footman's hand. It wasn't the servant's fault his master was bombastic and rude. Still, the man's accusation rankled.

Tomorrow you'll return, and you'll find that missing painting. You'll show Montgomery, Sir Michael, and Lorenzo Lotto's ghost that you are a capable investigator.

Chapter 2

"Do you think we dare go down to the breakfast room?" Agatha sagged onto the foot of Juliette's bed. She wore her dressing gown and slippers still, but looked remarkably fresh considering the late hour at which they had retired last night. "I cannot imagine the state of mind Father will be in this morning."

"He has had a dreadful shock. One moment he's host of a fabulous party, and the next he's staring at an empty crate where an expensive painting should be." Juliette stretched her arms above her head, pressing back into the bank of pillows.

Agatha toyed with the end of her braid, curling it round her finger. "He'll be like a badger with a sore paw this morning. You see if he isn't. He has a dreadful temper when he's riled." She flipped the braid over her shoulder and drew her feet up, wrapping her arms around her knees. "Let's talk of something more interesting."

"And by more interesting you mean . . ." Juliette grinned.

"Viscount Coatsworth?" Agatha blushed. "He was so attentive. Two dances, and he said he would have sat with me during the refreshments, if the painting hadn't been stolen and the evening destroyed." She ended with a scowl.

"Destroyed might be a bit strong." Though Juliette had to wonder what the newspapers would say about the event. The theft would surely dominate the pages, but perhaps someone would spare an inch or two of print for their debuts?

"Do you think we'll receive cards in the morning post? Or even posies or chocolates?"

"I would be shocked if the viscount didn't send some memento to you. When we call on the dowager, be sure to bring your notes and cards so we can answer them properly. And your calendar. We'll have to compare invitations and form a plan."

"It's awkward not having my own mother to take me round, to chaperone and the like. Though I suppose no dark cloud is without its silver linings. If my mother hadn't passed away, my father never would have sent me abroad for schooling, and I wouldn't have met you. Or at least I wouldn't have met you until we both made our debuts, and then I might have been so jealous of how pretty and graceful and nice you are that I might not have wanted to be friends." Agatha laughed. "But we've shared hair ribbons and homesickness and history books, and now it's like we're sisters."

"When my mother returns from Heild Manor, things will be easier." At least that was what Juliette hoped. "You are pleased with the dresses she had made for you and all the invitations she's accepted on your behalf? Your father gave her full run of your schedule for the Season, but if there's something you want to do or don't want to attend, you must promise to say so."

"I'm thrilled with the little bit I know so far. I don't know which I'm more excited about, the masquerade ball or the opera, and that's just this week." Agatha bounced off the bed and twirled, her nightgown and wrapper belling out. "Parties and outings and soirees and shopping and teas and strolling Rotten Row."

"With Viscount Coatsworth?" Juliette teased, throwing back the coverlet and wincing as cold air hit her bare feet.

"Perhaps." Agatha picked up a fan, flapping it open and fluttering it beneath her chin. "What about you? Did any swains pay you particular attention?"

Belting her wrapper and tucking her toes into lamb's wool slippers, Juliette shrugged. "None in particular. I met several nice men. My parents had arranged for Mr. Selby to lead me out for my debut dance.

You saw him last night. He is the man your father commissioned to acquire the Lotto painting."

"Why on earth would your father choose a tradesman for your debut dance? And someone so much older than yourself? I would have thought he would have picked someone like that German duke who was causing such a stir. Duke Heinrich von Lowe." She stiffened, bowed sharply at the waist, and clicked her heels. Or would have, if she wasn't wearing soft slippers.

"He was cutting quite a path through the guests, wasn't he? I heard all sorts of rumors and gossip." Juliette untied the string holding her braid and unwound it, tilting her head to the side. "As to Mr. Selby, I believe my father chose him to remind me that I should benefit from meeting a wide variety of people. My parents often have artists and professors and inventors and the like at their social events, and they've encouraged me through their letters to broaden my mind. I look forward to seeing Mr. Selby again and learning more about what he does." She hit a snarl, and the brush jerked out of her hand.

Agatha picked up the brush from the carpet. "Have you thought of cutting your hair? Not that it isn't beautiful, but it's so very long, and the latest styles are much shorter. It would curl more if it wasn't so heavy."

"I don't want to cut it. My mother's hair is just as long, and my father loves long hair. I don't mind not being up to the minute with the latest fashions. I like what I like." It put her in mind of the Duke of Haverly, with his unfashionable yet flattering hairstyle.

Agatha set the brush on the table. "I'll get dressed, and we can brave going downstairs. Perhaps Father has already finished breaking his fast, and we can eat in peace."

The maid assigned to Juliette waited in the little dressing room, and while she arranged Juliette's hair for the day, Juliette studied her reflection in the mirror. Agatha was full to the brim with excitement about Viscount Coatsworth, and they'd touched on the German duke, but neither had mentioned the individual who had caught Juliette's attention the most.

The Bow Street officer.

Mr. Daniel Swann.

Now there was an occupation that would provide fascinating conversation over dinner, she judged. What did a police constable do? How did one conduct an investigation? She had observed him questioning the help, not being cowed by any of the peers, not buckling in the face of Mr. Montgomery's strident accusations and insults.

Perhaps, when her parents returned, she should ask them to invite him to one of their dinner parties. Wouldn't that cause tongues to wag?

Agatha and Juliette braved the breakfast room. Mr. Montgomery sat at the head of the table, hidden by a newspaper. At their entrance, the paper folded down on one corner.

"Don't get up, Father." Agatha hurried around the table and touched his shoulder. "How are you feeling this morning?"

"You've taken your time, lolling about upstairs." His chiding was affectionate. "I've been up since dawn. Already composed several letters and discharged them about the city." He patted his daughter's hand. "I am unimpressed by actions taken last night to retrieve my property, and I've said so to the appropriate authorities. Good morning, Lady Juliette."

"Good morning." A footman held a chair for her, and the moment she was seated, a footman set a filled plate at her place. "I didn't get to tell you last night how sorry I was that your painting was stolen. I cannot believe someone would have the temerity to use the party as a distraction to break in and rob you."

Agatha motioned *no* with her hand, grimacing, but it was too late.

"I can believe it. London crime is getting worse and worse, and what are we doing about it? Nothing. A handful of officers to police the largest metropolis in the world? It's preposterous. I know many who bleat that having a paid police force will infringe upon their liberties, but those same individuals are the first to cry foul when they are the victims. It's becoming more apparent all the time that what we're doing is not enough. Unless Parliament is made to see, we will descend into chaos. More and more of the upper classes will have to hire their own protection. Especially if last night's performance is what we can expect from Bow Street. Sending a youth barely dry behind the ears, and what does he do? Muddle around questioning the guests and looking into places he has no business, and what did it get him? A return of my property? No." His face reddened, and his voice rose as he ranted. The paper crinkled in his fisted hands. "I sent round to Bow Street with my feelings made plain. I want action, not incompetence." The cutlery jumped as he pounded the table.

Agatha leaned back, putting her hand over her eyes. Juliette regretted opening this particular door, but now that she had, she must walk through it.

"Surely you didn't expect Mr. Swann to pluck your missing painting out of thin air? He is but one man, and I'm certain he's doing his best." Juliette surprised herself by rising to the defense of someone she'd barely met. But justice was important to her, and it seemed grossly unfair to accuse a man of incompetence when he'd had so little time to investigate. "If you give him time, I'm sure he will find the culprit and return your property."

Mr. Montgomery slowly relaxed into his chair, his hands opening, a patient smile smoothing his face. "My dear, it is kind of you to defend him, but you are very young and impressionable. Let the men deal with this issue. Would you like me to read what the papers had to say about your debut? That would be much in keeping with what is appropriate for young ladies."

Juliette feared he was about to reach out and pat her hand. Everything in her bristled at his patronizing tone, but she must remember that he was her host, her elder, and her best friend's father.

"No, thank you. I am assuredly capable of reading the articles myself. I will go over them this afternoon, I'm sure. Perhaps when Agatha comes by to receive callers with the dowager and me."

"Oh yes, I suppose you'll want to whisper and giggle over all the gossip." He snapped open his paper again, disappearing behind the print. "I'll be at the mill offices for the rest of the day, but home again for dinner, all right, Agatha?"

"Yes, Father."

Agatha saw Juliette off with promises to see her in a few hours, and Juliette settled back into the carriage for the short ride from Eaton Square to her parents' townhome on Berkley Square. Tiredness pulled at her limbs, and she stifled a yawn. She had found it difficult to sleep last night, wishing she had opted not to stay overnight at the Montgomerys'.

Because no one was in the carriage, she indulged in speaking her mind aloud. "Today you were supposed to start a new chapter. With the bustle of presentation and the debut behind you, you were supposed to be able to focus on really getting to know your parents and becoming a credit to them."

Disappointment was only a short step from resentment, she found. For years she had made excuses, to her classmates, to her teachers, to herself. Her parents wanted the best schooling for her, so sending her to Switzerland made sense. With the war raging, it was safer if she stayed at school and out of harm's way, so she had stayed . . . for years. It was their duty to see to their estate and the people who lived on it, so it was understandable they weren't there to greet her upon her return, that they had missed her presentation and her come-out ball. How did she honor her parents as God intended when their decisions thwarted the desires of her heart? When their actions made her feel as if she were always secondary in their thoughts?

"You do like to sail close to the wind, don't you? It's like you cannot help yourself, lad." Edward Beck knocked the dottle out of his pipe into the dish on his desk. "I'm not in the office five minutes this morning before I hear the news. The guv was fair raving. Seems the gentleman whose house you barged into last night looking for his lost painting wasn't happy with the way you treated his guests, and why wasn't his property recovered yet? Since you've had all of about six hours to find it?"

"Me, on the outers with Sir Michael?" Daniel pressed his palm into his chest, sending a mock-surprised look to his mentor and friend. "However shall I bear the shock?" He tossed his cloak onto the hook behind his chair and settled his hat atop it. "I believe when it comes to our esteemed guv, I could return His Majesty's reason to him whole and unharmed and Sir Michael would find some way to fault me." He pulled out his desk chair and leaned on the back with both hands. "Mr. Montgomery, the victim in last night's theft, said he'd let my superior know of his dissatisfaction, and it appears he is as good as his word. And barely after sunrise too. When did you get back, by the by?"

"About the same time the complaint came in. I nearly collided with Montgomery's messenger in the doorway." Ed rubbed his hands down his face, stifling a yawn. There were no set hours for an officer of the Bow Street Magistrate's Court. You went where the cases took you, and you worked until they were done. No two days the same. It was one of the things Daniel loved most about the job.

"Mr. Swann." Owen Wilkinson, one of the office boys, stuck his head into the room. "Sir Michael demands you in his office without delay." His young face bore a sneer. He had taken in their boss's disdain of Daniel and adopted it for himself, wearing it like an ermine cloak. "He's not best pleased that you are so tardy in appearing this morning."

"Fine." Daniel hadn't even sat down yet. He checked the clock—7:20. With the exception of Ed and himself, none of the other inspectors had arrived yet.

"He said not to waste his time."

The pointed stare set Daniel's teeth on edge. "I'm on my way. While I'm gone, make some coffee, then check the files. I want everything we have on art thefts and other stolen property in the region of Eaton Square."

Making tea and coffee was definitely within the office boy's list of responsibilities, but he always performed the task with ill grace, as if such menial work was beneath him. Owen scowled at Daniel.

"And, Mr. Beck"—the young man's tone and expression changed—

"he requested your presence as well, if you will." He practically genuflected. Ed had the most seniority amongst the Bow Street officers and was held in high esteem. Even Sir Michael showed him at least a modicum of deference.

Ed winked at Daniel. He tossed his pipe onto the desk, gave his cravat a twitch, and preceded Wilkinson out of the room. Daniel followed, his heart knocking against his ribs.

"Come in," Sir Michael barked when Ed tapped on the doorframe. "Good morning, Mr. Beck. I trust you tidied up the affair in Sussex?"

"Indeed, Sir Michael. The highwayman was apprehended with the stolen goods, and the local magistrate has heard the case and handed down his sentence. Justice is swift in that parish." Though he wasn't casual in Sir Michael's office, Ed was neither cowed nor obsequious. He stood relaxed, hands clasped behind him. Years of experience and success in his position afforded him the luxury of being at his ease in the supervisor's office.

"Excellent. That's what we need more of around here. Efficiency and professionalism."

Daniel hovered in the doorway until Sir Michael invited him in.

"Ah, Swann, where have you been? Stop loitering in the hall. Where is your report on the Montgomery matter?"

"I have not yet written up a report, Sir Michael." His fingers curled into his palms. "The investigation is not yet concluded."

"Well, what information do you have? Why must I chase you to find out? A report of your progress should be sitting on my desk this minute." He rocked back in his chair and steepled his fingers, glaring at Daniel.

"I have only this quarter hour returned to these premises. I was out all night on the matter."

Sir Michael shot him a vinegar-laced glare. "Mr. Montgomery sent me a most strident letter this morning pointing out the deficiencies in your methods. How dare you trouble the elite with your questions? It's clear the painting was stolen by someone hired for the social event last night. A waiter or footman or cloakroom attendant. Why then did you detain nearly a hundred party guests?" Sir Michael spoke as if to a simpleton. "And not just any guests, but the crème of society?"

"Sir, I have been taught that everyone is a suspect until they aren't. I was merely employing what I believed to be good police techniques." Daniel forced himself to stand still.

"And who told you such a thing? 'Everyone is a suspect until they aren't.'" Sir Michael scoffed.

Ed spoke up. "I believe it was you who told us that, Sir Michael, when we were looking for the miscreants who were stealing ladies' purses in Hyde Park. Turned out to be a pair of young jackanapes from the gentry and not the guttersnipes everyone supposed, remember?"

Daniel swallowed a laugh as Sir Michael's face reddened. He picked up a stack of papers and butted them together.

"Hmm, yes, well. What progress have you made?" He glared at Daniel.

Daniel gave a short synopsis of the information he had gathered, consulting his notebook from time to time. "At approximately ten thirty, with all the guests looking on, the crate was opened, and it was revealed that the painting was not inside. Upon examination, the crate had been opened from the bottom, and the painting removed sometime between its arrival at half five or thereabouts and the discovery of the theft at half ten."

"And? How did you proceed?"

"I obtained a guest list, and I questioned the servants, as well as conducting a search of the house in case the painting had been secreted away for later removal when there was less scrutiny."

"And this is another point where you have raised Mr. Montgomery's ire. How dare you search his house and invade his private quarters? He tells me you had the audacity to search not only his bedchamber and dressing rooms, but to enter his daughter's suite?" He gripped the edge of his desk and leaned forward. "Have you lost your reason?"

"Sir, what good is a search if it is not thorough?"

"What good did your 'thorough' search do? You don't imagine that Miss Montgomery stole the painting from her father, do you?"

"No, sir, I do not. However, there were several new ladies' maids who were unknown to the rest of the staff, having been brought into the household upon the homecoming of Miss Montgomery from abroad. I thought it prudent to search the areas to which they had access during the party."

Sir Michael was silent for a moment, and Daniel dared risk a look over at Ed. His blue eyes twinkled, though his face remained neutral.

"What else did you discover?"

"A bit of packing material was found under a skylight on the third floor of the residence. Perhaps the painting, which was packed in shavings, was taken out that way." Daniel consulted his notes once again. "The coach drivers parked on the street were questioned." He was careful not to mention that he'd delegated that task to a civilian. "The only gentleman who left the party early was . . ." He found the name. "Sir Bertrand Thorndike. It appears Sir Bertrand was in his cups and required assistance getting into his carriage. Several of the drivers witnessed this. Nothing else remarkable occurred outside."

Daniel waited for his supervisor to criticize, belittle, or otherwise tear down the work he'd done so far, but in the end, Sir Michael merely glared.

"So you admit defeat then? I knew the case was beyond your capabilities."

Stung, Daniel protested. "Sir, I am not defeated. I have had the case for less than half a day. It is my intention to canvass the local receiver shops to see who might traffic in artwork, make contact with my informants to ascertain who might be capable of housebreaking in the middle of a party, and begin making my way through the party guests. I've requested records to be brought on thefts in the Eaton Square area and any known art thefts on file. I shall look for commonalities to see if a pattern emerges."

"A fine plan, but I believe so much work is beyond your ability to execute." Sir Michael nodded. "Now that a more experienced inspector is available, I believe it is time to turn over the investigation. Beck, you will take charge of the case. Swann, you will assist if Mr. Beck so requests."

Heat pooled along Daniel's collarbones. "But, sir, this is my case."

Ed spoke up. "Sir, the lad's done a fine job to this point. I would have done exactly the same on this investigation. It seems a shame to take the case from him. Perhaps I can act as his assistant on this matter. He's earned the right to lead."

The temperature in the room seemed to fall. While it pleased Daniel that Ed was taking his part, he didn't want his friend and mentor to risk Sir Michael's unpredictable ire. No sense in both losing their positions.

For what seemed a decade or two, no one spoke. Daniel took his cue from Ed and stood his ground without moving.

If Sir Michael took the case from him, there would be no others. Daniel would merely be biding his time, picking up the crumbs of other investigators, as he had been doing the past two years. When his twenty-fifth birthday came in a few weeks and his patronage ended, Daniel would be tossed out of the Bow Street office to fend for himself.

Sir Michael heaved a mighty sigh, fiddling with a quill, as if reluctant to make a decision. At last he spoke, grudgingly. "For the time being, you two will work together. Swann, you will remain in charge of the investigation as long as I feel you are doing everything possible to bring it to a swift conclusion." He pointed his long, bony index finger at Daniel. "But remember, I will remove you if I feel you are making no progress. Now get out of here, both of you. I'm a busy man."

Daniel followed Ed down the hall, his footsteps sounding loud in his ears. At the doorway to the office, Ed jerked his head toward the street entrance. "Get your coat, lad, and let's get to it. You heard the guv. You're in charge."

As they stepped out into the brisk January morning, Cadogan eased his coach to the curb. "Ah, thought I might find you here." He touched his brim.

"Don't you ever sleep?" Daniel's breath hung in a frosty cloud.

"Don't you?" Cadogan shot back. "Where to, gents?"

"Belgrave Square. We'll start with the other debutante and her family. I don't feel like bearding Mr. Montgomery just yet." Daniel dug into his cloak pocket for a shilling. "Earl Thorndike's house."

"What do you know about the earl and his wife?" Ed asked, adjusting his hat and straightening his coat as Cadogan slapped the reins and they were away.

Daniel tried to put faces to names. "Nothing. Their daughter was one of the debutantes, but they weren't at the party. Lady Juliette Thorndike, her name is." Brown hair, brown eyes. Pink lips and softly rounded shoulders.

A nudge from Ed brought him back to the matter at hand. He consulted the guest list from the ball. "Isn't that odd? Why wouldn't they be at their daughter's party?"

"I've no idea. I didn't know they weren't until I studied the list and found they weren't on it."

"Something to track down, for sure."

"Do you think the thief is on this guest list?"

Blowing out a breath, Ed shrugged. "I hope not. Seems we have to prove things twice over when it's someone from the aristocracy. Nobody bats an eye if we point the finger at a servant or tradesman or dockworker, but even a hint of scandal from 'our betters' and the hue and cry is raised." He gave a broad grin. "I pity the poor man who has to take charge of this mess."

"I can always tell Sir Michael that it's too much for me and he'll toss it right to you." Daniel looked out of the side of his eyes at Ed.

"No, thank you. Why do you think I fought so hard for you to keep the case this morning?" Ed grinned.

Belgrave Square, which was lined with trees and expensive townhouses and shops, sat north and a bit east of Eaton Square, genteel and prosperous.

Daniel rented rooms, or rather his patron rented rooms for him, in a boardinghouse in the Charing Cross Road, a ten-minute walk to the Bow Street offices. Soon he would have to seek new lodgings, as his constable's salary would not reach to paying his current rent. If Sir Michael had his way and pitched him out of the office, Daniel would have to find a position and a new home quickly, since he had little in the way of monetary reserves.

The carriage rocked to a stop in front of a set of high steps leading to a glossy black-painted door.

"I hope they're awake after the late night." Ed swung the carriage door open. "I don't imagine they will be too pleased to see us in any case."

Daniel followed him onto the pavement. "They will have to endure our presence. Why is it that we coddle and pamper aristocrats when, if this was a fishmonger and his wife, we wouldn't think twice about barging in and getting the answers we seek?" He nodded up to Cadogan. "We should be finished in under an hour. I'd be obliged if you waited."

"I'll be here, guv. Anything I can do for you in the meantime?" He rubbed his red nose. "Didn't mind the bit of sleuthing you put me up to last night."

Avoiding Ed's questioning gaze, Daniel shook his head. "Nothing just now."

"Right." Cadogan wrapped his cloak more tightly around himself and settled in to wait.

As they trudged up the steps, Ed answered Daniel's question. "Because a fishmonger and his wife won't trot round to our superiors complaining about our methods, and even if they did, they'd get short shrift with the guv."

"So everybody is a suspect unless they have enough influence to make our lives difficult?" He flipped his truncheon end over end and caught it with a satisfying smack to the palm.

"Lad, sometimes I despair of you. Everyone is a suspect, but you have to tailor your methods to get the best results. Aristocrats don't take kindly"—he paused to use the brass door knocker—"to being accused and inconvenienced. If you want to leave here with the information you seek, then use some of those brains you cultivated at university. Whenever you're on a case, you act as if you're a mallet and everyone around you is a peg to be pounded."

As Daniel formed a retort, the door opened a few inches, and a dour-faced old man pierced them with a stare. "We're not receiving visitors."

"We're not visitors."

At Ed's scowl, Daniel modulated his voice.

"Sir, we are investigators from Bow Street." He consulted his notebook. "We're here to see Sir Bertrand Thorndike and Lady Juliette Thorndike please."

"Investigators?" He drew back, grimacing, as if he'd smelled food that had gone bad. "Why is it that you feel you can march up the front entrance like invited guests? I must insist you use the servant's entrance. We cannot have tradespeople traipsing through the front door." He pointed to the staircase going down to the left of the front entrance and shut the black lacquered barrier with a brisk bang.

Daniel shot Ed a glare. "And I'm the one who should polish my manners?" How dare the butler shoo them away like common street urchins? He raised his fist to pound on the door, but Ed tugged his sleeve.

"Put away your dudgeon, lad. It's just a flight of stairs."

Cadogan, who had climbed down from the carriage to stand at his team's heads, averted his gaze, but a smile played about his lips. Daniel marched down the front steps, slammed open the gate to the lower stairs, and descended below street level to the servants' entrance. Before he could knock, a young woman opened the door and bobbed a quick curtsy.

"Help you gents?" she asked.

Daniel introduced himself again, and they were granted entrance. The young maid led them down a tiled hallway and into the servants' dining room. As she turned to take their hats and cloaks, a woman entered through a swinging door, and Daniel froze.

She was dressed in black with a white apron trimmed in lace and a white cap. Around the edges of her face, gray intermingled with dark curls, and lines of care bracketed her mouth. She looked older than her forty-three years.

"Mr. Swann and Mr. Beck, ma'am. From Bow Street." The maid introduced them.

When her eyes met his, she stopped, the chatelaine at her waist chiming gently against the folds of her apron.

Ed handed over his cloak and hat and blew on his hands. "Aye, it's a rum un out there today. Cold as a miser's heart, it is."

"Good day, gentlemen. I'm Mrs. Dunstan, the housekeeper. How may we be of service to you?" She stared hard at Daniel, giving a slight shake of her head, sending him a bold message.

He understood what she wanted. And he hated it. But he would obey her wishes, as he had for all these years.

"We've come to make inquiries of the family regarding events of last night."

She relaxed a fraction, and he knew he'd read her correctly. "If you will follow me, gentlemen, I shall see if the family is receiving."

She led them upstairs into the foyer near the front entrance, where they had been only moments before, but on the other side. The table by the door bore several posies, wrapped gift boxes, and envelopes. Gifts for the young lady of the house? She had made her debut the previous evening. As pretty as she was, it stood to reason young swains would be lining up to shower her with gifts and invitations. The butler showed no remorse for the winding path he'd sent them on, his sallow jowls unmoving as he took their measure.

The butler and housekeeper whispered together, eyeing Daniel and Ed while they spoke. Eventually, the butler disappeared into a room off the foyer, and the housekeeper, with a long look at Daniel, returned the way she had come.

Daniel watched her, unsure what to think. Her refusal to acknowledge him stabbed his heart, and his face grew hot. Clearly nothing had changed in twelve years.

Finally, the butler emerged once more. "This way, gentlemen."

He gestured for them to enter, and Daniel found himself in a drawing room. Pale-yellow wallpaper, blue upholstery and drapes, and white wainscoting. The very picture of taste and elegance. The room was both formal and somehow restful. Weak winter sunshine filtered through the lacy shear panels behind the drapes.

"The officers from Bow Street, sir." The butler bowed and closed the door behind him.

A man stood near the fireplace, half turned away from them, his elbow on the mantel and his hand over his eyes. When he spun around, his hair was mussed and his eyes red rimmed.

Daniel raised his truncheon a few inches. "Mr. Swann. Bow Street. And my associate, Mr. Beck. You are Sir Bertrand Thorndike?" He must tread carefully here so as not to earn another reprimand, either from Ed when they got back in the carriage or from Sir Michael, if someone should lodge another complaint. But he also must get the information he needed.

"Yes." He winced at the sound of his own voice. If what witnesses last night said was true, his head must be splitting right now. He'd sewn the wind of drink and now reaped the whirlwind of a hangover.

"We need a word with you, and with Lady Juliette. And with the earl and countess as well." He thought he had made that clear to the household staff, but he'd restate their mission if that was what it took to have the correct people brought to them.

"That won't be possible, I'm afraid." Sir Bertrand took a seat in a high-backed chair and crossed his legs, putting his hand over his eyes again. "My brother and his wife have been called away to their estate in Worcestershire. They left a few days ago and are not expected back for some time."

"An odd time to leave the city, isn't it? Before their daughter's debut?"

Sir Bertrand waved his free hand. "*Noblesse oblige.* Duty called. My brother has always put the needs of the estate above his own pleasures. There was something at Heild House that only he could set right. Might I inquire as to what you wish to question them about? I suppose it has to do with the theft my niece told me about this morning? Though they could not be of any help, as they were not in London at the time."

Ed shifted his weight. "I understand you had to leave the party early, sir? A bit of, shall we say, indisposition?"

"You could call it that." Sir Bertrand swallowed and pressed his fingertips to his temples. He sagged back into his chair, avoiding the light from the windows.

"Sir, is Lady Juliette at home?" Daniel asked. Time was wasting on this investigation. The guest list was long, and if the people he needed to interview weren't here, he must press on.

"Lady Juliette has retired to her room." He kept his eyes covered. "I doubt she can add anything to your inquiries. And I know I cannot. I left well before any crime was committed. I need a drink. Perhaps a bit of the 'hair of the dog that bit me' will sort this pounding headache."

Disgust tightened Daniel's abdomen. The man was a wastrel, so inconsiderate, he chose to become sotted on a night that should have been a celebration of his niece.

"Nevertheless, sir, we will need to speak with Lady Juliette ourselves."

Sir Bertrand opened his eyes, his lids redder than Daniel had first supposed. "Gentlemen, I'm perishing for a drink, but my brother has locked the liquor cabinet and given the keys to his new dragon of a housekeeper. The butler has insisted upon plying me with an entire samovar of coffee this morning, which has done little other than to make me jittery and irritable. My niece is in her room, most probably weeping that her parents have abandoned her to face her debut season alone, or because she has been put into the care of myself, who neither sought nor wanted the job."

Daniel's mouth tightened. The man was also a cad.

"Uncle Bertie, you exaggerate on both counts."

Daniel stiffened to attention as Lady Juliette Thorndike entered. Ed smartened up his stance as well, but her uncle remained in his chair. He gave a weak flap of his hand and then covered his eyes once more.

"Gentlemen, welcome to our home. I am sorry you are here on such a poor errand and that my parents are not here to greet you. I trust my uncle has made you welcome. Please, do sit down."

She moved across the room and nudged her uncle's knee as she passed, as if reminding him to mind his manners.

"Apologies, my dear. My head is in a dreadful state."

"And you've no one to blame but yourself. Sit up and behave. The sooner we answer these men's questions, the sooner they may be about their business." She twisted the ring Daniel remembered from the previous evening as she frowned at her uncle. For all her uncle's accusations of her crying, her face bore no trace of tears.

"I've already told them we have nothing to add. I don't know why they're still here."

"Mr. Swann? I apologize for my uncle Bertie. However, I do feel he's correct in his assertion that we have nothing to add to what you've already been told. I'm mystified as to who would steal Mr. Montgomery's painting. I wish you well with your search, but I know nothing about the theft."

"Lady Juliette, can you think of anything unusual that happened at the party last night? Anyone acting suspiciously, anything out of place?"

She perched on the edge of a divan. "No. Everything went to plan until Mr. Montgomery took us all to his picture gallery. I didn't know most of the guests, having been away at school for several years, but I noticed nothing out of the ordinary. Dancing, socializing, some card playing in one of the side rooms."

Ed leaned forward. "Lady Juliette, what time did you arrive at the Montgomery house yesterday, and were you present when the painting was delivered?"

She paused, tapping her pursed lips. "I arrived midafternoon. I'm not certain of the exact time. I heard the painting being delivered . . . I mean, I heard the footmen carry the crate upstairs. Mr. Montgomery was speaking very loudly, excited about his acquisition, no doubt, and he directed the delivery of the painting upstairs, right past our dressing rooms. Agatha, Miss Montgomery, told me what the commotion was, and I'm afraid I didn't give it another thought. I had no idea her father was going to unveil the piece during the party, and I'll confess, I was not enamored of the notion. It seemed to take the focus off his daughter and put it squarely upon himself."

It took the focus off her as well. Daniel studied her up-to-the-

minute dress, her carefully arranged hair, the golden ring on her finger. She had everything. The finest schools, the finest clothes, the best
opportunities.

And yet Daniel felt she was withholding something. The way she
didn't meet anyone's eyes, the way she gripped her fingers together
until the skin showed white. "Why did your parents not stay for your
debut ball? What could have meant more to them at their estate than
seeing you properly brought out? Are you perhaps at odds with them?
Any reason why they wouldn't want to be here?" The timing of their
departure was so odd, and Daniel didn't like oddities in an investigation. Each one must be explained to his satisfaction before he could
let it go.

Lady Juliette flinched, and Ed sucked in a breath.

Sir Bertrand jerked, as if prodded out of sleep. "I say, that's nothing
to be asking a young lady. She is in excellent standing with her parents, and if you suggest otherwise, I'll send round to your superiors to
inform them of my opinion of your techniques. Neither of us had anything to do with the theft of that wretched painting. Now, go question
someone else and leave us alone." He sat up straight and then seemed
to regret it, clutching his temples and swaying.

Lady Juliette's eyes glowed hot, and this time they met Daniel's.
"Sir, you have overstepped with your suspicions. As my uncle says,
there is no correlation between the theft and my parents' travels. What
could possibly be the motive for myself or my uncle to be involved?
You can see from our circumstances"—she waved her hand to encompass the lavish room—"we have no need to steal. My parents were
called away to Heild House for a matter that arose on their estate.
There is nothing dubious about their departure. There is nothing to
find with the Thorndikes that will possibly aid your case."

The look she gave Daniel made him wince inwardly. He admired
her defense of her family, but he didn't totally believe her. He never
believed a witness, because he was a detective, and the first rule of
investigations was that people lied to detectives. He believed nothing
until he verified it.

"Where is your parents' estate in Worcestershire?" He took out his notebook.

"Why is that relevant?" She sent a look toward her uncle.

"Just to complete our records." He held the pencil poised over the paper. "I can get the information elsewhere, but it will be quicker coming from you."

Sir Bertrand pushed himself to his feet. "The estate is near the village of Pensax. I'm sure my brother and his wife will return as soon as they are able. Assuming you haven't already apprehended the thief, you can open an investigation into their movements."

"My uncle is right. It's senseless to waste time questioning guests who clearly had nothing to do with the matter." Lady Juliette rose, and Daniel and Ed followed suit. "There must be better avenues of inquiry for you to pursue."

She was right, but Daniel didn't want to let them off the hook easily. There was something amiss here, some undercurrent of tension between the uncle and niece that he didn't understand. Was it merely that he had been blind drunk at her debut that caused the friction?

She twisted her ring once more and looked at the ornate clock beside the fireplace. "Gentlemen, if you will excuse me, I am expecting callers this afternoon, and I must prepare. Uncle Bertie, are you going to receive guests with me, or would you be better off in bed?" Exasperation laced her words, and Daniel didn't blame her. Sir Bertrand appeared to be a weak reed to lean upon.

The butler showed them out through the front door, which gratified Daniel, but piqued him too. Was it that they were being treated better, or that the housekeeper had wanted to avoid encountering them again?

After all, as Daniel's mother, she'd been avoiding him for the past twelve years.

Chapter 3

HOURS LATER, JULIETTE CLOSED THE door on the last caller of the day, who walked to her carriage with Agatha and the dowager. An afternoon of entertaining under the sharp eyes of her chaperone had worn her out. No one had stayed beyond the polite thirty minutes, but there had been a steady stream all day.

When the knocker sounded, she groaned. Had someone forgotten something?

Without waiting for Pultney, she opened the door.

"Lady Juliette. Is your uncle at home?" The Duke of Haverly stood on the step, already tugging off his gloves.

"Come in." She stepped back, bending her head around the door to see his mother's carriage pulling away from the curb. "Uncle Bertie is hiding in the library. It's been a trying day, beginning with a visit from the police."

Pultney appeared as if on cue and took the duke's wraps.

"His Grace is here to see Uncle Bertie. Will you show him to the library?"

She escaped to her room to rest before dinner. Thankfully, there was nothing on the social calendar for this evening, and she could have a quiet night in.

As she walked up the stairs and down the hallway to her chambers, she thought back through the ladies she had met today, the way the dowager had comported herself, and wishing her parents had been present. A hot coal of resentment flickered to life in her middle. They should be here with her, or they should have sent for her to join them in the country. This continued separation only increased her feelings of abandonment. What was in the country that was so much more important than being with a daughter they hadn't seen in seven years? Was the fault in them or in herself? The duke had mentioned Bertie's handling of the situation. Was there more there, or was she being too tender?

Thoughts of the other visit of the day drifted in. She'd put the police inquiry to the back of her mind most of the afternoon, but now she took out those memories and examined them. Did the detectives really believe the absurd notion that her parents' departure from London and the theft of the painting were somehow related? Her parents had departed well before the painting had even arrived at Mr. Montgomery's house.

And yet that younger detective had stared at her, as if he could look inside and know all her secrets. As if he was sure she was keeping something from him.

If her parents were here, they would sort out that young man. Her father was blameless in the matter. He had a tremendous sense of right and wrong, of fair play and justice, and he'd taught his daughter to feel the same. She wanted the detective to find Mr. Montgomery's painting and for the miscreant who stole it to be properly punished according to the law, but she also wanted Mr. Swann to do it the right way. Not throwing out wild accusations about innocent people, trying to elicit a reaction.

If only she could enlist her father's help. Instead, her parents and God had abandoned her to the meager assistance of Uncle Bertie. Not even at boarding school, so many hundreds of miles away from her family, had she ever felt so alone.

In her room, she flung herself facedown across the counterpane. What did it matter that her behavior wasn't ladylike? There was no one to see, no one to care. Her father told her God counted every hair on her head, but it certainly didn't seem He noticed her now. Burying her head in the brocade bedcover, she tried to relax her muscles. The fragile strings binding her self-control pinged and snapped one by one until the tears threatened to escape.

She hated to cry.

How was she to navigate the next little while without her parents? And how long was a little while? What if they remained in the country for weeks? Or months? Her entire Season? Her mother was supposed to be here to guide her. They were supposed to become friends and confidantes, allies, and cohorts.

Her father was supposed to be here to support and protect her, to tease and amuse, to give his wisdom and insight as she made choices that could very well affect the rest of her life.

And they were ensconced at the country estate, oblivious to her wants and needs, putting duty ahead of her.

Or was she wrong to judge them so harshly? She had never had the responsibility of an estate. Bertie couldn't even reliably tell her what the issue that arose had been. If it really was a catastrophe that only they could head off, then it was right that they had gone, and she was being selfish to wish them here.

But she still wished it.

Juliette rolled over and opened the bedside table drawer, withdrawing two packets of letters. One had been tied with a pink bit of lacy ribbon, and the other with string.

Her mother's letters were full of advice and tidbits of life. She had shared the latest dress trends and snippets of news amongst her wide circle of friends, of her experiences at the opera, plays, and house parties. They were lighthearted and fun, but tucked amongst the more frivolous orts were serious passages about growing up and how to balance emotions with facts, how to recognize sincerity in a friend, and how to protect oneself from those who would take advantage. Motherly chats that filled in small measure the lonely places in Juliette's heart. Chats dispensed by letter that Juliette had hoped to relive in person the minute they were reunited.

Juliette's father's letters were a far different proposition. From the time she could read, her father had written her weekly. Always in a different code that she must first decipher, his letters growing more complex as she grew older. At first they were pictures strung together, then mixed up letters, then symbols and ciphers. How eagerly she had anticipated his newest epistles. Once she had become adept at cracking his codes, she had begun to write back to him in codes of her own. It was a delightful secret world shared only by the two of them.

His letters had been full of his favorite things, horses, dogs, fishing, boating, the latest scientific progress, interesting bits he'd learned in his various studies. And stories of what they would do when her schooling was over and they would be together. How he would buy her the best horse in the country so she could accompany them fox hunting each fall. The people he wanted her to meet, the places he wanted to take her. They would go fishing in Scotland and walk the beaches of Brighton, explore a Roman ruin in Cumbria, and set up a friendly competition against one another at archery when they all returned to the family home in Worcestershire.

While most of the girls at the exclusive finishing school in Switzerland had bemoaned parents they felt were too old to understand, too overbearing, too . . . everything, Juliette had never felt that way. Her parents were the epitome of all she hoped to become—elegant, intelligent, kind, interesting.

If she ever got to be with them, that is.

She ran her thumb along the edges of the letters as tears blurred her vision. She blinked hard and took a few deep breaths to beat them back.

God, why? Why are You asking me to delay my dreams? I haven't asked for anything extravagant. I just want to be with my parents. If Uncle Bertie wasn't so stubborn, I would have gotten on a coach and headed to Heild Manor right away. Guilt trickled through her. She had been given instructions through Bertie from her parents, and they would expect her to obey, to be a credit to the Thorndike family, and to await their return with patience and grace. This whining alone in her room was unseemly and letting down the family.

She replaced the letters in the drawer and pushed herself up from the bed, shoving her disheveled hair out of her eyes, ignoring the hairpins that fell onto the spread. She hugged her arms across her middle. Outside, sleet clicked against the windowpanes. At least the weather matched her mood.

Her eyes fell on the row of music boxes on the carved shelf over her writing desk, cherished gifts from her parents, one for each birthday. Porcelain, enamel, wood, brass, each different in construction. Each beautiful and delicate, just like her mother. Curiously, each music box played the same song, a portion of Mozart's "Eine Kleine Nachtmusik: A Little Night Music."

It was her mother's favorite piece. Though Juliette knew she would never play as well as the countess, she had worked long hours at the pianoforte learning the piece to surprise her parents.

Would she have the chance to perform it for them?

The walls of her bedchamber began to close in, and she flung open the door, storming down the hallway with no destination in mind. She couldn't deal with Uncle Bertie at the moment, wherever he had gotten off to, and she absolutely knew she couldn't face her parents' suite at the back of the house.

An upstairs maid, carrying a stack of folded linens, passed Juliette, and a footman followed her with a coal hod in each hand. The staff were strangers to her, which only made Juliette feel all the more lonely.

She turned away from the stairs and crossed the landing to the double doors behind her, opening them and slipping into her mother's favorite room in the house, the music room.

Soft rose-colored walls, white wainscoting, and delicate plasterwork on the ceilings. Yards of highly polished oak floors scattered with oriental carpets, and settees and chairs in muted gold upholstery. A harp, a pianoforte, a violin, a flute. Her mother was proficient at all, and especially gifted at the harp. She also possessed a fine singing voice. Juliette's earliest memories were of her mother singing as she entered the nursery each morning.

Juliette sat at the piano, fingers resting on the keys, eyes staring at the fallboard, which had been painted with a spray of flowers. Everything about the instrument spoke of her mother's taste and style. The keys were smooth and cold, and when she pressed them, they felt stiff and nonresponsive.

The chord echoed in the empty room. She pressed her lips together and let her hands drop into her lap.

Using only her index finger, Juliette slowly played the opening notes of the Mozart tune. One measure, two, three, and at the end of the fourth, a barely audible click came, sending a vibration through her fingers, and a small door opened on the side of the pianoforte. A weak thump sounded as a fabric-wrapped parcel fell out of the now open compartment onto the rug.

———— ⁂ ————

"How many blind alleys can one man go up?" Daniel climbed into Cadogan's carriage after yet another failure to get information from a receiver's shop. None of the receivers had caught even a whisper of who might have taken the painting, nor could any of Daniel's informants speculate who would want to steal it. None of the pawnbrokers he'd questioned even dealt in artwork. Their shops were filled with basic household goods, pocket watches, painted fans, shoe buckles, and the like. Practical things pawned by desperate people or pickpockets and petty thieves, not fine art. The shops bordered the territories known in London as rookeries, warrens of shacks, tenement buildings, and hovels where the poor crowded in and tried to survive. Not a hospitable environment for a piece of fine art . . . or a Bow Street runner.

"No luck, then?" Ed moved his feet as Daniel took the bench opposite.

"Not a speck. What did you find? Did Mr. Montgomery insure the painting?"

Ed had gone to the Montgomery house to question the staff and look into their backgrounds.

Ed shook his head. "He said he intended to go to his broker to increase the policy on his collection, but he hadn't arranged the new addition yet."

"Too bad. Wouldn't that be a tidy end to the case? Insurance fraud? Clap on the darbies and carry him off to Newgate." Daniel sighed. "I can't seem to envision a model of our criminal. Who had access to the painting? Who had the ability to steal it and either get it out of the house or hide it sufficiently that a search wouldn't reveal it? And who had the contacts to move it and shift it on for profit?"

Consulting his notebook, Ed scratched his gray side-whiskers. "I've gotten no results looking into the backgrounds of Montgomery's staff, both permanent and temporary. I did get an earful from Mr. Montgomery, however, about how we were less than useless, disrupting his staff, chasing our tails, and more of that ilk. I kept my head and 'yes, sir'-ed him a lot. He seems the type to like that."

"I don't know how you held your tongue. It's not as if *we* stole the painting. It's his property, and he couldn't manage to hold onto it for more than a few hours." Daniel scowled. He abhorred the way some aristocrats treated the Bow Street officers like common trash but then set up a hue and cry the moment they needed something or felt they had been wronged. Most of London, in fact, seemed to distrust the police, seeing them as some sort of deterrent to their freedoms rather than a protector of them.

The window behind Daniel's head slid open. "Where to, guv?" Cadogan asked from his perch on the driver's seat.

"Clerkenwell. Turner and Rathbone Dealers in Fine Arts." He handed a slip of paper with the address through the window over his shoulder. "Perhaps"—he shrugged—"we can learn something of the painting's current whereabouts through its origins. And two birds with one stone, since the man who procured the painting for Montgomery was also a guest at the party." The carriage lurched, and he braced his palms on the seat.

"Anything you studied up there at university teach you about what we're looking for? I can just about tell a portrait from a landscape, but after that, one painting looks much the same to me." Ed grinned. "Not like you young rascals with the gowns and tassels and the like, stuffing your heads full of book teachings. Us old relics learned through doing, not reading."

Daniel raised one eyebrow. "I might be glad to have all that education behind me when I apply for a job as a clerk or personal secretary once Sir Michael finally boots me out of Bow Street. I fear he's marking the days on his desk diary until he can finally rid himself of my presence."

"Seems a rum thing to do to you, lad. Dunno why your guardian set up such a daft scheme."

Ed was the only one Daniel had told about the structure of his guardian's wishes, though not the identity of said guardian. He himself didn't even know who his patron was, nor why he had taken an interest in Daniel's life. He only knew the man . . . or men . . . had governed his life since he was old enough to go to boarding school.

And his mother had gone along with their wishes. In spite of his pleading, begging her not to send him away. She had been firm. It was for his own good. They'd both get on better apart. She wanted him to go.

So at the tender age of twelve, he'd been taken from his home and his only family and deposited in a boarding school amongst the sons of the aristocracy and wealthy, ostracized, sometimes bullied, mostly ignored. He'd turned to books and athletics, pouring himself into both to assuage his loneliness.

The stipulations of the agreement were clear, and he'd been told them from the outset. He'd gone over them so many times in his mind, he could quote them verbatim.

All communication would be handled through the London solicitors Coles, Franks & Moody.

He would never seek to discover his patron's name.

He would conduct himself well at all times and never give his patron reason to regret the agreement.

He would never join the military.

He would sever all ties with his mother and become the ward of his patron.

In return, he would be educated, clothed, housed, and employed in the career of his choice up to his twenty-fifth birthday. On that date, all patronage would cease.

It had been the stipulation that he must cut off contact with his mother that had angered Daniel the most, both that this mysterious patron would demand it and that his mother would agree to it. She must have been glad for the opportunity. As an unmarried woman, having an illegitimate son hanging about had held her back in life.

Seeing her at the Thorndike house had been a shock. She went by Mrs. Dunstan now? Had she married? And now that he knew where she was, and he was so near the end of his patronage, would it be permissible for him to contact her? Did he want to, knowing she had sent him away?

Was this something he was obliged to report to Mr. Coles? He was due to see the solicitor in the coming week to receive his quarterly stipend. Would meeting his mother, however accidental or unintended, jeopardize his employment at Bow Street?

To this day, Daniel wasn't certain why he chose to become a Bow Street officer. Perhaps it was a bit of rebellion, a desire to shock his unknown patron? But not that solely. He also wanted to do something good with his life, something important.

During his last year at university, he had been unsure of which direction to take, what occupation to propose to his patron, but then Edward Beck had come to Oxford to investigate a suspicious death. Daniel, whose lodgings were near the canal where the body was found, observed the investigator, befriended him, and was intrigued by the position. He followed the case from beginning to end, even attending the trial at the magistrate's court rather than his lectures in order to see the killer brought to justice.

He didn't know what promises or payments or threats had happened behind the scenes to get him the job of his choice, but once he had chosen his path, his mysterious patron had seen to it that Daniel was employed at Bow Street a mere week after earning his degree in history and art from Pembroke College.

And he'd been the thorn in Sir Michael's side ever since.

The carriage bowled up to Turner and Rathbone, a broad brick building situated between a watchmaker and a lace shop. Across the street were a bookbinder, a wine shop, and the Horn and Hound pub.

"All a far cry from the rookeries, isn't it? Upscaled commerce." Ed took the measure of the street, looking up at the art dealer's sign swinging in the cold air. He doffed his tall hat to a pair of young ladies coming out of the lace shop.

"I wouldn't mind finding lodgings in a neighborhood like this." Daniel noted the publican sweeping his stoop. "I'll be looking for new rooms soon enough. Perhaps the bookbinder needs a clerk."

"Nonsense. You should set yourself up as a private inquiry agent if Sir Michael gives you the boot. You were made to keep the peace and unravel puzzles, son. You have a knack for this job. Many times you've seen something I haven't, or thought of a different approach that wound up cracking a case. I'll admit, when you first arrived on the job, you were as green as spring grass, but you've grown into the work."

A private inquiry agent? Daniel paused. He'd never thought of that. Could he support himself thus? It might bear looking into. Though his heart was in Bow Street. If only he could solve this case and earn Sir Michael's respect.

Stepping up to the art dealer's door, Ed tried the handle. The door didn't budge. Locked. "Shades on the door and windows. Can't tell if anyone's in there or not."

"Perhaps they've stepped out?" Daniel looked down the street. Every other business on the avenue was open for trade. "Tea break?" It was midafternoon, after all.

Ed rapped on the glass, but no one answered his summons. "Maybe there's someone around back? Do these places have storerooms or offices? I've never been inside an art dealer's shop before."

They rounded the end of the block and entered the alley behind the shops. At the far end, a hunched teamster drove his wagon away from them, canvas tarps covering a tied-down load of goods. Over the rattle of the wheels on the cobbles, Daniel said, "Narrow space for such a big wagon. He must be a good driver to wend his way through here."

They found the back door of the art dealer's, and it stood open a few inches. Ed put the flat of his hand on the panel and pushed it back. "Is anyone here?" He stepped inside, and Daniel followed.

They were in a large room with high windows up near the eaves, which let in narrow bars of light. The room smelled of wood shavings and dust.

It didn't take much light to note that something was terribly amiss. Crates were knocked over, packing material spilling everywhere. Daniel's boots crunched on broken shards of china and porcelain. A painting leaned against the left-hand wall, slashed to ribbons.

He caught Ed's eye. Ed put his finger to his lips and jerked his chin toward the doorway on the far side of the storage area. Faint light crept through the crack beneath the door, but no sound came from the room beyond.

Daniel nodded, tightness creeping over his muscles. Was the vandal still here? His truncheon slipped from his belt into his hand in a way he'd practiced many times.

Picking their way through the detritus as quietly as possible, they crossed the cluttered room. Each took up a position on either side of the door, and Ed drew his truncheon from beneath his cloak.

He pointed to Daniel and then to the doorknob. At his nod, Daniel grabbed the handle and thrust the door open.

Ed barged through, Daniel right on his heels. The older detective stopped so abruptly, Daniel crashed into his back.

"Ooomph." The air rushed out of Daniel, and he bounced to the side. "A little warning next time wouldn't go amiss," he chided, righting his hat.

Then he saw what had caused Ed to halt in his tracks.

A man lay sprawled on the floor of the cluttered office, half a foot of knife hilt protruding from his chest.

Chapter 4

THE PARCEL HIT THE CARPET with a substantial thud, and for a moment, Juliette thought she'd broken the pianoforte, that somehow she'd managed to knock a piece out of it.

Leaping from the bench, she rounded the end of the keyboard and stared at the trap door on the side of the instrument and at the square bundle on the floor.

She lifted the little door, and as she shut it, a small click sounded, some sort of internal fastening. The craftsmanship was astounding. The door disappeared into the wood pattern of the piano case. One would never know it was there.

The bundle on the floor was wrapped in a navy velvet bag with gold drawstrings, and the Thorndike family crest had been embroidered on one side of the bag. She'd seen this bag before, or one like it, years ago when her parents had been preparing to leave Heild Manor for London yet again, and the house had been in an uproar with packing.

Her mother's clothes had required several trunks, and valises and bandboxes lay open and spilling their contents. Maids bustled, the housekeeper ordered everyone about, and Juliette had perched on a footstool in the corner of the dressing room, watching the chaos and wishing her parents weren't leaving her behind, as they had so often. She must have been seven or eight at the time.

Father had entered the dressing room from his own connecting door, a velvet drawstring bag in his hand.

All movement stopped. Juliette straightened in her corner. She didn't see her father often, for he traveled frequently, but to her, he was the most amazing man in the world.

He crossed the room and bussed Mother's cheek, squeezing her arm and staring for a long moment into her dark eyes. A familiar sensation of warmth and safety crept over Juliette.

Then he handed Mother the velvet bag. "Are you sure this is all you want from the safe?"

"Yes, darling, I've plenty of other baubles already packed." Mother took the bag into her lap.

"Who is this little mouse hiding in the corner?" Father looked over his shoulder at Juliette. He winked at her, and she hunched her shoulders, happy he'd acknowledged her.

"Come here, Juliette," Mother beckoned. "I'd like you to see these. You'll wear them one day, after all."

Juliette slipped off her footstool and came to stand beside her mother, letting her fingers glide over the whisper-smooth cloth of her mother's skirt and releasing her perfumed scent.

Father took the bag and opened it, sliding out a black box and handing it to Mother. She opened the lid, and Juliette sucked in a breath. Against a bed of white satin lay a necklace of deep-blue stones strung together with diamonds.

"The Thorndike Sapphires, sweetling." Mother put her arm around Juliette and drew her into her side. "A wedding gift from your father." She looked up at him with such love in her eyes that it made Juliette's chest ache.

The childhood memory swirled away, leaving only the feelings behind.

Now she clutched the velvet drawstring bag as she stood in the middle of the music room, the ache from that long-ago day expanding and deepening until it nearly consumed her.

Opening the bag, expecting to see the contents from long ago, puzzlement struck her. This was no jewelry box. A slim leather-bound book slipped out of the cloth. Embossed with gold filigree, its gilt-edged pages were secured with a lock of some kind.

Why had her parents hidden a book in a musical instrument? She shook the bag, and a single slip of paper fell out.

Darling Juliette, you clever girl. Solve the puzzle, open the book, and everything will be made known to you. Your loving parents.

A rush of interest surged through her mind. She loved a puzzle, a challenge. Finally, some communication with her parents. It was just like her father to give her something to occupy her mind until they returned.

She hitched her skirt and sank onto the brocade settee, slipping off her shoes and tucking her feet beneath her hem. The lock was metal, with a row of small cylinders etched with symbols. Four cylinders, each with five different symbols. She did a quick calculation. That meant 625 possibilities.

They weren't letters or numbers. What were they?

Springing to her feet, she raced upstairs with the book. She was halfway to her room before she realized she had forgotten her shoes. No matter. She could retrieve them later. Rummaging in her handkerchief drawer, her fingers closed around her quizzing glass. Agatha had gifted her the glass for a jape their first year at school when Juliette had complained that their French instructor always wrote with such a small, cramped hand that she couldn't make out if he meant *cheval*, which was horse, or *chevel*, which was hair.

If only it weren't so dismal outside. What she needed was a fair bit of sunlight. Still, she went to the window and looked at the symbols through the magnification of the glass.

Miniature coats of arms. She recognized the Thorndike family crest on the first cylinder, but the others were unknown to her. How was she going to crack this code?

The library. In Juliette's experience, if there was something she wanted to know, someone, somewhere, had authored a book on the subject. Or one of the newest fads in literature, the monograph. Her father had written to her about both collecting and writing monographs, trading them with his friends and colleagues, and how much he'd learned from them.

Perhaps somewhere along the way he had acquired a monograph on heraldry? She could only hope.

The library was deserted when she reached it, and she was grateful that Uncle Bertie had taken himself off somewhere. Had he concluded his business with the duke? If so, he was probably nursing his intermittent hangover.

She opened the library drapes to allow some light into the room, but she still needed a taper to peruse the shelves. Her father had eclectic taste in reading material, as well as a rather haphazard cataloging system.

Or did he? The books weren't arranged by author or title or subject, but rather by . . . language? Latin, French, Italian, German, English, Russian. There were some in what was possibly Chinese, and even a handful in Arabic.

After an extensive search, she discovered *A Complete Body of Heraldry* by Joseph Edmondson. She dragged the heavy book from a bottom shelf and took it to her father's desk.

Taking up pen and ink, she searched for a sheet of foolscap to take notes. If she could identify each crest, perhaps they would give her the clues to unlock the book. Of course, she could have taken the mysteriously locked book to Mr. Pultney, the butler, and asked him to cut it open, but she was reluctant to do that. Her father's note had said to solve the puzzle, not to work around it. He wouldn't have taken the easy way out and cut off the lock, she was sure. He would have used his brain and his resources to work it out on his own. Besides, she may wish to lock it up again once she uncovered the code.

With the illustrations in the heraldry book and her quizzing glass, she painstakingly identified each coat of arms, first by the family it represented and then by the individual parts of the achievements of arms.

Leopards, stars, lions, roosters, helmets.

The mantlings, the crests, the shields, the supporters.

And the overall design on the shield. Per pale, per fess, quartered, canton . . .

She blew out a breath, looking at her notes. Was there a pattern here? Was the combination alphabetical? Territorial? Color coded?

The Thorndike coat of arms was on the first cylinder and seemed the logical place to start. After that she tried the others that also had leopards.

No results.

She tried by shield style, by crests, by supporters, by shire of origin. No results.

Frustrated, she sat back. Was she truly going to have to try all 625 combinations? That would be a process of elimination, not truly solving the puzzle. It would feel like cheating.

Or failure.

Studying her lists again, she tried to approach the problem from a different angle, as she had often done when decoding her father's more complex letters. What if it wasn't the images but rather what they represented? Words rather than symbols. Perhaps they spelled a word? Perhaps it had to do with the family names or family mottos.

She tried every combination of the first letters of the family names, trying to spell words. Then she began on the mottos, both in Latin and in English.

When she was ready to give up all hope and admit defeat, she tried one more. The lock clicked sweetly over and snapped open.

Thorndike, whose motto was "Rose amongst Thorns"; Cardigan, which was "On Grace Depend"; Geddes, which was "Seek Greater Things"; and Pattison, which was "Envy Is an Enemy to Honor."

The first letter of each motto spelled ROSE.

Rose amongst Thorns. Rose. The first word in the Thorndike motto.

She opened the book, only to be faced with another puzzle.

The writing was her father's, but it was in a code they'd never used before.

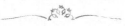

"Meet one Mr. John Selby, agent for Turner and Rathbone Dealers in Fine Arts. Guest of Mr. Montgomery. I met him last night." Daniel squatted on his heels beside the body.

"He sold the painting to Montgomery?" Ed sifted through the scattered paperwork on the floor.

"Yes. I gathered it was a commission for that particular painting, and Selby took care of procuring it." Daniel tilted his head to look at the knife hilt. He'd never seen anything like it. Silver, with a curled handle inlaid with stones. Were they real jewels? If so, the weapon was worth a fortune, and no thief would have left it behind. A petty thief would have taken it in any case, sure to get something for it at a receiver's shop.

"If the killer brought that with him, we're looking for a very wealthy suspect. If it was a weapon of opportunity, something that was for sale here in the gallery, then we're not looking for a thief. There must be some other motive." Daniel made a few notes as he studied the room, trying to envision what had happened.

"Or we're looking for a thief who got interrupted by our corpse here, panicked, grabbed whatever was to hand, and then fled without taking the weapon with him," Ed reasoned.

"Why the destruction then? And did that happen before or after the murder?" Daniel asked.

"There's paperwork strewn beneath the body, so you'd have to say the mess happened before the murder. But there are porcelain shards atop him, so the breakage happened after."

"So the killer was looking for something? He gets surprised by Mr. Selby, grabs the dagger, kills him, and then goes on the rampage destroying the artwork?"

Theories. That was all they had.

"I don't suppose Mr. Selby will be very helpful when it comes to details about the Lotto painting now." Daniel sighed. "How long has he been dead, do you think?"

Ed touched the body's cheek. "He's not completely cold. And the blood's still fairly fresh."

"He left last night at the same time as most of the guests. He was checked off the list at the door when he went. That was at nearly one or a bit after." Where had Selby gone after he'd left Eaton Square?

Daniel straightened. The coroner would be here soon, and hopefully his examination of the corpse would yield some clues.

The art dealer's office was a whirlwind of strewn papers. The desk drawers had all been upended onto the floor, and the chair would make fine kindling. He went into the front gallery space that faced the street and stopped, struck by the sheer wreckage.

A sculpture had been tossed from its plinth, bits of marble breaking off, and the bulk of the figure hitting hard enough to gouge splinters from the wooden floor. At least two large urns had been smashed, hurling shards of porcelain like shrapnel into every corner. And to Daniel's mind, the worst offense to the artwork, every painting had been subjected to a blade, ribbons of canvas drooping in the frames. Dutch portraits, English landscapes, Italian iconography. The vandal had been indiscriminate in his destruction.

Which led to the obvious question. Why? The value in this room alone would feed a gang of thieves for a decade. Why destroy the art rather than steal it? Did this murder have anything to do with the stolen Lotto, or was it an odd coincidence?

Daniel didn't believe in coincidences. The theft and the murder were too unusual not to be related, and when you threw in the timing of each, it strained credibility to think they weren't somehow connected.

A rattling of the front door spun Daniel around. Keys clanked against the lock, a quick click, and the door opened, flapping the shade in the door's window. A young man stepped inside, removing his hat, and when he looked up, he froze.

In a fraction of a second, his mouth opened, and he sucked in a breath. The valise he carried hit the doorsill with a thud. His eyes met Daniel's, and he whirled, grabbing the doorframe to propel himself outside once more.

Before he could escape, Daniel yelled, "Wait! We're the police. From Bow Street."

The young man stopped on the curb, still tensed to run.

Daniel showed the man his brass truncheon, bright because he polished it regularly. The truncheon was like a badge of office for a Bow

Street detective, handy for keeping the peace, plus a good place to roll up a warrant and stow it inside when necessary.

The young man approached the entrance, his eyes darting from painting to sculpture to broken pottery, then back to Daniel. His mouth worked, but no sound came out. His already pale complexion lightened further, and he swayed, holding onto the doorjamb.

"Wha . . . wha . . ." He blinked. "What happened here? Mr. Selby will be beside himself. Whatever will we tell poor old Mr. Rathbone?"

"Sir, who are you? Do you work here?"

The only response was more wide-eyed staring and a gaping mouth.

"Sir?" Daniel spoke sharply.

"I beg your pardon." The young man released his grip on the doorframe and wiped his hand on his trouser leg. "My name is Joshua Rickets. I'm employed here." His wrist flicked to encompass the gallery. "Where is Mr. Selby? He'll be furious. He was after Mr. Rathbone last autumn to let him install one of those new burglar alarms, since we've been getting in higher quality and more valuable pieces lately, but Mr. Rathbone wouldn't hear of it. Too expensive, he said. And didn't we have night watchmen patrolling Clerkenwell? Oh yes, Mr. Selby is going to be angry."

The words seemed to pour out of Rickets like ale from a mug.

Ed appeared in the doorway, holding aside the curtain that separated the gallery from the office. "Who's this lad?"

Rickets all but leapt out of his skin. "Oh, sir." He put his hand to his chest, as if to hold his heart in place. "I had no idea there was more than one of you here. Please tell me you are also from Bow Street?"

Daniel nodded while trying to place Rickets's accent. "What is it you do here, Mr. Rickets?"

"Oh." He looked down at the bag at his feet and picked it up once more. "I started out as a general assistant, moving things in the storeroom, delivering purchases, keeping some of the records. Then I moved up to selling here in the shop and then to buying things from local auctions, but recently Mr. Selby promoted me." His chin rose a fraction. "I'm the new acquisitions buyer for the firm. I travel throughout

England and abroad, purchasing artwork, both on speculation and on order. I just returned from my first trip to the Continent."

"When was that, Mr. Rickets?"

"Just this morning. I was supposed to arrive in a week ago, but I missed my ship in Genoa and had to take another. I'm glad it was arranged for Mr. Selby to meet the *Adventuress* and take possession of the artwork I'd purchased." He stepped into the gallery, toeing aside a pottery shard and closing the door. "I do hope he won't be too angry with me for missing the ship and allowing our purchases to travel on to England alone. They are valuable pieces, and I would hate to think of them falling into the wrong hands. There are some devious people working the ports these days." Digging out a handkerchief, he wiped his forehead and took another long look about the mangled room. "When Mr. Selby arrives, he's going to be devastated. I cannot predict what he will do. He is a man of uncertain temper." He leaned slowly to the side and set the bag on the floorboards. "Perhaps I should begin to clean some of this, to lessen the impact, if you understand my meaning?"

"No, you must not touch anything." Daniel edged around the broken statue. "I'm afraid I have some upsetting news. Mr. Selby must have surprised whoever did this, and the thief attacked him." He'd never had to inform someone of a death before. Was he doing it right? Was there a right way?

"Is he all right? Where is he?" Mr. Rickets swayed, as if the news was a body blow. "Poor Mr. Selby."

Daniel let the silence stretch out. Finally, when Mr. Rickets failed to draw the correct conclusion, he cleared his throat. "I'm sorry, but Mr. Selby is dead. He was killed sometime today."

"Killed?" The word came out a choked whisper. "Here?" A vacant, shocked expression dropped over his face, like a shutter. He trembled from head to foot. "Who? Who did it?" White showed around his eyes, and he fastened his stare on Daniel. "Is it safe here? Did you catch the man?" His throat lurched.

"Mr. Rickets, you're safe for the moment. The killer isn't here. I need you to remain calm." The man's jitters transferred to Daniel, who felt his skin crawl. "I'm afraid I need you to help us determine what, if anything, is missing."

He seemed not to hear.

"Mr. Rickets." Daniel looked at Ed, who shrugged. A clattering in the back room had Ed turning around to investigate. How was Daniel going to get this immobile, terrified clerk into the office with the body still there? "Wait here."

Turning, he reached up and removed the curtain rod from the doorway, let the wooden curtain rings slide off, and took the drape into the office to spread over the body. He returned to the gallery and took the young man's arm, leading him through the doorway. He suspected Mr. Rickets had been promoted beyond his ability to bear responsibility and was now paying the price for his ambition. He seemed a man better suited to taking orders than giving them, and Daniel had to wonder how successful he had been on his own in Europe.

Though Daniel tried to march him straight through the office to the stockroom beyond, it was slow going, as Mr. Rickets couldn't seem to look away from the shrouded form. He nearly contorted himself looking back over his shoulder when they emerged into the storage area.

Ed stood with a pair of men. One held a stretcher upright, his hand wrapped around one handle, leaning on it. "Coroner's here."

"Can you deal with that?" Daniel gestured to Mr. Rickets, who still looked as if he couldn't put one foot in front of the other without help.

When the coroner's men disappeared into the office, Daniel asked, "Can you tell me if anything is missing? What should be in this room that isn't?"

Mr. Rickets shuddered, raising a shaking hand to his face. "It's all so terrible. Does Mr. Rathbone know?"

"Not yet. What about Mr. Turner?"

"He passed away years ago, before my time. Back when Mr. Selby was the new clerk. Mr. Rathbone is very old, bedridden. Mr. Selby had charge of everything here. What will happen to the gallery now?"

"We'll inform Mr. Rathbone, if you will supply us with his address. But we can do that later. For now, please concentrate. Is anything missing?"

Turning, the man looked from one crate to another, from the shredded paintings on the wall to the dented silver bowl that lay on its side in the middle of the floor. He spread his hands, helpless. "I don't know. I've been gone a long time, nearly four months, on this buying trip. I have no idea what Mr. Selby bought or sold in that time."

"Once the coroner is finished, could you help us go through the paperwork? Perhaps the purchases are recorded there?" Daniel groaned inwardly. How long would it take to sort and catalog the inventory?

A man strode into the storeroom from the back alley. He wore a tall hat and shiny boots, and he carried a notebook and pencil. A truly impressive pair of side-whiskers sprang out from his jaw but did nothing to shield the man's rodent-like teeth sticking out at an odd angle. "Bill Beakey, from the *Clerkenwell Courier*. Is it true there has been a murder here?"

"Get out." Daniel stepped forward. He didn't need some newspaperman barging in and getting all the facts wrong and stirring up the neighborhood. Sir Michael was firm in his instructions that his detectives were never to talk to the press. If a statement needed to be made, it would come from his office.

"Thir, the public has a right to know. Has there been a murder? That is a coroner wagon outside." He wrote quickly, his eyes darting from one ruined painting to the next. "Vandalths? Thieveths? Do you have any idea who did thith?" He lifted a ribbon of torn canvas with the end of his pencil.

The man's lisp made it hard to understand what he was saying, but Daniel had heard enough. "Sir, I must ask you to leave. There will be an official statement from the Bow Street offices later today, I'm sure."

The reporter edged toward the office and quick as a flash ducked into the space, with Daniel on his heels.

"You cannot be in here." Daniel grabbed the wiry man by the upper arm, shot an apologetic glance at Ed and the coroner, and hustled the reporter out of the room.

"The people have a right to know." He wriggled, but Daniel held on.

Over the man's protests, Daniel hurried him to the door to the alley, pushed him outside, and closed the door. He leaned against it, lest the man try to return.

"Tapestries."

"Pardon me?" Daniel sucked in a deep breath. He'd forgotten about Mr. Rickets.

"Tapestries. There should be four tapestries from Belgium. They were sold to the Royal Opera House for display in the hall that leads to the most expensive boxes. They were a special purchase, a commission, and Mr. Selby sent me to Brussels especially to buy them." He mopped his head with his handkerchief, sweating in spite of the chill from the open door. "I apologize. I really am not myself."

Daniel made a note. Tapestries.

"How much is something like that worth?"

After a moment, Mr. Rickets said, "They are quite large, from the seventeenth century, and woven by a master." He named a sum that had Daniel's head spinning.

"I do hope they have been delivered and paid for and are safe from whatever happened here." Mr. Rickets touched a chipped picture frame. "If they have been stolen, I don't know how this business will survive. I don't know how it will survive without Mr. Selby. You will catch whoever did this, won't you?"

Daniel nodded, but he wondered if he was up to the task. First a theft, and now a murder. The stakes were rising.

Chapter 5

"Juliette, may I come in?" Uncle Bertie's voice came through the door, but she barely heard it.

Her bedroom looked as if a stationer's shop had exploded, with papers strewn, tacked, and dropped everywhere. Her mind raced from one possibility to the next—letter groupings, patterns, repetition of symbols.

The answer was here, and she was close. The entire afternoon, she'd pored over the pages of the mysterious book, trying one approach after another to decipher the code.

Uncle Bertie knocked again. "Juliette, I'm coming in."

He didn't wait for permission, but when he opened the door, he remained on the sill. "What is all this?"

She looked up, shoving her hair away from her temples. Ink stained her fingers, and she glanced in the mirror on her dressing table. A black smudge decorated her cheek.

"What?" Her concentration broken, it still took her a moment or two to come back to her present circumstances.

He gestured to the papers. "What are you doing?"

"Working." She grabbed the book and swung her feet over the edge of the bed. "Have you seen this before?"

He had changed into evening clothes, and he looked crisp and fresh, as if he'd never heard of overindulgence in drink. His eyes were clear, and his speech precise. "Where did you get this?" He flipped through the opening pages. But only the first page had any writing. The rest were blank.

"It tumbled out of the pianoforte. I played a few measures of Mother's favorite song, and bang. A door opened, and the book fell out. It's in Father's handwriting. I've been trying to break the cipher. Look, he left me a note." She showed him the scrap of paper challenging her to find the answers in the book.

Bertie raised his eyes. He studied her face, frowning, and she remembered the ink smudge. And her disheveled hair. And that she hadn't changed for dinner.

Rather than chide her, he asked, "Have you made any progress?"

"I think so." She scrabbled through the papers on the bed, some sheets she'd used for trial and error decoding, and some of the letters from her father in all the various codes he'd used. "The code most nearly like what is in the book resembles this letter, a simple cryptogram. The letter was a single transposition code, and I wonder if the book isn't the same. Or possibly a double transposition, but if that's the case, it will take me much longer to break."

She stopped. Would Bertie understand anything she'd said? After all, the letters from her father had been a private game between the two of them, and Bertie had probably never tried to decipher a code in his life.

"Your father wrote to you in code? While you were away at school?"

"Yes, for as long as I can remember. When I was very small, he wrote in pictures, then in simple codes, and then more complex. It was for our own amusement."

"That's amazing." Yet he didn't sound surprised.

Looking at the book he held, she noticed something she hadn't seen before. From this angle, it appeared . . . yes. There it was. The gilded edges had been painted. If one bent the pages just right, a picture would appear. "Look." She took the volume and pushed against the edges of the long side, angling the leaves backward.

The picture appeared. Heild Manor, the Thorndike ancestral home in Worcestershire. And in the very corner of the picture, so tiny she had to use the quizzing glass, a short string of letters, perhaps the key to the code?

Pbfiy

She snatched up a clean sheet of paper, uncapped the ink on her desk, and reached for a fresh quill. "If P-b-f-i-y is code for Heild, the rest should come easily."

Bertie leaned against a bedpost and crossed his arms, watching her work.

"This makes no sense. Could those letters stand for 'manor' or 'house'?" Why couldn't she do this? She'd had such hopes.

"He's laid the groundwork for you in the games he sent. What other five-letter words were important to your father?"

"I don't know." She wanted to throw something. For a few hours the code-breaking had pushed aside all else, but frustration at her parents' absence came rushing back. "If they hadn't run away to the country, I could ask him."

Bertie sat on the end of her bed, clamping his hands on his knees and leaning forward. "They aren't here to ask, and from this note your father left, he wants you to solve this yourself. Focus. Eliminate distractions and concentrate on the problem before you. I need to know what this book contains, and you are the one who can figure it out. What word might your father use that has five letters? A word that is important to him?"

Why was Bertie so interested? Why did *he* need to know? It was a puzzle given to her, not him. She cast her mind about, shuffling through the coded epistles she'd received from her father. Until she thought she might know.

Jules. His nickname for her.

Once she had the initial letters in place, she looked for the patterns that would help her fill in the rest. Double letters, repetitive short words like "the" and "and." Places where a capital letter in the middle of a sentence indicated a proper noun.

Yes, yes! Letters became words, which became sentences.

As she completed more and more of the text, her pen slowed.

"What does it say?" Bertie came to look over her shoulder.

She read it aloud. "'If you are reading this, Jules-girl, I applaud you. It means you are ready for the next step. You are at a place in your life where you will have to choose your path, and you will know what is right for you. But you must choose with your whole heart, because there is no turning back once the step is taken. We are proud of you, and know that we will all be reunited someday, in London, at Heild, or in heaven. Tell your uncle Bertie that he must open the door for you, and he must tell you the truth. Your loving father, T.T.'"

"Open the door?" What did that mean? What truth? She looked up and back at Bertie. And what would her tosspot uncle know of it? Though satisfaction at solving the puzzle gladdened her, she still felt an enormous emptiness. The message felt ominous, with a touch of finality. Even if Bertie knew something of the truth mentioned in the note, why should he be the one to tell her? Why wouldn't—or couldn't—her parents?

The code must have been written recently. The ink was fresh, the pages pristine. It wouldn't make sense if it had been written years ago when she was a little girl.

Were her parents speaking of her debut season, her introduction into adulthood? She was at a point in her life where she would be making decisions about her future. Selecting whom to marry stood at the top of the list, and she must choose carefully because such a decision could not be undone. And Uncle Bertie would now be the one to open doors socially for her, to guide her through the process?

What a farce. How was she to rely upon Uncle Bertie when he'd been tap-hackled most of the time since she'd returned to England?

Bertie backed away from her desk and sank onto the featherbed. He had a faraway look to his expression, and Juliette turned on her chair, resting her arm along the back.

"I never thought I would be the one to have to do this. I thought your parents would decide when you were older." He turned to look at her.

A tinge of exasperation colored her tone. "Uncle Bertie, I'm not a child. I will have some say in this. I'm not expecting you to become my duenna."

His brow furrowed. "What are you on about?"

"About you being my guardian until my parents return, and of you having a role in my selection of a suitor. That's what the letter says. Choose with my whole heart what cannot be undone. On the brink of choosing the path my life will take?"

He tilted his head, and he actually smiled, his shoulders relaxing. "If only that was it, I wouldn't feel so daunted. I wish your parents were here. I wish they had not saddled me with this burden." He held up his hands. "Don't take umbrage, girl. I don't mean you. Oh, hang it, just come with me."

"I'm not dressed for dinner. You'll have to give me a bit of time."

"We're not going to dinner. Bring the book and follow me." He hoisted himself up by holding on to the bedpost and left her room.

He strode down the hall, and Juliette hurried after him, clutching the book to her chest. He went past her parents' suite, past his own apartments, and at the far end of the passageway, he stopped before a wall sconce with a shiny silver reflector. Reaching up, he pulled down on the sconce, and a click sounded. The wall moved, pivoting to become a door.

Juliette blinked. A secret doorway?

"I believe *this* is the door your father wanted me to open for you." Bertie pushed the panel of wallpaper and wainscoting open. "Hurry up before someone sees."

She slipped through behind him, and he closed the entrance, plunging them into darkness. Eyes open wide, she could still see nothing until he moved again, and a small louvered window appeared above them. He'd opened a shade to let in the weak evening light. A staircase emerged from the shadows, and he took it.

Each tread was heavily carpeted, and their feet made no sound. At the top a small landing turned, and he paused, his hand on a brass doorknob. His head bowed, and he appeared unsure.

Juliette touched his arm. "Uncle Bertie?"

As if coming to a decision, he straightened. "If this is our Rubicon, so be it." He bent in the low light, fiddled with the complicated knob, and opened the door.

Juliette wasn't sure what she expected, a dusty, musty attic space? Something in storage her parents wanted Bertie to give her?

But as she stepped into the room, she felt as if she'd fallen through a tear into another world. "What is this?"

Bertie lit a lamp, then another and another until the room was illuminated. The space covered the entire top of the house, with areas partitioned off but still open. There were no windows, no dormers or skylights, save for narrow, horizontal panes of glass up under the eaves that would provide next to no light but perhaps might supply some ventilation.

In the area nearest her, a large flat space of wall had been painted black, and next to it, another had been covered with padded cloth. The black section had been written on with chalk, and the cloth portion held maps and charts and lists, each fastened in place with pins. A desk sat before them, covered with books and papers.

In another area, what appeared to be a tangle of glass beakers and tubes and pipes, with bottles and jars and containers, each bearing a paper label. Odd instruments lay scattered on the bench, with more notes and paper filling a pigeonhole rack nearby.

At the far end of the large space were mats and weapons and fitness equipment.

All of this Juliette took in quickly, yet none of it made any sense. What was this place? How long had it been here?

Uncle Bertie finished with the lamps and came to stand before her. He took the book from her, placed it on the desk, and cupped her shoulders. "There's something I must show you. Promise me you will never tell a soul about this room. Promise me that even if you choose to reject every bit of what I'm about to reveal to you, that you will hold the secret dear and never breathe a word of it. You have no idea how many people's lives you will put at risk if you cannot keep your own counsel about this."

His grave tone sent a shiver through her.

"Do I have your word?"

She nodded.

"I must hear it aloud. Promise me."

"I promise. What is this all about?" Lives depended upon a secret room in her parents' house? What were her parents and uncle up to? She twisted the ring on her right hand. Would she get used to being stunned on a regular basis, or would nothing surprise her again after the day she'd had?

"Sit." He guided her to one of the chairs near the desk. When she was seated, he drew a tall, rectangular object shrouded in a black sheet from near one of the support pillars that marched down the room. Slender wooden legs peeked from beneath the cloth. When he'd placed it before her, he removed the covering.

Her mouth dropped open. Her hands went lax in her lap.

There was no mistake. Mr. Montgomery's voice, laden with pride, describing the details.

It was the painting.

The stolen Lotto.

On an easel.

In her parents' house.

In a hidden room.

And Bertie had sworn her to secrecy. A trickle of thought became a torrent. "Tell me you did not steal that painting. Tell me you are not a thief. Tell me you did not rob my best friend's father." She shook her head. "Why? It isn't as if you need money. Or do you? Were you merely bored and looking for a thrill?"

But how could he have stolen the painting when he was so drunk last night he didn't even make it to the refreshment break before being sent home?

"I am not a thief." Bertie put up his hands. "Well, perhaps a sort of thief, but hear me out."

"You stole the painting?" She was on her feet at his admission. What was she going to do? She had lied to the detectives who had questioned her about her family. She had slept in the Montgomery house, eaten at their table this morning, and all the while, their property had been in her parents' house?

"Sit down. I will explain everything."

"You had certainly better." And the minute he was finished, he was going to find some way to return that painting to its rightful owner, and she didn't care how he did it.

"This"—he waved to include the entire attic space—"this is the 'War Room,' Juliette. I know your parents planned to tell you eventually, but now it looks as if the burden falls to me. You need to know that you come from a long line of spies and agents for the Crown. Your ancestors have served every monarch since William the Conqueror, doing what needs to be done to preserve the kingdom and its rulers."

She couldn't even take in what he was saying. Spies and agents? Uncle Bertie? Her parents? He must be jesting. Or he was still sotted.

"Well, to be fair, not every monarch. Things did get a bit sticky upon occasion. Bloody Mary, for example. The family had to do a bit of clandestine espionage against the Crown in that case, but it all worked out in the end." Bertie shrugged. "Listen, my dear, I know this is a weighty bit of information to take in, and I wish I didn't have to spring it on you like this, but your parents aren't here, and I need your help."

"Help with what? And what does this painting have to do with anything? How on earth did you manage to steal it?" What sort of fabrication was he spinning here? Her parents weren't spies. They were just . . . parents, albeit absent ones.

"I stole the painting. I used the ruse of being drunk to get out of the house, to have several people witness me leaving. But first I stole the painting, got it up to the roof through one of the skylights, and after the party ended, I climbed the outside of Montgomery's house and retrieved it. You were probably asleep two floors beneath me when I fetched it down off the roof."

"But why steal it at all?"

He blew out a breath. "I must confess that I lied to you. Your parents are not in Pensax at the estate. They are . . . on a job . . . I think. I hope. They disappeared so quickly, and at such a momentous moment for you, the urgency must have been great. Only a job, a mission, would be so critical that they would miss your homecoming. But neither myself nor our superior know what caused them to flee." He held up his hands.

Her heart jumped into her throat. "You don't think they're . . ." She couldn't finish the question.

"No. I don't, and I don't want you to entertain such notions. They are both experienced agents, and for what I can only assume is a serious and important reason, they have gone underground for the time being. We had an inkling that danger was on the horizon, and they must have gotten wind of it and felt it necessary to hide until it's sorted out."

"What danger?" Panic hooked its claws into her windpipe and throttled it. "Where are they?"

"That is unknown at the moment. But they are together, and they are working on this case from their end, of that you can be certain. I suspect they saw trouble coming, and rather than stay here and pretend it wasn't happening and put you at risk, they disappeared until it could be taken care of."

"Without leaving word?" That seemed unnecessarily cruel. "What is the nature of this danger? And what are we to do?" She waved her hand to encompass the large room. "How can we help my parents fix this so they can come home?"

"That's where the mission comes in. Our handler in the special branch of the Home Office received intelligence that a very dangerous agent who we have been after for years had compiled a list of suspected and known spies from several of the Sixth Coalition nations. My handler sent one of his best agents, code-named Leonidas, to France to intercept the list if possible. From what we have pieced together, Leonidas learned that the list was being brought in by a courier to be sold to someone working in one of the foreign embassies here, but that the foreign agent didn't trust his courier not to double-cross him, and he divided the list, encoding it and secreting it into a shipment of artwork being brought into the country. Leonidas was able to catch up to the agent, but when he traced him to the port in Genoa, he found someone had killed the man. That same someone also killed Leonidas. We suspect the courier got greedy and killed his partner and then panicked to find a British agent so close to discovering him. The bodies were found in Genoa. That was the reason your ship was delayed leaving port. We were beginning to put a lot of this together before you arrived, but more has clarified over the past few days.

"You met the art dealer, Mr. Selby. He brought the painting to Garfield Montgomery's house before the ball. We don't know at this point if he's a pawn or if he's involved, but my handler thought it would be a good idea to keep an eye on him."

"Mr. Selby? I danced with him." Had she shared her debut dance with a spy? A possible traitor? How would she ever look Mr. Selby in the eye again and not let on that she knew? The scope of this secret grew and grew until she felt it taking up all the space in her mind.

"Your father thought you might be able to draw him out, get him to talk, perhaps allow him to pursue an acquaintance and possibly gain an opportunity to see what he knew."

Juliette didn't know what to feel about this. Her father had planned to use her? Like . . . bait? For a mantrap? How could he? Had she ever really known either of her parents?

"The plan was that once Tristan and Melisande told you about your family history, they would allow you to decide if you wanted to continue in their trade. You certainly have the right to refuse. No one is obligated, especially not you. This inheritance has been passed down from fathers to sons for nearly eight hundred years, but this is the first generation in the direct line where there is no son to inherit."

No son. Her parents had never let on their disappointment that she hadn't been born a boy, nor in their inability to have more children. And all this time, they must have not only mourned that there was no male heir to inherit the title, but that there was no son to continue the family tradition of service to the Crown.

She reached for the code book. Yet, in that letter from her father, he had said she would get to choose her own path, and that he was proud of her. She had cracked the code to open the book all by herself, and she had deciphered his message. Did that mean he hoped she would choose to follow them into their secret life despite being female?

He had said there could be no turning back once she made her choice. She would either take up the challenge or have to pretend she knew nothing about it for the rest of her life.

"Each piece of artwork is supposed to contain a string of the code, and the code, once deciphered, lists spies and agents at work in Europe. Tristan is the code breaker in the family, not me. I'm better at burgling and getting about the city unseen. However, he has been training you to follow in his footsteps for years. With Tristan away, I need your help. If the list falls into an enemy's possession, it will spell disaster. There is every chance that your parents' names are on the list, and mine too. If the list is transferred by the courier to the buyer, we will be revealed as spies, as will the names of several of our allied countries' operatives, and we will almost certainly be targeted for execution by whatever foreign government procures the names. We must find the information, to keep it out of the wrong hands and warn any of the spies at risk. I suspect that your parents have gone after the courier, the man who murdered Leonidas and who stands to gain financially by selling the list. Only through stopping him, and obtaining the entire list, will our safety be guaranteed."

Her heart lightened at the knowledge that her parents had not abandoned her for nothing, even as the weight of responsibility settled around her like a cloak of granite. If the list was made public, it would put an end to the many generations of service to the Crown. If the wrong person acquired the list, it could mean death to anyone on it. Her parents would be in danger. Uncle Bertie would be in danger. For all she knew, she might also be in peril. Guilt by association?

Had everything in her life been leading to this moment? This choice? Had God been directing things to put her in this place for this purpose? But . . . would He ask her to enter into a life of deception?

To pretend to be one thing, while being someone totally different in reality? If she chose the path of her parents, she would begin to bring about the relationship she had always longed for, wouldn't she? And yet would she someday be placed in the position of lying to her husband and children?

Could she dash away and leave her babies behind to go on some daring adventure for the Crown?

Could she lie to her husband and lead a double life, keeping secrets and telling falsehoods on a daily basis?

Could she find herself having to send her children away to boarding school . . . possibly for years . . . for their own safety?

Could she, at some future date, turn her back on her hypothetical husband and children when they needed her?

But if she chose not to help Uncle Bertie, she was, in fact, turning her back on her parents, who were real and in the here and now.

She had no real choice. She must continue their work. Whatever the cost.

"And you believe the painting was one of the pieces used to smuggle part of the code into the country?" She would focus on the problem before her and consider the ramifications later, just as her father had taught her.

"Yes. It came from aboard the *Adventuress*, the very ship you traveled on to get home. The artwork had been sent to Turner and Rathbone and Mr. Selby. Here I had been haunting the docks for days hoping to intercept the coded art, and I found you instead. Later I was able to obtain an inventory of the shipment, and I believe I know the whereabouts of most of the other pieces."

Bertie studied the Lotto. "I've been over the painting in detail, however, and I can't find anything that resembles a code."

She got to her feet, her knees like wood, and approached the Lotto. Standing back a few feet, she studied it as a whole, then removed her quizzing glass from her pocket and stepped to within a few inches. Raising the glass, she examined the painting.

"Perhaps it's like many of my father's codes. You must approach it from an unconventional angle in order to learn its secrets." She tilted the magnifying glass one way and another as she passed it over the cherub, the bride, the groom, the background, the wedding ring. Nothing seemed unusual. The varnish was undisturbed, the impasto even across the surface, the paint in good repair.

"I've been over and over it." Bertie's frustration leaked into his tone. "The painting should contain some bit of code, but there's nothing there."

"Have you taken it out of the frame?" She stepped back, blinking against the dryness in her eyes created from staring so hard.

Bertie paused in his pacing. "I have not."

Removing the painting took nearly half an hour, as they didn't want to damage the work or leave traces of tampering. Juliette spread a cloth on the table to lay the painting upon, careful not to disturb the keys in the corners of the stretcher. Bertie produced a badger hair brush from the work bench and carefully dusted the edges of the painting.

"You take the painting, I'll take the frame?" Juliette asked, bending to inspect the joinery of the carved wooden frame.

When she was nearly ready to give up, she found it. Etched into the rabbet, barely visible, a short string of random letters and symbols. Maybe twenty characters in all?

"It's here." Her fingertips brushed the indentations. Excitement and relief zinged along her skin. This proved that everything Uncle Bertie had told her was true. The spy work, the coded messages, the list of international agents. Validation that her parents were doing important work. Did that justify their treatment of her?

Bertie crowded next to her.

"Can you make it out?"

"The letters I recognize, but I've never seen some of these symbols before, and there isn't enough of the code here for me to be able to decipher it." She straightened. What good was finding the code if they couldn't read the message?

"We'll have to find the rest of the artwork that bears the coded names."

"How do we do that?"

Bertie gave a half smile. "By using the list of inventory from Turner and Rathbone."

Her interest pricked, she leaned forward. "How did you get that inventory list? Surely Mr. Selby didn't just hand it over, especially if he is part of the conspiracy."

"I acquired it, and that's all you need to know. Suffice it to say, I got very little sleep last night, what with running all over London."

"How will we procure the rest of the items to search for code?"

He held up his hands. "Slow down. *We* aren't going to get anything. I will try to purloin the items, and you will pretend nothing has happened and go about your social engagements as planned. The dowager duchess will no doubt call upon you tomorrow to make arrangements. I cannot involve you in anything more than helping me decipher the code once I have the pieces in my possession. That is your only concern. That and never telling a soul about any of this."

Did he seriously believe that she would be content to play the debutante while her parents' lives and their true identities were in peril?

"No. I can help more than that." She reached for the journal containing her father's coded message to her. "This." She tapped the book. "This says it is my choice, my decision which path I will take, and that you are responsible now to show me how. I'm ready. I want to continue the family trade, and I want to help my mother and father. They've been forced into hiding until we find the entire code, and the sooner we do that, the sooner they can come home." Desire burned in her chest. Which surprised her. How could she want something so much when she hadn't even known about it an hour ago?

"You cannot help me right now. People will expect you to act like a normal girl during her first Season. Attend parties, make new acquaintances, be seen, be attended to by possible suitors. You must behave as people expect, or they will think something isn't right."

"And meanwhile, you go about stealing artwork all over the city?"

"Yes, but not overtly. I've developed a reputation for drinking and bucking convention. No one will expect me to behave differently. I will continue to pretend to be a gin guzzler. You'd be surprised how much access that behavior gets me."

"Pretend? So you aren't really a drunk?" Which explained how he was able to put on and take off his hangover earlier today.

"Of course not. What kind of spy would I be if I was falling down drunk all the time? Drunks don't keep secrets, nor do they have the stealth, balance, or control to housebreak or burgle or get into and out of tight spots without being seen."

"But your eyes were red, and you had such a headache when the detectives were here."

"A small matter of a bit of black pepper on the fingers, rub the eyes, and there you have it." He produced a tiny vial from inside his coat and opened it, holding it under her nose. She jerked away as the sharp bite of peppercorns filled her senses. Her eyes watered, and she blinked hard.

"As to the headache, those can be feigned, you know." He squinted, putting his hands to his temples and groaning softly.

"What a relief. I wasn't certain how I was going to navigate all of this"—she waved at the painting and the code book—"and your drinking."

"I reiterate, you are not going to navigate any of this. I appreciate your help, and I will rely on you to assist me in breaking the code once we have enough of it to work with, but until that time, you are not a spy. You are not going to help me with fieldwork. You are nowhere near ready for such a step."

He was right, which chafed. "Then help me get ready. Teach me whatever it is you think I need to know in order to do this work."

His head tilted a fraction as he studied her, and her heart squeezed. The motion reminded her so much of her father, his brother. Oh, she missed him.

"Fine. When this is all over, we will begin your training."

"Or you could begin right now." She twisted her ring.

"I cannot. I have to go out."

"Where?"

"One thing you must learn, my dear, and you may as well start now. You must not ask too many questions. I come and go from this house often and at odd hours, and I am rarely at liberty to say where or why. If you need to know, I will tell you, and if you do not, then I won't." He tapped her on the nose.

She swatted his hand away. "Remember, what is sauce for the goose is sauce for the gander. Perhaps I will come and go as I please without informing you."

"We're not in competition with each other. I truly cannot tell you where I am going tonight. If you want to commence your training as a spy, I suggest you head to your father's library and start reading up on art history. I have a feeling we might need to know more than we currently do in order to gather all the pieces on the inventory."

He told her she would become a spy, and now he wanted to send her back to the schoolroom? She suppressed the desire to roll her eyes, for she sensed if she did, he might regret sharing all he had with her. Perhaps he was hoping she'd lose enthusiasm for the work if she had to do some hard slog.

He didn't know her at all if he thought she'd be put off that easily. She had lived abroad for seven years, excelled at her classes, managed to get herself and her friend home without assistance, and came from a long line of Thorndikes with mettle. She would not let down her forebears.

And he underestimated her if he thought she wouldn't find some way to join him on his forays into the spy world. After all, it is what her father had trained her to do.

Chapter 6

"Mr. Rickets is less than useless right now. He seems to be in complete shock. How can you spend months on the Continent, at the tail end of a war no less, acquiring commissioned artwork and not remember what you bought?" Daniel scraped together another pile of paperwork from the gallery's office floor, adding it to the stacks he and Ed had compiled. In the twenty-four hours since discovering the body, all he had done was inform people who needed to know. Thankfully, Sir Michael had been out of the office, so Daniel was spared that ordeal. "All I could get out of Rickets was that he bought some tapestries for the opera house. He promised to try to write down any other items, if he remembered them. I hope he has calmed himself before I call around to his place later today."

Ed skirted the area where the body had been removed the day before. "To be fair, he has suffered a blow. It isn't every day you find your guv has been murdered and your place of employment destroyed. I've seen it before with witnesses. So traumatized, they're never the same again. Perhaps after he's had a bit of time to grow accustomed to the new situation, he will remember more details." He lifted a broken desk drawer. "How are we going to make sense of this stramash? It looks fit for the ash heap."

Leafing through lists and invoices, Daniel checked for dates. Perhaps they could reconstruct the records chronologically, which might help them pinpoint what was missing or what the killer might have been searching for before he was interrupted. "I wish Owen was here. I'd put him to work organizing all this paper."

"There's an idea." Ed chuckled. "You're the lead investigator. If you need personnel, send to Bow Street for them. There's a room full of clerks and office staff at your command. If you need other help, grab the closest night watchmen, send to the local magistrate, or conscript aid off the street. Give orders. Don't wish and palaver. What do you want to do next?"

Daniel rubbed his palm on the back of his neck. In spite of wanting more responsibility and freedom in leading his own investigation, it would take time to become accustomed to being in charge. He'd spent the past two years carrying everyone else's papers. What did he want to do next? He cast his mind back to the cases he'd been involved in, however peripherally, trying to remember what other Bow Street officers had done.

"Take the guest list." He drew it from inside his coat front. "Begin questioning the rest of the Montgomery guests, and see if you can talk to Montgomery again. Find out what you can about the timeline, from when he first wanted to buy the painting until last night. The theft and the murder have to be related. It's too coincidental for them not to be linked."

Ed ran his finger and thumb across his moustache, eyes thoughtful.

Doubt seeped through Daniel's chest. "You don't think that's a good course of action?"

"No, lad, I think questioning the guests and learning more from Montgomery is the right way to go. I just wonder if you should keep your mind open to the thought that maybe the murder isn't linked to the theft. Different parts of the city, and it's a big jump from stealing to killing. We don't know much about this Mr. Selby. Maybe he wasn't a good fellow. Maybe he was trifling with some man's wife. This could be a jealous husband, or maybe he reneged on a gambling debt. It's a danger for an investigator to make assumptions, and narrowing your theory of the crime so quickly forces you to make assumptions. It's early to be drawing conclusions."

Daniel recognized this for wise advice. "You're correct, as always." He dropped the sheaf of papers onto the workbench. "I will go to the coroner's office and see what we can find out from Dr. Rosebreen's examination of the corpse. On your way to Eaton Square, could you stop in at Bow Street and apprise Sir Michael of these developments and send our sweet office boy over here to begin organizing this office?"

Ed grinned. "I cannot decide if you're being efficient sending me rather than going yourself, or you just want to avoid both Sir Michael's questions and Owen's scowls."

Daniel chuckled. "Perhaps both."

They left Turner and Rathbone's, parting ways at the corner. Daniel leaned into the cold wind and searched for a carriage. The street was crowded for a Sunday, and a ring of curious onlookers had taken up station across the road in front of the pub.

The journalist was nowhere to be seen. How quickly the scavengers assembled. He must have followed the coroner's wagon right to the scene of the murder. Was that his job every day? Haunt the mortuary and try to wheedle his way in to get information?

Daniel's arrival at the coroner's office chilled him as much as the January wind. Cheerless brick coated in soot, few windows, and an overall sense of gloom, the building reflected its purpose. A small metal sign affixed to the door was the only indication of the building's function.

A clerk in a stark office shrugged at Daniel's introduction and pointed. "He's about ready to start." A long tiled hallway with doors opening right and left at regular intervals bisected the building. "You must be new. Haven't seen you here before." The clerk shuffled papers. "First time seeing a body opened up? Might want to stay close to the door. But don't lose your breakfast in there. I'm the one who has to clean it up. Make for the back alley if you feel sick."

Daniel gripped the knob of his truncheon, stuck in his belt. "I'll be fine." Something about this man reminded him of Owen. A junior office employee, taking airs above his station. Supercilious.

Or was Daniel being unjust? Perhaps it was merely a friendly caution.

"That's what most people say. A few minutes later, I'm getting out the mops and buckets. Third on the right," the clerk instructed. "Dr. Rosebreen is in there now."

Bracing himself, Daniel entered the room the clerk had indicated. The smell of death was about the place, and he hoped he would remain composed. He had never been to an autopsy before. His role in the rare murder cases taken by Bow Street had always been too peripheral to require him to attend the procedure. He wouldn't give the smug clerk the satisfaction of seeing him get sick.

Dr. Rosebreen, a slender man of forty or so, with sandy hair and light eyes, looked up from the body. Mr. Selby lay unclothed, covered by a sheet to the waist, on a table made of wooden slats. The knife had not been removed, and a shiver went down Daniel's back and through his legs. The dead man seemed so inconsequential now. Not as he had been when he was alive, vital, moving, with a will of his own. He was now at the mercy of the doctor, the investigator, and eventually the sexton of a church to see to his burial.

They had been unable to find any family, and the elderly gallery owner hadn't been able to recall whether his employee had living relatives or not. Most of the time, the old man hadn't seemed to hold onto a thought for more than a minute.

Mr. Selby's landlady had little to say as well. He kept to himself, paid on time, and caused no trouble. A search of his rooms revealed little other than that he had a wide taste in reading material. No letters or personal correspondence, just the occasional tailor's bill or cobbler's receipt. When Mr. Rickets was able to compose himself better, Daniel would inquire as to Mr. Selby's personal life.

Daniel surveyed the bleak coroner's exam room. Tiles covered the walls, and high up opposite the door, a barred frosted-glass window let in light. The room was unheated, and his breath misted the air. Just as well it was cold and smelled mostly of vinegar and carbolic. What must this place be like in high summer?

"Good morning." Rosebreen held up his hand in greeting. In spite of the cold in the room, he wore no coat. His sleeves were rolled to the elbows. "I'm just getting started, so I haven't much information for you yet." He plucked an apron from a hook beside the counter, dropping the neck loop over his head and reaching for the ties.

"That's fine." Daniel remained by the door, as per the clerk's instruction, looking anywhere but at the corpse. Someone cleared their voice behind him, and he jumped.

"Ah, Foster, are you ready?" Dr. Rosebreen beckoned.

A short, round man with a moustache that nearly hid his mouth stepped into the room. He pushed what appeared to be a pulpit on wheels. A bottle of ink rested in a well on the top, and a quill and paper lay on its slanted surface.

"My assistant, Mr. Foster."

The clerk pushed his portable writing desk across the tiles, every step echoing off the hard surfaces in the room, and took up his station in the corner, leaving plenty of space for the doctor to move around the table.

"The lavender, if you please, Mr. Foster." Rosebreen readied his instruments.

The clerk opened a cupboard, removed a wooden box, and took off the lid. He shook the contents, which made a rustling sound, and set the box on the counter. The strong herbal scent of lavender buds warred with the medicinal smells.

"Very good. I find the lavender helps." Rosebreen nodded to Foster.

Daniel drew out his notebook and pencil.

"Let's begin, shall we?"

What followed was both fascinating and harrowing, but thankfully, Daniel didn't disgrace himself. There would be nothing at which the front desk clerk could cavil. He focused on the facts and not what was happening, listening to Dr. Rosebreen describe his findings and the faint scratching of Mr. Foster's pen against the paper as he took notes.

At last the procedure was finished. On a side table, the murder weapon lay in a box on a bed of cotton. Dr. Rosebreen covered the corpse with a sheet, leaned back against the counter, and lit a cigar. Puffs of smoke screened him from Daniel's view for a moment and then cleared toward the ceiling.

"Conclusions?" Daniel asked.

"Whoever did this is strong. Or motivated. Or both." The doctor studied the glowing end of his cigar. "That blade measures approximately eight inches, and it was buried to the hilt in our victim's chest, nearly going all the way through. Hard enough that the guards on the hilt indented and bruised around the fatal wound. It isn't all that easy to bury a knife into someone's chest. There's the breastbone and rib cage to maneuver. But our killer either got very lucky, or he's had some training. Perhaps he is a soldier, or former soldier? Or a physician?" Rosebreen shrugged. "Our killer struck to the left of the breastbone, with the knife blade horizontal, punching it through a gap between ribs and directly into our victim's heart." He used his cigar as a mock weapon, holding it in his fist like an ice pick, plunging it into an imaginary opponent. "From the angle of the blade, I would guess our victim was standing and that the attack came from the front. There's no real way someone could have stabbed him over the shoulder in a sneak attack with enough force to bury the blade like that."

"And Mr. Selby just stood there and let it happen?"

"There is only the one wound on the body. No cuts on his hands, no sign that he tried to defend himself. Either our victim was caught completely unawares, or he knew and trusted his attacker, letting him get so close there was nothing he could do at the germane moment to ward off or escape the attack."

"Indications at the scene were that the murder happened in the midst of the gallery being ransacked. There were office papers strewn under the body."

Dr. Rosebreen picked a piece of tobacco off the tip of his tongue and flicked it to the floor. "I think you're definitely looking for a man. I'm not sure a woman would have the physical strength to bury the knife in his chest like that, nor be tall enough. And you're looking for a man of average or better height. The knife had only a slight downward angle."

Daniel made a few notes. "Anything else?"

"Other than the stab wound, Mr. Selby was in excellent health. He hadn't eaten in several hours, and the body showed no signs of rigor mortis. He hadn't been dead all that long when we arrived to pick him up. I'd put your attack sometime between midnight and noon yesterday."

"Can't you narrow that time?"

The doctor shook his head, knocking ash into a metal dish on the counter. "That's a shorter time span than most murder investigations. The body was discovered quickly, which makes my job easier. Sometimes I can't pinpoint the time of death within a week." He shrugged. "Come to my office, and Mr. Foster will bring you a copy of his report in a few minutes."

Foster trundled his writing desk into the hall, and Dr. Rosebreen led the way out of the room. Daniel paused in the doorway to look back at the body of Mr. Selby. It seemed wrong to just leave him there, though a sheet covered him from head to foot.

"Mr. Swann?" Dr. Rosebreen called from down the passageway.

Daniel tucked the box containing the murder weapon under his arm and went to Rosebreen's sanctum. His brows rose. He could never work in such . . . clutter.

Shelves lined every wall, and on every shelf were specimen jars full of oddities and bits that he didn't want to identify. Papers. Books. Instruments. And the pervasive smell of cigar smoke.

Perhaps the man smoked to cover other odors in his workplace. The thought made Daniel queasy. He should stick to the lavender.

"What is the procedure now, with the body?" Daniel felt he should know this, but such things had never come under his purview before. Did they keep the body until the case was closed?

"Once you notify his closest relative, they can come here or send someone from their church to claim him. We can keep him for a few days because it's cold at the moment, but if no one claims him before the end of the week, we'll see him interred." The doctor shuffled some papers. "His clothing looked quite fine, so I assume he must have some assets. If he does, then the burial will be covered out of those funds. If there is no money, the Crown will see him interred in a pauper's cemetery somewhere in London."

A sad end. Familiar outrage sparked in Daniel's belly, the desire to find justice for someone who had been wronged in the ultimate way.

Foster appeared, a clutch of papers in his hand. A man's life reduced to a few facts and suppositions that would go into a file.

Daniel took his leave of the morgue, wishing he could shake the sense of oppression that followed him out into the chill air.

"You aren't going to tell me how you obtained this inventory of the artwork?" Juliette read the invoice again. She and Uncle Bertie stood in the War Room, and though it was afternoon, the lack of natural light made it difficult to tell the time of day. Juliette had spent a restless night lying awake thinking of all she knew and didn't know, going back through her childhood to see if she could pick up on any clues she may have missed as to her parents' true identities, wondering where they were now, and dwelling on all she needed to learn. It had been a chore to prepare for and attend church, but Uncle Bertie said she must, to keep up the illusion that nothing was amiss.

"No. If you're going to join the family business, it's important that you understand that information is compartmentalized. If you don't need to know something in order to perform your function, then you probably won't be privy to it." Uncle Bertie clasped his hands behind his back, pacing the open space before the desk.

Juliette nodded, but frustration pushed through her chest. "Who decides what I need to know? What if I need to know something you haven't told me, and I get into a tangle?"

He shrugged. "The flow of information is one of the most critical objectives of spy work, and the lack of a crucial piece has been the downfall of many an agent. We do the best we can. The longer you are in the service, the more information, the more contacts, the more responsibility you will have. Which is why you must start out in increments. You have neither the training nor the network to reach very far just yet. You've much to learn, and you'll have to grow up quickly."

"What if you have to break the law to get information?" Could she do that? Bertie had broken the law stealing Mr. Montgomery's painting, but he fully intended to return it as soon as possible. Did that make what he had done acceptable?

Had her parents broken the law in their work? She shook her head, trying to clear it of doubt and uneasiness. They had raised her to know that lying was always wrong, citing the Ten Commandments' admonishment to not bear false witness. And yet they *had* lied. Everything she had learned in the past twenty-four hours threw all she thought she knew about her mother and father into question.

Juliette had always seen the world as rather black and white, right and wrong, with no gray areas. One followed the rules of Scripture and society, and one did not stray off that clearly defined path. Was reality less simple? Was there ever a situation in which it was acceptable to lie? Or did her parents know it was wrong and just count on the mercy and forgiveness of God later?

"The laws for agents of the Crown are somewhat more . . . fluid, shall we say, than for the ordinary subject. Our superiors work those things out, often after the fact, so that we don't wind up in jail. That being said, there are still some things that are not justifiable, even for a spy, so don't think you can toss caution to the wind and do whatever you wish."

"It all seems rather murky and clandestine." She could not imagine her parents operating under such circumstances. If they could be so successful on the fringes of the law, had she ever truly known them? If she hadn't discovered the hidden codebook, would they have ever made her privy to their secret life as spies? "Lying and skulking about, deceiving people with your words and actions. How can you justify such behavior?"

Uncle Bertie's face composed itself into long-suffering lines. "Did you think everything would be done in the open air, straightforward and forthright? You're talking about some of the most dangerous men and women in the world, willing to do anything to get what they want. Some for patriotic and fealty reasons, and some for less noble motivations like money or revenge. Loyalties are intricate and complex and sometimes contradictory. Information is the coin of the realm in the spy kingdom, and if you are going to enter into the fray, you need to shed your naïve notions and face reality. What we do is seldom straightforward or clear-cut. But we do them to protect our nation and our king. If you cannot sign on for that, then you should bow out now and forget you ever saw any of this." He waved his hand, his eyes hard, his tone uncompromising. "Grow up and realize that there are things in this world that don't fit your tidy little parterre garden of ideas."

Abashed and properly chastened, Juliette wanted to cringe. She had sounded like an outraged adolescent rather than an adult spy-in-training. The lines around her parents' integrity were now blurred, but that didn't mean their characters were besmirched, did it? *Focus on the task at hand. Sort out feelings and thoughts later.* She fell back on her self-defense pattern of compartmentalizing. *Think about it later.*

"So where do you start with this list?" She held up the lined invoice from an art dealer. Turner and Rathbone, Clerkenwell, with nine items, beginning with the Lotto. The list of pieces sent to England, which, according to Uncle Bertie, contained the coded names of international spies. A brown splotch of something marred the lower left corner of the page, but she didn't think the stain covered any writing. What was it? Coffee? Ink?

"We'll attempt to locate each piece." Bertie picked up a letter opener and rotated it in his hands. The opener was fashioned like a medieval sword, and it caught the light. His hands were long fingered and dexterous as he toyed with it.

"We?" Juliette paused. "As in you and I?"

Bertie nodded. "Yes, we. As much as I wish I could keep you out of this, I cannot see a way to get my hands on all those pieces without help." He held up his hand. "Before you get giddy and giggly, listen to me. You have no training. You have no experience. You must agree to do exactly as I say at all times, and if you are in danger, you must flee. Don't look back for me. Your safety is paramount. When your parents return, I will not be responsible for telling them how I lost you by thrusting you into the fray before you were ready."

His words both sobered and excited her. He would include her in the mission. "So help me get ready. Teach me." She put the list on the desk and spread her arms. "You say I don't know the first thing about spy craft. Well, what *is* the first thing?"

Bertie whirled, his coattails flying out, and threw the letter opener, whizzing it past Juliette's head into the wall behind her. The blade hit with a thwack and quivered. She jerked away, stumbling and grabbing at the back of a chair to save herself from an undignified sprawl.

"The first thing to know about spy craft is that danger is everywhere and that anything can be a weapon." Bertie tugged his waistcoat back into place, his voice calm. "You must be aware of your surroundings and keen to possible danger at all times. If you're serious about training, let us begin. One of the skills you must perfect is that of the dead drop. Leaving information as inconspicuously as possible, allowing another agent to retrieve it, also inconspicuously."

He walked past her to retrieve the letter opener. "Pick up the list."

She turned to the desk, but the paper was gone. Not on the surface, not on the floor beneath the desk, not behind the chair.

When she straightened, Uncle Bertie held the paper before her nose. She hadn't even noticed him taking it. "When you can abscond with something that is in plain view and deposit it out of sight in a public place, you'll be ready for your first dead drop. It's all about distraction and sleight of hand."

For the next hour, Juliette practiced under her uncle's critical eye. He demanded perfection, critiquing her movements, instructing, showing her again and again. At last he relented. "With practice you might be competent in a year or so." His wink took the sting out of the comment, and she loosened her muscles enough to laugh.

"I shall endeavor to keep your high praise from going to my head." She dropped a quick curtsy.

"Let's move on to picking pockets." Bertie rolled a dressmaker's dummy from a corner to the center of the room. A woolen cloak hung from the form, complete with patch and slit pockets. Around the hem of the cloak dangled tiny brass bells on silk threads.

"Take the purse from the pocket without ringing the bells." Bertie stood back, arms crossed.

Juliette inhaled deeply and forced herself to relax as she let out the breath. Flexing her fingers, she circled the form, looking for a telltale bulge that would indicate which pocket was her target.

All the while, she felt Bertie's scrutiny. If she couldn't master these basic skills to his satisfaction, would he refuse to let her partake in the mission? Would he end her training, call her hopeless, and strike out on his own?

Forcing such thoughts from her mind, she called upon all the hours she had spent perfecting card tricks while at school. Her pianoforte teacher had instructed her to play with whist cards for an hour each day to make her fingers dexterous and supple. She could cut a deck and shuffle with one hand, pull a single card from the center of the stack without disturbing the rest, and deal from the bottom of the deck without detection. Concentrating fully, she dipped into the right hand seam pocket and withdrew a fat leather purse. Not a chime to be heard.

With a grin, she brandished the pouch. "Well?"

Bertie shrugged. "Beginner's luck?" He took the purse and put it into the inside breast pocket of the cloak. "Try again."

This was more of a challenge, and if the dressmaker's form had been a person, there was no way she wouldn't have been noticed, but by slow stealth, she removed the purse, again without a sound.

Bertie tapped his lips with his finger. "You have unplumbed depths, young lady."

Flushed with success, she turned a pirouette. "What's next?"

"What's next is, I suppose, your first lesson in disguises." Bertie shoved the dressmaker's dummy out of the way with his toe, setting all the bells jingling. "The item on the list that we're going after next is the maquette."

"What is a maquette? I've never heard the word."

Bertie leaned against the edge of the desk. "When a sculptor begins work on a new piece, they often cast or carve a small model of the design, to test proportions and scale and the like. The model is known as a maquette. Most are destroyed once the final sculpture is finished, but if the maquette remains, and it is of a famous statue, it can be very valuable."

"What is this particular maquette depicting?"

"A statue of Saint Mark by the Italian sculptor Donatello. The finished sculpture is nearly eight feet tall, but the maquette is only about twenty inches, and it was cast in bronze, so it's heavy. The maquette differs from the sculpture in that it is a finished piece. The statue sits in an alcove high on the exterior of a church in Florence, and because it wasn't intended to be seen from the back, only the front of the statue was carved in detail."

"How did you learn this?"

"Your father's extensive library is a very handy resource." He tapped a stack of books beside him on the table. "I—we—need to know as much as possible about each of those items in order to plan for their retrieval."

Retrieval. Not theft. Did his calling it something else salve the conscience?

"What will happen to the stolen pieces after we are finished with them?"

"We'll obliterate the code and return them to their rightful owners."

"How? We cannot just arrive by coach, pop out and say 'Thank you. Sorry. Here you are.' And hand them the pieces."

Bertie shook his head. "Don't be absurd. It will take creativity, ingenuity, and a fair bit of stealth to acquire the pieces, but returning them will require no effort at all. We'll arrange for a message to be channeled to that young Bow Street detective looking for the painting that a cache of stolen goods can be found at a certain location, and"—he snapped his fingers—"case closed."

In the meantime, they would need to avoid attracting the attentions of that detective lest they be caught and bunged into Newgate to await trial for theft.

What had she gotten herself into? This was all a far cry from debut dances and new ball gowns.

She picked up the paper once more. The inventory that held the key to her parents' and Uncle Bertie's safety would dominate the next few weeks, and possibly longer. "Where is the maquette now?"

"It was purchased in Italy for Lord and Lady Bickford. I understand that Saint Mark is the patron saint of the linen guild or weaver's guild or some such, and since Lord Bickford has made his fortune in the textile industry, he fancied owning the piece when it came up for sale."

"Lord and Lady Bickford are hosting a ball tomorrow night. The invitation is on Mother's writing desk, and the acceptance has been sent."

"That's correct. The maquette will be in their house."

"And you propose to steal the statuette during the party? Like the painting? While everyone is distracted?"

"In a manner of speaking, yes. I cannot repeat my falling-down-drunk routine. Two art thefts carried out in an identical manner only a few days apart will be difficult enough. If I make another spectacle of myself in order to leave early, even the thickest Bow Street detective will make the connection, and our Mr. Swann does not appear to be stupid. I propose that we attend the ball, and I will not pretend to be drunk, and we will find some way to either examine the maquette or remove it once we arrive. I can't say exactly how we will accomplish this, because I've never been in the Bickford house before, nor do I know exactly where they're keeping the maquette. This will be in the nature of a reconnaissance mission."

"The ball is fancy dress. What costumes will we wear?"

"Your mother saw to all of that when she accepted the invitation. The costumes will arrive this afternoon, I believe. Remember, if anyone asks, your parents have been called away to Heild and will return as soon as they are able. In the meantime, they wished you to carry on under the watchful eye of the dowager, and you are quite pleased to do so."

Juliette picked up the letter opener. "You do believe my parents will return, don't you?"

"Until we know otherwise, we will operate on that premise." He pushed off the desk, taking the letter opener and the list from her hand. He stabbed the point of the opener through the paper and into a support post.

Chapter 7

WHEN THEY ARRIVED AT THE Bickfords' home Monday night, Juliette felt she was smothering in her heavy dress. Mother had chosen a Tudor gown with a high white lace collar, stomacher, and heavy velvet skirts sewn with pearl beads. She could hardly move quickly in this cloth cage.

Yet the costume helped her feel as if she truly were someone else, which gave her confidence in playing her role as debutante. After all, how hard could it be to locate the statue, find the code, and if necessary, get the statue out of the house?

Uncle Bertie followed her up the steps to the front door, his saber rattling at his side. Dressed in the green uniform of the 95th Rifles, his pewter buttons caught the light from the coach lamps beside the entrance, and his boots gleamed.

"Remember," he whispered. "Act naturally, but make your way around the house and see if you can find the maquette. Though it's possible you won't need to hunt. If it's here and Bickford's proud of it, the statue might have pride of place somewhere."

"And I am to let you know when I find it?" They stood in the crowded foyer, noise swirling around them as party guests took off their wraps and exclaimed over costumes. "Where will you be?"

"I'll be around, probably searching rooms you cannot get into. The smoking room, for instance. If you don't see me, don't worry. It's possible I can get out of the house with the statue, and if that is the case, don't look for me. We'll meet up at home. Just enjoy the party, check in often with the dowager, and don't fret. Above all, don't do anything to jeopardize yourself or call attention to your actions. Better to fail at tonight's mission than scuttle the whole works."

Uncle Bertie, once they had delivered their cloaks to the attendant, escorted her to the dowager's side and tendered her into the older woman's care.

The dowager studied Bertie from boots to immaculately combed hair, and her mouth tightened. She'd obviously heard of his proclivity for drink, and she was not inclined to be indulgent.

He bowed. "Your Grace, I am most grateful. Juliette, enjoy yourself and listen to the dowager. She will steer you right." He nodded to Juliette and disappeared into the crowd.

"We'll present you to your host and hostess and then see about finding you a dance partner." The dowager squared her shoulders, as if launching a military campaign, determination exploding from her every movement. "Where is Miss Montgomery? She was here a moment ago."

They wended their way through the growing press of people. A hand snaked through the crowd and clutched her arm. Juliette stifled a squeal.

"There you are. I've been waiting for you to arrive. Would you ever have thought?" Agatha squeezed her arm again. "We're at a fancy-dress ball." She glittered in a gown covered in turquoise paillettes. Her red hair glowed, and her eyes shone. She looked like the mermaids of lore, waiting to sing her siren song.

"You look wonderful."

The dowager, who was dressed as . . . a dowager . . . predictably puckered. "I wish I had undertaken your chaperonage in time to advise you as to acceptable costumes. You're drawing too much attention to yourself for a debutante. I know it's the accepted thing to be allowed to wear colorful garments at a fancy-dress ball, but that might be a tad too far."

Agatha's inner light dimmed, but Juliette turned to the dowager. "I think she looks beautiful and striking and interesting. Her costume was chosen and designed by my mother, and I think it's perfect."

The dowager sputtered and backtracked. The Countess of Thorndike was known for her impeccable taste, and if she thought the dress the right choice, it would do the dowager no favors to disparage it to others. "Of course. I only meant . . . that is . . . It's time to meet the Bickfords. Come along."

Juliette's dress brushed the floor, her skirts full, taking up more room than any dress she'd worn before. It flared from her waist, and the tight corseted bodice kept her back straight. She had to turn to see around the edges of the high lace collar that stood up along the sides and back of the neckline.

She had not been in the ballroom two minutes before she saw it. The maquette stood on a marble pedestal between the two French doors that led out into the garden. There it was, in plain sight of all the party guests.

Before she could notify Uncle Bertie, the dowager partnered her with a man dressed as a cavalier. He gave her an appraising glance, and she had to resist rolling her eyes. Thankfully, he wasn't a talker, and she could be alone with her thoughts as they went through the dance patterns.

How was she supposed to get close enough to examine the maquette, or if necessary, to steal it, when fifty people reeled and quadrilled their evening away within steps? They would have to abort the mission, and Uncle Bertie would have to use stealth and the cover of darkness to get into the house and make off with the bronze man.

Agatha danced with Viscount Coatsworth, and she looked blissful. The viscount, dressed as a cavalry officer, looked elegant and sure of himself. By dancing with Agatha yet again, was he openly declaring his intent to pursue her?

Juliette turned a small circle in the dance, catching sight of the statue again. It was impressive, a dull bronze, but with such detail. How much did it weigh?

The dance ended, and she curtsied to her partner and allowed him to lead her back to the dowager's side. Agatha joined them, flushing prettily as the viscount bowed to her and took his leave.

"Viscount Coatsworth—he asked me to call him Alonzo, isn't that wonderful?—said I made the most beautiful water sprite he'd ever seen. I didn't even have to explain my costume. He guessed it right off. He's most clever, you know."

"Your Grace, may we go to the refreshment room?" Juliette asked after waiting for a break in the dowager's conversation. "I'm parched."

The dowager turned from the woman to whom she had been speaking. The refreshment room door was within eyesight of the divan where she sat. "Yes, but don't be gone long."

"May we bring you anything?"

"I'll wander in there later. Mind your manners, girls." She eyed them sternly before turning to her companion. "It's such a responsibility, bringing out girls, isn't it?"

They walked arm in arm across the ballroom. With so many people and lamps and fires in every fireplace, the house had grown quite warm. As they passed the maquette, one of the footmen was discreetly opening the French doors to allow for air to circulate. Uncle Bertie stood a few feet away from the little statue, and he smiled at her benignly as she went by.

Agatha paused in the doorway of the refreshment room, clearly awed. A table ran the length of the far wall, laden with delicacies. Salmon, and cold tongue, and Scotch eggs, and aspic jelly. Cakes and biscuits and trifles. At one end, a footman stood ready with a silver ladle beside an ornate punch bowl.

Juliette accepted a cup of punch from a footman and made her way to a small table.

Agatha followed, chattering away. "I couldn't think where Alonzo— did I mention he asked me to call him Alonzo? That surely has significance, doesn't it?—anyway, I couldn't think where he had gotten to, and then up he popped and asked to partner me for the first dance."

Did Uncle Bertie have a plan in place now that he knew where the maquette was in the house?

"He even whispered in my ear that he hoped I would be attending the opera tomorrow night."

Would he give her a signal when he was ready to make his move?

"I assured him I would, since Father has already made arrangements. Which is what I wanted to ask you about. I don't know if your mother already made plans for you, but I hope you can come." Agatha leaned close and put her hand on Juliette's arm. "To the opera, I mean, as our guest? Father's making up a party, and Duke von Lowe himself has agreed to come. It seems he and Father have some business dealings, and he came to the house this afternoon for a meeting. He's just the thing right now, so sought after, and he's coming to the opera with us. Isn't that wonderful? I made certain Father asked Alonzo too."

Did Uncle Bertie expect her to get near enough to the maquette to see if the code was in plain sight on it somewhere, or would he try to view it himself?

"You will come, won't you?"

Should I ask Lord Bickford about the statuette? If he's proud of it, he might show it to me and talk about it long enough that I might get a good look. Or would it be better to leave it and not draw attention to myself by asking after it? If we do manage to get it out of the house, the detectives are sure to ask if anyone has shown any undue interest in the piece.

"Juliette, I don't believe you've heard a word I said. What are you woolgathering about?"

"Pardon?"

Agatha laughed and gripped Juliette's forearms. "What is the matter with you? You've been distracted all night." A stricken look came over her face. "Oh, how silly of me, of course you have. You must be so disappointed that your parents had to leave, but they'll be back soon, I'm sure. Here I've been blathering on without even asking how your first dance went or anything."

"I'm the one who should apologize. I've a few things on my mind, it's true, but there's no excuse for not paying attention. You said something about the opera?"

"I beg your pardon, ladies. May we sit with you?"

Duke von Lowe himself had approached their table without notice. He bowed, clicking his heels together. He wore his military uniform rather than a costume. He looked distinguished, and from close up, Juliette had to admit, very handsome. His fair hair gleamed in the lamplight, and humor lurked in his blue eyes.

Agatha gave little notice to the duke, instead patting her hair and smoothing her dress while smiling at his companion, the dashing Viscount Coatsworth.

"Yes, of course." Agatha scooted her chair to the side to allow them to take the other seats at the little table.

"May we get you something to drink? Perhaps something to nibble on?" Coatsworth asked before he sat.

"No, thank you." Juliette touched her punch cup, still full. "We're well looked after."

Though Agatha made room for Coatsworth beside her, he opted for the chair next to Juliette. Agatha's shoulders drooped, and she sent Juliette a questioning look.

"You look very fetching this evening, ladies. A water sprite and a Tudor aristocrat. Excellent choices." The viscount leaned close, and if Juliette hadn't shifted in her seat, he would have brushed her shoulder with his.

The duke settled next to Agatha. "It is good to see you again, Fraulein Montgomery. Lady Juliette, we have not yet had the introductions." He raised his brows toward Agatha.

"Oh, of course. Juliette, this is Duke Heinrich von Lowe. Your Grace, may I present Lady Juliette Thorndike." Agatha hurried through the introduction. "Lady Juliette and I are the best of friends. We were at school together."

The duke looked from Juliette to Agatha, an appreciative look in his eyes. "Lady Juliette, I was sorry to hear your parents were made to travel. I had been looking forward to meeting your father. I was told he is a man of varied interests and very congenial. I hope he will return to London before I must depart for my own country." His speech was precise, with the distinct pronunciation of middle Europe. Juliette had heard the accent and inflection for years in Switzerland and had no trouble following along.

"I'm pleased to meet you. I hope your stay in England has been pleasant." She sipped her punch not because she was thirsty, but to have something to do with her hands. Now that she was out of the ballroom, she wished she hadn't left. What if Bertie needed her and she was trapped in the refreshment room?

"Your costume is most becoming, Lady Juliette. One would think you had stepped out of a painting."

She touched her lace collar. "Thank you."

"Not just any painting, but one that could hang on the wall in one of my castles. You should have your portrait painted in that dress. I met a painter last evening at a dinner given by the Duke of Haverly. A Herr Hamish Sinclair. A relative of the duke's, I understand. According to the Dowager Duchess of Haverly, Sinclair has painted the portraits of the most influential members of the nobility that England boasts. Have you met Herr Sinclair?"

Juliette shook her head. "No, but the dowager has mentioned him."

Coatsworth, as if he believed von Lowe had monopolized enough of the ladies' attention, again leaned close to Juliette.

"How fortunate that you have brought up your chaperone. I noticed you only danced the first set. Is that your preference, or has no one had the courage to ask for another? If it is that you lack offers, I present myself as the solution to this terrible wrong. You must allow me to lead you out. Where is the dowager so I may ask permission?"

Juliette tightened her grip on her cup. What should she do? Agatha clearly had first call on Coatsworth, and it was a breach of friendship to pay too much attention to a friend's quarry. Not that Juliette had any designs on Coatsworth's affection. But it would be rude, wouldn't it, to refuse his gallantly delivered request?

"Ah, Coatsworth, you are beating me to the prize. I had intended to ask Lady Juliette for a dance myself." The duke gave a rueful, playful glare. "But, I shall happily turn my attentions to Fraulein Montgomery. Fraulein, would you do me the honor?"

Anxiety made Juliette's corset feel unbearably tight. She had not consented to a dance, and yet here she was being led out of the refreshment room by the viscount. Waves of unhappiness rolled over her, sent by Agatha. Juliette glanced back over her shoulder, bunching her brows and hunching her shoulders to silently plead her case with Agatha.

Her friend's mouth twisted in a "what else can we do?" expression. She shrugged and put her hand on the duke's arm, her dress tinkling as she rose.

They entered the ballroom once more, and Juliette breathed a sigh. With the French doors now open, the room was no longer unbearably stuffy. Which was just as well, since even more people had arrived.

There were costumes of all kinds, but the most eye catching was a woman dressed as a Russian empress. She wore a high-piled white wig, elaborately curled, topped by wafting ostrich feathers of bright blue. Her dress had a stomacher, wide panniers, and much lace and ornament.

But most striking was that a brace of Borzoi hounds preceded her on leashes. The lean, needle-nosed dogs stalked the ballroom, their tongues lolling and their eyes bright. People made way for the woman, who had rather strong features and a sizeable beauty mark on her right cheek. As she passed Juliette and the viscount, she muttered something to the dogs in . . . Russian?

"Quite a cosmopolitan guest list, is it not? I heard some members of the Russian ambassador's household might attend tonight." The viscount watched the feathers wend their way above the crowd. He led Juliette onto the floor, and they took their places in the lines of dancers.

Juliette tried to concentrate on the steps and her partner, but each time she turned toward the French doors, she spotted the maquette. It was almost as if the little statue mocked her. It was within reach, but it might as well have been in the West Indies for all she could do about it.

"What do I have to do in order to keep your attention?" Coatsworth asked as they met and promenaded down the room.

She focused on his face. "I do apologize. I am somewhat distracted."

"I asked you to dance so that I might put to you a question."

They parted for the next movement of the dance, and her heart hitched. A question? She neither wanted nor sought the viscount's attention, for she would do nothing to hurt Agatha, who was clearly besotted by the handsome young man. What could he possibly wish to ask her?

When they rejoined, he bent his head close to hers and whispered, "Does Miss Montgomery enjoy riding?"

Juliette faltered, nearly missing her turn to pirouette. "Agatha?" He wanted to ask about Agatha? Relief made her light-headed. "Yes, she does."

His grin split his face and reached his eyes. "Splendid. Does she ride well enough to hunt, or is she more of a trot-around-the-park rider?"

"She's no Dick Turpin on Black Bess, but she can acquit herself well."

"And you? Are you an equestrienne as well?"

"I love to ride, especially over fences."

"Thank you for the information." He grinned conspiratorially. "Perhaps we shall have to arrange something."

Juliette's spirits lifted. Coatsworth was still interested in Agatha, and there might be a social engagement that involved riding in their future.

But as she spied the maquette on its plinth there in plain sight, her chest tightened. Bertie stood mere feet away, speaking with Lord Bickford. Together they approached Donatello's replica in miniature, and Bickford nodded. Bertie reached out, but Bickford put his hand on Bertie's arm.

Drat. That was the moment. Uncle Bertie could have examined the piece, gathered the string of code, and they would have accomplished tonight's mission. The dance steps whirled her away, and she lost sight of them both.

The music ended, and she was just making her curtsy to the viscount when a shout erupted, quickly drowned by the barking of large dogs. A tray crashed to the floor, and women screamed.

The viscount took Juliette's hand and tugged her behind him, putting himself between her and whatever danger had invaded the party. People pushed and shoved, moving back from the happening, and like twin bolts of gray lightning, the Russian woman's dogs shot across the ballroom, chasing a hissing, yowling black cat.

The menagerie skidded through the musicians. Chairs scraped, sheets of music flew, men scrambled, and odd squeaks and wails came from the pianoforte as the pianist climbed atop the instrument to avoid the onrush.

The dogs' nails clicked and clattered on the polished dance floor. The cat, seeking escape, careened around the corner of the room where the chaperones sat. The matrons flapped and scuttled like hens discovering a fox in the coop, their lorgnettes, fans, reticules, and quizzing glasses tossed away in their haste to escape.

Footmen took off in pursuit of the animals, but the agile cat darted here and there, and in a burst of inspiration, latched onto the drapes, climbing at great speed to the pelmet, where it crouched, hissing and puffing up its fur. The dogs leapt and barked, slavering and showing their teeth, but the feline was out of reach.

Juliette peeked over Coatsworth's shoulder, stifling laughter. The Russian woman was gesticulating and shouting in Russian, but the dogs paid her no heed. Footmen darted here and there, trying to grasp the trailing ends of the leads but wary of the snapping fangs.

What a debacle. Lady Bickford had subsided into a chair, with her women friends fanning her with handkerchiefs and plying her with smelling salts. A servant with a broom shooed the dogs toward the open French doors, but the canines were adamant they were not leaving without their feline friend.

Juliette scanned the room, wondering what Uncle Bertie was making of the debacle.

He was nowhere to be seen.

Her eyes flew to the statue, and she rounded Coatsworth to check on it.

It was gone.

"Are you quizzing me for a reaction? Because if so, I don't find the humor."

"As I live and breathe, I'm telling the truth." Cadogan tossed the note on Daniel's desk. "I was waiting outside Lord and Lady Bickford's house, cuz I had been hired for the evening to take Mr. and Mrs. Albright to a party there. This gent come running out, all panting and wild eyed, and said to fetch a policeman. Another piece of art has been stolen. Someone went for a night watchman, but one of the toffs from the party came out with a note, looking for a driver to fetch an officer from Bow Street. I stirred up Lola and Sprite and trotted here quick as I could. Figured you'd still be working. You're always working."

"Was it another painting?" Daniel reached for the note, opening the stiff, heavy paper. This surely was no coincidence.

"No, a statue. Some little saint or something." Cadogan's cheeks were red, and he edged toward the stove in the middle of the room to hold his hands to the warmth.

Daniel glanced at the scrawled summons, stood, and reached for his cloak, truncheon, and hat. He had been going over the papers and reports the office staff had compiled when they'd organized the contents of the art dealer's office. The detectives' room had been empty and dark save the single lamp on his desk, all the other officers having gone home for the night.

He liked the solitude and peace while he worked.

The search of Turner and Rathbone had brought forth a mountain of paperwork. There were piles of correspondence, invoices for a new office chair, whale oil for the lamps, and lumber for packing crates. There were ledgers for payroll and the rent on the building and profit and loss statements. What was conspicuously absent was any form of inventory. Not from the past month, year, or even decade.

Mr. Rickets, when consulted, said of course there were inventory sheets. They were kept in a green file box until the end of the year, when they were taken across the street to the bookbinder's for binding together. The completed inventory books were kept on the shelves above Mr. Selby's desk.

But the shelf was bare. Someone had taken every book, and the green file box was nowhere to be found either.

Daniel was no nearer discovering who had stolen the Lotto painting than when he'd begun.

And now another piece of fine art had gone missing?

He climbed into Cadogan's cab with a feeling of déjà vu.

The neighborhood Cadogan drove to was less prestigious than Eaton Square, but still respectable. The houses were not as tall, the streets not as wide, but inside the Bickford residence, the few guests who remained were attired even more lavishly than at Montgomery's. There were . . . costumes . . . of all descriptions.

A fancy-dress ball.

Lord Bickford rushed toward him, his coattails flapping. A small man with gray hair, he made little movements with his lips, even when he wasn't talking. "Oh dear. Oh dear. My statue. It's gone. Just vanished. How could this happen?" He throttled his hands.

"Someone find Lord Bickford a chair," Daniel ordered. "Before he faints."

Hands reached out and guided the host to a seat.

Daniel took a count. A bare dozen people remained. "Is this the entire guest list?"

"Oh, no. When folks heard the police had been sent for, they started leaking out the house like water. Nobody wanted to be detained for hours like last time."

"I need a complete list of those who attended." How was he supposed to take witness statements when his witnesses scattered to the four winds? "Where is the watchman who was called?"

A red-cheeked man in a navy coat edged forward. "That's me, sir."

Mindful of Sir Michael's warnings, Daniel handed the watchman his notebook and pencil. "Take the names of each of the remaining guests." He turned to the small group. "Once you've given your name and address, you are free to go." So many had already left, and if these people were anything like the Montgomery guests, they had seen nothing, knew nothing, and were adept at sticking to the theory that it was a servant or housebreaker.

Daniel returned to the host of the party. "Describe what was stolen, please?"

"A maquette of a statue of *Saint Mark* by the sculptor Donatello." Lord Bickford's hands fluttered.

Daniel knew from his university studies what a maquette was and who Donatello had been, but he raised his eyebrows, as if he'd never heard of them before, encouraging Lord Bickford to say more.

But the man was clearly at a loss. He shrugged, touching his cheek with his fingertips and looking around, as if the statue would materialize if he just wished hard enough.

"Oh, for pity's sake." A woman, clad in glittering gold that shimmered when she moved, stepped forward. "I'm Lady Bickford. The statue is about this high." She spanned her hands nearly eighteen inches apart. "It's bronze and heavy, and it was sitting in the ballroom. We haven't even owned it properly for a week, and my husband paid what I consider to be far too much for it." Lady Bickford had ebony hair that surely must be dyed, given the wrinkles on her face and the creped nature of her hands, and she seemed to have a fine disdain for her husband. She glared at Daniel. "What is this city coming to when a person can have their home robbed in the middle of a party?"

"Where did you acquire the piece?" He addressed Lord Bickford.

"Turner and Rathbone."

Daniel would have been shocked if he had said any other name.

Clearly something was going on here that was more involved than an opportunistic theft by a temporary servant. Was the theft of the maquette a further complication to his case, or would it show commonalities that could lead to the apprehension of the thief?

"Was this a piece purchased specifically for you, or did you buy it after seeing it in the gallery?"

"I learned about the statue through Mr. Selby, and when he said he was sending a buyer to Europe, I asked him to get it for me if he could." Lord Bickford turned hopeful eyes to Daniel. "You will get it back, won't you?"

"We'll do our best, sir. Did you hire temporary staff for this party?"

"Of course we did. Our regular staff couldn't hope to keep up with everything for such a large gathering. There were more than fifty guests." Lady Bickford spoke as if Daniel had rocks for brains. "You don't know the first thing about fine entertaining, do you?"

He knew more than she thought, just not from her side of things.

"I will need a list of your staff, both temporary and regular." A thought struck him. "And the paperwork, receipts, anything you have that pertains to the stolen item. I will need those too. Now, can you please describe exactly what happened and how the statue came to be missing?"

They moved into the ballroom, which wasn't as large as Montgomery's but still substantial enough for the number of guests said to have attended. Daniel surveyed the room, noting the scattered chairs where the orchestra had sat, the bedraggled panel of drapes, and the scratches on the floor as Lady Bickford told the story. In one corner a footman knelt, picking up broken glass and piling it on a silver tray while a maid wiped spilled liquid with a rag.

A crime of opportunity, or a carefully planned and executed raid?

"Who was the woman with the dogs?"

"A guest from the Russian embassy. We sent an invitation for the ambassador and five guests, and she was part of his party."

"You don't know her name?"

"No, but she was with the Russian ambassador."

As if that made her of sterling character.

French doors flanked an empty pedestal, and Daniel had to wonder at the brazenness of the thief or thieves. Why not wait until the dead of night, pick the lock on one of the doors, and steal the statue with no fanfare or danger? It was a matter of a few steps at best, in, out, and gone. Though if it were a crime of opportunity, snatching the statue during the fauna fray made sense.

"Is the statue always kept here?"

Lady Bickford snorted. "No. This is what pride gets you. I told him when he bought it that the only place for it was in his safe. It was too valuable to leave lying about. But he had to bring it out for the party so people could tell him how impressed they were. Which is silly, since most people wouldn't know fine art if they tripped over it in the street." She flipped her wrist. "And now it's gone. A fortune wasted on a hunk of bronze. All we have to show for his extravagance is empty air."

"That's not true. I insured the piece against theft." Lord Bickford straightened. "Mr. Selby recommended it, especially as I had told him I wanted the piece on display at this party. And when Montgomery's painting went missing, I went right to Lloyd's that next morning and insured the statue against damage or loss."

"Praise be, you did something right. We can get our money back at least." Lady Bickford raised her hands.

Daniel added "insurance fraud" to his list of motives, but unless the Bickfords were better actors than they seemed, he couldn't make himself believe it. Still, it would bear checking out.

"The doors were open during the party?" In spite of the chill outside?

"It got very warm. Gloriana ordered them opened." Lord Bickford touched the pedestal with a longing expression in his eyes.

"I did not order them opened," Lady Bickford snapped. "I thought you did. You were standing right here most of the night, ignoring your duties as host and hoping someone would come by and ask you about your precious statue."

His neck reddened, and for a moment his eyes blazed. The old fellow had some fight in him after all. "I never told anyone to open the doors."

"Who did?" Daniel asked. "Would your butler do it on his own?"

"Of course not. He's too well trained." Lady Bickford looked as if she'd just kissed a lemon. "My staff does not get above its station."

Gritting his teeth, Daniel took a moment to inhale and keep his composure. "Did anyone attend the party that you weren't expecting? Did anyone bring a guest?

"No one would show up without an invitation." Lady Bickford

puckered. "None of our friends would be so uncouth. Why are you asking such crude questions? Though I suppose it is to be expected. Police work not only infringes upon the liberties of the people, but it is undertaken by such common people."

"My dear, please. We want him to do his best to find the statue. He won't do that if you insult him."

"I don't want him to find the statue. I want the insurance money," she snapped.

"Was anyone expected to attend but didn't?" Daniel kept his voice neutral. Lady Bickford had jumped to the top of the suspect list by her own admission.

"Almost everyone who was invited attended. There was only one couple who sent their regrets. The Earl and Countess of Thorndike were called back to their estate for some reason." Lady Bickford shook her head. "I cannot imagine. Why employ an estate steward at all if you have to go haring back to the country at the drop of a hat? It speaks to poor management, that's what."

Daniel knew nothing about estate management from the owner's perspective. He'd spent his early years on an estate, but it had been as a boot boy in the main house, or mucking out and exercising the earl's horses, or carrying bushel baskets of potatoes into the root cellar for the head gardener. His mother had been domestic help, seamstress, maid, assistant to the cook, sometimes baby nurse, anything the family wanted or needed. From the day he realized he was not like other children, that his lack of a father made him somehow less, a burden, an embarrassment where others were concerned, he did his best to earn his keep, to help out however he could so that people would like him and perhaps forget that his mother was never married.

"Well? What are you going to do? Stand there woolgathering, or find out who did this? Or better yet, tell Lloyds there is no hope of getting that wretched thing back and that they must pay out our claim." Lady Bickford put her hands on her hips, staring at him expectantly.

Jerked back to the present, Daniel tried to appear as if he hadn't been daydreaming. "I will need those lists of guests and employees as quickly as possible. If you have a secretary who can provide them while I am here, that would be optimal. If not, please compile them tonight and have them delivered to the Bow Street Magistrate's Court first thing in the morning. Now, I would like to look outside." He went to the closest set of French doors and grabbed the knobs, but the doors wouldn't open.

"A bit like tipping the pitcher upright again when all the water has run out, isn't it?" Lady Bickford shrugged. "My husband ordered the doors locked *after* the statue was stolen."

The butler was summoned with the keys.

"These doors need a key even on the inside? Are all the doors in the house that way?"

"Yes. I want the house to be very secure at all times." Lord Bickford puffed up his chest, took one look at his wife, and deflated. "I didn't order the doors to be opened, and I only had the statue out of the safe for a few hours. This isn't my fault."

"If you will accompany me?" Daniel asked the butler. Once they were outside and out of earshot, he asked, "Did you open the doors during the party?"

"No, sir. I was delayed seeing to a guest who had spilled a drink on his shirt. The doors were closed when I left the ballroom."

"Who has access to the keys?"

"All the keys for the house are hung on a board in the servants' dining room."

Where anyone could get at them. What passed for security in some houses was laughable.

"How long were you gone from the ballroom?"

"Perhaps ten minutes or so? I took the gentleman upstairs to milord's valet to see what could be done and returned as soon as I could. When I arrived back, the doors were all opened, which I thought a bit odd considering how chilled it was outside."

Daniel took a quick gander at the small terrace, the stone steps, and the walled backyard. If someone stole the statue and climbed over the wall with it by himself, he would have to be equal parts agile and strong.

Perhaps he wasn't looking for one individual, but a gang? A quick search of the files at Bow Street had turned up nothing in the way of gangs dealing in fine art, but there had been some houses broken into last fall that were purported to be the work of a gang operating out of the St. Giles rookery. But their thefts had been limited to small items like jewelry and coins. Had they graduated to larger crimes?

He entered the house again. "Lord Bickford, did anyone show any undue interest in the statue?"

The aristocrat shook his gray head slowly, his shoulders bowed. "Not a soul seemed to care except Sir Bertrand Thorndike. He asked if he might examine it up close. I was so pleased he was interested, but before I could tell him about it, that infernal cat got into the room and the evening was destroyed."

"Sir Bertrand was here?"

"Yes, and his niece, Lady Juliette," Lady Bickford said. "Such a nice young woman. A debutante. Viscount Coatsworth seemed most taken with her. He was attentive during their dance, and I had a chance to speak with my good friend the Dowager Duchess of Haverly, who is acting as Lady Juliette's chaperone in her mother's absence, and she was very pleased at the number of suitors asking for an introduction to Lady Juliette. Even Duke Heinrich von Lowe seemed interested." Lady Bickford bit her lip, as if her speculations and gossip tasted sweet.

A flare of something uncomfortable, but which Daniel refused to name, lit his chest. Coatsworth dancing with Lady Juliette. The man rubbed him the wrong way, but Daniel couldn't exactly say why. He'd only met the viscount briefly a few nights ago, and not under the best of circumstances.

"What condition was Sir Bertrand in?"

"Condition? He was immaculate." Lady Bickford drew herself up, her neck stiff. "Why do you ask?"

"He wasn't the worse for drink?"

"Certainly not. There were spirits on offer in the card room, but I can assure you, no other alcohol was served. I don't host those kinds of parties."

Chapter 8

"THE TROUBLE IS, EVERYBODY SEEMS to know everybody." Daniel compared the guest list of the Montgomery and Bickford parties. "More than a quarter of the names are duplicates. I've interviewed party guests until my head aches, and no one saw anything. They were all watching the dog and cat show."

"Anybody know where the cat came from?"

"Burst in through the open door. Bad timing that it happened right in front of two large dogs."

"Bad timing or good? A diversion created to spirit the statue away, or an opportunist who saw his chance?"

"No way to tell just yet." Daniel tossed the papers onto his desk. Pages and boxes and files had piled up around his work area, and it was driving him mad. He liked order, needed it to keep his thoughts clear.

"What about the servants' list?" Ed asked.

"That's no help either, because there are no commonalities there. Not one of the temporary servants hired by Mr. Montgomery also worked during the Bickford party."

Ed leaned back in his chair, tapping his finger against his lips. "Are you sure? Is there a way to check that the temporary servants actually gave their real names when applying for the position? Is it possible that the same person, using a different name, was at both residences?"

Daniel paused. "They were supplied through a hiring agency.

Different agencies. If they lied to the agency about their name, how would we go about proving it or finding them?"

"Maybe bring the butler and housekeeper from Montgomery's house to the station and get the temporary workers from the agency who supplied them to Bickford's and see if anyone recognizes anyone?"

"Can you arrange that?" Daniel asked.

"I can try to track people down, but what will you be doing in the meantime?"

"I'm heading over to the opera house to talk to the manager. The only item Mr. Rickets managed to stammer out that he bought for sure on this trip was a set of tapestries that are supposed to hang in the opera house hallway that leads to the Royal Box."

"That's a good idea. Perhaps the manager's paperwork can shed some light on the case."

"More than Bickford's did. He had a copy of the invoice, though he didn't want to show it to me at first. I think his wife is right. He paid a ridiculous amount for the maquette. Beyond that, he had no other information. He fetched the statue himself from the gallery when he'd been notified by Mr. Selby that it had arrived, and nothing seemed out of the ordinary to Lord Bickford. Selby wasn't behaving unusually, the gallery was as it should be, and nothing indicated anyone was in danger."

Owen strolled into the office, dropping a sheaf of papers onto Daniel's desk and placing a paper-wrapped bundle on Ed's. "Evening, gents."

Ed unwrapped his parcel to find a hot pie. "Did you bring one for Mr. Swann?" he asked the retreating back of the office boy.

"He never asked me to," Owen shot back before disappearing into the hall.

Pursing his lips, Ed broke the pie in half and handed part across the gap between the desks. "That youngster is in for a rude awakening someday."

Daniel took the offering, letting Owen's poor manners roll off. "If he was nice to me, I might die from the shock. How did you fare questioning those in the neighborhood of the art gallery?"

"Nobody saw anything." Ed bit into the meat pie, closing his eyes in pleasure, chewing and swallowing before going on. "Either they are deaf and blind, or no one wants to get involved. The only bit of information I could get out of anyone was that a wagon blocked the entrance to the mews for half an hour that morning, and no one could find the driver."

"There was no wagon blocking access when we arrived. Do you think it had anything to do with the murder?" Daniel tasted the pie, inhaling the meaty aroma. He hadn't eaten for hours, too busy gathering information to think about a meal. He should take better care of himself, or he would run out of strength when he might need it.

"The publican across the street said he looked out and it was there, and he looked out a bit later and it was gone. Thought the driver might have been loading barrels, maybe from the butcher's shop around the corner?" Ed shrugged. "It might be something. It might be nothing. If there was nothing stolen from the gallery, why would you need a wagon?"

Daniel thought back. "There was a wagon pulling out at the far end of the mews when we arrived on the scene." But they had been too far away to make out any details on the driver, the team, or the contents of the dray. And it had been moving at a child's pace, hardly fleeing the scene of a murder. "With no inventory books to look through and Mr. Selby deceased, we can't tell if anything is missing from the gallery. Mr. Rickets is supposed to come in early tomorrow morning. Hopefully, he has gathered his wits enough to be coherent."

Having tried twice to interview the art buyer over the last forty-eight hours, Daniel fought frustration that Mr. Rickets had been "too upset" to respond. Daniel was out of patience and would have to demand answers. For now, he had other clues to chase.

As he gathered his cloak and hat for the quick trip across the street, a lithe youngster with a dirt smudge on his nose bounded into the office. "There a Mr. Swann here?"

"That would be me."

The boy dug in his pocket and pulled out a well-creased envelope, holding it in one hand while extending his other palm. "Letter for ya."

Daniel tossed a penny his way, which was deftly caught and secreted into a pocket before he could blink. The letter jutted out, and the minute Daniel took it, the boy was away.

"Love letter?" Ed asked, finishing the last of his pie and chuckling.

"Lawyer letter." Daniel read the terse note. The solicitors Coles, Franks & Moody, serving in their role as mediator between himself and his patron, instructed him to attend the Ash Valley Hunt one week from now to ride Beauden's Best, a thoroughbred for sale. Prospective buyers would be at the hunt, and his patron, as a favor to the horse's owner, wanted Daniel to ride the animal to show it off. He'd performed the service many times, for many different owners, all brokered by his patron through the solicitors.

How was he supposed to fit in jockey-for-hire duties with his investigation? Yet he would have to find a way. Though it wasn't written in the "rules," it was understood that Daniel would do as his patron asked whenever possible.

Though he was forbidden from searching for his patron's identity, he couldn't help but try, passively, to put together the clues. But he'd not yet been able to suss out the identity of his patron through the jobs he required Daniel to do. The horses he rode to order always belonged to different owners, and no trail of information ever led back to a single repeated source.

Frustrating for an investigator to be so stymied.

Like he was on this case.

"Sir Michael will want a report on his desk at sunup. I'd best see about those tapestries."

"If we don't find a solid lead soon, the press will be baying for our blood." Ed returned to his witness statements.

"And on that cheerful note, I'll see you for the Rickets interview on the morrow."

Juliette enjoyed the opera, unlike so many of her friends who went only to be seen and because it was the cultured thing to do. This would be her first visit to the Royal Opera House, and in spite of her evening's mission, she was looking forward to the performances.

She smiled as she climbed into the dowager's carriage. "Good evening, Your Grace."

The dowager eyed her critically before her stern expression broke into more pleasurable lines. "Good evening, Lady Juliette. I have had a letter from your mother at last, thanking me for taking you under my wing in her absence."

Juliette's heart should have soared at the news, but she had, at Uncle Bertie's urging, penned the note herself, pretending to be the countess so the dowager would spread it abroad that the Thorndikes were indeed at their country estate.

"Your mother is such a gracious woman, and so stylish. She pens a very nice letter as well, most precise and accurate in her penmanship. And punctilious as to her manners. Her remarks about my chaperonage were most gratifying, I can assure you."

Juliette's conscience pricked. Though stern and outspoken with her views, the dowager had been kind, and Juliette, who believed in integrity and truthfulness, chafed at the new role she'd adopted.

Was it right to lie if your motives were good? Would God look favorably upon their endeavors if they lied and stole and deceived to accomplish them?

What wouldn't she give for a long conversation with her parents about these struggles? Their advice would be invaluable and perhaps give her wavering conscience somewhere to stand. If only she truly knew where they were.

They rode in silence to Agatha's house, but that was where the silence stopped. Agatha climbed into the carriage like an awkward colt, dropping onto her seat beside Juliette with a giggle.

"I do appreciate you calling for me. I intended to ride with Father, but he's running terribly behind, and I can't really blame him. Father has had a visit from Sir Michael Biddle himself from the Bow Street Magistrate's Court to assure him that everything is being done to find his painting, and would you ever guess? Mr. Selby, who was at our party, the man you danced with during the opening set, Juliette, and who sold Father the painting . . ." She stopped for breath, her hand pressed to her bosom. "He was murdered." Her eyes, wide and glistening, sought Juliette's. "Someone broke into the art gallery in the early morning after our party and killed him."

Juliette gripped the window frame. Blood rushed from her head, lightness blossoming between her ears.

Mr. Selby was dead? Murdered?

"Are you sure?" she whispered, her voice cracking.

"I am. Sir Michael told Father that the murder might have something to do with the stolen painting and they were investigating. He even asked Father his whereabouts after the party dispersed and his movements the next morning. I was able to tell Sir Michael that Father never left the house until after nine the day after our debuts, because we both saw him and broke our fast with him."

Juliette closed her eyes, willing the swirling in her head to cease so she could think. Mr. Selby was dead. Murdered in his shop.

Coldness crept along her limbs. Someone she had met, with whom she had laughed and exchanged pleasantries, was now dead.

And the painting he had sold from his gallery now resided in the attic of her parents' townhouse, stolen from its rightful owner. No, not stolen, removed. Removed for a time for a good reason.

Not just the painting, but the statuette too. When she'd arrived home from the Bickfords', she'd raced upstairs to the hidden room to find Uncle Bertie balancing the maquette on his knee, studying the depiction in miniature of Donatello's *Saint Mark*.

"The code is hidden in the hem of his robe." Bertie pointed to the bottom of the figure. "Not obvious, but there nonetheless."

"How on earth did you get a cat into the ballroom?" Juliette removed her cloak. The lace collar of her costume itched, but her curiosity itched more. "If you were aiming for maximum chaos, you hit the bull's-eye."

"I didn't do it." He grinned. "It was a beautiful thing though, wasn't it? There I was, contemplating how I would get the statue out of the room without detection, and wondering if I would have to do a little housebreaking tonight instead, when the entire room erupted. I feel we should send some kippers around to the Russian embassy for those dogs."

Juliette sagged onto a chair. "It was all happenstance? You didn't orchestrate it?"

"I had nothing to do with that cat's arrival. How did the party end? I nipped out to the garden, hid the statue, and nipped back in time to commiserate with poor Bickford on the theft. It's just as well I was able to snatch it when I did, because Bickford was moaning that he should have kept it in his office safe where it usually resided. Safecracking is vastly more difficult than simple housebreaking. And who knows when the statuette would be out in the open again."

"In all the pandemonium, I didn't realize you had come back into the Bickfords' house." Juliette leaned forward to study the code scratched faintly into bronze. "That agent must have been in a hurry when he scratched this message. It's terribly hard to read."

"He created the code, so he would be able to read it better than most. Perhaps the indecipherability is intentional to thwart a decoder."

Juliette considered this, feeling the bump of her garnet ring beneath the satin of her evening gloves. She wished she had changed out of the Tudor gown before racing upstairs.

"My superior has sent an agent to the Continent to follow the trail from that end. And to bring the body of Leonidas home."

They were quiet for a long moment, before Juliette stirred.

"How did you get the maquette from Bickford's to here without being seen?"

"It was a close-run thing. I left with the majority of the party guests, and I watched you depart with the dowager. I found a place to observe from down the street, and when the detective arrived, I knew they would occupy everyone in the house. What I hadn't counted on was Mr. Swann deciding to have a good look outside at precisely the moment I had leapt the back fence to retrieve the statue from the bushes where I had hidden it." Bertie pointed to the damp patches of dirt decorating his evening trousers. "I dove behind the yew hedge, and Detective Swann stopped only five feet from me. If he had discovered me, I had no plausible story as to why I was hiding in the shrubbery. I regretted not pretending to be sotted at the party, but Bickford and a dozen others had seen me sober and in my right mind only a half hour before." He set the heavy bronze on the desk. "I thought you'd be home long before I was."

"I thought so too, but the dowager wanted to go inside at Agatha's to give her regards to Mr. Montgomery. I suspect it was actually to glean what information she could about the painting theft and to gossip about the maquette, but I'll give her the benefit of the doubt." Juliette stripped off her gloves finger by finger. "Let me have a go at the code. Perhaps there's enough to begin to decipher it."

But try as she might, she had made no headway. This string of symbols was even shorter than that on the painting. She had puzzled over it so long that she'd dreamed of the symbols and groupings and had awakened unrefreshed this morning.

As the carriage to the opera bowled along, she could only think that all the while she had been dancing and laughing and contemplating a theft, Mr. Selby, who had sold both pieces, had been dead.

A shaft of doubt sliced through her. Uncle Bertie had produced a list of the encoded artwork on Turner and Rathbone stationery, but he refused to say where he got it. Where else could he have procured it except the gallery?

Surely Uncle Bertie wouldn't have killed someone to get that list. Would he?

Shivering, Juliette wrapped her cloak about her. No, she wouldn't believe it.

But how could she really know? Less than a week ago, she had lived in blissful ignorance of her family's true legacy and actions. Now she was lying and stealing and keeping secrets as if she'd done so all her life. She was practicing picking pockets and locks and balancing on narrow beams to simulate walking a ridgepole, all in anticipation of having to break in or get away without detection.

What did she really know about her parents and her uncle if they had hidden so much from her already?

Another shiver racked her spine.

But murder was an altogether different proposition.

"Juliette, haven't you heard a word I've said? You've gone into a trance." Agatha nudged Juliette. "Isn't it awful? I mean, murder. Who would do such a thing? One must be a complete scoundrel and evil person to kill someone, don't you think?"

"Miss Montgomery, I do beg you to stop speaking of such terrible things. It isn't seemly. You shouldn't even know about such events, a young girl like you, and your talk of murder and killing has upset Lady Juliette." The dowager dug her hands deeper into her fur muff, pinching her lips. "Lady Juliette, do put your feet on the hot stones here. You look positively pasty with shock."

How the dowager could see in the relative darkness of the carriage was beyond Juliette, but she obeyed, placing her slippers on the burlap-wrapped heap between them on the floor.

"Let us talk of more pleasant things. I understand Duke Heinrich von Lowe will be attending tonight and sitting in our box, as well as Viscount Coatsworth. You're each garnering some delicious attention for debutantes, I must say. Last night at the Bickfords' bash, both of those gentlemen approached me about furthering their acquaintances with you." The dowager had a smug tinge to her tone, as if she were somehow responsible for the good impression the girls were making upon the *ton*. "I think your parents will be pleased."

"Father said he would meet us at the opera house, as he had to finish his meeting with Sir Michael. Father entertained dignitaries from Russia at one of his mills today. I think some of the same persons who were at the Bickfords' last night. Wasn't that awful? Those dogs?" Agatha collapsed into giggles.

"I must say this Season is off to a peculiar start. One wonders what might occur next. At least nothing untoward will happen at the opera. I'm glad your father got this party up tonight. I don't often get to see an opera. My son, the duke, abhors the art form, and he's let his box go." The dowager shrugged, as if to say her son's oddities were not her fault.

Juliette tried to bring her mind to bear on what the ladies were saying, but she kept circling back to Mr. Selby's murder and Uncle Bertie's having the list of art and artifacts in his possession only hours later.

Light blazed from the windows and braziers along the street in front of the Royal Opera House as their carriage pulled to the curb. The pillars stretched toward the night sky, flanking the entrance.

Juliette composed herself as they walked up the steps. Agatha clutched her arm, oblivious to Juliette's inner chaos.

You must remember your task tonight. It's not just to be seen having a normal Season. You must find those tapestries and examine them.

Reminding herself of her mission both focused her mind and put her nerves on edge. Would any of this ever come easily to her? Did her mother still have bees' wings flapping under her skin when she received new orders from her superiors?

They made their way through the grand foyer, surrendered their wraps at the coat check, and all the while Juliette searched for the tapestries. Though the hall was splendidly decorated, no hangings graced the foyer.

Where else might they be? And how could she search without being obvious?

They made their way up the staircase to the right, and when they turned into the hallway behind the boxes, her senses prickled. Along the outer wall, opposite the velvet curtains separating the boxes from the passageway, someone had painted a landscape mural that ran the length of the hallway.

Since the tapestries were not in the foyer, they were most likely in one of these halls behind the boxes. How many halls did that mean?

The box Mr. Montgomery had reserved for the evening was nearly half-full when they arrived. The dowager made her way toward the front row of chairs as if by right. Juliette followed her to take the measure of the opera house.

Four tiers of boxes encircled the auditorium. That meant four long halls on each side of the building, plus the shorter halls along the rear of the boxes facing the stage head-on. Twelve passages to investigate.

She put her hand on the brass rail and leaned over. A queer feeling swirled in her head as she looked down three floors to the pit below, and she straightened, sucking in a quick breath. Heights didn't frighten her per se, but she didn't like them much.

The curtains behind them parted, and more guests arrived. Juliette nodded to Duke Heinrich and made her way to Agatha's side.

Viscount Coatsworth edged around the duke to approach Agatha, who flushed prettily and rounded her shoulders to reduce her height. Juliette touched her arm and straightened her spine, reminding Agatha to stand tall and be proud.

"Good evening, ladies." Coatsworth bowed. "You look well. One hopes tonight will be a simple entertainment with no catastrophes or excitements beyond those on stage." He grinned. "After our last two parties, I could use some normality."

Duke Heinrich bowed and clicked his polished boot heels together. "Lady Juliette, Fraulein Montgomery."

They took their seats, and a hush came over the crowd as the curtain rose. For short stretches, Juliette enjoyed the music and the pageantry, but for the most part, her mind raced.

What had Mr. Selby known? Was he privy to the knowledge that his artwork was being used to smuggle information? Had that knowledge gotten him killed?

Did Uncle Bertie have anything to do with Mr. Selby's death?

At the first intermission, no one left the box, much to Juliette's consternation. She was hemmed in by Agatha on one side and Duke Heinrich on the other.

"Opera is very popular in my country. My family built an opera house in Frankfurt." The duke spoke modestly, but Agatha was clearly impressed.

"I love the opera," she offered. "We went several times in Lucerne, didn't we, Juliette?"

Viscount Coatsworth leaned forward. "I say, ladies, have you been invited to the Ash Valley Hunt this next weekend? If not, would you come as my guests? We've a party going down, and I understand you both ride quite well?" He seemed to want to get the conversation off the duke's family wealth and influence. "It's going to be a cracking good time. The Ash Valley pack is one of the best in the country."

"That sounds delightful." And it would be, if only to get Juliette out of London for a weekend. She could use the time to breathe and perhaps not think of everything going on in the secret lives of agents and spies.

"We'll travel down there on Sunday. It's only a couple hours' drive from London. The hunt is on Monday, a week from now, and we'll attend the Hunt Ball on Monday night. Then we'll all troop home on Tuesday. I'm sending my horses down this week, and I can send mounts for you as well."

"Thank you. I will ride my mother's mare, Fabiana, but perhaps Agatha will need a hunter?"

"Are you attending, Your Grace?" Agatha asked the duke.

"Ja, I have been invited. So many kind invitations have arrived. Some even for summer, though I do not know if I will be still in England at that time. How far is it to Brighton? I have been invited to spend time in a summer cottage in Brighton."

"I love Brighton." Agatha clapped her hands, her eyes shining. "The sea air, the beaches, and the parties. I haven't been in ages, but when I was a girl, my parents had a house there, and we went every summer. Do your parents still have a home in Brighton, Juliette?"

"Thorncliff." She nodded. "It's near Brighton but not in the actual town. Farther west along the coast." She panned the milling crowd below, and her eyes linked with those of someone she recognized.

Mr. Swann, from Bow Street, stood in an aisle, looking up at their box. An odd quiver went through her at the intensity of his gaze. It felt as if he could see right into her mind. Could he tell she knew exactly where the artwork he sought was being kept? Was her face giving away her secrets?

She broke eye contact, hoping she looked bored and disinterested, as if perhaps she hadn't recognized him.

When she glanced back, he was gone.

———⟨❦⟩———

By the second intermission, Daniel was bored out of his skull. He didn't speak Italian, and he didn't know the story being told on the stage. It all seemed overdone and too flamboyant for his tastes anyway.

When he'd come to speak to the manager about the tapestries, the man had been too busy. It was opening night of a new show, and he had no time for detectives making a nuisance of themselves. He would talk after the performance.

Then, as if realizing he was being rude, he had softened. "Sir, please see tonight's performance, and we will discuss your concerns in my office after the show. You will be my guest for the evening." He assessed Daniel's attire, which was clean, expensive, and in style, but hardly eveningwear, and snapped his fingers. An assistant appeared, as if out of thin air.

"Ned, see that Mr. Swann has a very good view of the stage from the pit. Near center front. He is my guest."

And Daniel had found himself in the fifth row center, blocked in on either side by opera enthusiasts, waiting for the final act to begin.

He'd been on the verge of refusing the offer and stating he would return later, when he'd spied Lady Juliette Thorndike entering the foyer.

Her dark, luminous eyes seemed to take in the grand room like an amazed child. Had she never been here before?

What was it about her that fascinated him? Was it that she was more than a comely woman? He'd seen pretty girls before and not felt this pull. Was it that she seemed intelligent in a way that he had supposed aristocratic young ladies were not? Which was wrong of him, he admitted, to assume they were all empty headed, caring only about fashion and themselves and the impression they were making on one another. Though in his encounters with aristocrats, that had been his experience.

Or was he being a fool, spinning fantasies where there was no foundation? She was well out of his sphere, he was deeply involved in a case that would most likely make or break his career, and he had no interest in following up on a brief acquaintance with a debutante who probably wouldn't even acknowledge his existence had they met under normal circumstances.

"So why did you stay for the opera?" he whispered to himself. "Why did you stare up at her box during the first intermission until she met your gaze?" Heat crawled across his collarbones, and he ignored the stare of the man to his right, embarrassed at getting caught talking to himself.

When the final bow had been taken and the crowd began to disperse, Daniel waited in his seat. The manager would be busy for a while yet. Casually he let his eyes move from box to box. Jewels glittered, satins shone, feathered headpieces wafted.

In Lady Juliette's box, Mr. Montgomery had arrived, his linens gleaming white against his dark coat, and the deep timbre of his voice drifting over even the babble of the crowd on the auditorium floor.

At the rear of the box, the German duke held open the curtain for the guests to precede him into the passageway. Daniel rose to his feet and headed toward the foyer.

Not to catch a glimpse of a certain young lady, he chided himself. But because he needed to see the manager in his office.

An usher directed him down the correct narrow corridor and to a door marked with the manager's name and position. Daniel opened the door and stopped.

Three heads turned, the manager's, Duke von Lowe, and . . . Lady Juliette.

"I beg your pardon. I didn't realize you were engaged. I'll wait outside." Daniel began to back out, but the manager held up his hands.

"No, no, you will save me a trip. This gentleman and lady have asked to see the tapestries as well. You can come with us." The manager beamed, sweat standing out on his scalp through his sparse hair. "It has been such a successful opening night, and we're so very proud of the tapestries. It will be a pleasure to show you."

Neither Lady Juliette nor the duke appeared to think it a pleasure, but they didn't demure. How could Daniel ask the manager about murder and thievery in front of a lady? Perhaps he could bide his time. The aristocrats would look their fill of the tapestries, and he could get about his business with the manager after they'd gone.

They were led up the left-hand staircase from the foyer, where many of tonight's audience lingered, sounding like a flock of seagulls on the mudflats at low tide.

"We've only just gotten them hung up in time for the performance tonight. Imported from Belgium. They were most expensive, but so beautiful," the manager prattled over his shoulder as he went up the plush carpeted stairs. "Originally we thought to hang them in the private hallway that leads to the Royal Box, but then so few people would be able to view them. So we put them in the anteroom here on the second floor, where people mingle during the intermissions."

They walked through a curtained doorway, Daniel in the rear, and viewed for the first time the four tapestries.

Rectangular, taller than they were wide, with muted colors. Around the borders, spaced evenly between bars of ribbons and greenery, different crested shields marched. Cherubs, each covered discreetly with flowing ribbons for clothes, climbed boughs, perched on drums, and floated in the air around a large coat of arms in the middle of each tapestry.

The duke stood back, one elbow perched on his crossed arm, his hand at his chin, studying them all. Lady Juliette, however, walked right up to the first one, stopping only inches away.

"They were created in Brussels, in the great tradition of Belgian weaving, originally commissioned for a Spanish family in the sixteenth century." The manager's chest swelled. "The directors are most proud to have such artistry on display. They are publishing a booklet that will be for sale over all of London for those who are not fortunate enough to be able to see them for themselves."

The manager went on, speaking to the duke about the opera house, tonight's performance, and the many pieces of art that decorated the building's walls.

Lady Juliette's dress rustled as she moved, and when Daniel joined her before the first tapestry, he caught the scent of roses.

It took him back to his childhood, working in the gardens at the estate. The head gardener had a fondness for roses, and he'd taught Daniel how to prune and fertilize and water, but mostly how to enjoy the blooms.

Daniel learned the valuable lesson that one could appreciate beauty no matter how poor you were. There were things that no man could take away from you, be you king or servant, and an appreciation of creation was one of them. It was something Daniel tried to remember each day, though finding creation to appreciate was more difficult in the city than when living on the estate.

"Why are you interested in the tapestries, Lady Juliette, if I may be so bold as to ask? Had you heard of them before coming tonight?" Daniel kept his voice low, pitching it under the speech of the manager. He studied her profile as he waited for her answer. Her skin was darker than most English maids. Not that he minded the richness of her complexion. No, it only served to intrigue him.

"I did know of them prior to this evening. I made the acquaintance of Mr. Selby, an art dealer, and he mentioned the tapestries to me in passing. I only learned today that he was tragically killed. Such a shame. But it was Duke Heinrich's idea to ask to see them tonight, as he had heard of them as well and wondered how they compared to tapestries hanging in some of his family's castles in Brandenburg." She moved on to the next hanging.

Daniel glanced at the duke, but he was still talking with the manager, barely looking at the artwork. His family had more than one castle?

"Are you making any progress on those thefts? Agatha said Sir Michael Biddle visited her father about the matter today, and poor Lord Bickford was beside himself about that little statue that was stolen. Surely something like that can't have much value. It was so small."

She had spoken rather coolly of Selby's murder. Weren't women of the *ton* supposed to be susceptible to fainting or a fit of the vapors when learning of distressing things? "Value is not set by size. If so, boulders would be exorbitant in price and diamonds would be negligible. Value is set by the worth of an item to someone who cares about it. A child values a penny more than a king values a guinea."

"Lady Juliette, the dowager will be waiting for us. I don't like to hurry you, but she is not a woman who appreciates waiting, I do not think," the duke said.

"Just a few minutes more. These are so beautiful. And the weaving is so close. It stops the mind to think of how many thousands of threads and the planning that must have been done to create such a depth of color and such lifelike expressions."

She stood close to the fabric, as if counting the individual threads of which she spoke. When she neared the center coat of arms, she paused, her hand coming up to almost touch the wool and silk.

"Aren't you too close to enjoy the tapestries? You cannot see the picture if you stand so near." The duke put his hand on her elbow.

She resisted for a moment and then relented. "Of course. And you are right—we should be on our way. The dowager will be growing impatient."

"Do you not wish to study the fourth tapestry?" the manager asked. "It is my favorite. The stags and unicorns are so beautiful."

"Perhaps another time." She put her arm through the duke's. "Thank you so much for the private peek. They're truly wonderful. I shall have to tell my parents about them when they return to the city."

With a short nod to Daniel, she let the duke lead her away.

Left alone with the manager, Daniel suggested they return to his office. Once there, he addressed the reason for his visit.

"The thefts Lady Juliette mentioned are why I am here. I want to caution you that two items from the same shipment of art as these tapestries were stolen this week. I would encourage you to remain vigilant and inform your night guards to do the same. I do not know what the connection is between the thefts, but it is beyond the realm of likelihood that they are coincidences."

"I heard of the robberies, but I had no idea there was any connection to our tapestries." The manager pulled his chair out from his desk and sat down heavily. "Do you think someone might want to steal our new artwork?"

"I don't know. I came out of an abundance of caution and to ask if you could tell me what you know about the buying process, the shipment, or anything related to the purchase. Did you approach Mr. Selby, or did he approach you? Do you have any of the paperwork connected to the sale?"

The manager was already turning to a file drawer behind him. "I believe it was someone on the board who first mentioned the tapestries. Where he got the information, I am not sure. I only attend the beginnings of board meetings in order to give my reports, you see, and then I am excused. Perhaps, though . . ." He paused in his rummaging. "Yes, here we are. Minutes of board meetings for this year."

Pages of closely written script thumped on the desk. "When was that?" He rifled through them. "Ah, maybe this is the one." He held up a long sheet of foolscap to the lamp. "Yes. Here it is. The idea was first proposed by Lord Gravesend. He's a collector himself, and I understand he had commissioned Turner and Rathbone to purchase some items for himself on an upcoming buying tour. The representative from the art dealership had mentioned the tapestries and suggested them as a possible acquisition for the opera house." He looked up from the paper. "The motion was made, discussion followed, a price was set, and the motion carried."

The representative from the art dealership who was now dead.

"Do you have an invoice or provenance or other paperwork about the tapestries themselves?"

"Yes, of course." More rummaging. He produced a dark-brown folder. "It's all in here."

Daniel looked at the papers inside. Everything seemed in order. Mr.

Selby's signature on the invoice. The price, which, like the maquette, boggled the mind. The letter of provenance from the dealer in Brussels.

"Who arranged the transport?"

"Turner and Rathbone. They agreed to terms with the board, and when the tapestries arrived, they were delivered here. We weren't sure when they would come. Shipping hasn't been easy for many years, but with the defeat of the French, things have opened up again. I wasn't hopeful they would arrive before opening night of the Season, but I was pleased to be wrong. I sent round a thank-you note to Mr. Selby personally at the gallery when they were delivered."

Daniel hadn't come across that note yet in all the office paperwork. But who would steal something as innocuous as a thank-you note? It must be in the boxes yet to be sieved.

He thanked the manager for his time and left feeling he'd gone up a blind alley once more. The tapestries must not have anything to do with the thefts, though he was glad he had warned the manager to be on his guard.

More questions than answers had arisen from his visit.

But foremost in his mind was why Lady Juliette Thorndike had been interested in three of the four tapestries.

"It was right there. Tiny but unmistakable. My heart was pounding so loud, I'm surprised the detective couldn't hear it." As Juliette made her report and copied from memory the symbols from the tapestry onto her worksheet, her pulse skipped in her veins. She dipped her quill in the inkwell on the battered desk in the War Room, concentrating on reproducing the code correctly.

"I don't know whether you are brave or idiotic. What possessed you to invite the detective along for the inspection?" Uncle Bertie paced before the desk, his hands behind his back.

"I wasn't the one who invited him. It was the manager. He showed off those tapestries like they were his newborn children. The detective arrived in the office as we were going upstairs to see them. I was prepared to wait until most of the people had left, claim to have forgotten my reticule, and then slip upstairs, but Duke Heinrich intervened. He said he'd heard about the new artwork and suggested we see the manager about viewing them."

Bertie's head came up, and he stopped pacing. "The duke suggested the viewing?"

Juliette nodded. "Look, some of the symbols are repeated." She held up the paper, tapping her chin with the feather quill. "Now we're making progress. Repetition and patterns are the keys to breaking a code."

"Well done, but go back. It was Duke Heinrich's idea to see the tapestries?"

"Yes. He excused the two of us from our party, with the dowager's permission, to ask the manager about seeing them. No one else in the group wanted to go, though the duke invited everyone."

"Did he examine them with you?"

"He stood back to observe them, and he spoke with the manager while I got close to the tapestries. Mr. Swann stood beside me, but he seemed to be looking . . ." She ducked her chin, her cheeks warming.

"Yes?"

Glancing up, she tried to put on a cloak of casualness. "He seemed to be looking at me more than at the tapestries." Her chin came up.

Bertie pinched his upper lip, his eyes clouded. "You'd do best to avoid the detective. He's sharp brained and not your average plodding night watchman. He's making inroads on the case, though he isn't aware of that just yet. If we aren't careful, he'll slot enough pieces together to uncover what we need kept secret." He straightened, consulted the list pinned to the post with the letter opener, and pointed to one line.

"The next item won't be difficult to obtain, and it won't be clandestine either. But it will need to be procured by you."

She leaned forward. "What is it and how?" Anticipation feathered across her skin.

"It's a jade dragon. Rare enough, and it is up for public auction.

Tomorrow afternoon at Barrett and Company Auction House. I want you to go there, purchase it, and bring it back here. Your cover story is that your father's birthday is coming up soon, and he is interested in anything he can find coming from the Orient. You think the jade dragon will make the perfect gift." He waved his hand. "And it's more than plausible, since my brother has given a lecture at the Lyceum on Chinese art, and he wrote a monograph on the subject not long ago as well."

"Not that I mind going, but why me? Wouldn't it be more appropriate for you to buy it or to accompany me? Where will you be?"

"I have another brief mission for my superiors. I shouldn't be gone more than three days, but if I am, do not worry, and do not attempt to locate or acquire any other pieces from the list." His voice sharpened. "Promise me. You've had some success here early on, but that is no reason to think you're an accomplished agent."

Knowing he was correct, but still feeling taken down a peg or two, she fought a tinge of rebellion. "I promise. But I've never been to an auction before. What should I do?"

He spent the next little while going over the procedures and cautioning her again not to draw undue attention, to use her cover story, and to come straight home again with the dragon.

"How much am I supposed to spend?" she asked. "I mean, how high should I bid?"

"As high as it takes to win." He reached into his jacket pocket and pulled out a long, narrow envelope. "This is a letter from our solicitors, Coles, Franks, and Moody, instructing the auctioneer to send the bill to their offices for payment. It's a letter of credit that should far exceed the price of the dragon." He handed it to her. "When it comes time to pay for your item, show it to the auctioneer's clerk."

"Do you think we'll be able to find all the pieces on the list?"

"I don't know. We'll try. We need enough, anyway, to break the code they include. The more we find out and the more code we have to work from, the better our chances are. Information is the key. And the more pieces we have, the fewer our enemy will. And the less code he will have in order to try to break it. The stakes are very high."

The question that had hovered in her mind all evening rose to her lips, but it wouldn't come out. How did one ask one's uncle if he had committed murder to obtain much-needed information?

Uncle Bertie, dressed impeccably, with elegant manners and an insouciant manner, couldn't possibly have killed anyone. It was unthinkable.

Or was it just unbearable to think about?

Chapter 9

"TELL ME ONCE AGAIN, HOW did you decide which pieces to purchase?" Daniel pinched the bridge of his nose, wishing he had another cup of coffee. After a late night, he'd been up before dawn to go over his interview questions for Mr. Rickets, who had appeared promptly at seven at the Bow Street Magistrate's Court for his overdue interview. A Mr. Rickets who was most loquacious but seemed to circle his answers for a long time before revealing them. The interview was already into the second hour.

The art buyer was more composed than the last time Daniel had seen him but still nervous as a feral cat. He swallowed and fidgeted, picked imaginary lint off his coat, fingered his watch chain, and shifted his feet under his chair. Was this his habitual manner, or was he disconcerted by being questioned by detectives?

"Mr. Selby, God rest his soul, has—had—contacts on the Continent who told him when certain pieces were coming up for sale, and he had customers here who were sometimes looking for specific items. It was his practice to go round his best customers before going to the Continent and asking if there was anything on his list they might be interested in, or if there was something they were looking for particularly. These might be individuals, like Mr. Montgomery, who wanted the Lotto painting, or Mr. Bickford, who wanted the statue, but it might also be an organization, like the Royal Opera, who asked us to purchase the tapestries. But there might be something in an auction catalog that Mr. Selby didn't have a buyer for just yet but thought he could sell, so he would agree on a limit price with Mr. Turner and would buy it on speculation, as it were."

"But this time, rather than go himself, Mr. Selby sent you?"

"Yes. He and Mr. Turner thought it best that I get the experience, especially now that the war is over and travel is easier. I've been to the Continent before, with the army. And I speak French, Italian, and Spanish, though my Spanish isn't the most flash. Mr. Selby was most impressed with my linguistic ability. He thought it would be an asset in negotiating. I was honored and, if I'm honest, anxious to do a good job and please Mr. Selby. Becoming one of the buyers for Turner and Rathbone comes with not only a raise in pay but a considerable cache of prestige in the art world." He smoothed his lapels. "Much more impressive than being a shop assistant in a gallery, you see?"

Daniel looked over at Ed, who had his elbows on the table and his laced fingers propping up his chin.

"Where did you travel on this trip?" Ed asked.

"Oh, many places. I was gone for months. Spain, Italy, Belgium. I never spent the night in the same place. Mr. Selby had a rigorous schedule laid out for me. It was another reason he said he was sending me in his stead. He disliked travel at the best of times, but he'd wrenched his back one day moving things in the storeroom, and the thought of all that coach travel made his bones ache."

"Did you keep much money in the art gallery?"

"Oh no, most of our transactions happened at the Bank of England. The sale would be agreed upon at the shop, but Mr. Selby would accompany the customer to his bank for the actual transaction. There was a bit of petty cash in a box in the office, but only enough to purchase things for the day-to-day running of the gallery or to pay a delivery driver when we needed to transport an item to its new home."

Owen sat at a small table in the corner, writing notes on the interview. His pen scratched lightly on the pages, but otherwise he sat still. Daniel had to give him credit. He was fast and legible, and his records were impeccable. It was his impudence that grated, not his skill.

"Did Mr. Selby have any enemies? Anyone who might wish to do him harm?"

Mr. Rickets fussed and fidgeted as he thought about his answer. "Mr. Selby wasn't like that. I mean, he was rather boring on the whole. He didn't excite anyone to the point of shouting, much less to murder. He was ordinary. Good at his job, reliable, a good boss. I cannot imagine anyone wanting to kill him."

Daniel consulted his prepared list of questions. What else could he ask? Thus far, he'd discovered nothing that lent itself to finding Mr. Selby's killer, and several things that seemed to indicate he hadn't an enemy in the world.

Yet the man was dead, someone had killed him, and someone had stolen the inventory lists.

"Have you been able to remember what else you purchased on your trip?"

"Oh, my, yes. I am sorry my mind was so blank before. It was the shock, you see. Poor Mr. Selby, God rest his soul. And the state of the gallery. I don't know if we'll open the shop again. Mr. Rathbone is so old now, and to have to start over. He lost so many beautiful pieces to that wicked vandal." His nostrils flared. "It's disgraceful that someone would act with such wanton wickedness, destroying beautiful pieces of art that never harmed anyone."

Not to mention killing Mr. Selby. God rest his soul.

"What else did you buy then? And for whom?" Daniel prompted.

"Oh yes. Well, specifically, I bought some table silver and jewelry at an auction in Pau, and several items all in a lot at a villa in Lombardy whose owner had a propensity for betting on bad cards and needed to pay his creditors. There was a very curious collection in Zurich that had items from Africa and other odd places. I don't think Mr. Selby had buyers for those pieces, but he did enjoy artifacts from around the world. Some were intended for auction here if I could get them for a low enough price. And one particular item he was most insistent that I purchase. A first folio of Shakespeare that had been taken to France at the beginning of the war by an aristocrat who evidently thought war was going to be a pleasant junket. When he was killed and the camp overrun, the folio fell into enemy hands. Mr. Selby had tracked the folio to a book dealer in Marseilles, and he had a buyer here willing to pay a king's ransom for it to be returned to England, where it belongs. I don't know which pieces went where, as Mr. Selby liked to keep that information to himself. He was closed mouthed when it came to sharing information about our clients. I think he feared another dealer might pinch his customers if word leaked. He didn't tell me who the items were for, and I didn't ask. It was strictly need to know, you understand.

"I know there were some other oddments here and there that I bought, but the paperwork was with the shipment, and Mr. Selby would have received those documents when he took possession of the crates at the quay." His mouth twisted. "I was frustrated to have missed the departure in Genoa." He fingered the buttons on his waistcoat. "I had heard there was a Sevres jardinière for sale, which I thought I could purchase and still make it back to port on time. The owner was a determined Genoese who wished to sell but did not wish to negotiate. He also wished to drink wine, and he would not drink alone. We imbibed, and I hoped that when he was inebriated, I might get him down to a better price. Alas, he had a head for wine, and I do not. I got nowhere in the negotiations, and I fell asleep at his table. By the time I awoke, my ship had left port and my head wanted to leave my body." He winced and rubbed his temple. "I was afraid Mr. Selby would be upset that I did not return with the shipment, and rightly so, as it was very valuable. That is why I was so nervous when I came into the shop, having to face Mr. Selby and tell him that I missed the boat—on two counts."

He sighed, his shoulders slumping. "I didn't appreciate what a fine man he was until it was too late. I couldn't have asked for a better employer." He sniffed and blinked, digging for a handkerchief and blowing his nose with a loud honk. "If Mr. Rathbone doesn't reopen the store, I don't know what I will do."

Daniel looked at Ed, raising his eyebrows. Did he have anything else to ask?

"The jeweled dagger wasn't something you purchased while on your buying trip?" Ed indicated the box beside him on the table, the box that contained the murder weapon, the sight of which had nearly sent Mr. Rickets into a faint.

Rickets composed himself, rubbing his palms on his thighs and staring at the wall to his right. A shudder went through him, as if he could still see the dagger. "No. It must have been something Mr. Selby obtained for the shop while I was in Europe. Possibly from an individual, but more likely from an auction house." He shuddered again. "I've never seen it before, and I don't want to see it ever again."

"What auction house did Mr. Selby use? To sell things you bought on speculation?"

"Barrett and Company almost exclusively. They have a wide range of clients and handle most every type of art and antiquity."

"They would have a record of items they had sold for Turner and Rathbone, wouldn't they?" Daniel asked. Perhaps they could get an approximation of the inventory of the art dealership through the auction company.

"Of course. I can't imagine why someone would want to steal our inventory books. Most of the current inventory was destroyed by that wanton, wicked—"

"We understand." Daniel had no desire to go over that again. "Thank you, Mr. Rickets, for coming in today. If we have further questions, we will contact you." He pushed his chair back and folded his list of questions, tucking it into his breast pocket.

Rickets seemed taken aback at the abrupt end of the interview, but he gathered himself enough to give a weak smile and nod. "I hope I've been of help to you. Please apprehend whoever did this soon. I'm afraid to be in the gallery by myself knowing there is a madman on the loose."

When he'd departed, Owen shook the ink drops off his quill, capped the bottle, blotted the papers, and butted them together. Ignoring Daniel, he handed the pages to Ed. "'Ere you go, sir. Nice and tidy. That man can talk for England." He rotated his wrist and flexed his fingers. "I thought he'd never stop."

"Thank you, Owen." Ed examined the papers. "That will be all for now."

Owen nodded and sauntered out of the room, whistling softly.

"What do you think?" Daniel asked Ed.

"I think we heard plenty and didn't glean much." Ed slid the box with the dagger toward himself. "He doesn't seem to know anything that would point us in a solid direction. Mr. Selby had no enemies that he knew of, they'd received no threats that he was aware of, and he encountered nothing unusual on his buying trip."

"So we're no further ahead, and Sir Michael will be expecting an update this evening."

"What next?"

"You're going to contact the agencies who supplied the extra workers for the Montgomery and Bickford parties and see if anyone recognizes anyone else."

"What will you do?"

"I will visit Barrett and Company Auction House. It's the slimmest of leads, but it's the only one we've got." Daniel followed Ed out of the interview room.

Most days, the six detectives who called Bow Street Magistrate's Court their home base were scattered across London and sometimes across the country, but today there was a full house.

Thomas Fyfe had his boots on the corner of his desk and his chair tipped back at a precarious angle. Pipe smoke wreathed his head, and his waistcoat strained to cover his substantial middle. Many a scoundrel had underestimated both his brains and his brawn to their peril.

Edgar Piggott, a wiry man of just over five feet, cleaned his nails with the sharp end of a pushpin. When Daniel passed his desk, Edgar jerked his chin in a hello, but any smile he might have given was hidden by his legendary moustache.

Tolliver, whose given name was Matthias, barely glanced up from the neat stacks of paper on his desk, but Andrew Jamison bounded up and clapped Ed on the shoulder. "Greetings, Beck. How's the war against crime going? Word is, the pup got his first case, and it's a cracker." He winked and elbowed Ed, jerking his head at Daniel. "Ah, makes a tear come to the eye it does, seeing our little lad growing up like he is."

"All right." Daniel grinned. "How long do I have to work here before I'm no longer 'the pup'?"

Jamison spread his hands, as if the answer was obvious. "Until someone greener than you gets hired on."

Ed handed Daniel the interview notes and took his hat and cloak from the pegs on the wall by his desk. "I'll let you know what I find."

Daniel nodded and took his own garments. Jamison perched his hip on the corner of Daniel's desk and crossed his arms. "So tell me about your case, me boy-o. A theft linked to a murder linked to another theft? And all caught up in the aristocracy?"

"You seem to know a lot already."

"Word gets around. Sir Michael seems a bit . . . unsettled? Is it the case or the detective? Why isn't Ed in charge?"

Daniel's hackles rose. "I am a capable detective, and I can handle my own cases." That this was the first one he'd been given charge of shouldn't signify. "Now, if you don't mind, I have an actual lead to follow and cannot spend the rest of the day gossiping." He clapped his hat on his head and swirled his cloak in a practiced manner so the many capes fell across his shoulders just so.

Jamison raised his hands in a conciliatory gesture. "Easy there, lad. I meant no offense. Sure you can handle a case on your own, and well past time you had one. I only meant to let you know we're all here if you want to bounce some ideas around. We all play on the same team, lad." He swept his arm wide to take in the other detectives, who nodded agreement. "Sir Michael can be a thrawn de'l when he's in a mood, but don't let him knock your confidence. We'll help if we're needed, and we'll watch from the side if we're not."

Shame flickered in Daniel's chest. "Right. My apologies." They were good men who didn't deserve the rough side of his tongue. He'd not earn their respect if he couldn't take some good-natured quizzing from time to time. "I appreciate the assistance."

Cadogan's cab waited at the curb. "Need a ride?" He'd blanketed Lola and Sprite against the chill, and their breath hung in misty clouds before being swirled away toward the river.

"Know where Barrett and Company Auction House is?"

"Aye. Climb in."

The auction house was an understated brick building on the outside, but the interior spoke of wealth and taste. Walnut paneling, plush Axminster carpets, and subdued but ample lighting in the foyer.

A well-dressed clerk raised his head from his paperwork. "May I help you, sir?"

Daniel introduced himself. "I'd like to speak to a manager, please."

"There is an auction in progress, sir, and the manager won't be available for some time."

"This is a matter of some urgency." Why did he seem to choose to arrive when managers were at their most busy?

"So is an auction that will produce thousands of pounds, sir. You are welcome to go into the gallery and observe the proceedings. I will tell the manager you are here, and if there is a break, he will come to you."

Daniel slid his pocket watch into his hand. He supposed he could wait a few minutes, and he'd never been to an auction before. "Very well."

The clerk showed him to a side door, and he slipped into the gallery. The room was only half-full. Perhaps the clerk had overestimated bringing in thousands of pounds today.

He took a chair along the wall, putting his hat and cloak on the empty seat beside him as the auctioneer murmured on about a pair of cloisonné vases. Daniel leaned in to hear, and the opening bid would have impoverished him.

He refrained from rolling his eyes, but only just, leaning back against his chair and folding his arms to wait.

A head turned, and his gaze meshed with Lady Juliette's.

But even more astonishing was the woman to her left.

"I'm sorry I'm late. It seems to be a perpetual state with me. Where are we going?" Agatha landed in the carriage beside Juliette and stopped speaking, her brows rising.

"Agatha, this is Mrs. Dunstan, our housekeeper. The dowager wasn't available to accompany us, and I didn't think she would enjoy the excursion anyway. It's just shopping, after all, so I asked Mrs. Dunstan to accompany us. I don't have a ladies' maid yet, since Mother had to leave before we chose one, and Mrs. Dunstan said she didn't mind getting out of the house for a while."

As much as Juliette would have loved to go on her own to bid on the next item, Uncle Bertie had said to obey all conventions, which included taking a maid with her when she went out. It was he who suggested the housekeeper, in fact.

"I see," Agatha said weakly. "If I had known the dowager was unable to come, I would have brought my maid so your housekeeper wouldn't have been inconvenienced."

"I'm sure Mrs. Dunstan will be an excellent chaperone. It's not as if we're going to get up to anything scandalous. A few errands and some fresh air." Did bidding on a sculpture that might contain a secret code harmful to the realm constitute scandalous?

Mrs. Dunstan nodded. "I won't get in your way, Lady Juliette. Pretend I'm not here." She looked out the window, giving the girls at least the pretense of privacy. Juliette had never been comfortable with the notion that servants should be seen and not heard and that unless one was addressing them directly, one should act as if they weren't there at all. That they were part of the furnishings and functions of the house, not people in their own right.

Thankfully, her parents had never believed that either, nor acted upon it. Those they hired were people with lives and feelings and ideas. They were neither better nor worse than anyone. The employer-employee relationship was built on mutual respect and was an equal exchange. A fair day's wage for a fair day's work, making certain that courteous treatment went both ways.

When it came time for Juliette to set up her own household, she intended to operate along those lines.

"What's on your list to accomplish today?" Juliette asked Agatha.

"I simply must stop by Catrin's today and pick up my riding habit. If we're going to the Ash Valley Hunt, I want to look my best. And I've got a beautiful new gown for the Hunt Ball. What are you going to wear?" Agatha dove in on her second-favorite subject.

"I shall have to look through my wardrobe. I know Mother will have covered every contingency, and if not, I can borrow something from her dressing room. A groom is taking Fabiana from the stables here down to Ash Valley on Thursday in plenty of time for her to be rested and ready for the hunt on Monday."

Mother wouldn't mind Juliette riding her mare, but hopefully she would return to London before the hunt and all would be well. Worry spiraled through Juliette's middle. The process of procuring and decoding the art pieces was stretching into eternity. The longer it took, the more likely that someone else could break the code. It was possible that even now it was too late. Worse, the longer her parents remained away, the more bleak the possibilities. Had they been captured? Were they even now dead, as Mr. Selby and Leonidas were? Surely God wouldn't allow anything to happen to them just as she was coming home, just as she was beginning to know them without pretense. *God, protect them wherever they are.*

Perhaps when Uncle Bertie returned, he would have news?

"I had another place I wanted to stop before the dressmaker's, if you don't mind." *And a letter of credit burning a hole through my reticule.*

"The milliners? The glovers? Or do you need new stationary? I'm having calling cards printed. I don't like the ones I chose last week as well as I had hoped. There's a new style at the stationer's with scalloped edges that I just adore." Agatha dug in her reticule. "Look at these. What was I thinking? They're so drab." She held up a perfectly good bit of pasteboard with her name printed in beautiful script.

"Actually, I'd like to visit an auction house."

Agatha's brows rose and arrowed together. "An auction house?" She sounded as if Juliette had suggested calling upon Mad King George. "Whatever for?"

"My father's birthday is approaching, and he's taken an interest in studying things from the Far East. There's an item coming up for bid that I want to get for him."

"What item? Can you not send someone to buy it? Are ladies welcome in an auction house?"

"Of course we'll be welcome. It isn't like Whites or Boodles. It's open to the public. The item I want is an ornament for Father's desk. According to the catalog, it's a dragon carved from jade. Not too big, but heavy, to weigh papers down. I think he'll love it." He would love it if she could get it, because of the code. But unlike the painting and the maquette, which must be returned as soon as possible, he would be able to keep the dragon because she was purchasing it with his own money. That, at least, sat lighter on her conscience.

"The only auction I can remember was one near the Haymarket, where they were selling livestock. It was noisy, smelly, and crowded." Agatha plumped back against the squabs. "Father took me when I was small, and when Mother found out, she blistered him but good."

"This won't be like a livestock auction." At least she hoped not. She'd never been to an auction at all, livestock or not.

Barrett and Company turned out to be more like a Mayfair salon than an animal barn. Understated elegance greeted them, and while no one was openly rude, curious stares followed the ladies through the foyer.

Agatha nudged Juliette and whispered, "I don't see another woman anywhere."

Mrs. Dunstan stood to the side with Agatha while Juliette approached the clerk, showed her letter of credit, and signed her name. He handed her a bidding card with a number on it. "Keep this with you to show the auctioneer if you happen to win an item. He'll record it, and we'll use it when you are ready to pick up your purchase." He snapped his fingers, and an elderly man in a green waistcoat and breeches and white hose that wrinkled around his thin legs shuffled forward. "Allow one of our ushers to show you around."

"Would you care to look over the items available today before the bidding begins?" His voice rasped softly. "Or perhaps some refreshments? Coffee, tea, and cakes are laid on in the anteroom just here."

Juliette peeked into a roomful of small tables and a serving board along the far wall. While not laden as for a banquet, it was certainly lavish enough. Men stood in small groups, and a blue haze of smoke hung near the ceiling. Heads turned as they stood in the doorway, and eyes widened. One man hastily stubbed out his cigar and fanned the air about him, as if trying to hide the evidence.

Juliette smothered a smile. She wouldn't intrude upon their sanctum. "I would like to see the items up for auction if I may?"

"Certainly." The usher led her to another room adjacent to the auditorium, where three rows of items awaited their turn to fall under the gavel. Two lines of tables covered in white cloths sat against the long walls, while a selection of larger items stood in the center of the room.

Remembering Uncle Bertie's instructions, she didn't go straight to the green dragon. Instead, she admired a set of table silver, a collection of Venetian glass ornaments, and a cased clock that must be six feet tall.

"This place might be open to the public, but there seems to be a dearth of female patrons. Look at this. Who would buy something like this?" Agatha stopped before an escritoire of unusual proportions.

It really was awful, at least half a century out of date. What would one do with such a piece? Where could one put it that it wouldn't dominate a room?

Mrs. Dunstan stayed a few feet behind, watchful but unobtrusive as they studied the different lots. Halfway down the room, they came to the jade dragon.

An attendant stood nearby, and Juliette asked, "May I touch it?"

He nodded, stepping close and lifting it for her, his white gloves gleaming. He must wear them to prevent leaving finger smudges behind. A small tag fluttered from a string looped around the dragon's head, and he read from it.

"Lot number twenty-two, jade on an onyx base. It's heavy." He kept hold of it, even as he placed it in Juliette's hands, assisting her with the weight.

It was solid and cold, and the eyes stared blankly at her. The artist had inserted ivory teeth into the open mouth, and long, carved whiskers folded back along the face. Horns draped toward the neck, and the entire figure appeared ready to leap from the base and scamper about the room.

She studied it from every angle as quickly as she could, lest someone think she was too interested in the piece and thus drive up the price.

Nothing resembling a code emerged from the scales or spines or coils of the dragon body.

"Should I get you a quizzing glass?" Agatha teased. "You're looking at it as if you expect it to bite you. Come see these snuffboxes. They've got the most amazing landscapes painted on them, and so tiny. Do you think my father might like one?"

Juliette nodded her thanks to the attendant and moved down the line. At the next table, she admired a fine pen and ink set and a pair of silver-backed brushes.

"Shall we find our places?" she asked when they had circled the room. While they had been in here, no one else had shown any interest in the dragon. Perhaps it wouldn't be too costly to win.

They took chairs near the front, and Juliette sat between Agatha and Mrs. Dunstan. Men crowded in. Some used the seats, but more stood around the perimeter of the room.

The first few items produced little in the way of excitement from the bidders. Was this normal, or did having women present throw the men off their stride?

Agatha shifted in her chair. "This is awful. We'll leave right after your lot comes up, won't we?"

"Yes, of course. We'll go right to the dressmaker's so you can pick up your order."

A rustle went through the room as the next piece was brought out. A landscape painting by Sir Joshua Reynolds.

The bidding grew intense as two gentlemen on opposite sides of the room raised again and again. When the price reached three hundred pounds, Agatha gripped Juliette's wrist. "Never mind leaving early. This is fascinating."

The man seated on Agatha's right leaned forward. "The bidders are Mr. Love and Mr. Galesford. They own competing galleries, and each must have a client eager to own this painting. I wonder who has the higher limit? They are famous rivals."

Agatha breathed in, her eyes round. "I had no idea auctions could be so lively."

The painting was eventually knocked down to Mr. Galesford for 325 pounds. Mr. Love glared at Galesford, who shrugged and turned away.

Juliette shifted in her seat, anxious now that the dragon's time on the block drew near. She surveyed the room. Would anyone bid against her? It was impossible to tell from looking at the faces. Some appeared bored, some conversed in low tones, and some studied their catalogs.

Her eyes linked with a familiar face, and she stopped breathing.

Detective Swann sat in a chair along the wall, staring at her.

Why was he here? Was he following her? Did he know anything about her mission today?

His gaze flicked to her left, and his face hardened.

She glanced to where he was looking but could see nothing. The only person on her left was Mrs. Dunstan, and the rest of the row was empty.

Perhaps he had just thought of something unpleasant.

The gavel banged on the next item, and she forced herself to look at the dais. It was time. The attendant carried the dragon up to the platform and set it on the small table.

"Lot twenty-two, dragon of Chinese jade, onyx base. Believed to be two hundred years old. We'll open the bidding at fifty pounds."

Before Juliette could raise her hand, someone behind her bid.

"Fifty pounds. Thank you, sir. Now sixty?"

Anxiety gripped her. She had hoped to bid unopposed, and now it appeared she would have to make choices, and quickly.

The attendant who had shown her the piece looked at her, and she nodded. He spoke to the auctioneer. "Sixty, sir, from the lady in the center."

A murmur and stir went through the room. A lady was openly bidding.

The auctioneer found her and nodded, mild shock touching his features.

"Sixty. Thank you, ma'am. Now seventy?" He looked over her head to the back, and Juliette resisted the urge to turn around.

Show no interest in the other bidders. Give the impression that they don't matter, that you will keep raising all day if you have to.

Uncle Bertie's instructions played through her mind. She affected a neutral expression, but her hands sweated.

She could feel eyes staring, but most of all, she could sense the detective's scrutiny. What would he make of her bidding on the dragon? Did he know it came from the same shipment as the painting and the statue? If so, was she ripping aside the curtain of secrecy the Thorndikes had kept so carefully closed for centuries?

Yet she must have the dragon, and she had a solid cover story should he question her.

One hundred pounds, one twenty, one fifty. Each time when the bid was to her, she lowered her chin a precise amount, keeping her eyes on the auctioneer.

The man bidding against her spoke from the back. "Three hundred pounds." His voice had an edge to it, authority, as if he were bored with toying and had now gotten serious.

It was an immense raise, probably designed to scare her out of bidding.

"Juliette . . ." Agatha breathed out. "Surely not."

But she must have it. And two could play his game, whoever he was. She would not be cowed. "Five hundred pounds."

Her spoken bid hit like a brick through a window. Quaking in her midsection, she ignored the gasps and murmurs.

The auctioneer paused, leaned to his side, and whispered in the ear of one of the assistants, who sped from the room.

"A moment please," the auctioneer said.

The assistant returned presently with the clerk who had given Juliette her bidding card.

The clerk and the auctioneer conferred in low tones, looking over their shoulders at her from time to time. The clerk nodded once and then again, whispered something to the auctioneer, and stepped back.

"Lady Juliette Thorndike?" the auctioneer said, his voice rising. "You are aware that you have bid five hundred pounds?" He spoke as if she were a simpleton, trodding heavily on the *hundred* in case she thought she had offered a mere five pounds. As if she had bid in error and had no concept of money.

"I am well aware." It irked her that he had needed confirmation of both her identity and her ability to pay and yet still felt the need to explain the situation to her. He hadn't done the same for the gentleman in the back who'd bid against her. "My bid stands."

He rubbed his hands on his trousers. "Very well. Five hundred pounds is the bid. Sir? Will you raise?"

Silence. Heads turned, and Juliette did as well, unable to stop herself.

But whoever had been her opponent had gone. Several men in the back of the room indicated the blank space where he must have stood.

"All done at five hundred, then? Once, twice . . ." Bang! The gavel hit the podium. "Sold to Lady Juliette Thorndike for five hundred pounds."

She let out a breath. She'd done it.

The dragon was whisked from the table and carried away.

"Now what?" Agatha asked.

"We see the clerk and retrieve our prize." Giddiness washed over her. Gathering her reticule, her bidding card, and her self-possession, she rose and followed Mrs. Dunstan down the empty row of chairs. Another item was being bid upon, but Juliette felt she garnered more stares than the Venetian glass on the block.

She risked a look back over her shoulder to Mr. Swann. He had gotten to his feet, but a man had approached him and was leading him through a door on the far side of the auction room. The detective's eyes followed Juliette until he turned through the door and out of sight.

"This way, Lady Juliette." The clerk made clearing motions, though no one stood in their way, and they found themselves in the auction house office.

She signed where asked, giving Barrett and Company permission to take her letter of credit to her lawyers for payment.

"A pleasure, Lady Juliette. It isn't often we get a lady of your quality gracing our auction house. You've bought a lovely piece. Did you know you were bidding against Sir Wilfred Barr? He is the buyer for the British Museum. They are looking to expand their collection of items from the Far East, and he had hoped to procure the dragon today. It's a brilliant example of jade carving, and dragons are most popular with the general public."

A twinge pinched her heart. She loved museums. Perhaps, when this was all over, they could gift or loan the dragon to the museum. But for now, she must get it home and find the hidden code.

Stepping outside, carrying the heavy jade, she turned into the breeze so her bonnet's brim wouldn't bend. "The carriage is just down the street."

Agatha held her cape with one hand and her hat with the other. "Why does it seem so much colder here than in Switzerland? And this wind. It cuts right through me."

"I think it's the dampness. It gets into your bones." Juliette checked to see that Mrs. Dunstan was still with them, but when she turned forward again, three men stepped from an alley on their right and blocked their path. With what had to be a practiced maneuver, they surrounded the three women and pushed them into the narrow passage between the buildings.

"Hello, duckies. Hand it ovah." The middle one, with a dirty face and gloves with more holes than wool, held out his hand.

"I beg your pardon," Agatha retorted. "Get out of our way."

"You misunderstand our intent. We ain't leaving without it. Now give." One brandished a knife, while another smacked a cudgel into his palm. The man with the cudgel moved to cut off any escape to the rear, while the man with the knife leered and waved the blade like an extension of his hand.

Juliette looked around them, but the alley was deserted. She held out her reticule. There wasn't much in it anyway, and certainly nothing worth getting anyone hurt over. "Here. Take it and be gone."

"Not that, you ninny. That fancy green stone is what we was sent for." He pointed to the dragon in the crook of her arm.

"No. Go away and leave us alone." She tightened her grip, the onyx base digging into her ribs. "Take our purses before we scream."

"Can't do it, love. We got orders. 'Get that dragon, no matter what.'"

The one with the knife stepped forward, jabbing his blade dangerously near Agatha's face. "Don't want to get your looks ruined, do ye?"

Agatha whimpered and backed away, only to be shoved from behind by the third man.

"Barney, don't do nothin' foolish. Give them a chance to think it over. They'll do the right thing." The leader held out his hand once more.

Mrs. Dunstan put her hand on Juliette's arm. "Milady, perhaps you should do as they ask."

A quick assessment of the odds, their position, and the possible consequences produced only one choice. Juliette handed over the dragon. The leader snatched it close and shoved past them toward the far end of the alleyway. The man with the cudgel followed on his heels, but the bladesman paused, reached for Juliette's arm, and sliced through the strings of her reticule. He grinned and relieved Agatha of her bag as well.

"Don't let no opportunity go to waste, I say." He touched the knife to the brim of his hat with an impudent grin and disappeared at a run.

Shaking, Juliette brushed a stray curl off her cheek. How could she get the dragon back?

"Jules, you're bleeding." Agatha sounded aghast.

She glanced at her wrist, and a wave of light-headedness hit her. Her knees turned to pond water, and she wobbled.

Agatha wrapped her arm around Juliette's waist. "Here, lean on me. Mrs. Dunstan, do you have a handkerchief?"

Wooziness wafted through Juliette's head and traveled straight to her stomach. She had never liked the sight of blood, especially her own. Berating her weakness, she allowed Agatha to lead her into the street while the housekeeper clamped a square of white linen against her dripping wrist.

"What's happened? Are you all right?"

Juliette opened her eyes. Detective Swann strode toward them.

"We were robbed," Agatha blurted out. "And she's injured."

"I'll take her. Go fetch your carriage." The detective took command, and Agatha surrendered Juliette and hurried down the street.

Mr. Swann's strong arm came around Juliette's waist, and she leaned against him. He was solid and muscular, and . . . he smelled nice.

You really are light-headed, you bacon-brained nit. Pull yourself together and stop being so missish.

"I'm all right. It's just a cut. I'm sure it isn't serious." Especially if she didn't look at it. She hoped she sounded steadier than she felt. The assailant's knife must have been very keen, for she'd felt nothing when he'd sliced at her purse.

Mrs. Dunstan kept hold of her wrist with the stained handkerchief, but she had her body angled away from Juliette and the detective. Was she squeamish as well? If so, Juliette didn't blame her. In fact, she applauded the woman for helping when the sight of blood clearly disturbed her too.

"We'll get you settled in your carriage, and you can tell me what happened."

Passersby paused and then hurried along the sidewalk. Where had they been when Juliette was being robbed?

"Not to worry," Mr. Swann assured them. "She's just feeling a bit faint."

The carriage arrived, and Agatha swung open the door. Her face was white, and some of her hair had escaped its pins to hang in red hanks from her temples.

"Have the housekeeper get in first, and I'll hand her up to you," the detective instructed.

Why didn't he address Mrs. Dunstan herself? Juliette bristled. Was he one of those who thought domestic servants beneath him?

Before she could gather her tongue enough to say something, she was lifted by strong arms into the carriage. The detective followed swiftly, taking the seat next to her and reapplying the pressure to her wrist with his own handkerchief this time. He lifted the edge of the cloth, squinted at what lay beneath, and pressed down again. His hand spanned the entire circumference of her wrist, and his skin seemed dark against the handkerchief. Dark like Juliette's.

Was he of Welsh descent too? He probably hadn't gotten teased about it like she had. She laid her head back against the seat and closed her eyes.

"You haven't lost much blood, milady. And the cut is not too deep. I don't believe you will need stitches, though you should have your physician round to look at it." His deep voice, so close to her ear, did funny things to her middle. Though that could be the dizziness, of course.

"It's not blood loss that makes her weak," Agatha offered. "It's the sight of blood. One time, when we were at school, I tripped while we were walking in the woods, and a stick scraped my palm. I didn't think I would be able to get her back to the chalet. I had to wrap my hand and keep it in my pocket out of sight the entire way back."

Juliette's stomach lurched just remembering it. Some people were afraid of spiders. Some people hated heights. Her nemesis was the sight of blood.

Not an ideal weakness for someone who wanted to become a spy.

Daniel felt as if he'd missed a step in the dark. He'd been racing out of the auction house, eager to get back to Bow Street with his information on the allotment sent by Turner and Rathbone for this week's sales, when he'd encountered Lady Juliette and Miss Montgomery staggering out of an alley.

He'd taken Lady Juliette into his arms, ignored "Mrs. Dunstan" as best he was able, and sent Miss Montgomery for their vehicle.

Lady Juliette had fit into his embrace perfectly, and he chided himself for even thinking such thoughts when she was clearly in distress.

Her wound appeared superficial, though her phobia did not.

"How did this happen?"

"We were set upon." Righteous indignation colored Miss Montgomery's words. "Three men, and one of them had a knife. They pushed us into the alley and demanded we give them the green dragon Juliette just purchased as a gift for her father. What is London coming to? Housebreakers, thieves, ruffians. We were accosted in broad daylight in a respectable part of the city. Something must be done about the lawless element."

The words seemed strange on her tongue, but Daniel suspected she was quoting her father. Mr. Montgomery had said something similar. Several somethings, as a matter of fact.

"Can you describe the men?" He kept hold of Lady Juliette's wrist, firmly but gently, where it lay on his thigh, and it wasn't unpleasant. She smelled of rose blossoms. Not just any roses, but spring roses after a long winter. The kind that made a man glad he was alive.

Lady Juliette stirred, taking a deep breath. "One of them was called Barney. He was the one with the knife. Blue eyes, reddish-brown hair. And missing a front tooth."

Daniel's senses perked. "Was there another one with a sap? Short fellow with pockmarked skin?"

"A sap?" Agatha asked.

"A short leather-wrapped stick with a loop around his wrist? A cosh or a cudgel?"

"Yes," Juliette said as Agatha nodded. "But neither of them were the leader. He was tall and thin as a park fence rail. They were all dirty and ragged, but the leader was filthy." Her nose wrinkled, and her mouth twisted. "He demanded the jade dragon."

The gears in Daniel's mind meshed and clicked. "I believe you ladies have encountered Dirty Dave Figg. His associates are Barney

Messenger and Ratter. If Ratter has a Christian name, I've never heard it. He used to be a ratter before he turned to criminal pursuits. They're getting bolder if they've ventured out of the rookery at St. Giles into Chelsea. They're usually found swilling gin in a pub along the Oxford Road."

"What's odd is"—Miss Montgomery leaned forward against the rocking of the carriage—"that dirty one said he had been sent for the dragon and wasn't supposed to return without it."

Lady Juliette jerked, and her hand came up as if to stop her friend's speech, but Miss Montgomery either didn't see the gesture or ignored it.

"How did they know Juliette had purchased it? They wouldn't have been allowed inside the auction house, not in their state."

Daniel pounced on the information. "They said specifically they wanted the dragon. It wasn't a random robbery?"

"Perhaps the man I was bidding against brought insurance against not winning?" Lady Juliette offered. "He had them wait outside the auction house to steal what he couldn't buy?"

That was possible, though improbable. There hadn't been much time between that man losing the bid and the robbery. Though the man had left before Lady Juliette. Had he been giving instructions to his henchmen?

"That makes no sense," Agatha offered. "The clerk told us the other bidder was Sir Wilfred Barr, and he was bidding for the British Museum. If he had the piece stolen from you, he certainly couldn't put it on display at the museum, or everyone would know he'd come by it dishonestly."

Again Juliette made a cutting-off motion with her uninjured hand, but it was too late. Why was she so desperate to keep her friend silent?

And how did what he'd learned from Lady Juliette and Miss Montgomery fit with what the auction house manager had told him?

Chapter 10

JULIETTE SAT AT HER DRESSING table and eyed the neatly wrapped bandage on her right wrist. Though Agatha had begged her to send for a physician, Juliette had asked Mrs. Dunstan to clean and bind the wound. Not even to herself would she admit she didn't want a doctor for fear he would say she needed stitches.

Now that the wound had stopped bleeding, she was clearheaded and it was time to assess her options.

If only Uncle Bertie were here to advise her . . . or to forbid her to go on the mission she had set for herself tonight. She would go alone, as she should have done today. Agatha, while a lovely friend, had proven a liability.

Why did she have to be so chatty? Why had she shot down Juliette's alternate theory of the crime and pointed Mr. Swann in the direction Juliette least wanted?

Juliette had sensed his mind working, taking in the information Agatha had spilled like an ewer. He was intelligent and an experienced investigator, and he had to be gathering all the bits and putting them together as a road map to the answers he sought.

But Juliette was intelligent too, and she had more of the pieces of the puzzle than he did. She knew the reason artwork was disappearing. She knew where the stolen items were now, and she had the list of the rest of the art that contained the code.

Someone out there had sent those miscreants to steal the jade statue, so they must have at least a partial list of the artwork too. The same person who killed Leonidas? And Mr. Selby?

The notion made tonight's mission both necessary and urgent, and she should stop dithering and get on with it. She went downstairs to the breakfast room, where she'd asked dinner to be served. No sense eating alone in the vast dining room, and she didn't want to have to change for the meal either.

"Mrs. Dunstan, thank you for your help today. I am sorry you were involved in such unpleasantness." Not the least of which was the detective's treatment of her housekeeper. He'd ignored the woman's existence, even speaking about her rather than to her.

"See that your housekeeper sends for the physician," he'd said when he'd delivered them home.

Mrs. Dunstan had been standing right there, but she might have been a potted palm for all the notice the detective had given her.

It was a blot on his copybook, and it disappointed Juliette out of all proportion. She wanted him to be a better man. She wanted him to be as noble as he seemed at first. Which was ridiculous. Why should she care about the character of a police officer, particularly one she was attempting to outwit?

Eating quickly, she ran through her plan for the night, and before she lost her nerve, she went up to the War Room to prepare.

Along one of the walls, cabinets held a wide and varied wardrobe and disguises of all types—wigs, false teeth, skin patches, dresses, suits, shoes, hats. Everything one could need to transform oneself into someone unrecognizable.

It amazed her anew at what her parents had kept secret from her for so long. Would she get the chance to know them, to discuss all of this, to work alongside them someday in the future? Or would she forever have to discover things about them after the fact if they never returned from their mission?

Uncle Bertie had said disguises were something for the advanced spy, and she would get to those lessons much, much later.

"'Needs must when the devil drives,' Uncle Bertie," Juliette muttered.

She sorted through the clothes, taking out a dark-green dress of plain muslin, many times patched and wearing thin in places. She added a dingy cap trimmed with wilted lace, a pair of sturdy boots in need of a polish, and a tatty shawl of brown wool. She hoped she could pass for a charwoman on her way home from work.

She then turned to a cabinet her uncle had declared she was even less prepared for than the disguises closet.

The doors were heavy, because each held an iron rack fastened to the inside. Tugging them open, she studied the array of weaponry at her disposal. Knives, pistols, chains, blatant and obvious, but also lesser known menaces like sharpened stars of metal for throwing, and a glove studded with brass spikes. There were spring-loaded knives, pistols that attached to sleeve holsters, and a small rack of glass vials that contained she knew not what.

She shuddered and selected a small knife that fit into the pocket of her dress.

Venturing into a rookery at night had to rate as one of the most nonsensical things she had ever attempted. Neither the tomfoolery that she'd gotten up to at boarding school, nor the rudimentary lessons she'd been given thus far into spycraft, had prepared her for arming herself to go in search of thieves in their home patch.

But—she studied her reflection in the full-length mirror—if she wanted to enter into the family business, and if she wanted her parents' identities as spies to remain secret from foreign governments, she had no choice. She had to retrieve what she had lost.

Her mother wouldn't shirk this duty just because she was scared, and neither would Juliette.

Perhaps tomorrow she would present Uncle Bertie with both the jade dragon and a tale of her bravery.

And perhaps you are the biggest fool in Christendom.

Cold wind sliced through the thin shawl, and she rued having to leave her heavy cloak at the house as she ventured out on the street. Her cheeks stung, and her nose burned. The lace cap she wore offered no protection against the chill. Fog hung in the air, a mist so thick you could almost drink it, creating fuzzy halos around the braziers and streetlamps.

Tucking her hands inside the shawl, she put her head down and hurried on. It was half eleven and dark as pitch between the small puddles of light that came from behind the window glass of houses along the road. The weight of the dagger in her pocket thumped against her leg as she walked. She'd say one thing for the disguise cupboard. The shoes she wore might not look like much, but they were comfortable and suitably heavy if she should need to kick someone.

Kick someone. She shook her head. A fortnight ago she would have been shocked to even think such a thing, and now she considered the skill a boon?

The neighborhoods changed the farther she walked, from fancy townhouses and beautifully tended squares to row houses and then tenements. Shops crowded together with narrow fronts and small windows, and upper stories hung over the street, blocking the moonlight.

Detective Swann had said the men she sought were often found in gin houses along the Oxford Road. But which one? Could she slip into such places searching for the right men?

She had no notion of accosting them, but only to follow them to their place of residence, wait until all was quiet, and break in to get the jade dragon back. If it was still there. *Please don't let them have handed it off to whoever sent them after it in the first place.*

Was God listening, or had He abandoned her like her parents had, trusting her to find her own way through this thicket of skullduggery?

A creature scuttled across the alley near her, and she choked down a scream. What had sounded like a reasonable course of action in the warmth of the townhouse now seemed madness. What had she been thinking? It wasn't too late to abandon her plan.

A lamplighter strolled near, his torch over his shoulder, a can of whale oil dangling from his hand. He didn't look at her, and she realized that in this outfit, in this neighborhood, she was nearly invisible.

A strange sensation, since she was used to being noticed. Even as a child, because of who her parents were, people had shown deference, acknowledged her, or at the very least had been curious.

It was an odd feeling, and yet a wee bit freeing, to be someone else for a while.

Litter scudded the street, and she wrinkled her nose as a musty, dank smell came from a dilapidated building. People passed her, but they kept their heads down, not meeting her eyes, and she realized she would stand out if she didn't do the same.

Eeriness crept over her. Was someone following her? She heard no footsteps, but the sense of eyes on her, of being observed, but in a menacing way, prickled the back of her neck. Gooseflesh that had nothing to do with the temperature flashed along her skin.

Don't speed your footsteps. Stay calm. It's probably nothing.

Ahead, a sign squeaked on its chains over a scarred door. The Anchor and Lamb. A gin house? Light spilled from the front window, but the fog and darkness swallowed it quickly. As she neared, she dashed a look over her shoulder.

Something moved in the shadows several yards behind her, but what? Was it her imagination, which had been working far too hard from the moment she left the house? Or perhaps someone going innocently about their business?

Her mouth dry, she reached for the door handle.

"Get out. Go away. You don't belong here." A beggar woman stepped out of the narrow space between the pub and the building beyond. Her Irish accent was thick, and she brandished a stick. "This is my patch." The muted light from the window fell across the woman's face. Filthy hair hung in her eyes, and a large wart stuck out on the tip of her nose. As she stepped close, Juliette retreated, but the stench of the woman's clothes swirled around her thicker than the fog.

The beggar raised a gnarled hand, long nails ready to gouge. "Be gone, Oi said!" She let out a shriek that curdled the blood. Juliette put up her hands to ward off the woman. Surely someone inside the pub had heard the scream. Wouldn't they come to her aid? But the door remained stubbornly closed.

Juliette's heart caught in her throat, and she dodged the first swing of the stick and wasted no time getting away. The gruesome cackling wrapped around her and propelled her down the street away from the woman. Grabbing up her hem, she ran, but though she abandoned the area the woman considered "her patch," the beggar did not give up the chase. She seemed to be almost herding Juliette with her pursuit.

Juliette's feet pounded the cobbles, and she marveled that her pursuer could keep up. The sturdy shoes she had fancied would serve her well now weighed several stones, and a stitch developed in her side. Why wouldn't the woman cease her chasing?

Up ahead, the lights from the Oxford Road shone in blurred globes. She was nearly out of the rookery. But a man stepped out of a doorway and stood square on the pavement. If Juliette continued, she'd run straight into him. His arms came up, and she knew he meant to grab her. At the last moment, she ducked, swerved, and ran down a side street.

Ahead, light spilled onto the pavement from an open door. The sign over the entrance showed a severed pig's head on a barrel and the script The Hog's Head. A man in a threadbare coat leapt from the doorway just as Juliette arrived, and two men in pursuit barreled after him. The second man collided with Juliette, his shoulder crashing into hers, sending her staggering into the street.

After leaving Lady Juliette at her townhouse, Daniel had flagged a coach, ordering the jarvey to speed along to Bow Street. Lady Juliette seemed much more in control of her faculties. Her wrist would be sore for a few days, but it should heal quickly.

He put his hand over his eyes. When had he last slept? He couldn't remember. The last thing he had imagined himself doing was coming to the aid of a damsel in distress like some overblown chivalric knight.

And to rescue the young woman who had stalked the edges of his thoughts for days . . . madness.

Not to mention encountering Mrs. Dunstan, his mother, crowded into a carriage with him, each trying to ignore the other as best they could. Her from indifference, and he from anger.

She looked well. Better than when she'd thrust him away as a youngster. A nice dress, a nice bonnet, smooth skin, and clear eyes. He remembered her as thin and drawn with worry, always keeping her head down, never speaking until spoken to when she worked as a maid. But she had been light and happy and caring when they were alone. Which made her betrayal all the worse.

His mother had made certain he had food, even if she went hungry. That he had a place to sleep, clothes to wear. She'd worked long hours, never shirking, never complaining, but it must have rankled, having to care for him when other women on her same wage scale had only themselves to see to, and they were allowed to live in the big house free of charge. His mother had rented a cottage out of her meager wages, because no children could live in the servants' quarters, especially not by-blows like him.

She must have been thrilled to be shut of him when the mysterious offer had come. The letter had arrived one day, and the next he had been on the mail coach, heading to a boys' school in Kent. Barely time for him to plead with her not to send him away, but enough time for him to realize she couldn't wait for him to go.

The dictates of the agreement were etched into his mind, especially the one that said he was allowed no contact with his mother. It might have been painful once, but now he had no issue with the requirement. He didn't want to speak with the woman who had rejected him.

He shut the door on those memories. *Focus on the case at hand.*

The carriage rocked to a stop in front of the magistrate's court, and he tossed a coin to the driver as he hurried up the stairs.

Ed met him in the hallway.

"I was giving a report to Sir Michael. Wasn't much, but he was asking."

"How did he take it?"

"Said we had more negatives than positives. We'd ruled out plenty of people, but we hadn't ruled in anyone."

"Perhaps that is about to change. Can we use one of the interview rooms? I want to walk through the case, and I want privacy." Daniel unbuttoned his coat. "Owen, bring paper, ink, and pushpins to room C."

For a moment, it appeared young Wilkenson was going to refuse, but his insubordination would only go so far. With a pinched mouth and sullen stare, he turned on his heel and marched away.

Daniel went to his desk, hung up his coat, and piled papers into a stack. "I want to break down the case as we know it and narrow the suspects. I have more information, and I want to see what you think of it."

Ed gathered the pages from his desk and followed Daniel into interview room C, which boasted the largest table.

"The manager of the auction house was not keen on talking about his clients. I had to threaten a warrant for his records before he divulged. I gather they're known for their confidentiality, and their clients, buyers and sellers can remain anonymous if they wish."

"What did he tell you?"

"There was only one item up for auction today that came from Turner and Rathbone. Mr. Selby himself delivered it to Barrett's a week ago, and he was eager to get it in the earliest auction."

Ed's brows rose. "Did he say why Selby was in such a hurry?"

"I gather the buying trip cost the gallery more than they had intended. Whether Rickets overspent or things cost more than they anticipated is anyone's guess, but selling this item quickly was meant to recoup some of that expenditure. The auction house manager had a handwritten receipt from Mr. Selby, putting a reserve of one hundred pounds on a carved jade dragon from China."

"Did it realize that price?" Ed's eyes widened. "Who buys such things for so much money?"

"You might want to sit down." Daniel stopped stacking pages on the table and waited while Owen came in and laid blank paper, an inkwell, and two new quills down.

"Anything else, sir?" he asked Ed.

"Tea for both of us, and a couple of meat pies from the vendor on the corner." He set a shilling on the table. "And get one for yourself."

When the door closed behind the office boy, Daniel said, "The dragon sold for five hundred pounds."

"Five hundred?" Ed dropped into a chair. "Are you quizzing me? No one would pay five hundred pounds for a hunk of green rock."

"Lady Juliette Thorndike would."

Ed's mouth opened, but no words came out.

"And what's more, she had it in her possession for only a few minutes before it was stolen. At knifepoint. I came on the scene outside the auction house only moments after it happened. Lady Juliette was bleeding and faint, and I got her into her carriage and took her home. Miss Montgomery was with her, and she told me what happened." He gave a quick report.

"I think we should pay Dirty Dave and his friends a visit, don't you?" Daniel drew up a chair. "As soon as it gets dark, they'll come out of hiding and start soaking up gin. No point in looking for them before nightfall. They're holed up somewhere in the rookery, and it wouldn't pay to go in there without an army."

"They'll probably turn up at The Hog's Head, if I know Dirty Dave. He likes one of the barmaids there." Ed had gathered himself, and his eyes were intense. "Dave and his bunch don't have two original thoughts to rub together. Whoever sent them is the man we really want. I know I said to look for other motives before jumping to conclusions, but I've changed my mind. It stands to reason that whoever is stealing the artwork is also the one who killed Selby."

Daniel fished through the papers until he found the one he wanted. "No family has been found to claim Selby's body, so the coroner released it to Mr. Rathbone's butler. He will arrange the burial. The magistrate's court is likely to turn over Selby's estate to Rathbone, who will see that all outstanding bills are paid."

"What do you want to do with all this paper?"

"Make some sense of it. Get it organized and summarized. I want to make a timeline of events, of Selby's movements the last week of his life, and I want to write a list of those who could still be our killer."

"Why did you want pushpins?"

"I have to see it, to fix it in my mind, so I'm going to tack the pages to the wall as we go."

He uncapped the ink bottle, dipped the quill, and wrote "Incident Room" in bold strokes. "This goes on the door, and no one but you, me, or Sir Michael enters from now on." He took a pushpin from the bowl, opened the door, and drove the pin through the paper into the door on the outside.

"Sir Michael will have a fit or two about the holes in the walls and doors."

"Not if we solve this case quickly. I'll offer to have the plaster repaired once we're done." Daniel threw off unnecessary concerns and concentrated on putting what he knew about the case into chronological order.

After a couple of hours, he had a better handle on what they knew and on what they suspected, but nothing pointed a big black arrow at any single suspect. Frustrating.

When it was full dark, they wrapped up against the cold and set out for St. Giles. Daniel made sure he had both his truncheon and his pistol tucked into his belt. "Let's start at The Hog's Head, like you suggested. If Dirty Dave isn't there yet, the barman might know where we can find him. Plenty of information passes through that pub every night. At least half of my informants call that their local."

"Mine too. The Hog's Head is a clearinghouse of criminal connections." Ed turned his collar up, clutching his stick in his beefy hand. The brass top caught the lamplight. "The fog's rolling in. Going to be a bad night."

The Hog's Head was crowded, a fire roared on the hearth, and ale flowed down throats by the frothy lakeful. Daniel eyed those closest to the door, hunched around tables or sitting along the walls on long benches. Several he knew from encounters petty and criminal, and one or two he suspected he'd meet for similar reasons in the near future.

Conversations ceased, the click of the dominoes stopped, and a few shoulders hunched up around ears, as if the men didn't want to be seen.

Ed wove toward the barman, not bothering to hide his truncheon, the easiest way to identify a Bow Street detective. Daniel stayed near the door, watching the twenty or so patrons, none of whom would meet his eyes.

A barmaid with blonde hair escaping her mobcap stood in the opening at the far side of the room, a tray against her hip and a pitcher in her hand. Was this the woman Dirty Dave was sweet on?

"Haven't seen him. Not in at least a fortnight." The barman shook his head, sloshing a wet rag on the counter. "And I don't like your kind coming in here and upsetting my customers."

"What about Barney? Have you seen him?"

"Him neither."

"Do you know where they're likely to be?"

"I ain't their social secretary. I don't watch for 'em to come, and I don't miss 'em when they're gone. But even if I did, I wouldn't tell the likes of you lot."

A subdued huzzah went up from one of the back tables, and Daniel slipped his hand under his coat to the pistol at his waistband.

"Why don't you shove off? You ain't getting served here, and you ain't getting answers." Turning his back on Ed, the barman reached up for a tankard.

Ed leaned forward, grabbed the man's shoulder, and spun him back, fisting his hand in the man's shirtfront and hauling him half over the bar.

Several of the patrons rose, but Daniel drew his pistol and shook his head, motioning with the barrel for them to sit back down. One fellow caught his eye, sitting in the far corner in the shadows. A disreputable hooded cloak hid his expression, but he had a stillness about him that put Daniel's senses on alert. He sensed this was the most dangerous man in the room, and he positioned himself to keep him in sight.

"I believe we got off on the wrong foot, mister." Ed's voice was deceptively calm. "You seem to think I'm asking idle questions and that I might not mind if you don't cooperate. Let me disabuse you of such a notion. If you think the two of us are troublesome, wait until we bring every Bow Street officer, clerk, magistrate, and delivery boy into this establishment and make The Hog's Head our new base of operations. We'll gum up your works until you won't have a customer left in the rookery." He kept his fist locked in the man's collar, speaking to him from only inches away.

Daniel hid a smile. Criminals took in Ed's silver hair and the wrinkles creasing his face, and they underestimated both his strength and his will. Any moment his black truncheon, with the brass tip bearing more than one ominous dent, would tap the barman on the nose, and he would rethink his choices.

"You want to cooperate now, don't you?"

Red suffused the barman's face, and he scowled, a fleck of spittle appearing at the corner of his mouth.

"Oh, for the love of all that's British." The barmaid stalked over, smacked the tray and pitcher on the counter loud enough to make everyone jump, and jammed her hands on her rounded hips. "Enough. Dirty Dave hasn't been in tonight, and he isn't likely to neither. He's run up a tab he can't pay, and if he shows his face, the coin will be taken out of his hide. I told him not to come back until he can deliver some blunt We're not a charity here." She eyed a few customers who looked away.

The door beside Daniel opened, and a man stepped through, his collar up, hat pulled low. He stomped his feet, looking at the floor, before raising his head. Daniel could only see part of him, as the door stood between them, but Ed took one look at the man and dropped the barman.

"Hello, Barney. Been looking for you." He started toward the newcomer, and Daniel wrenched the door back.

Barney spun and shot out into the darkness with Ed on his heels. Daniel followed, his blood leaping, eager for the chase, when he collided with a figure that loomed out of the mist.

Assuming it was one of Barney's compatriots, he staggered a few steps to regain his footing and raised the pistol he still held.

Whoever he had hit lurched into the street, splashing into an icy-cold puddle in the gutter. A mobcap went flying, and a mass of dark hair . . .

A woman!

Daniel jammed the pistol into his waistband and went to help her. A quick glance told him Ed and Barney had disappeared into the fog.

"I'm so very sorry, ma'am. Please, forgive me. Let me help you." Of all the clumsy things to do, barging into a woman and knocking her down like a ninepin.

Grasping her elbow, he tugged her upright. With a groan, she shoved the hair out of her eyes, and his heart stopped.

Lady Juliette Thorndike . . . dressed like a fishwife, roaming the streets of St. Giles after dark?

"What are you doing here? Of all the nonsensical behavior! Are you hurt?" He marched into the street and snatched her cap from the cobbles. "Is this some sort of game you're playing? Amusing yourself by venturing into the rookeries? Are you alone, or are your friends somewhere nearby sniggering?"

He thrust the cap into her hands, grabbed her by the elbow, and marched her toward the nearest streetlamp half a block away. Shock and anger mingled. What was she thinking? How could she be so careless? Or simpleminded? What was she playing at?

She clutched the cap to her chest, her shawl trailing over one shoulder, and her breath came in gasps. Twice she looked behind her, and her eyes were wide and unfocused.

He had pity on her and slowed his steps.

And he remembered that she was a lady, the daughter of an earl.

They reached the corner and stood in the muted circle of light under the post. "Are you injured?"

She shook her head, pushing her hair out of her eyes and putting the cap on once again. A smear of dirt marred her cheek.

"Would you care to explain yourself?" He unbuttoned his coat and draped it around her shoulders. He withdrew his truncheon, wrapping the loop around his wrist and his fingers around the leather grip.

"I wanted my dragon back." She lifted her chin, her eyes sparking. "I heard you say the men who stole it frequented this area, and I wanted to find them."

She really was simpleminded. A pity, for she had seemed intelligent upon first meeting. Perhaps he should apply to have her admitted to Bedlam.

"What did you intend to do? Approach them and politely ask for your property back?"

"Of course not. I'm not simple-wit. I had a plan." His coat dwarfed her, nearly dragging the ground.

"Which was?"

She clamped her mouth shut, glared at him, and was saved from answering by the arrival of Ed, dragging Barney by the scruff of his neck.

"This young man has had a change of heart. He believes he would rather share information with us than a cell in Newgate Prison. Isn't he a clever lad?" Ed shoved Barney toward Daniel, dug in his pocket, produced a set of darbies, and clapped them on his quarry's wrists around the light pole.

"Now we can talk at our leisure. I've no mind to go haring about the rookery anymore tonight." Ed pushed his hat back. "And who is this waif?" He pointed his truncheon at Lady Juliette.

"You've met her before. May I present Lady Juliette Thorndike, daughter of the Earl of Thorndike, and debutante." Daniel loaded his voice with sarcasm. "Found wandering the streets of St. Giles like a vagabond."

"I wasn't wandering. I was running. Because I was being chased by an Irish harridan who wanted to dent my head with a cudgel." Her back straightened. "I owe you no explanation. I merely wanted to get my property back. It was a gift for my father, and I spent a great deal of money on it."

"I see." Ed sent Daniel a "calm yourself" look. "Perhaps young Barney here can help with that." He poked Barney in the middle of the back with his stick. "Can you not, Barney? You remember the lady, don't you? You met this afternoon."

Jaw set mutinously, Barney mumbled something.

"What was that? We can't hear you." Ed poked a bit harder.

"We had orders. Take what we stole to a receiver's shop, get a bit of brass for our trouble, and don't tell no one." He rattled the darbies against the light pole, but they were firmly locked.

"Which receiver's shop would that be?"

"Hawthorne's on Wells Street."

Ed questioned Daniel with a look.

"I know the place. Hawthorne lives above the shop."

"Then let's toddle round, shall we?"

Daniel fisted his hands. "I have to see Lady Juliette safely home. And we have a prisoner."

"I'm not going home. I am going to this Mr. Hawthorne's shop. If that's where my dragon is, then I'm going to go fetch it," Lady Juliette declared.

The ridiculousness of this situation wasn't lost on Daniel, but it didn't make him feel like laughing. "If you're coming, you're in for a walk. Wells Street is a fair stretch of the legs."

Ed unlocked Barney from the lamppost but snicked the open darby to his own wrist. "Lest you get any funny ideas."

Daniel took Lady Juliette's arm, not because she might escape but because it seemed unchivalrous not to. What could she have been thinking? And where did she get such awful clothes? What had she planned on doing if she found the men who stole her property? Thinking of all the harm that could have come to her, he found himself growing angry again.

"You're hurting me."

He relaxed his grip. "Beg pardon, milady," he said through stiff lips.

By the time they reached the receiver's shop, Daniel's teeth were nearly chattering. Without his coat, he was like a shorn lamb in a spring gale.

The windows were dark on the ground floor, but one story up, firelight flickered around the edges of a drape. Ed hit the door with the end of his stick. "Open up. Bow Street officers. We have a warrant."

Barney's head whipped round. "You don't have no warrant. You didn't even know about this place until I told you."

"Don't worry. They almost never ask to see it." Ed shrugged, whacking the door again.

Footsteps and the clinking of a chain sounded on the far side of the door, along with a heavy thump. Hinges creaked, and the door opened a few inches. "Whatcha want? We're closed. Come back in the morning." A beaky nose appeared briefly and then jerked back as he went to slam the door.

Ed put his booted foot into the opening and shoved. "Can't come back. We're on urgent police business."

"Open up, Hawthorne. It's Detective Swann."

Hawthorne's shoulders slumped, and he stepped back. "Come in then. Quick. Won't do for the neighbors to see runners on the doorstep. Gives the place a bad tone."

He held a candle aloft and wore a dressing gown and slippers. "Got me out of bed, you did, with your bellowing and stomping about." Shuffling toward the back of the shop, he took up his familiar place behind the counter.

The room was jammed with merchandise. Display cases of watches and cheap jewelry, silk shawls, shoes, snuff boxes, small furnishings. Anything desperate people could raise a few shillings on.

But Daniel wasn't interested in any of those offerings. Hawthorne kept the valuable objects, the ones most likely to have been gotten illegally, behind the counter out of sight.

Ed drew Barney forward. "This lad says he brought you an item earlier today and that you paid him and his mates for it."

Hawthorne was already shaking his head. "Never seen him before."

Daniel sighed. "Seem the night for it, doesn't it, Ed?" He leaned on the counter. "Let's not play games. I'm tired, and I'm cold. If I have to lay about this place to search it, lots of things are going to get broken. And at the end of the night, you'll be in the gaol, and I'll have what I came for." He waved his hand to take in the curtain-draped shelves behind Hawthorne. "I wonder how much of your inventory will match the lists of stolen goods that come into Bow Street frequently? There are terrible penalties to be exacted for those who traffic in purloined property."

Hawthorne tightened the belt on his robe and smoothed the hair over his ears. "Now, now, there's no need for threats. I run a clean business here." He seemed to notice Lady Juliette for the first time. "Who's the dolly-mop?" He ran his tongue over his crooked teeth and leered.

Daniel smacked the countertop with his truncheon to regain his attention. "She's not your concern, but keep a civil tongue in your head, or you'll find your eyes rattling about in your skull. I want what you bought from this man today. I want a green stone carving. Where is it?"

For a long moment, Daniel stared at the pawnbroker. The candlelight cast odd shadows on his face. Finally, Hawthorne shrugged. "I got a note yesterday describing the item. Said someone would deliver it to the shop and I was to pay them five shillings for their trouble. I should keep the item out of sight until it was called for by a Mr. Smith. That's all I know."

He bent out of sight behind the counter, and Daniel put his hand on his pistol grip in his waistband. One never knew what someone might do when they felt cornered, and Hawthorne was certainly cornered.

"Here. Take it and be gone." The green dragon hit the counter with a *thunk*. The ivory teeth shone dully, and the eyes stared blankly at the far wall.

Daniel hefted it, touched his hat brim, and turned toward the door. "Much obliged, Hawthorne."

"What am I to tell this Mr. Smith when he arrives?" Hawthorne protested.

"When was he supposed to come by?"

"He never said. Not directly. Just that someone named Mr. Smith would retrieve it and until then to keep me mouth shut."

When the four of them stood on the curb again, with Daniel holding the dragon, he said, "We need to put someone on this shop to watch for 'Mr. Smith.'"

"Good idea. I'll take Barney here to the warden at Newgate until he can go before the magistrate, and you take the lady home. When I get back to the office, I'll get a man to keep watch here."

Daniel and Lady Juliette had to walk a fair bit to find a carriage for hire, and it didn't even surprise Daniel that it was Cadogan who showed up first. It was almost uncanny how often the jarvey was available when Daniel needed him. The man seemed to make a habit of being wherever Bow Street men were. Daniel supposed it made a change from waiting outside pubs and theaters, but it did seem odd. Perhaps he would ask Ed what he knew about Cadogan.

They disembarked in front of the Thorndike townhouse, and before they could mount the steps, the front door opened.

Sir Bertrand Thorndike stood in the doorway, lit from behind. Without a word, he stepped back and bade Lady Juliette to enter.

Daniel waited while she handed back his coat, and he passed her the stone carving. "I bid you good evening, Lady Juliette. In the future, I would advise you to stay out of police business and trust the Bow Street detectives to retrieve stolen property."

"Understood. Good evening, Mr. Swann." And as regally as a princess, she lifted her hem with one hand, squared her shoulders, and walked up the steps into her house.

Daniel and Sir Bertrand shared a long look before Sir Bertrand closed the door, shutting out the light.

Juliette preferred not to relive the events of the evening, particularly the lecture and the layering on of guilt Uncle Bertie provided at the end. He had strode the open space of the War Room and held forth for longer than was comfortable before relenting and putting her to work on the jade dragon.

The stone statue proved as stubborn as Uncle Bertie, but in the end, she won—at least the fight with the dragon.

After examining it under strong light with the most powerful magnification at her disposal and finding nothing resembling a code, she thought to attack the base instead.

Solid black onyx, with no adornment. Or was it solid? She pressed, twisted, and slid her fingers over the base from every angle, and finally a soft scrape of stone on stone sounded as a side panel slid off, revealing a compartment.

An empty compartment.

Frustrated, she lowered the statue to the table and leaned back, covering her eyes. It was nearly dawn, Uncle Bertie had gone to bed hours ago, and she had wasted the time she should have been sleeping.

When she lowered her hands, the dragon seemed to be mocking her with his ghoulish grin.

Resignedly, she picked up the removable panel to replace it on the base when something rough met her fingertips. She turned over the rectangle of onyx.

There it was. Two lines of code carved into the stone lip of the little door.

Moving the reflector behind the lamp on the table, she brought the brightest light to bear, copying the symbols and letters onto a piece of foolscap.

Relief poured over her. Her errand hadn't been for nothing. She hadn't risked her life in the rookery, disappointed Uncle Bertie, or nearly ruined everything by crashing into Detective Swann without reward.

Detective Swann. He had been so angry with her. And yet he had helped her retrieve her property. He had given her his coat when she was freezing, and he'd seen her safely home.

His coat had smelled of citrus and cloves.

Odd in a policeman. Putting clove oranges into clothing cupboards was a trick her father's valet used to keep the clothing fresh smelling. Where had the detective learned the custom?

Chapter 11

"I AM GOING TO ENJOY MYSELF." Agatha adjusted her reins and then her veil. "I am not going to fret, worry, or do anything to take the enjoyment out of this hunt. And I most definitely am not going to fall off my horse."

"It is going to be a good day. Why do you think otherwise?" Juliette stood back as the groom led over Fabiana, her mother's chestnut thoroughbred mare. Another groom stood ready to give her a leg up.

"I just have an odd feeling. I didn't sleep well, and I dreamed I fell off into a huge mud puddle, and everyone around me was laughing. I feel like all my most awkward tendencies come out when I'm on a horse. Other people seem to have grace and rhythm when they ride, but I feel like a sackful of fireplace pokers jutting out at odd angles."

"Nonsense. You look lovely, and you'll do just fine. That riding habit is the height of fashion, and the green brings out the beautiful tones in your hair."

"No one else has seemed to notice," Agatha muttered, and her eyes went to Viscount Coatsworth, who was checking the girth on his mount. "I had hoped he would issue an invitation to be my escort at the ball tonight, but thus far he's been too busy laughing and posturing with his friends to notice me."

Ah, so that was it. Alonzo hadn't paid Agatha enough attention, and she was miffed and feeling insecure. Juliette wilted a bit inside at the prospect of propping up Agatha's self-confidence all day. She was exhausted from her escapades of the last few days and lack of sleep, not to mention the weight of Uncle Bertie's disapproval of her actions. That she'd retrieved the stolen dragon hadn't mollified him. He'd even threatened to stop her involvement in the case altogether.

And days of training and wrestling with the encoded messages with little result had worn her down.

As she was assisted into the saddle and hooked her leg over the top pommel, she felt another pang of longing. Her mother should be riding Fabiana right now. Where was she? Was she safe? Uncle Bertie seemed confident that her parents would return, but it had been almost two weeks. How long could she maintain her hope when there was no word?

Her father should be here too, riding one of his many excellent hunters.

This should have been their first hunt as a family. A sense of aloneness blew through her. Her parents had kept hidden from her the most important part of their lives, and they had asked Bertie to lie to her about where they had gone. So many lies. Was Bertie lying to her now with his assurances that her parents would come back as soon as they were sure the danger was over?

If her family could lie to her about this, what else had they lied about? Was everything they told her a lie?

And what about You, God? You promise never to leave or forsake us, but I feel forsaken. There is no one to trust. Can I trust You?

Guilt pinched her heart. It was blasphemous to question God, wasn't it? But what if what you saw and felt didn't agree with what you had been told? If her parents had lied to her about so much else, had they lied about the trustworthiness of God?

Around her, the bustle went on as if she weren't having a crisis of faith. The field of twenty or so assembled and milled in a grassy field awaiting the start.

The pack, released from the kennels, bounded and circled the master of hounds, giving the occasional bay, tails lashing the air. The whips spread out, and the huntsman conferred with the head groom.

Duke Heinrich edged his rangy bay close to Juliette's mare. "It is a good day for a hunt, ja? A good day to be out of the city. The fog this last week was . . . I had heard stories, but to experience it for myself." He shook his head. "Today is much better." He raised his face to the sky. Sunlight bathed his features, and Juliette responded to his smile with one of her own, tamping down her uncertainties.

"It has been a good week to be home by the fire," she agreed.

"I wish I had been, but my duties here in England are many. I was at meetings with your cabinet ministers, discussing the new boundaries for France and Germany now that the war is over."

Juliette shifted her skirt aside to adjust her stirrup leather, letting the strap out another hole. Fabiana stood rock still, only mouthing the bit and swishing her tail.

"I didn't realize your duties were so serious. National borders must be complicated to decide."

The duke smoothed his moustache. "I am only one of many who were there last night, and I do not have much authority. I suspect I was invited because of my title and my family, not because someone thinks I have special insight into the matter. It is often the way of things when one is from a powerful family, no? The title is more important to people than the person who bears it?"

Juliette nodded. "My father has said many times that people are more important than their titles or their occupations. I think that is why he enjoys inviting people from all walks of life to his dinner parties. He says it forces some who wouldn't mingle otherwise to learn about one another. When a duchess has to sit beside a penniless poet, they both find out that there is more to someone than their income or influence. Or when a professor from Oxford and a proprietress at Almack's really talk to one another, they find out that each person has something to offer to society."

The duke looked over her shoulder. "Or when a *Polizist* joins a local hunt?"

Juliette twisted to look behind her, and her heart flipped. *Polizist.* Policeman.

Detective Swann settled into the saddle of a blood bay stallion that stood at least seventeen hands. Mr. Swann wore impeccable riding clothes, boots that gleamed in the sun, and a determined expression.

Anxiety pressed against her chest tighter than her stays. What was he doing here? There was nothing here pertaining to his case . . . except her.

Heads turned and brows went up as he circled his mount. The bay was an impressive animal, and the detective looked well atop him. But he was certainly an anomaly amongst the aristocratic field.

"Herr Swann!" The duke stood in his stirrups and motioned for the constable to join them. Juliette pulled the veil down from the brim of her hat to hopefully conceal her expression.

She shouldn't be so happy to see the detective when they had opposing objectives. Every moment today she would have to be on her toes, not appearing evasive if he should ask her something, and yet giving nothing away that might jeopardize her ultimate mission.

"Good morning, Lady Juliette, sir." Mr. Swann guided his horse alongside Fabiana, who sidestepped at his approach but calmed quickly with just a touch to the reins.

"That is an impressive mount, Herr Swann. Is he yours?" the duke asked.

"No. I am riding him for someone else. His name is Beauden's Best, and he's for sale. The owner wanted him given a run today. There are several potential buyers here who would like to see him over fences before they put in an offer."

"He is for sale?" The duke took a closer look. "I will be watching to see how he goes. I have many horses at home in Germany, but I could always use a few more. And new bloodlines, *ja*? Who is the owner, Herr Swann?"

"I don't know. My instructions came through a solicitor's office. You can inquire at Coles, Franks, and Moody if you're interested."

"You don't know who owns the horse? Yet you're riding him?" Juliette asked.

"It's complicated. I was hired by the solicitors to show the horse to best advantage." Mr. Swann shrugged. "It's not the first time. I do jobs quite often for them." His mouth firmed into a straight line, and the muscles of his jaw tightened, as if he gritted his teeth.

Juliette looked away. He probably needed to supplement his pay somehow. Bow Street officers must not make much money. He must be forced to take cases or work on the side to make ends meet. Their speculation was probably causing him embarrassment. She sought to change the subject.

"Will you attend the Hunt Ball tonight?" She was looking forward to a social event where she didn't have to worry about stealing something or examining something for more clues, where she could enjoy herself with no undercurrents. And she had been asked by Duke Heinrich for two dances and to be his dinner partner, with the dowager's approval, of course.

It almost seemed wrong to be having fun when her parents were in hiding and her uncle had a mission laid on for tonight.

Hopefully, Uncle Bertie would be successful in his hunt. He planned to obtain two pieces of artwork in one night, which she thought overly ambitious, especially as he had been adamant that breaking into a museum and absconding with their newest acquisitions was a job for one person only. Hopefully, by tomorrow morning, with the fragment of Egyptian papyrus and the carved eagle statue in his possession, they would have enough of the code that she could crack it.

But until then, she would do as he asked and play the innocent debutante, enjoying the day on horseback and the evening dancing and dining.

"I have been invited by the master of hounds to attend, but I will probably decline and go back to London. My boss, Sir Michael Biddle, while satisfied we managed to get your stolen dragon back to you in a timely manner, is not best pleased that I took this day off. If the lawyers hadn't leaned on him, I wouldn't be here right now."

The pack of hounds moved across the downs, and the field gathered into a loose order. Agatha rode beside Viscount Coatsworth, and she flashed a smile over her shoulder at Juliette. All was right in her world once more.

Fabiana trotted, shaking her head and snorting, knowing what was to come and keen to get on with it. The duke rode with a steady hand and secure seat, but he seemed stiff in the saddle, militarily correct.

Mr. Swann, however, knew what he was about. His long legs encased his mount's barrel, and he kept his hands low. With a longer rein than most, he rose and fell in the stirrups to the cadence of his mount, his body catching the rhythm with apparent ease.

The horse's bright coat reflected the light, and his mane blew back in the breeze created by his movements.

"He is an excellent horseman on a magnificent horse." Duke Heinrich kept his horse parallel to Juliette's. "He is a good man too. I like him."

It pleased Juliette that the duke would treat Mr. Swann as an equal. Others of the hunting party had not welcomed the detective, turning their horses aside, but not the duke.

The day was as exciting and pleasant as Juliette had hoped. The hounds latched onto a scent, and the field flew the hedges, stone walls, and fallen trees, galloping across pastures and following the baying of the pack.

Mr. Swann was nearly always toward the front, both because his horse was of fine quality and speed and because he needed the most people possible to see the animal in action. Juliette's mare was sharp and full of run, and she had no difficulty keeping up.

Duke Heinrich wasn't a natural over fences, but he was brave, and he stayed near Juliette for most of the chase. Of Agatha and the viscount, Juliette saw almost nothing after the first fence, but she didn't worry. There were plenty of riders in the field to look after each other.

When the pack finally ran the fox to earth, they bayed and scrabbled and dug around the hole the fox had created for his den, but they were unable to roust him. Juliette was relieved. The fox would get away today.

The master of hounds dismounted, calling off the dogs and dispensing pats and praise in equal measure.

In spite of the winter air, Juliette's cheeks were warm from exertion, and steam rose of Fabiana's withers. She patted the mare's sweating coat and kept her walking in circles as the rest of the field caught up to the frontrunners and the pack.

Agatha's eyes sparkled, and she waved to Juliette. The viscount was still at her side, so perhaps he had asked to partner her tonight after all.

A brace of men on horseback separated from the field and approached Mr. Swann's mount. They conversed for several minutes before Mr. Swann nodded and pointed to the northeast.

Duke Heinrich's cheeks were red and his eyes lively as he walked his horse. "A glorious day. And we have tonight to anticipate." He inclined his head at Juliette. "I cannot tell you how delighted I am to partner you. When I spoke to the dowager, she was also most pleased."

A faint alarm bell rang in the back of her head. He was not seriously thinking of courting her affection, was he? She had promised herself that she would not consider marriage during her first Season, and she felt doubly so now without her parents being present.

The duke was pleasant, handsome, and cosmopolitan, but he stirred nothing in her beyond a cordial friendship. And he would return to Germany, while she would remain here in England. She had no desire ever again to be that far away from her family.

Her eyes darted to Mr. Swann aboard the showy bay. The detective was handsome and interesting . . . and dangerous. He stirred in Juliette feelings of excitement tinged with guilt. His purpose was to dig out secrets and hers was to keep them hidden. There could be no future for them together, even if such a thing would enter his head, but it was fun to daydream.

He glanced up and caught her looking at him. She turned away, adjusting her veil, feeling the warmth rising in her face.

Mr. Swann maneuvered his horse closer. "Two of the interested buyers would like to observe this fellow more closely on the ride back to the kennel. We'll be returning over part of the course rather than following the field back via the road."

"A good idea. May we join you?" Heinrich asked. "I would like to see him more myself."

Pleased to be included, Juliette patted Fabiana's neck. "I would enjoy that."

The ride back over fences was even better than the hunt. With no pack to worry about, they could go at a fair canter and in a reasonably tight group. The two buyers hung back at first, then moved away from the jumps to the side to get a better view of the action.

Juliette put Fabiana to the hedges, and the mare met them beautifully. They soared over a stone wall and loped easily up a slight grade. They were halfway to the top of the rise, two lengths behind Mr. Swann, when she realized the duke wasn't beside her. Easing back on the reins, she turned her chestnut in a wide arc.

The duke's horse, riderless, trotted across the field, blowing and kicking. Juliette ripped off her glove, put her fingers to her lips, and let loose with one of her most unladylike yet useful tricks, a piercing whistle.

Mr. Swann was half a furlong up the hill, but her blast reached him, for he slowed from a canter to a trot, then to a walk, steadying his eager mount.

Juliette headed for the last fence, where the duke was picking himself up from the ground. "Are you all right?" she called.

"*Ja*. It was my fault. I didn't see the stride, and he chipped in at the last minute and threw me off balance. We must get him back and check him over." The duke's hat had tumbled off, and he'd lost his crop. A smear of mud decorated his cheek, and when he went to get his belongings, he limped.

"You are injured." Juliette began to dismount, but he waved her to stay in the saddle.

"I landed rather hard on my knee, I fear. But there is no need to worry."

Mr. Swann galloped past in pursuit of the runaway, and he skillfully managed to corner the animal along a thick tree line and grab the reins. The two buyers trotted up, and after checking the horse over, they boosted the duke back into his saddle.

"Take it slowly, sir," Mr. Swann said. "We'll walk the rest of the way."

"We've seen enough," the younger of the two buyers said. "We'll consider our bid and contact the solicitor's office."

When they reached the kennels, grooms helped the duke and Juliette dismount, but Mr. Swann vaulted lightly from his horse's back and slipped the reins over the bay's head. He spent time patting and talking to the horse before a groom led him away.

"Herr Swann, a moment of your time, *bitte?*" The duke stood on one leg, his other toe barely brushing the ground. "I would ask a favor of you."

The other riders who had gone out that day had hung around the stables laughing and talking, but now they drifted toward the club-house. Agatha paused on the path, looking over her shoulder and beckoning to Juliette.

Juliette made an in-a-minute gesture. She would wait for the duke and accompany him to the hunt headquarters.

"Yes, sir?"

"I was to partner Lady Juliette to the festivities this evening, but alas"—the duke indicated his injured knee—"I will be unable to fulfill my duties. I would ask that you stand in as my replacement?"

Mr. Swann looked quickly to Juliette, and she closed her mouth lest she appear too shocked.

Not that she was averse to attending a hunt ball with the detective, but could she spend an entire evening in his presence without divulging even a hint of her secrets?

You're a fool of the first water. You should have said you had to return to London, and therefore, though you regretted it mightily, you would not be able to partner Lady Juliette tonight.

Daniel tugged on the white gloves he hadn't worn since the last formal at Oxford and checked his cravat in the mirror of the men's cloak room. Around him wealthy, influential men, many of them titled, made final checks of their appearances.

He wished Duke Heinrich had asked Lady Juliette her preference before he'd declared his wishes that Daniel partner her tonight. She surely must be disappointed that her new escort was of such lowly status, and if given a choice, she would have declined. There were many more qualified men who would have been eager to serve as her partner.

Still, he was no coward, and he would keep his promise to the duke. It stung a bit that the duke had asked him in an offhanded manner, probably because he felt safe to have Daniel escort the lady, since he didn't consider Daniel a rival.

Music from the large meeting room turned ballroom for the evening drifted through the door. Daniel had never been to a hunt ball. He was prepared, however, since the solicitors had encouraged him to attend. His mission was clear. Speak with the buyers, talk up the horse he had ridden today, and secure their offers. He was grateful he had brought the correct clothing with him.

He had his patron to thank for being here, and also for the clothes. For the past nearly thirteen years, he'd had no say in his wardrobe. Every six months he'd been ordered to turn up at a tailor's for measurements, and shortly thereafter new clothing had been delivered to his place of lodging. Uniforms for school, formal wear, riding gear, outerwear, shoes, boots, hats, gloves, smallclothes. All luxurious and expensive and all chosen by someone other than himself.

In under a month, all that would change and he would be on his own, supporting himself through what he made at Bow Street and whatever private cases he could scare up. A niggle of uneasiness dug into his gut. He'd never taken care of himself solely, always having had someone else to rely upon.

Stop it. You're a grown man with experience and skills, and you will fare just fine. You've been kicking against your patron's goads for years, and now you'll get your chance to be free of his strictures.

Joining the stream of men heading to the ballroom, he walked down the stairs to the main floor. On the opposite staircase, the ladies descended from their dressing rooms, and he searched for Lady Juliette. She had been gracious at the time of the substitution in partners, but perhaps she had second or third thoughts and regretted agreeing.

Daniel waited in the foyer, ignoring the curious glances of the women as they passed by.

"I say there, Swann, did the stallion give you a good feel over the fences? I'm considering putting in a bid, but I want a careful jumper, you know?"

Drawn into a knot of men, Daniel gave honest, precise answers to their questions, but he kept glancing up the steps.

When Lady Juliette appeared on the landing above him, he sucked in a breath and forgot what he was saying.

She was stunning.

Her gown of soft white glistened with silver beads, and she had threaded a white ribbon through her upswept curls. She carried a fan looped over her wrist, and she wore that gold ring with the red stone over her long white gloves.

A soft smile touched her lips, and her eyes, so dark they glistened, locked with his. His heart thudded against his waistcoat. She was a rare beauty, and brave—albeit a trifle foolish with that bravery— kind, and intelligent. She would make someone a perfect bride someday.

"Swann? Does he chip in if you don't give him plenty of direction?"

He shook his head, trying to remember the threads of the conversation. "He's fine. Natural jumper. Careful but bold. If you'll excuse me, gentlemen." He left the buyers without a backward glance.

When she reached the bottom step, he held out his arm. "Good evening, Lady Juliette." Did his voice sound as strained to her as it did to him?

"Good evening, Mr. Swann." She inclined her head. "Or should I call you Detective?"

"Perhaps, since we are well acquainted now, after having gone racing about the rookery at night together," he murmured close to her ear, "you should call me Daniel."

Mischief and humor lit her face. "Let that be our little secret . . . Daniel."

He liked the sound of his name on her lips. Those rosy, bow-shaped, perfect lips.

Stop it. You'll make a donkey of yourself. God didn't see fit to make you a gentleman, and you are aspiring to well above your station. If she knew you were a by-blow whose mother worked as her housekeeper, she would never speak to you again.

"I believe I should present you to the dowager, who is my chaperone. She has spent the afternoon shopping in the village, and she has not adjusted well to the change of plans when I informed her. The duke sent a note to her with his apologies, and he's gone back to the city to recuperate." Lady Juliette's fingers tightened on his arm, and he didn't know if that meant she regretted the change of plans, the dowager's reaction, or that the duke would be absent this evening.

"Lead the way." *Stop second-guessing motives. Take a break from the police work and enjoy yourself for once.*

The dowager sat with the other chaperones, dressed in black but with diamonds at her throat and ears. She straightened in her chair as they approached, and Daniel was reminded of the panel of black-robed professors at university before whom he had defended his thesis.

Her mouth was as tart as a Spanish blood orange, and she eyed him from hair to shoe tips. But he'd encountered her type before, and he would earn no points by playing the sycophant.

"Your Grace, may I present Mr. Daniel Swann, who is kind enough to stand in for Duke Heinrich for the evening. Mr. Swann, Her Grace, the Dowager Duchess of Haverly." Lady Juliette made a small curtsy to the dowager who inclined her head.

"A pleasure, Your Grace." Daniel bowed.

She puckered. "I cannot say I am pleased with the substitution, but what can I do? I was not consulted. Two dances and the dinner hour. That is all. If I had been given proper warning, I would have found a more suitable partner. A *policeman* of all things." She tapped her black lace fan into her palm. "I will be watching."

Daniel offered Juliette his arm and deliberately kept his walk slow and steady lest he give in to the urge to scamper away from the dowager's glares.

"A formidable woman. As good as a dragon guarding the gate of the damsel's castle."

"She means well, and she takes her duties seriously. Beneath all that bluster, there's a rather dry wit, and I suspect a secretly tender heart." Lady Juliette shrugged at the skepticism he put into his expression. "It's true."

"She hides it well. I suspect a squad of detectives couldn't gather enough evidence to convict her of having a tender heart."

Miss Montgomery went by on the arm of Viscount Coatsworth, and her mouth opened. She tugged her partner's arm, and they halted. "Juliette, what is this?"

"I didn't have time to tell you. The duke suffered a minor injury and cannot attend tonight, so Mr. Swann was kind enough to take his place." She sounded bright and happy, but Daniel wondered if it was an act.

"I see." Miss Montgomery blinked, and she spoke slowly, as if she did not see but was trying to avoid being rude.

"Come along, Agatha. The lines are forming." The viscount turned his shoulder to Daniel, cutting him out of the conversation. "Lady Juliette, when you've fulfilled your obligations, we'd be pleased if you'd join our party."

Heat built in the pit of Daniel's stomach. Fulfilled her obligations, as if she were merely doing charitable work by partnering him but would soon be free to join her own set.

Lady Juliette seemed not to notice the condescension in Viscount Coatsworth's tone and smiled brightly. "That's very kind of you. We shall have to see what eventuates."

He could feel eyes on them as he led her to their place in the line. She appeared cool and unruffled, but his heart banged against his chest. He should not be so distracted by flashing eyes and curving cheeks, rosy lips and graceful movements.

But he was.

Completely captivated.

The music started, catching him by surprise, and he jerked, a half step behind the rest of the dancers. *Just what you need, lad, to crash into someone or trip over your own feet from minute dot.*

Lady Juliette pretended not to notice his clumsiness, inclining her head and circling him with elegance.

If someone had asked him later, he wouldn't have been able to describe the rest of the set. He concentrated only on not making a rube of himself and not letting on that she disturbed him so.

When the last song ended, he didn't know if he was relieved or disappointed.

"It's warm in here, isn't it?" She flicked open her fan. The curls at her temples moved in the breeze she created, and her floral scent wafted toward him.

"Would you care for some refreshment? I could fetch you something to drink."

"Let's go together." She put her hand on his arm, and he led her through the arched doorway into the refreshment room.

White painted shelves lined one wall, holding ribbons, cups, trays, and other trophies won by members of the hunt club. On the end walls, paintings of horses and hounds were separated by brass wall lamps. And down the center, a long white table of edibles.

Holding a cut-glass cup of punch, Lady Juliette moved to one of the paintings. Daniel joined her.

"George Stubbs was the greatest equine anatomist painter in history." Daniel studied the light and shadow that delineated every muscle of the thoroughbred in the painting. "I once had the opportunity to visit the Marquess of Rockingham's home and view Stubbs's painting of the marquess's horse, Whistlejacket. Amazing talent, and a beautiful horse."

"You know paintings?" She sipped her cup, her delicate brows rising only slightly in polite interest, not shocked disbelief.

"I studied art and history while at school."

"Where did you attend? I went to school in Switzerland, first an academy, then finishing school."

"Boarding school in Kent and then Pembroke College at Oxford."

This time the brows went higher. "My father and uncle attended Merton College in Oxford."

She didn't ask, but he thought he should tell her, to remind himself not to be distracted, to remind himself that he should nip his interest in her while it was still in the bud.

"An unusual path for a detective, I know. Not many Oxford graduates wind up in Bow Street. But it gets worse. I am the illegitimate son of a domestic servant from Norfolk. My mother was a housemaid, and I have no idea who my father was. I was plucked from my home at twelve by an anonymous stranger, sent to school, educated and provided for, and given my choice of professions. Next month, on my twenty-fifth birthday, all support from my benefactor will cease and I will have to live solely on my salary as a detective." He watched for her reaction, sure she would now excuse herself. Would she be polite or aghast? Ashamed to be seen with him?

"You seem to be making a good fist of it. What led you to become a detective? Did studying art and history prepare you for working out of the Bow Street Magistrate's Court?"

Had she not heard what he said? He was baseborn, a by-blow who didn't even know his parentage.

"History is a great teacher for many disciplines. We must learn from history, or we will be doomed to reenact it. History teaches you perspective and consequences and the truth about mankind." He stopped, as he was in danger of sermonizing on his favorite topic.

Yet she didn't seem bored. "And your interest in art?"

He shrugged. "It began as a small boy at our parish church. The stories told in the stained-glass windows. I learned those Bible stories through the artistic depictions before I could even read. Then when I went to work as the bootboy in the manor house, I loved looking at the paintings and portraits, wondering about the scenes and the people. When I had the opportunity to study art, it spliced easily with history." Why didn't she bolt? And why was he still talking about himself?

"Ah, there you are, Lady Juliette. Your chaperone is anxious that you should return to her at once." Viscount Coatsworth inserted himself between Daniel and the lady, with his back to Daniel. "Allow me to see you safely back to her side."

Lady Juliette deftly avoided the hand he sought to put on her arm and moved around the viscount. "Thank you, sir, but Mr. Swann will see to the duty. We have one more dance to share."

Daniel tried not to look smug as she took his arm while handing her punch cup to the affronted Coatsworth.

And yet as he inhaled her floral scent, he reminded himself that their paths lay far apart, and he would do well to remember his place. She had been kind when learning the truth about him, but that didn't mean their relationship—such as it was—would go any further.

They had only just returned to the ballroom when Owen Wilkenson entered through the foyer, his hair tousled and his cheeks pink. He had the grace to skirt the dancers, but he bumped into several onlookers as he made his way around the room to Daniel and Lady Juliette. When he arrived, he was out of breath.

"Mr. Beck sent me to fetch you and the lady here." He gulped. "There's been a break-in at her family's home, and several staff members were injured. Mr. Beck said to fetch you straight away, and he sent me in Cadogan's cab. The men who are working outside told us we couldn't come up the drive, as we didn't have an invitation, so I gave them the slip and ran all the way."

Two men clattered into the ballroom, eyes hard, one carrying a stick. "There he is, the blighter."

Lady Juliette's hand had tightened on Daniel's arm, and she gave a gasp. "A break-in? Who was hurt?"

"Dunno, milady, but I would be obliged if you'd tell these men I'm with you." Owen skipped aside, evading the grasp of one of the men.

"Enough, gentlemen. I'm from Bow Street, and this man works for me." Daniel held up his hand. "We'll be leaving now and taking him with us. You may go back to your posts."

Staff at the Thorndike house had been hurt. An empty feeling opened in the pit of his stomach.

Was one of those staff members his mother? *Please, God, don't let her be hurt.* He brought himself up short. He hadn't prayed in awhile. Was it fair to do so now, when he needed something? He and God had a rather formal relationship, almost a don't-bother-me-I-won't-bother-you status. When he had been wrenched from his mother so many years ago, and then told by the school's chaplain that God had blessed him, it had frozen a place in his heart that he rarely acknowledged.

He'd stopped praying that God would let him go home. Mostly, he'd stopped praying.

Chapter 12

SOCIAL CONVENTIONS MADE JULIETTE WANT to scream. She could see the value in some, but in an emergency, they should be thrown off.

"You cannot go haring off to London with that policeman. You have no chaperone. The dowager isn't going to leap into a carriage in her evening gown. And she's not going to let you go without her. Have some sense, Juliette." Agatha held onto her arm.

"Aggie, I am going, and that's that. You may inform the dowager that I had no choice and that I found a suitable companion to accompany me in order to observe the conventions." Though where she would get someone like that, she had no idea.

"Come, Lady Juliette. We must go now." Detective Swann had his cloak, hat, and his brass-capped walking stick and shifted his weight from boot to boot beside the hunt club's front door.

"Of course I'm coming. I'll get my wraps." She hurried up the stairs to the ladies' dressing room, with Agatha following, protesting all the way. Inspiration dawned as she accepted her cloak.

"Miss, would you be willing to accompany me to London tonight? I'll pay, of course, but I need a maid for the evening." She addressed the young woman who had been looking after the dressing room. "I know you've been hired here, but I will pay the hunt club for your time, and I'll pay you an additional fee."

Within moments the head waiter had struck a deal that allowed Juliette to take Miss Fischer, the maid, with her to London and to put her up for the night. Juliette would arrange the maid's transportation back to the village tomorrow.

The four of them—Juliette, Daniel Swann, the office boy, and Miss Fischer—piled into a carriage that now waited in the front drive.

"Evening, Cadogan. Fast as you can."

"Aye, sir. Lola and Sprite will get you there." He shook his reins, and they were off.

"Lola and Sprite?" Juliette asked as she rocked back in the seat.

"The horses. Cadogan is a familiar cabbie, usually hanging around Bow Street or Drury Lane looking for fares. I travel in this carriage often." Detective Swann settled himself next to his coworker. "Lady Juliette, this is Owen Wilkinson, who works at the magistrate's court."

"Mr. Wilkinson," she said. "What can you tell us about what happened at my home?"

The young man knuckled his forelock. "Milady, I was tidying the office, preparing to go home for the night, when a man rushed in. He said there had been a break-in at a house on Belgrave Square and that there were injuries. I told him someone would be there soon, and I went to Mr. Beck's house. His place is closest to Bow Street. Together we went round to the address. Mr. Beck took one look and sent me to fetch Mr. Swann."

"Do you know who was hurt?" Mr. Swann asked. "And how badly?"

"I dunno. I didn't even make it into the house before Mr. Beck sent me on my way."

Mr. Wilkinson sounded defensive, as if he wasn't to blame for not having all the answers Mr. Swann sought. Juliette sensed tension between the two, but she held her tongue, her mind on her home.

The carriage rocked and jolted, and they made good time in spite of the lateness. In just over an hour they had reached the Chelsea Bridge and trundled over the Thames. In Belgrave Square, lights blazed from the Thorndike house windows, and Juliette hurried up the stairs as Mr. Swann paid the driver.

The front hall looked as it should, nothing missing or damaged. Light spilled from her father's library, along with the sound of voices.

She stopped on the threshold. The room was a shambles. Books had been tossed from shelves, paintings ripped off the walls.

"Ed, what do you know?" Mr. Swann tugged off his gloves and tucked the walking stick under his arm.

"Looks like they were after a safe or strongbox." Mr. Beck indicated a walnut panel that had been swung open behind the desk. His gaze swept over Daniel and Juliette in their eveningwear, his brows rising. "Lady Juliette." He inclined his head.

Juliette hadn't even known that panel existed.

"They went at it but didn't get it opened. Looks like an axe maybe?" Mr. Beck fingered one of the gashes in the paneling.

Juliette studied the iron-banded door that had been built into the wall. Several shiny gouges and dents decorated the front, but the Vexier combination lock still clung to the hasp, foiling the robbers. The strongbox safe was nearly four feet tall and two feet wide, and it must weigh several hundred pounds. What did Father keep in there?

The Thorndike sapphires, among other things?

"Who was injured?"

"The butler and the housekeeper. They were the only ones here at the time."

"How badly?" Mr. Swann's voice sharpened. "Where are they? Have you questioned them?"

"Easy there." Mr. Beck made damping motions with his hands. "There's someone with them downstairs."

"I want to talk to them." Mr. Swann turned so quickly, he nearly bumped into Juliette, his cape swinging and the hem wrapping around her briefly.

"I'll come with you."

Though it was her house, the detective went ahead of her to the doorway to the servants' area on the ground floor. She remembered that he'd been in the house before and must have been brought through this way.

When they reached the servants' dining room, Juliette stopped. The butler, Mr. Pultney, sat with his head in his hands, his collar open, his hair disheveled. He murmured something, but Juliette didn't catch what it was. Mrs. Dunstan, the housekeeper, had a towel to her lip. The towel was splotched with blood, and Juliette's knees wobbled. Mrs. Dunstan looked up, her white cap askew and eyes staring.

Across the table from them, with one booted foot on the seat of a chair, a man leaned. Juliette knew him. That hair was distinctive. It was the Duke of Haverly.

"Good evening, Your Grace."

He straightened and put his foot on the floor. "Lady Juliette. I was supposed to meet your uncle here tonight, but he's late. As usual. When no one opened the door, I grew worried and let myself in. I'm glad I did, since it seems the household was in need of aid."

Mr. Swann approached, but stiffly, as if his knees had lost their bend. "Did anyone see who did this? What happened?"

The duke explained. "I found the place empty and the library is a mess. Seems thieves broke in. They found only the housekeeper and the butler in residence. They roughed up Mr. Pultney here and tied him up, shoving him into the wine cellar. They forced Mrs. Dunstan to show them where the valuables were kept. When she wouldn't, they encouraged her to comply with their fists." He indicated the bloodied towel.

Juliette looked at the far wall and took some deep breaths.

"That's fine, Your Grace, but I'd like to hear it from them." Mr. Swann had a notebook and pencil in his hands, but he looked at the butler. "Mr. Pultney?"

"There were two of them. Big men. Bigger than me by a fair bit. I opened the door because I knew the duke was expected tonight, and they rushed right by me." He sounded ashamed. "I couldn't stop them. The door hit me in the shoulder, and I fell."

"Where is everyone else tonight? The footmen, the maids?" Juliette asked. She went to the sideboard and filled two glasses of water from the pitcher there and brought them to the table.

"Sir Bertrand gave the rest of the staff the evening off. He'd purchased tickets to a minstrel show at a theater in Covent Garden, and he wanted everyone to go. Mr. Pultney and myself could look after his lordship ourselves for a few hours, especially as he intended to be away for part of the evening." Mrs. Dunstan lowered the cloth and revealed a split and swollen lip.

Juliette closed her eyes, nausea gripping her. She groped for a chair and sank onto it.

"Here, let me," Mr. Swann said, his voice gruff. He took the cloth from Mrs. Dunstan and dampened it in cold water from a pitcher on the sideboard. He sat beside the housekeeper and dabbed at the cut.

Juliette's insides shook as she watched him, his hands tender, though his expression was fierce. Her house had been broken into. Her staff had been injured. With everything in her she wanted to run upstairs and see if the sanctity of the War Room had been breached, but with detectives and dukes running about the place, she had to wait.

Where was Uncle Bertie now? He had been intending to procure two more items from the art gallery list. What if he waltzed in unaware, holding a carved eagle and a scrap of Egyptian papyrus that by tomorrow would be reported stolen? How could she warn him?

"They ran past you, sir?" the detective asked.

"It was like they knew there were only two of us here. They didn't ask about anyone else." Mr. Pultney ran his hand over his sparse hair, and his fingers trembled.

"Do you think they were watching the house?" the duke asked.

Mr. Swann's mouth tightened, as if he didn't appreciate being interrupted, but he said nothing. What did one say to a duke, after all?

"Perhaps. It was not half an hour after everyone left for the theater that they barged in."

"They locked you in a room down here?" Mr. Swann picked up the small notebook and stub of pencil he'd laid on the table to help Mrs. Dunstan and made notes, barely looking up when he talked.

"One of them did. The other shouted at Mrs. Dunstan. 'Where's the safe? Where's the safe?' And he grabbed her by the arm and hauled her down the hallway." The butler took a sip of water, nodding his thanks to Juliette. "The one tied my hands behind my back, shoved me into the wine cellar, and put a chair under the knob so I couldn't get out."

The detective raised his eyes but said nothing to the housekeeper, letting the silence lengthen.

She finally stirred. "When they had Mr. Pultney locked up, they made me show them the safe. I didn't want to tell them, but one of them had a knife, and he said, did I want to die for another man's belongings? I tried to think what Himself would want us to do."

Himself was Juliette's father, a term of respect her mother had given leave for her staff to use.

"I took them to the dining room. I showed them the silver safe hidden in the wall there." She touched her lip and winced. "That's when one of them hit me. Said not to be daft, they didn't want teapots and platters. They were after bigger treasure. Where was the earl's personal safe?"

Thieves not wanting silver? They must not have known what else the dining room safe held. There was a complete dining service for twenty-four, all rimmed in gold. A former Earl of Thorndike had commissioned the set when he had entertained King William and Queen Mary at Heild House in Worcestershire more than a century ago.

"I told them I didn't know where any other safe could be. I'd never seen it." Her tongue came out to explore the split. "That's when one of them hit me again. I know sometimes people say they see stars when they take a blow to the head, but it's true."

The pencil snapped, and everyone startled. Fury blazed from Mr. Swann's eyes.

Juliette took Mrs. Dunstan's hand, hoping she didn't think the detective was angry with her. "What happened next?"

"They dragged me with them into the library. I couldn't see well with my eyes tearing up, but they started throwing books off the shelves and banging on the walls. They found a second safe." She turned to Juliette. "I swear I didn't know it was there."

Juliette squeezed her hand, her mind taken off the blood and centered solely on the remorse in the woman's eyes. "I believe you. And don't worry. My father will not blame you for any of this. He would much rather give away all he owned than have one of his staff put into harm's way." Though she'd never heard him say it, she believed it was true.

"When they couldn't get the safe open, they marched me upstairs. They went through your parents' bedchambers and Sir Bertrand's. Sir Bertrand's room looks out onto the street, and they must have seen the duke's carriage arrive. The one with the knife pushed me into Sir Bertrand's dressing room and pushed a dresser in front of the door."

"I came inside then." The duke put his foot up on the chair seat again. "Though it took a bit of searching, I eventually heard Mr. Pultney kicking the door down here and released him, and we located Mrs. Dunstan. I sent my driver to Bow Street, and the three of us"—he indicated the butler and housekeeper—"did a quick walk through the house to make certain no one else was here and to try to ascertain what might have been taken."

Mr. Beck called down the stairs to the servants' dining hall. "Sir Bertrand Thorndike has returned. He's coming up the front steps now."

"Will you be all right?" Juliette asked the housekeeper. She must warn Bertie, if possible, not to show the items he'd stolen tonight.

"Yes, milady. The rest of the staff will be home soon. If Sir Bertrand needs anything, ring the bell."

"If he needs anything, I'll tend to him myself. You have the rest of the night off. When the cook gets home, have her make you some tea, then get some rest."

She led the way upstairs, and when she reached the entrance hall, Bertie leaned against the doorframe in the open doorway, his hair hanging in his eyes, and his lips slack. He raised his chin a fraction and winked at her before dropping his head again.

"Well, aren't you a pretty sight?" She put her hands on her hips, playing along. "Here we've been in crisis, and you've been in your cups." She checked his person, but she could see no evidence of the items he had gone out to retrieve. Had he stashed them somewhere?

"Wha' crishish?" He wobbled.

"Our house was burgled. The police are here, Mrs. Dunstan is injured, and you're staggering drunk. I despair of you, Uncle Bertie."

"Injured?" He blinked, waving his arm weakly. "Bad?"

"A split lip."

"Wha' got nicked?" He hiccupped.

"I don't know. I don't think anything was taken, but I haven't had time to do any sort of investigation into what might be missing." She spoke slowly and with intent so he should know she'd had no time to check on the War Room.

The duke strode over to Bertie's side and put Bertie's arm over his shoulder. "You need a cup of strong coffee." He sniffed and winced, leaning away. "Several cups, I think."

"I wouldn't bother trying to sober him up tonight. Can you help me get him to his bed? He can suffer the consequences of his debauchery in the morning."

"Who are these people?" Uncle Bertie waved toward Owen Wilkinson and Miss Fischer, who sat beside each other on straight-backed chairs in the foyer.

"They came home with me. Don't worry about them. Worry about getting yourself upstairs. I'll be up directly."

Weariness she didn't have to fake washed through her. The day had started bright and early. She'd had a full day of hunting, an evening ball, a cross-country rush in a carriage, and a burglary. She didn't think she could take much more today.

"Gentlemen," she said to the Bow Street detectives, "perhaps you might return in the morning? We'll be better able to assess any damage done, as well as provide an inventory of what might have been stolen. I must attend my uncle in the absence of his valet."

"Of course, Lady Juliette. Please lock the doors after us." Mr. Swann flipped his notebook closed, watching the duke and Uncle Bertie stagger up the staircase.

"Miss Fischer can stay here tonight, and I'll see she's returned home to Ash Valley in the morning."

He nodded. "Wilkinson, go fetch us a cab."

The young man eased to his feet, glanced at Miss Fischer as if reluctant to leave her company, and in a breach of protocol, sauntered out the door without so much as a by-your-leave in Juliette's direction. Detective Swann's mouth hardened, but he didn't reprimand Mr. Wilkinson in front of her. Juliette shook her head. Was the boy careless, or was he impertinent? Did he display bad manners to offend her or, as she suspected, to needle his boss?

"I'll be by in the morning," Mr. Swann promised. "Thank you for your company earlier in the evening. I'm sorry your day had to end this way. I'll let the night watchmen in this district know to look in on the house frequently throughout the night, but I don't expect any further trouble, especially not once the rest of your staff returns."

He and Mr. Beck left, and Juliette locked the front door. She leaned against it before remembering Miss Fischer.

"If you'll go downstairs to the kitchen, you'll find some remaining staff to assist you. Thank you for coming to my aid."

Juliette hurried upstairs once the girl had gone. She reached Uncle Bertie's room, tapped on it, and when beckoned, entered.

Bertie sat at his desk, his hair combed and his eyes bright. "Well, we seem to have kicked a hornet's nest, haven't we?"

Her gaze flew to the duke, but His Grace merely remained silent, leaning back against the mantel and crossing his arms.

"Don't worry about him. He's my supervising officer, and consequently yours."

"What? The Duke of Haverly is a spy?"

"You might want to keep it down," Bertie said dryly. "He's held on to that particular secret for a number of years, and I'd hate for it to get out now."

Juliette covered her mouth, her mind racing. One question that popped into her head that she just had to know the answer to or perish.

"Does your mother know?"

Marcus and Bertie broke into laughter. "No, Lady Juliette, and we must keep it that way. My mother couldn't keep a secret if promised the Crown Jewels."

Juliette subsided onto the foot of Bertie's bed. "If you're Bertie's supervisor, are you also my parents'?"

"I am. It's a recent promotion, with the retirement of my supervisor. And before you ask, no, I do not have any news as to their whereabouts. However, I am not worried." The duke's calm, rational manner soothed Juliette. He seemed in perfect control. "They will turn up when and where they are needed, and they have always enjoyed a certain amount of latitude to maneuver."

Could she trust the duke? After this would she be able to trust anyone? When and if her parents returned, could she truly believe anything they said? She was alone, though surrounded by people encouraging her to believe them.

God, what should I do? Where can I turn?

"We should concentrate on finding who is chasing the imported artwork besides us, because clearly someone is in possession of at least a partial list of artifacts." Bertie fisted his hand and tapped his thigh. "Not only did someone know in advance that the jade dragon would be up for auction at Barrett's, they sent thugs to steal it from whoever purchased it. Now that they know it was Juliette, they've sent more reprobates to burgle the house, ostensibly to retrieve it."

"How did they know it was on the list, if we have the original?" the duke asked. "You stole the inventory list from the art dealer's yourself. Who else would have a copy?"

"It has to be the courier," Bertie said. "The man who was supposed to transport the list and make the sale, but Fournier must have gotten suspicious and encoded the list, hiding it in the artwork. Perhaps with plans to send the code key once the payment had been made? Leonidas thought Fournier had grown to distrust his courier. It must be the courier who is now after the encoded artwork."

Fournier. It was the first time Juliette had heard the identity of the man who had assembled the list of Europe's most dangerous spies. Her parents and uncle . . . and she had to assume the Duke of Haverly as well.

She stiffened. "Uncle Bertie, you took the list from Turner and Rathbone's? Did you see Mr. Selby there?"

"Don't get yourself into a state. I stole the list, yes, but Selby wasn't there. I certainly didn't kill him. You know better than that. I never would have entered the gallery if someone was there. I was long gone before he ever arrived that night."

She wanted to believe him. "Then, was there a second copy of the list at the gallery?"

"I don't see how I could have missed it. I took every inventory book they had, and I went through the entire office. Packing slips, vouchers, suppliers, requests." Bertie yanked the end of his cravat. "Now that the detectives have gone, we should retire upstairs and see what's what."

They went single file, quietly, as they could hear other staff members returning belowstairs. As they neared the hallway that led to the War Room, Juliette stopped.

Mrs. Dunstan and Mr. Pultney stood before them, the butler holding a lamp. "Shall we go up, sir?" He motioned toward the concealed staircase.

Again, Juliette boggled. They knew?

"We'll talk upstairs, but yes," Uncle Bertie whispered in her ear. "They're also working for the agency."

"Why didn't you tell me?"

Bertie shrugged. "Need to know. And I was waiting to see if you would persist in becoming an agent, or if you would cry off. No point in telling you if you were going to bail out when things got tough."

Though she could see the logic in his explanation, it still irked her that he thought she would abandon the mission the moment things got difficult.

Mr. Pultney lit the wall sconces in the War Room, and Juliette dropped onto a chair. "For how long?"

The butler shrugged. "Nigh on thirty years, milady. Brought on to work with your father and to protect him and his family."

"And Mrs. Dunstan?"

"Nearly thirteen years now I've worked for the agency. I was placed into various households where I could easily pass along information to my superiors, and I've moved about a fair bit. The duke installed me here with your parents when he took over running things six months ago. Thought I might be useful, since there might be a new agent coming of age. Your mother agreed." She smiled, though not broadly, as she still nursed a split lip.

Juliette felt warmed inside. They had planned for her to take her place in the family business and had prepared someone to help mentor her.

The room was undisturbed, and the painting, the maquette, and the jade dragon were still there, in a row. Juliette's attempts to break the code hung on the wall. Each line was labeled with the artwork from which it had come, including the tapestries, which, thankfully, they had not needed to steal.

"What about the items you went in search of tonight, Uncle Bertie?" she asked.

"When I got to the museum, the papyrus and the alabaster eagle were gone. The display cases were smashed, the night guards scratching their heads, and the thief long gone."

The duke scowled. "Nothing else was taken? They didn't try to disguise what they were really after by stealing other things as well?"

"No. Most telling, isn't it? Whoever it is must be more concerned about getting the code than getting caught." Bertie's face was grim.

"How much of the code do they have now? Two or three lines? They can observe the tapestry codes if they know where to look, so we can assume the score, if you will, is nearly tied." Juliette pointed to her chart.

"What's left to obtain?" the duke asked. "And I shall dispatch someone to obliterate the code on those tapestries. No sense leaving them there for anyone to discover."

"Three things are left. A parure, a Shakespearian first folio, and a pair of silver candelabra." Bertie consulted the list pinned to the support post. "Two of those items were purchased by the same man, Lord Gravesend. The jewelry for his wife, the folio for himself." Bertie crossed his arms. "A straight-up theft, Marcus?"

The duke shook his head. "I know Lord Gravesend. That folio will be locked up tight. The only chance of seeing it is if he decides to show it to you." He turned to Juliette. "That's where you and my wife come in."

<hr />

"Is the break-in at the Thorndike house linked with the street robbery of Lady Juliette outside the auction house?" Ed Beck tipped back in his chair in the interview room Daniel had taken over for the investigation. "Which is linked to the theft of the Montgomery painting and the maquette by the Turner and Rathbone gallery, which is linked to the murder of John Selby?"

"It's too much of a coincidence to think it's somehow not all part of the same pattern." Daniel kneaded the back of his neck. In the four days since the break-in at the Thorndike house, they had chased every clue, each time ending in frustration and more questions.

The biggest lead, the mysterious Mr. Smith who was supposed to appear at the receiver's shop to retrieve the jade dragon, had failed to show. Ed had put one of his informants inside, posing as a shopworker, but the results had been a big fat nil. Had someone tipped him off that the dragon wasn't there and the police were?

"What are we missing?" Daniel asked for the hundredth time.

"Inventory lists from the gallery. Has Mr. Rickets come up with anything more? The man purchased all the items personally over a period of weeks on the Continent, and so far he has only been able to remember a few of the pieces?"

"He stopped by this morning." Owen straightened from his spot in the corner. "Brought another list with his apologies. Said he had given it some thought and wrote down what he could remember."

"Why didn't you say so? Where is it?" Irritation coated Daniel's voice. It had been a long day, and he had run out of patience. "Did you not think it was important, or were you waiting to bring it out when it was too late to do anything with it?"

Owen scowled. "You weren't here, nor was Mr. Beck. It's on your desk in the common room, properly dated and time-stamped."

Daniel's conscience niggled that he had unfairly snapped at the office boy, but he shoved it down. Owen was insolent and annoying, and Daniel wouldn't put it past him to withhold a crucial bit of information just to trip Daniel up.

But that was unfair. For all Owen's partiality and dislike of Daniel, he had never done anything to jeopardize a case.

To cover his feelings, Daniel left the incident room to fetch the paper from his desk. As Owen had claimed, it sat there front and center with the proper notations. He picked it up. More than thirty items were on the list; the painting, the maquette, the tapestries, and the jade dragon were all there.

There were no corresponding names of anyone who had purchased the items, but there were check marks and marginalia that read "Found destroyed in the gallery" beside several pieces.

Ed took the list and ran his finger down the column. He paused about a third of the way down. "Owen, please fetch the night sheets for the past week."

"Something interesting?" Daniel asked.

"Possibly."

They waited for Owen to return with the reports of crimes that had occurred in the last seven days, and when he did, Ed tapped one page. "There it is."

Daniel read where he pointed. "Burglary at the Platford Museum. Portion of Egyptian papyrus. Alabaster carved eagle statuette. No suspects."

"What's a papyrus?" Owen asked.

"It's ancient paper. This must be a portion of a scroll or document from Egypt." Daniel found the artifact on Rickets's list. "Pressed between two sheets of glass, acquired in Italy."

"And the eagle?"

"No details except it's carved from alabaster, which is a pale stone."

Two more pieces of artwork from the same shipment had been stolen. And on the same night as the break-in at the Thorndike house.

Ed was thinking along the same lines, for he asked, "Are these the same thieves who broke into the Thorndike house? To steal the jade dragon? It was part of the same shipment, from the same gallery."

"Possibly, but it seems more likely they are part of the same gang, since the break-ins happened at roughly the same time in different parts of the city. Was anything else stolen from the Platford?" Daniel asked.

Ed consulted the pages. "No. Just those."

"That's too much of a coincidence to be a coincidence. But why? Why those things in particular? Is this an elaborate attempt to ruin Turner and Rathbone? We've found no motive there. And nothing ties the artwork together except that it was purchased by Mr. Rickets in Europe at the behest of Mr. Selby. The pieces are all dissimilar. Of varying values. Different disciplines, subject matters, and several different clients. Some were bought on commission. Some were chosen for later resale." Daniel leaned against the table, crossing his ankles and bracing himself with his palms.

"They were bought by the same man, at the behest of the same art dealer, and shipped together from Genoa to London aboard the *Adventuress*."

"Have we checked on the ship or its crew? Perhaps someone saw or heard something?" Daniel asked.

"We can put Piggott and Fyfe on that in the morning, though the ship's probably long left port. Perhaps someone in the shipping office will have information. And Tolliver can follow up on the museum theft. I'm sure it's part and parcel of the pattern, but if it's anything like the rest of the robberies, there will be precious few clues. Still, we must do our due diligence. For now, I suggest we all go home and get some rest." Ed stood, pressing his hands into the base of his spine. "Some of us aren't as young as others." He gave a wry smile. "And the wife will be forgetting what my face looks like."

Guilt trickled through Daniel as he studied the list from Mr.

Rickets. It was easy to forget that Ed was married, that he had a life and family outside the walls of the Bow Street Magistrate's Court.

Daniel rented rooms in a boardinghouse a few minutes' walk from Bow Street. His landlady was a quiet gentlewoman who rarely said a word. Due to his unpredictable schedule, Daniel did not opt to include board with his room, and consequently he almost never saw his fellow boarders. His meals came from costermongers' carts or wayside inns or public houses.

What would it be like to return to a cozy home at night, to be greeted by a loving wife and children? He, who had lived in schools and colleges for years, and before that in servants' quarters and dilapidated accommodations his mother could get for near to nothing.

His mother. With a tight gut, he remembered her split lip, pale skin, and the way she refused to meet his eye. Anger burned bright, because that avoidance mirrored exactly how she had behaved when the solicitors had come to take him away as a boy.

She had turned her back on him.

"Swann."

Daniel looked up. Sir Michael, in evening dress and satin-lined cloak, stood in the doorway.

"Sir?"

"My office." He turned on his heel and disappeared.

Daniel sighed, bracing himself. He'd had the investigation for over two weeks now, and he still had more questions than answers. Time was escaping, and soon he would be twenty-five and his patronage, and probably his employment, would cease. If he was leaving Bow Street, he didn't want to go out with a loss on his record.

Sir Michael draped his evening cloak over the end of his desk and removed his white gloves. "I was across the street, taking in an opera with the Home Secretary, and I thought I would look in. While I admire your diligence in working late, I question your outcomes. Where are you on the case?" He sat in his green leather desk chair, and the springs squeaked.

"There have been some developments, sir. We've linked the theft of the painting to several other art thefts and to the murder of the art dealer. Last night two more pieces were stolen, this time from a museum. Thus far, five stolen pieces have been reported, with one item being recovered and returned to its owner."

"Do you have a suspect?"

"No, sir, not yet. We're searching for commonalities and motives, but thus far, nothing has presented itself." Daniel stood with his hands clasped behind his back. "We'd—I'd like to request permission to send Piggott and Fyfe to the docks tomorrow to investigate that shipment and arrival of the artwork. Every piece reported stolen has come from the same cargo load. There must be something else that links them."

"What about the murder? Are you any further there?"

"Sir, we've found nothing from Mr. Selby's personal life that would provide a motive for murder. Certainly none of the common factors have been unearthed. He wasn't in financial difficulties, he had not had a romantic entanglement, and he got on well with his employers and employee. He led a quiet life, occasionally rubbing shoulders with members of the *ton* as he provided them with art and advice."

"Any particular members of the *ton*?"

"Mr. Montgomery, obviously, but Lord Gravesend, Lord Bickford, and surely more that we cannot identify at this time, because the paperwork was stolen from the gallery. We've pieced together what we can of what remains, but there isn't much that links the art to specific buyers." Which had to be key, or else why steal the information?

"Motive, means, and opportunity. It all goes back to the basics. Go over everything again, and I don't need to remind you, time is moving on. I want results. The Home Secretary wants results, and the members of the aristocracy want to feel they and their belongings are safe." He narrowed his eyes. "Keep Mr. Beck up to date on everything to do with the investigation. If things don't break soon, he'll become the lead investigator, and you will be looking for a new place of employment."

"We're doing our best, sir."

"Your best might very well not be good enough, Mr. Swann."

Daniel hated that he agreed with Sir Michael.

Chapter 13

"MARCUS CAN USUALLY GET WHATEVER it is he needs. Including a last-moment invitation to a party." Charlotte, the Duchess of Haverly, grinned at her husband as they climbed the stairs to Lord and Lady Gravesend's home. "I just wish he could give me more notice sometimes."

Uncle Bertie bumped Juliette's shoulder and offered his arm. "At least with you in attendance, we are not in need of the dowager's services tonight, Charlotte. I know she's your mother Marcus, and a lady, but frankly, she rubs me up the wrong way."

"She can have a rather abrasive effect on people." The duchess spoke over her shoulder as the door opened and noise and light spilled out. "I remind myself she hectors because she cares."

"Is she still angry with me?" Juliette asked.

"We've managed to soothe her ruffled feathers somewhat by explaining that she could hardly leave Miss Agatha Montgomery without a chaperone, and she could not be in two places at once, and wasn't it clever of her to think of sending a maid with you and remaining with Miss Montgomery, thereby averting disaster for all?" The duke grinned. "I credit her with brilliance whenever I can. It mollifies her, and she alters her narrative to fit."

Juliette laughed, both at his handling of his mother and from nerves. They had arrived, and for the first time, their partnership had swelled to a team. She still struggled to realize that the Duke and Duchess of

Haverly were involved in the spy game. How many members of the aristocracy were counted among their numbers?

Lord and Lady Gravesend stood at the doorway to the drawing room, greeting guests. "Your Grace, welcome. So delighted to have you." Lord Gravesend bowed. "And your lovely duchess. We're honored."

Lady Gravesend had a tight look about her mouth. Was it because her husband had turned up mere hours ago and announced four more for dinner? Or was she nervous at having such a high-ranking peer in her home? Lady Juliette made her greetings and followed the Haverlys into the drawing room.

But not before she noted the peridot and diamond necklace, earrings, bracelet, and bandeau adorning Lady Gravesend. The parure they had come to investigate. But how could they get close enough to the jewelry to examine it when it was being worn by the lady of the house? Juliette caught Bertie's eye, and he shrugged and made a "later" gesture.

Of the other dinner guests, six of the seven were unknown to Juliette, though the Haverlys greeted them familiarly. The one she recognized brought an easing of her tense shoulders. Duke Heinrich von Lowe crossed the space and bowed, taking her hand. He had a slight limp but otherwise gave no indication of his fall.

"I did not know you would be in attendance. I am most pleased." He kissed the air a mere inch above her knuckles.

"How are you? Better, I hope?"

"Much. The injury was not as bad as I feared, and Viscount Coatsworth recommended a physician here in London who was most adept at treatment. Though I would not win a footrace, I can get around without too much trouble. I am glad tonight's entertainment does not include dancing." He shrugged apologetically.

Juliette could see why the ladies of the *ton* thought him handsome, and while she did too, her feelings for him did not lead her to desire anything more than friendship.

"Uncle Bertie, this is Duke Heinrich von Lowe, of Brandenburg.

We have attended several social events together, including the opera and the past Monday's hunt, though I confess it seems a long time ago that we were on horseback together. So much has happened in the interim."

Uncle Bertie looked the duke over, shook his hand, and turned away when Marcus asked him a question.

"Did something happen at the Hunt Ball? Was Mr. Swann not there to see after you?" The duke's brows came down.

"Oh, he was most attentive and helpful. It's just that we received word that my parents' house was broken into, and the detective accompanied me back to London to see to things. It's been a rather long week, what with checking to see what might have been stolen and helping our staff who had been injured."

"Thievery again? I had no idea London was such a lawless place. Many of the social events I have attended have also been the target of lawbreakers. It is most displeasing. Nothing like that would be allowed to flourish in my family's territory. We take a rather stern view of outlaws, and the punishments are most severe."

Juliette tapped her fan in her palm. "There does seem to be a rash of events, doesn't there? I wonder who could be behind it all?"

"Whoever it is, I hope that Detective Swann gathers them up soon."

Lord Gravesend and his wife moved around the room, and Juliette admired the lovely jewels twinkling around the lady's neck. Peridot was an unusual stone for a parure set, which in Juliette's eyes made them all the more beautiful. And Lady Gravesend's dark-green velvet gown accented them beautifully.

She twisted the garnet ring on her own finger, remembering her mother wearing the Thorndike sapphires. Thankfully, the thieves hadn't been able to open her father's safe. Though she was certain they had come for the jade dragon, they would not have been able to resist such a prize as those sapphires.

When would she see her mother wearing them again? Were her parents really all right, working to some plan of their own? And how would she feel when she saw them again? Why couldn't they at least send word? Uncle Bertie and the Duke of Haverly seemed unconcerned. Was it because they knew something she didn't? And could she spend a lifetime working for the government and keeping secrets from some, sharing them with others, and having to decide which was which? Would she ever be required to keep secrets from her parents? And eventually from her husband? Where was the line one would draw between truth and lie? Her mother had always urged her to honor God and be truthful. How did one keep secrets and still be truthful?

"Shall we go in to dinner?" Lord Gravesend asked.

Then began the ritual of pairing up according to rank. Lady Gravesend had clearly prepared and matched dinner partners quickly. Lady Juliette found herself on the arm of a Lord Highsworth, who was at least thrice her age but pleasant. When they were seated, she found herself across the table from Duke Heinrich.

Down the way, Charlotte, as the ranking woman present, sat beside their host, and Juliette studied her. She was an agent for the Crown, but only since her marriage. With an ease Juliette envied and wondered if she'd ever acquire, the duchess conversed with Lord Gravesend.

By the time the third course had arrived, Juliette wondered if they would ever get to the germane topic. She responded to her dinner partners and ate the food, but all the while she pondered how to get her hands on the code fragments in this very room and elsewhere in the house.

"I understand you captured quite a prize recently," the Duke of Haverly said. "Congratulations. A first folio from the Bard himself."

Lord Gravesend swelled a bit. "I never imagined I would get it, but when the opportunity to purchase arose, I couldn't say no."

"I was so happy for him," Lady Gravesend said. "He's admired the works of Shakespeare for as long as I've known him, and though he's collected rare manuscripts for years, the Shakespeare folio is the crowning jewel of his library."

"Speaking of jewels, yours are stunning," Charlotte said. "Most becoming. Are they family pieces?" Though she knew they were not.

"Oh, no, they were a gift from Harold, a sort of thank-you for supporting him in buying the manuscript." Lady Gravesend touched the necklace and beamed down the table to her husband. "He's always spoiling me. These came from Austria, I believe."

"Where did you unearth the Shakespeare manuscript?" Uncle Bertie asked. He raised his wineglass and took a long drink.

"I have some early copies of some of his plays. I love the dramas especially and *Hamlet* in particular. We saw *Hamlet* performed last Season, and I was transfixed. That night at the theater, I was approached by a man who works for Turner and Rathbone in Clerkenwell. He said he had heard I was a collector." Lord Gravesend's eyes glowed with his passion. "He said he had heard of a folio of Shakespeare's plays, the 1623 edition, at a book dealer's in France, and if I was interested, he would send his buyer to the owner with an offer." He speared a piece of grouse with his fork. "I gave him a generous limit as to what I would spend, and he was able to negotiate a good price. With the rest, he purchased, on my orders, a little something for Hester."

A "little something" like hundreds of pounds worth of jewels? He must have spent a packet on Shakespeare.

"My countess would love to see the folio. She's got an affinity for books," Haverly said. "She's been through my library in the country and is now making her way through the books at our townhouse. I've some rare editions, but nothing as spectacular as a first folio." He raised his glass toward his wife.

"Of course, if you're interested." Gravesend sat up a bit straighter. "I don't like to bore people with my hobbies, as I know they are not everyone's taste, but I'd love a chance to show it off."

Juliette's muscles eased. If she and Charlotte could find the code, they wouldn't have to steal the manuscript.

It was the jewels that presented the larger problem.

After dinner, Lord Gravesend led them back to the drawing room, where Lady Gravesend had prepared some card tables. "We'll begin the games, dear, while you show off your manuscript to those who wish to see it." She patted her husband's arm. "Don't be long."

Juliette joined Charlotte, her husband, Uncle Bertie, and Duke Heinrich.

Lord Gravesend practically skipped down the passageway to his library. "I'll have to ask you to wait in here while I retrieve it. It's too valuable to leave on a bookstand where all can see it."

Lamps were lit, and the smell of leather and paper and ink surrounded them.

Charlotte went to the nearest bookshelf and trailed her fingers over the spines, as if greeting friends. "This room is magnificent."

It was, too, with two stories of bookshelves. A gallery led around the upper story, reached by a pair of spiral staircases, one at each end of the room. Library ladders hung from brass rails along the crown molding, and large, comfortable chairs beckoned someone to sink into them with one of the volumes and escape into the pages.

Duke Heinrich took a slow stroll about the library, his hands clasped behind his back. Uncle Bertie followed his movements, and Haverly leaned against a desk, watching his wife with an indulgent smile on his face.

In a few moments, Lord Gravesend reappeared carrying a navy-blue box. "I am thrilled that you all wish to see my treasure. I'll tell you a bit about it. It was once in The Bodleian Library, but in the 1660s they decided to purchase a newer edition—the third, possibly—and remove this one from the collection. You'll see," he said as he set the box on the blotter of the desk, "that there is a hole in the binding where the book was once chained to the shelf. All the books, being so precious at the time, were locked by chains to the shelves, and to take one down, you had to unlock the row." He opened the flap on the box and revealed a rather nondescript, if large, brown leather tome.

Juliette's heart sank. She hadn't realized the book would be so big. How could they search the entire folio in the few minutes they had?

Lord Gravesend removed the book and placed it in a velvet-lined trough. "I had this specially made for the folio. The leather is understandably brittle after so many years, and the binding is fragile."

He opened to the first pages, and a portrait of William Shakespeare greeted them.

Mr. Shakespeares Comedies, Histories, & Tragedies.

'Published according to the True Original Copies.'

Charlotte stepped forward first. "May I?"

"Of course, with all care."

Gently she touched the heavy paper that bore age spots and ripples from former dampness. Slowly but rhythmically she turned the leaves. Juliette joined her.

"I love how books are created," Juliette said, touching the stitched binding that showed in some places, but in reality, looking into the gutter of each page to see if someone had penned a bit of code where the pages met. Charlotte concentrated on the printing itself.

They were no more than a dozen pages in when Uncle Bertie yawned. "That's a fascinating book, no doubt about it, but what say we all go play some whist? I'm feeling bold tonight."

Juliette straightened. They had more than a hundred pages to look through. Why was he rushing them from the room?

"Are you sure?" Haverly asked. "It's a once-in-a-lifetime chance to view something this special. I'd hate to deprive Charlotte or Juliette of the opportunity."

"I'm sure. A book's a book's a book at the end of the day."

Uncle Bertie's ennui irritated Juliette. Was this another of his plots and ploys?

He tapped the blue box the book had arrived in, his fingers moving erratically.

"Of course." Haverly touched his wife's arm, and she nodded, regret in her eyes. "Shall we join the others?"

Charlotte stepped back, smiling at Lord Gravesend. "Thank you for allowing us to see your treasure. Perhaps we can visit in the future to enjoy it again."

Duke Heinrich, who had waited to the side, bowed slightly. "I would like an opportunity, if you please. I will rejoin you in a few moments, *ja?*"

"Your Grace, why don't you escort the ladies back for the gaming, and I'll wait with Duke Heinrich," Lord Gravesend said. "He can take a look, and then I'll lock the book up again."

When they reached the passageway to the foyer, Uncle Bertie said, "The code was on the box, not the book. Under one of the straps. I need paper and pen before I forget it."

"There's bound to be paper and ink at the gaming tables to keep score," Charlotte offered.

They joined the card players, partnering up, and Juliette noted Uncle Bertie tucking a scrap of paper into his coat pocket. They were halfway through their first game when Duke Heinrich and Lord Gravesend reappeared.

"An amazing find. And in fair condition for so old a book." The duke flipped the tails on his coat out before he sat. "I could have looked at it for much longer."

Juliette agreed. She played a card, taking the trick, and Lady Gravesend applauded. The diamonds and peridots winked from her wrist, neck, and ears. So near Juliette could touch them.

How were they going to get a closer look?

"I hope you're ready for this." Uncle Bertie, clad all in black, guided her through the dark streets.

She did too. Her heart fluttered and skipped as she followed him through twisting mews, keeping to the shadows. Her feet, clad in soft slippers, made no sound, but they ached with cold. Her dress was pure cotton, black as ink, that made no rustle like silk might have, and it absorbed what little light came from the moon.

"I got a rough layout of the house from our visit tonight, but I've no idea where Lady Gravesend might keep her jewels. The folio was kept in a secure location somewhere outside the library, a safe or strongbox, so the jewels might be in the same place." Bertie drew her back into an alcove and pressed his finger to his lips.

Footfalls and the creaking of metal echoed off the cobbles. A circle of yellow light appeared, glowing from a lantern. A night watchman trudged by, his breath puffing out in the cold air. The handle of his lantern scraped and squealed as he walked, his head down.

When he had passed, Juliette let out her breath.

"Most night watchmen are good men, but they fall into a routine and pattern. You can often time it so you don't encounter them. They see the same buildings and streets over and over, and unless something is quite out of the ordinary that draws their attention, they don't notice. Boredom and routine are the death of perception and sharpness." Bertie led the way again.

He'd been explaining and teaching since they'd slipped from their home at two o'clock, a mere hour after they'd left the Gravesend party.

"Three o'clock is the best time for breaking in. The occupants have often retired and are in deep slumber by then. The household staff has cleared away from the evening's events, and after what would have been a very long day for them, are asleep. Night watchmen are cold and bored and unobservant at that hour, and the moon has waned, so there is less chance of being seen."

They neared the back of the Gravesend house. "How are we going to get in?"

"I'm going to climb." Bertie stopped beneath a deep overhang, studying the townhouse. One of a dozen on this street. Each had stables in the rear, with a place for a carriage and housing for grooms and coachmen.

Bertie pointed to a drainpipe attached to the brick. "I unlatched that first-floor window before we left, and I put a wad of paper into the latch to keep it from closing correctly. I'm hoping that with the late night, the butler didn't do a thorough check of all windows and doors, and that if he did, the latch appeared locked. When I get in, I'll come downstairs and open that door. You wait here out of sight, and don't worry if it takes me awhile. Moving quietly always takes longer than you think. Once we're inside, we'll split up and see what we can find. You focus on the downstairs, and I'll take the Gravesend bedchambers. If you find something you can't manage to unlock, wait for me to come to you. If you find the folio, obliterate the code. If you find the jewels, pocket them. Whatever you do, don't go in search of me. And if you hear noise from upstairs, get out of the house and back home. Don't worry about me. I'll be fine. Whatever happens, you must not be apprehended. Do you understand?"

He gripped her shoulder, his dark eyes glittering.

"I understand." She clutched the pocket on her cloak where the lock picks resided. "I'll be careful."

Slipping away like a mist, Uncle Bertie approached the house, and without making a sound, he shinnied up the drainpipe like a spider. Juliette held her breath as he reached the window. With great agility, he leaned out and raised the sash. It whispered up with the slight creak of wood on wood, and he disappeared inside.

Juliette waited, counting in her head, imagining him creeping along the hallway, down the stairs to the ground floor, through the service areas of the house, and finally to the back door. Then she added more time for stealth. He should be coming now.

Nothing.

She let a few more seconds tick by.

The door remained stubbornly closed. He had said to be patient, that it would take him some time, but it seemed an eternity since he'd entered. Had he been caught? Had he forgotten about her?

At last the door separated from the frame a crack. Relief crashed through her even as tension tightened. She was going to do this. It was real. She, a debutante from a respected family, was going to break in and rob people who had entertained her in their home.

God, how can this be right? I can't even ask Your protection and guidance, because this feels so wrong.

She eased across the cobbles, looking up and down the mews and seeing no one. Uncle Bertie stood just inside the door, and he closed it but left it off the latch. "Always leave your escape path free in case you have to leave in a hurry. I'm sorry it took so long. The stairs creak terribly."

They crept through the kitchen. A scullery maid slept on a pallet near the stove. She couldn't be more than twelve or thirteen summers, and she didn't move as they passed her.

Up half a short flight of stone stairs, and Uncle Bertie pushed aside the door that separated the service areas from the rest of the house. As Juliette entered the part of the house she had seen earlier that evening, she mapped it out in her mind.

"You find his study, and I'll head upstairs." Uncle Bertie edged to the wall, stepping where the treads were the strongest and least likely to creak. Like Juliette, he wore soft shoes that made no marks or sound.

With no candle or lamp, Juliette had to feel her way down the hall. She found a music room and a morning room, both doors standing open. Faint light came in through the tall windows, but it hovered near the glass and didn't penetrate the corners. She crept on. If she didn't find a study, she'd come back and examine those spaces more closely. At the end of the hall, she encountered her first locked door.

Kneeling, she dug the ring of skeleton keys from her pocket to try first. If none of them worked, she would use the lock picks. In the War Room with enough light and time, she had become adept at opening the various locks Uncle Bertie put before her, but now, with freezing fingers, tight muscles, and the threat of discovery, her hands fumbled.

Sorting through the keys, she chose one and inserted it. Wriggling and manipulating produced no results, and she moved to the next, shutting her eyes to concentrate. This time the lock opened with such ease, she didn't realize it at first.

She turned the handle, smothering a shaky laugh and opening her eyes.

The room had two tall windows that looked out on the street. Light from the streetlamp on the corner slanted across a desk, a rug, and a pair of tall chairs set before a fireplace. A screen had been placed before the fire, and the glow from the coals stood out red in the darkness.

Certain her heart had taken up permanent residence in her throat, she tried to swallow. Her father had a safe in the wall. Did Gravesend follow that leaning too? She tried the drawers on the cabinets, each one sliding out easily. Papers in neat files and bundles. A few rolled charts and ledgers.

The wall cupboard in the corner opposite the door was next, and this had a sizeable lock. Once again she employed her skeleton keys, but none fit. She resorted to the picks. The coals in the fireplace collapsed and settled, and she nearly went straight up into the air. Cold as it was, a trickle of sweat glided down her temple, and she wiped it away on her shoulder.

How was Uncle Bertie faring? He must be faster than she, with so much practice. Why wouldn't these tumblers fall into place?

The whisper of a shoe on carpet brought her up straight. Though it frustrated her that she hadn't been able to get this lock open by herself, at least Uncle Bertie could help her. She removed her tools from the lock, and at the last minute, as she turned toward the door, a shiver scampered up her spine.

What if it wasn't Uncle Bertie?

Better to be safe than sorry. She slipped behind the heavy drapes to the right of the cabinet. Every muscle knotted, she waited, peeping through the opening in the curtains.

The door eased back by increments. A small candle entered first, held in a gloved hand.

Uncle Bertie would never use a candle. She froze until she felt light-headed. *Breathe, or you'll faint.* She looked down to make certain her hem and shoes were hidden by the curtains, pressing back against the cold windowpane and thankful the drapes reached the floor.

"It's got to be in here. It wasn't in the library." The whisper, a man's, crawled across Juliette's skin. Not Uncle Bertie.

"Look around then. We've been here too long already. I don't like finding the back door open. It's almost like someone was laying a trap for us."

There were at least two of them. Who were they? Were they the same two who had broken into Juliette's house and injured Mrs. Dunstan? Her heart pounded in her ears, and her hands fisted, the lock picks poking her palm. What should she do? What if they found the jewels before she did?

What if Uncle Bertie crossed their path without knowing they were here?

File drawers slid open, and soft noises came from the area where Gravesend's desk sat.

"Anything?"

"No, you? He said it was as big as a tea chest. A blue box with hasps."

They were after the folio.

And they knew it was in a protective box and what color that box was. They had been informed by someone who had seen it firsthand.

One drew near to her hiding place. "It's as black as the inside of an ink bottle in here. I wish we could open the drapes and let in a little light."

Panic twisted through Juliette, and she closed her eyes.

"You won't let in enough to be worth it, and the candlelight would shine like a beacon to any night watchman passing by, you simpleton. What about that cabinet?"

Shuffling, a small thump, and a grunt. "It's locked."

"How secure? Can you force it?"

A rattle and a knock. "Not without making a lot of noise."

"We've looked everywhere on this floor. What if he keeps it upstairs?"

"Maybe we should break the lock, grab what's inside, and run for it? It will make some noise, but we can be out of the house before anyone gets down here."

"And what if the book isn't in there?"

"We'll tell him we couldn't find it. I already told him we could go after the book, but he was out of his head if he thought we could nab the book and the jewels at the same time. Not unless they were sitting together on the dining room table."

"I don't like this. We've been here too long as it is. Break the lock, and let's make a run for it."

What should I do? What should I do? What would Mother do? God, what should I do? Help me!

"Eh? Who's there?" A quavery voice sounded from the hall. "Is that you, Hester?"

Lord Gravesend? Calling for his wife?

A scuffling, bumbling sound of bodies hitting one another came from the other side of the curtain. Juliette dared a peek through the opening, and two dark figures collided in the doorway in their haste to get out, the candle in one of their hands dropping to the floor and going out. Heavy footsteps, a crash, and a door slamming.

A dark figure appeared in the doorway as Juliette reached to part the curtains, and she froze.

"Juliette, come with me now."

Uncle Bertie. She was so relieved, she wanted to cry. She hurried to him, and he grabbed her hand, pulling her down the hallway toward the front doors. "We can't go out the back. Those oafs must surely have wakened the entire staff with their plowing about."

They dashed through the front door, running down the street for half a block before Uncle Bertie slowed her to a walk. "Act calmly. If anyone stops us, we're an *accoucheur* and midwife coming home from a birthing."

Since Juliette didn't know the first thing about delivering a baby, she prayed no one would ask. How did he come up with these cover stories so easily?

"What happened?" Uncle Bertie led them diagonally across a square, hurrying over the grass under the bare branches of winter trees.

She told him in gasps, still breathless. "They were after the folio, and someone had described not only the book but the box."

"Lord Gravesend hasn't been shy about showing the folio to people, but how many could have seen it in the fortnight or so since he acquired it? You and I, and Marcus and Charlotte, for certain."

"And Duke Heinrich."

"Yes." Uncle Bertie walked quickly.

"I was near to getting that cabinet open, and I feel certain the book was in there. And probably the jewels too." Disappointment dragged at her. "We were so close."

Bertie pulled her into a shadowed nook as the night soil wagon trundled by. The odor smacked her in the face, making her gag. The job of shoveling out privies was considered so foul, the work could only be done under cover of darkness.

When the wagon had passed, Bertie released her arm. "We got close enough." He patted the pocket of his cloak. "The jewels were upstairs in Lady Gravesend's dressing room. Her maid was asleep on a cot, and I had just removed the last piece from the case when I heard a stair creak." They stepped out of the nook and continued along the street. "I was angry at first, thinking you hadn't heeded my warning about the stairs, when someone coughed, a male someone. It was time to get out of there, but I needed to find you first."

"I jumped behind the curtains when they came in. I thought it was you, but then I thought, what if it isn't? I didn't know what to do. Especially when they mentioned opening the drapes to let in some light."

"What would you have done?" he asked over his shoulder and she trotted to keep up.

"Hoped that I had surprise on my side, waited for the right moment, and then run for it. Neither looked to be physical specimens, and I believe I could have escaped and hidden outside. Better to have lost the opportunity to find the jewels than to be apprehended by fellow spies."

"You believe they were spies then, and not just thieves?"

She considered this, thankful to see they were nearing Belgrave Square and their home. "I believe we must proceed under the assumption that they are the henchmen of whatever spy sent men to break into our house and who arranged to steal the jade dragon after the auction. The same person who stole the papyrus and the alabaster eagle."

Arriving home, Juliette mounted the staircase to her chamber to lay aside her dark cloak.

Uncle Bertie left her at her bedchamber door. "Go to sleep. You can look at the code tomorrow. And brace yourself, because we'll probably get another visit from the police. We were dinner guests at a house that was burgled the same night. They're going to connect some points of commonality sooner rather than later, and we'll have to have a story ready."

Though she wanted to examine the necklace, she was so tired she could barely hold her eyes open. Tomorrow would be soon enough.

Tomorrow she might see Detective Swann.

And tomorrow she would have to lie to him . . . again.

Chapter 14

Daniel arrived at Bow Street feeling like a thundercloud. In spite of his exhaustion, he'd been unable to sleep. No matter which way he looked at it, nothing made sense. The office was buzzing along when he arrived at seven.

"Night reports are in." Owen slouched by. "I put them in the interview room this time."

"Is Mr. Beck here yet?"

"Came in. Went out. Said he'd be back soon."

"Fetch me some coffee, please."

The reports of which Owen spoke were the incidents of crime across the city, collected by night watchmen and citizens. He read through them, his heart heavy at so much lawbreaking. A woman attacked, a brawl at a tavern, a window broken, a store robbery. Every morning at least half a dozen crimes were reported.

His eyes locked on one line. Jewelry stolen from a house.

Scrabbling, he found the inventory sheets provided by Mr. Rickets.

There it was. Peridot and diamond parure, purchased in Denmark for a Lord Gravesend.

"Why do I feel," Ed said from the doorway, "that we're chasing a wisp o' mist?" He closed the door, then blew on his hands. "It's cold as a miser's heart out there. I went by the museum and questioned the two watchmen who were working the night of the theft. They reported that they were together when the items were stolen. They were having a cuppa in the guards' room, and they heard glass breaking. Went to investigate, and someone had thrown a rock through a window in the front of the building. Nothing damaged but the windowpane, but a few moments later, they heard more glass. Thought it was another window, but found it was a display case. The thieves came in through a cellar door. Broke the hasp with a pry bar. The watchmen never saw them."

Daniel pulled out a chair. "It's almost like we're chasing two different thieves. One is clumsy and brazen, robbing a lady on the street of her newly purchased auction item, breaking into that same lady's house and threatening her staff but not stealing anything, and now smashing glass and breaking door locks. But the other thefts are more . . . delicate? Precise? Nicking a painting in the middle of a debutante ball without anyone seeing. Stealing a statue from a crowded house with a cleverly designed and executed distraction that no one would see as deliberate. And you'll never guess. The jewelry from the art list? It was stolen last night. I'm heading to the scene now."

Ed reached for the door handle. "Which group murdered Selby?"

"The killing was chaotic and unplanned, and the damage to the gallery was substantial and appears indiscriminate, more rage than anything. But the theft of the paperwork was meticulous and thorough. Only items related to purchases made over the years was taken."

"Are we looking at two people from the same outfit but vastly different personalities and motives? Or are we looking at two different people with opposing motives and personalities?" Ed stepped onto the street and held up his hand.

Cadogan appeared, as if he'd been waiting for them at the end of the block, Lola and Sprite snorting and blowing. "Morning, gents. Where to?"

At the Gravesend residence, his lordship vacillated between irate and distressed, while Lady Gravesend sat like a stone statue at the end of the table.

"Never in my life has anyone invaded the sanctity of my home and stolen from me. We have locks on our doors. What are night watchmen for if they cannot keep subjects of this realm safe?"

"Sir, where were the jewels kept?"

"Last night they were in my wife's dressing room. Our valuables are usually kept in a locked box in a locked cabinet in my locked office, but last night it was so late when we said goodbye to our guests, my wife left them in her dressing room to be put away in the morning."

Lady Gravesend let out a small moan and put her hand to her trembling lips. Her husband rounded the table and clasped her shoulder. "It wasn't your fault, Hester. We should have been able to leave them on the parlor table overnight if we so chose. This is our house."

Daniel looked from the corner of his eye at Ed. Lord Gravesend's naivety had been punctured. Amazing that it had taken this long.

"Sir, was anything else stolen?"

"No, thankfully, though it appears they tried. I recently acquired a Shakespearian first folio, and though the cabinet where it was kept showed some marks that they attempted to get in, they didn't manage it."

Stiffening, Daniel consulted his notebook, flipping back through the pages to where he had copied the list from Mr. Rickets. "A first folio? Did you purchase it through Turner and Rathbone?"

"Yes. How did you know?"

"Sir, we're investigating a string of thefts connected to that business."

Lord Gravesend snapped his fingers. "Mr. Montgomery's Lotto painting?"

"Among other pieces, yes."

"So this wasn't a random theft? A housebreaker didn't decide to come in and see what they could find?" Lady Gravesend asked. "We were . . . targeted?"

"Milady, who knew about the jewels?" Ed asked.

"Last night was the first evening I had worn them. We had guests over for a party. I was so happy." Her fingers drifted toward her collarbone, as if she could feel the weight of the necklace still. "Before that I told no one. My personal maid knew of course, but she's been with me for more than ten years, and I trust her. She would never betray me."

"You hosted a party? Who attended?" Why were these people constantly entertaining? They opened their doors to all sorts, and showed off their treasures, and then were shocked when someone broke in to steal. Daniel held his pencil poised over his notebook to list the guests, but his mind hopped and skipped, reminding him of his lack of sleep and lack of results.

"Just a few friends. It was going to be small and intimate, just eight including us, but at the last minute . . ." She turned to look up at her husband, who stood behind her. "There were some additions."

Daniel raised his brows.

"Well, it seemed impolite not to invite them. He's a duke, after all." Gravesend pulled out a chair beside his wife and sat, lacing his fingers on the polished surface. "I ran into the Duke of Haverly at the club. I was telling Fotheringham about the folio, and I suppose I was going on a bit, but I was that excited. It's the find of a lifetime." His fingers tightened. "Haverly overheard, and he asked about it, very interested. To be honest, I was flattered to have someone of his rank impressed by something I owned. I asked him if he would like to come round to see it, and I invited him and his wife to dinner. When he said he would love to, but would I mind if the invitation also included two of his friends, because he had made dinner plans with them, and he told me who they were, I was delighted. Sir Bertrand Thorndike and Lady Juliette, his niece. Respectable people who would certainly be a pleasure to host."

A sinking feeling started in Daniel's gut.

"Did any of your guests show an interest in the jewels?" Ed asked.

Gravesend frowned. "No. Beyond a compliment here and there. You aren't suggesting that one of our dinner guests was responsible for this? That's preposterous. They're quality. None of them would have need of the jewels. They could buy diamonds if they wanted them."

But stealing them might be more fun. Daniel had suspected the thief might be stealing for the thrill of it or from some compunction rather than for monetary gain.

"Some of the guests were much more interested in the book than my baubles. Harold took them into the library and brought the book from his study to examine. The others came back fairly quickly, but I did wonder if Duke Heinrich would return in time to play cards at all." Lady Gravesend reached over and put her hand on her husband's wrist. "When you get talking about your passion for collecting old manuscripts, you can go on a bit."

He covered her fingers with his as if acknowledging the truth of her statement. "But he asked such interesting questions, time got away from us. The countess and Lady Juliette were intrigued at first too, but Sir Bertrand grew bored rather quickly. There doesn't seem to be much substance to that man. Unlike his brother, the earl, who has as keen a mind as any I've encountered, Sir Bertrand seems more interested in drink and idleness."

Daniel and Ed were shown through the house, both the lady's dressing room where the velvet-lined box that had contained the parure set lay empty, and the cabinet in the study that had nearly been breached.

"The slam of the back door awoke you?" Daniel consulted his notebook, trying to envision what had occurred.

"Actually, I believe it was a creak of a stair. When winter damp sets in, the wood swells and the stairs do moan and groan a bit. I thought I heard a sound on the stairs, and I sat up, but after a while of hearing nothing, I lay back down." Lord Gravesend jiggled the door on the locked cabinet. "I was almost asleep again when I heard a door slam. I'm sure it was the back door, but when I came downstairs, the front door stood open too. I went right to my study to check on the folio. There was a stub of candle on the floor in this doorway, and the scratch marks you can see here. I was so relieved that the manuscript was still inside. I and the footman who had also been roused locked the doors and checked the windows. There was a window in the upper hallway unlocked, but I don't think that's significant. With the doors open, who would climb up to get into a window? We returned to our beds. It wasn't until first thing this morning that my wife reported that her jewels were gone. We sent for a watchman, and he said he would report it to you."

"Do you think you'll find my jewels?" Lady Gravesend asked. "They were a gift."

"We'll do our best, ma'am." Ed touched his hat brim. "We'll be in touch."

When they stood on the pavement, Daniel caught Ed's eye. "It's too much to overlook. I think the guest list narrows our focus."

"But what is the motive? Like Gravesend said, they're all as rich as Croesus. Why steal when you can purchase?"

"Opportunity first, then figure out the motive. That's what you've always taught. If a person didn't have the opportunity to commit the crime, nor the means, then the motive doesn't matter," Daniel reminded Ed.

"I'm glad you've taken so many of my lessons to heart, but I don't like where this investigation is leading."

"Neither will Sir Michael." And neither did Daniel, if he was honest. Were one or more of the Thorndikes behind the thefts?

Ed took his leave at the corner, heading to question a few receivers' shops and fences to see if the jewels had turned up there, but more to cross it off the list than from any real hope of finding them.

On the ride back to the office, Daniel stared out the window, seeing nothing of the buildings flashing by.

Lady Juliette Thorndike had been at many of the places where a piece of artwork from Rickets's list had disappeared. She had been in proximity to nearly every piece that had gone missing. Was her uncle using her, a debutante, to get to the artwork?

Or was she a willing participant? The thefts had started shortly after her arrival back in this country, after all.

At the office he went to the interview room they'd commandeered.

Surely Lady Juliette had not stabbed Mr. Selby in the heart with a dagger. The idea was ludicrous, both from a character standpoint and a physical one. The coroner had said the attacker was taller than Mr. Selby and that the blow would have taken great strength. Neither of which he could ascribe to Lady Juliette.

Relief at his reasoning had him finding a chair. He propped his elbows on the table and studied the charts he'd pinned to the wall.

He might have been able to rule out Lady Juliette as a murderer, but did that absolve her of theft? What could possibly be her motive? She didn't need money. The Thorndike fortune was well known. She had an alibi for the museum break-in that was unassailable since she had been with him at the time. And she certainly hadn't robbed herself outside the auction house. She'd only just arrived in the country from the Continent. Was there a connection there? Had she been in contact with Rickets while the buyer was in Europe?

"Owen!" His shout rang down the hall. Noise in the office wasn't looked upon favorably, as detectives worked and court was held upstairs, but this time he felt an urgency that laid aside the rules.

The office boy stuck his head into the interview room. "What?"

"Send round to the Turner and Rathbone gallery for Mr. Rickets. I want him in this room without delay."

The office boy straightened, his eyes sparking interest. "You're sending me? To bring in a witness?"

"Unless you think the job is beyond you. Go." Daniel waved toward the front door.

Owen snapped a salute and vanished.

Bemused, Daniel shook his head. Did Owen secretly aspire to being a Bow Street investigator? Could that be the key to winning him over, giving him more responsibility than fetching coffee and reports?

He surveyed the stacks of paperwork, charts, lists, and maps they had collected over the last three weeks. With the days passing quickly until his patronage ended, would he solve the case in time? Would he be here next month to worry about Owen's moods?

Drawing out a new piece of paper, he wrote the questions he wanted to ask Mr. Rickets. The precise path of his travels, the order of purchases, any contact he might have had with Lady Juliette. Had he ever met Sir Bertrand?

He left room for other suspects because there were several who had been present at many of the same social gatherings. Miss Agatha Montgomery. Viscount Coatsworth. Even the Dowager Duchess of Haverly had been present at more than one activity. Not to mention Duke Heinrich. The night the Thorndike house had been broken into and Daniel's mother frightened, the duke had been absent from the Hunt Ball. What if his "injury" was a sham and he'd used it as a decoy to return to London to search the Thorndikes' house?

Did the German duke suspect that the Thorndikes were somehow involved? Had he searched their house for the stolen items because he knew they had been taken by Lady Juliette or her uncle?

Or had the man who wanted the dragon and sent thugs to rob Lady Juliette of it merely tried again to obtain it?

Was he looking for reasons for it not to be Lady Juliette because he liked her?

Perhaps it was time to lay a trap. With one item left on Rickets's list, he was almost out of bait.

"Mr. Rickets wasn't there. Not at the gallery and not at his house. When the landlord let me in, his place was destroyed. Looks like there had been a fight. The neighbor said he heard a rumpus a few days ago, but he's hard of hearing and dotty besides, and he couldn't remember which day." Owen rubbed his nose. "I tried the other neighbors, but they knew nothing, and then I went to the gallery. It was locked up tight. The pub owner across the street said he hadn't seen Mr. Rickets in nearly a week, and nobody's been in or out of the place since the investigators finished with it. I went round to Mr. Rathbone's house, but he hasn't heard from Mr. Rickets either. The old man was distressed, stuck in his bed like he is, not knowing what's happening to his business. He's still very upset about Mr. Selby getting himself murdered, and to be honest, I don't know how much use Mr. Rathbone will be in the future. He's acting very queer, and ready for Bedlam if he doesn't come back to himself."

"That was most enterprising of you to consult at the owner's place." Daniel wanted to give Owen his due.

"Do you think we're likely to find Mr. Rickets's body somewhere? Fish it out of the river maybe?"

Daniel dreaded to think so. "Maybe with the gallery being shut and his boss murdered, he took a job elsewhere?" But Daniel wished he knew where the man was. If they did arrest a suspect, Mr. Rickets would be required to testify at a trial.

Ed came into the room. "The report from Piggott and Fyfe on their trip to the shipping office turned up nothing. The paperwork was all in order and the cargo signed for by Mr. Selby, and Mr. Rickets, just as he said, was not a passenger on the ship. But look who was." He set the paper down before Daniel and pointed to two names.

Agatha Montgomery.

Lady Juliette Thorndike.

"They traveled on the *Adventuress*, the same ship that brought the artwork from Genoa to London on January 31."

Daniel tightened his jaw, pressing his tongue against the backs of his teeth. Another connection.

The case was building brick by brick, and the time had come to admit what was staring him in the face.

Lady Juliette Thorndike was somehow mixed up in this mess, and her uncle Bertie was most likely a murderer in addition to being a thief. He had been absent from the debut ball, ostensibly too drunk to hit the ground with a hat, but what if he had been stealing a painting and then lying in wait for the art dealer and killing him?

"Who bought those silver candelabra from Selby? That's our next stop. We find out and we'll find our thieves and killers."

Chapter 15

"This is it. The final piece. At least, the final piece we can hope to get our hands on." Uncle Bertie tapped his fist against the edge of the desk. He was resplendent in evening dress, prepared for tonight's entertainment at the Barrington home.

Juliette studied the chart affixed to the War Room wall. The code had been written in a column on the left side of the large sheet of paper, and she'd cracked part of it.

Bertrand Thorndike.

Marcus Haverly.

Two of the strings of letters had yielded to her attempts. If the letters had been grouped in the same manner as the names, it would have been easier. She'd manipulated the code she had in every direction she could think of, but she couldn't make her parents' names emerge.

Though she'd teased out two names, they did little good, since it had been highly suspected that those names were present anyway. It was the others, the four bits of code they had, and the one they were hoping for tonight, that would provide valuable information.

The code for Bertie's name had been on the jade dragon. Marcus Haverly's on the painting. That left the folio, the maquette, the jewelry, and the tapestries, and whatever was on the candelabra at the Barringtons' tonight. Which held her parents' names? She prayed it wasn't the papyrus or the stone eagle, since those were out of reach.

"Anything new on the code front?" Bertie asked.

"No. The agent, Fournier, must have distrusted his courier greatly. The code is complex. The symbols and letters aren't consistent from one name to the next. It's like there's a new code for each name. The 'e' and 'h' symbols are not the same in your name and Marcus Haverly's. That and having all the letters grouped in clusters of five has complicated matters. If my father was here, I know he could crack it."

"Fournier wouldn't have anticipated being killed before he could finish the mission. But there you are. As agents, we make plans and we make contingencies, but in the end, we're really just doing the best we can. The courier must have been angry when he learned the list had been divided and secreted onto so many different pieces of art in order to prevent the exact thing the courier was hoping to do—steal the list and sell it. Now he's forced to search for the artwork and possibly have to decode it himself if he doesn't have the key."

"Do you think whoever this courier is, he's working with the buyer now to obtain the pieces, or is he working alone?" Juliette asked.

"Impossible to tell. If he's made contact with the buyer, they might be working together. We won't know for sure unless or until he's captured.

"As for tonight, we must be bold. With the break-in here and the theft at the museum, things are coming to a head. We can't hope to sneak into the Barringtons' later tonight and steal the candelabra. The newspapers are baying for blood and the entire *ton* is on alert to protect their valuables. The Barringtons' have decided to hire extra security. We're going to have to grab the candelabras at the first opportunity, because if we don't, someone else will. Whoever is on the other side of this feels more like a common thief than a spy. There's no finesse, no elegance to his moves. He's swift, brutal, and he hires muscle." Bertie rose. "Let's go."

With perfect timing, the dowager's carriage rolled to the curb as they reached the foyer. "Will the Haverlys be in attendance?" Juliette asked as she accepted help with her cloak.

"No. It's just us tonight. Watch everyone, and watch for our chance. We won't have much time. I'll take one of them, and you grab the other. Hopefully, we can both escape without notice."

"Is the risk of getting caught greater than the value of the list?"

"Do you want your parents' names in the hands of foreign operatives?"

Which was answer enough.

He tugged on his gloves and held open the front door for her to precede him. "If we're caught, I'll take the blame, say I coerced you into helping me. I'll say it was a prank or something. While I'm explaining to the police, you can examine the candelabra, get the code, and go to work on it. I'll rely on Marcus and the Home Secretary to get me out of Newgate."

Juliette joined the dowager in the carriage. Uncle Bertie was taking his own conveyance, as he had somewhere he wanted to stop first along the way.

"Good evening, Your Grace."

"Good evening. I hope you'll stay through the entire evening this time. While I appreciate that you were needed at home, it was awkward for me to have to explain your sudden absence from the Hunt Ball."

"I apologize again. Thank you for coming with me tonight. Are you well acquainted with the Barringtons?"

"I am." The dowager spoke as if it was a silly question. "They are most refined. He is the third son of an earl, and she the daughter of a bishop. I've been to several events at their residence, and each has been lovely."

"Is their house large?"

"Large enough."

Juliette could almost hear the dowager's scowl. She had hoped for information on the layout and size of the establishment so she could begin to formulate some sort of plan, but it was clear the dowager was not in a talkative mood—at least not about anything Juliette wished to know.

"Are you an accomplished musician? Tonight's festivities will be of a musical nature, and I always enjoy myself more if my companions also enjoy music."

"I play the pianoforte."

"Well?"

"Well enough." Juliette had turned the phrase back on the dowager.

After a pause, during which the dowager sniffed imperiously, she said, "I understand your mother is an accomplished pianist."

"That is so." Juliette felt a twinge of remorse at her terseness, since her mother would have found a way to be gracious, even to a woman as prickly as the dowager. "Though I do not play as well as she, I am considered competent."

"I suppose that is all that is required of a young lady these days. I had hoped to present several suitors to your parents when they return from their estate, but thus far no one has offered for you yet. The German duke seems to be expressing some interest. Are there others that I should know about?"

Duke Heinrich had been attentive, it was true, but not to the point of actually courting her favor.

The man who most interested her would send the dowager into a fit of the vapors if Juliette mentioned his name. Daniel Swann would not be considered a proper suitor.

What would her parents think? Not that Mr. Swann had exhibited any interest in her beyond the scope of his investigation, and in any case, she was engaged in actively deceiving him, something that would put paid to furthering their acquaintance. But he did intrigue her. He had risen above his background to make something of himself. He was learned, intelligent, and kind under that businesslike exterior. She remembered him sacrificing his coat for her the night she ventured into the rookery alone. How he had scolded her even as he made certain she was kept warm.

"There is no one, and at the moment, I am not seriously considering anyone. I'd like to spend this Season free to enjoy myself and not worry about marriage just yet."

The dowager sniffed again. She could say a dictionary's worth of words in that mannerism. "You should always be worried about marriage. An advantageous marriage is the entire purpose of having a debut season."

Their arrival at the party was unremarkable, though Juliette was tense and watchful. *Calm yourself, or everyone here will suspect something isn't right.* Before she knew it, she was seated on a spindle-backed chair in a pale-pink music room, listening to Boccherini and wondering where the candelabras were.

She could see very little of the musicians, a pianist and a flautist. Seated in front of her was a rather rounded woman with hair piled high and topped with ostrich feathers that cut off the view of anyone behind her. She wore an alarmingly bright-yellow dress and used a cane. When she spoke, it was with a heavy accent. Was she Austrian? German? Slavic?

Juliette shifted, surveying the room without calling attention to herself. Duke Heinrich, who sat on her right, tilted his head in silent inquiry, and she gave a polite smile.

Agatha, on her left, sat still as a statue, the model of deportment. Not only was she seated beside Viscount Coatsworth, but the viscount's mother was in attendance. Just how serious were things becoming there?

Juliette felt badly. She'd been so distracted that she had missed the exciting things happening to her friend. Notes and invitations had arrived at the Thorndike house from Agatha, but Juliette hadn't answered the last few. It was a sign of both Agatha's good nature and her preoccupation with Coatsworth that she had greeted Juliette with a hug instead of hurt feelings.

Once all this was over, she would make it up to Agatha.

Leaning forward ever so slightly, she looked down their row. The dowager was near the end, and with a sigh, she spied Uncle Bertie along the back wall. Now she could relax. He would be in charge, he would give her the signal, and he would help her when the time came.

Every muscle tightened. Near the door to the hall, Daniel Swann leaned against the wall, arms crossed, face formidable.

What was he doing here? Was Uncle Bertie aware? Was Mr. Swann alone? She turned the other way and found Mr. Beck in the opposite corner.

What did they know? What did they suspect? Was it a coincidence they were here? Perhaps they were hired as the extra protection Uncle Bertie had told her the aristocracy was hiring just now.

She faced forward, staring hard at the ostrich feathers. It was clear the candelabras were somewhere else in the house. Juliette was stuck in the middle of a row, and she could hardly excuse herself without causing a scene.

When she looked once more toward Uncle Bertie, she crossed glances with the dowager, who was frowning with a pinched mouth. She flicked her fingers toward the music, silently ordering Juliette to stop fidgeting and pay attention.

At last the performance concluded, and the guests applauded. When Juliette looked for Uncle Bertie, he was nowhere to be found.

And neither were the detectives.

Lady Barrington led her guests into the dining room, where refreshments had been laid on, and Juliette took her first look at their quarry. Magnificent silverwork adorned with a dozen candles each, the candelabras stood at least a foot and a half high. More than two feet if you counted the tapers, each anchoring an end of the buffet table.

How much did they weigh? And how on earth would she and Uncle Bertie get them out of the house unseen?

Impossible. She moved to the opposite side of the room to await Bertie's lead.

Agatha squeezed her arm. "Can you imagine? The viscount's mother has invited me for tea. At the home of the earl, her father-in-law. Alonzo says his grandfather is eager to meet me. He's not doing well, confined to a Bath chair, so our visit won't be long, but still." She squeezed again, her eyes sparkling. "If he approves, then . . ." She lowered her voice and put her lips close to Juliette's ear. "I think Alonzo will make a formal offer for my hand."

Juliette's mouth fell open. She had missed a tremendous amount if the viscount was on the verge of a proposal. "And you're happy about this? Of course you are. You're glowing. But what a whirlwind. You've only known each other—what is it?—three weeks? Aren't you moving quickly?"

The brightness dimmed in Agatha's expression, and she loosened her hold on Juliette's arm. "I thought you'd be happy for me. But you've been so distant lately. Like you're preoccupied or something. We were meant to share this Season, do everything together, but you've gone off on your own more often than not." She blinked, her blue eyes clouded with doubt. "The dowager is pleased, and my father is pleased. I had hoped you would be as well."

"Aggie, I am sorry. Things have been at sixes and sevens, but I am happy for you. Just surprised, is all. In a few days we can sit down and have a nice long natter, and you can tell me all about your visit to the earl's home." She touched her friend's gloved hand. "Please forgive my inattention."

With her customary generosity, Agatha brightened. "We can go to Gunter's."

"Even though it's just across the square from my parents' house, I haven't had a chance to go there yet. I'm glad we'll go together." Where was Uncle Bertie? And where were the Bow Street detectives? Juliette felt she was performing on two separate planes, the debutante and the secret agent. Pray she didn't cross her lines.

The woman in the yellow dress and feathers went by, leaning heavily on her cane. Her dress had many-layered skirts that Juliette imagined would hamper more than ease her movements. Perhaps they were the style in the woman's home country.

Uncle Bertie entered the crowded room, his movements lax, his hair falling into his face. Juliette straightened. He lurched toward her, a glassy expression in his eyes.

"Zhuliette," he slurred. Eye-watering fumes of alcohol wafted off him.

Agatha wrinkled her nose and stepped back while Juliette grabbed his arm to keep him from falling.

"Uncle Bertie, really? Again?" She put exasperation into her tone. "It's barely half ten."

"I'll talk to you tomorrow, Juliette. I should return to the dowager, I think." Agatha couldn't get away fast enough.

Bertie leaned on Juliette. "Get ready," he whispered against her ear. "For what?"

He blinked slowly, weaving as he straightened. "Ah, Mishter Shwann, how do you do?"

"Sir Bertrand. Lady Juliette."

Daniel Swann's truncheon hung from his wrist like a lady's fan but with more menace. He looked from her to the candelabras and back again.

Guilt writhed through her middle and made her fingers tingle.

"Good evening, Mr. Swann. I didn't expect to see you here tonight."

"A little extra security. It seems that parties to which you two are invited are vulnerable." He spoke with a clenched jaw. "And Sir Bertrand, you can drop the facade of being drunk. I saw you splash a little drink from your flask onto your lapel and muss your hair before you staggered in here. What are you two plotting?"

Juliette looked at Bertie.

Uncle Bertie took his time straightening, and he gripped Juliette's wrist as he took Mr. Swann's measure. "Plotting, sir?" The slur was gone from his words, and he brushed his hair back from his brow. "I beg your pardon."

"It's not my pardon you should be begging. It's the forgiveness of half a dozen of your friends whom you have robbed of their possessions, though why is beyond me. You're rich enough to buy those things many times over."

"Is there trouble here, Herr Swann?" Duke Heinrich spoke behind them. He held a glass and a plate of nibbles, his brows raised.

"Nothing that should concern you, Your Grace. Sir Bertrand, Lady Juliette, perhaps our conversation would be best held in private?" He nodded toward the door into the hall where his colleague, Mr. Beck, stood.

Juliette glanced about the room, but no one paid them any mind except Heinrich, who looked uncertain.

"There is nowhere to escape. Go quietly, and I won't be forced to clap you in darbies in front of all your friends."

Restraints? How humiliating. Juliette's shoulders drooped.

"What are the charges? Feigning drunkenness?" Uncle Bertie surveyed the room.

"For theft and murder. Sir Bertrand, if you will?" Mr. Swann motioned toward the door. "Lady Juliette?"

Before she could take a step, a thunderous crash filled the room. People jumped, and a lady screamed. The woman in the yellow dress lay on the floor, and she had apparently grabbed the tablecloth on her way down, yanking trays of food and the punch bowl to the floor.

Silver platters and bowls bounced across the parquet, and one of the candelabras teetered and rocked. A footman reached for it, but not before two or three of the lit tapers fell. Hands reached out to snuff the flames, and others to assist the woman.

As they sat her up, her ostrich feathers, broken and bruised, toppled, and her hair tumbled down her shoulder. Two men helped her to her feet, and she moaned and looked at her food-splattered dress.

"*Was fürein Chaos. Ich bin so beschämt,*" she wailed.

Duke Heinrich went to her side. "*Bist du verletzt?*"

Footmen began clearing up the scattered food, and Lady Barrington, with red cheeks, urged people to go into the drawing room.

Detective Swann held Juliette and Bertie back, waiting for the room to clear, but when about half the guests had followed their hostess, another commotion broke out.

Four rough-dressed men barged into the room, brandishing pistols. Their faces were covered with masks, and their hobnailed boots rang on the floor. Taking advantage of the upheaval, they strode through the guests, shoving aside those in their way.

One stayed by the door, his pistol pressed against Mr. Beck's temple, his grip firm on the policeman's arm. Two went right to the candelabras, grabbing them up, dumping the lit tapers into the punch bowl, where they snuffed with tiny sizzles. The fourth held his pistol on Mr. Swann . . .

Who had reached for his own pistol and now covered the thief. "Put it down."

"Not likely." The thief switched his aim to Juliette.

Her throat parched. The end of that pistol looked bigger than a cannon's mouth.

"You, come here." He crooked one finger. "The rest of you, stay put. And you," he ordered Daniel. "Throw your pistol into that punch bowl."

Daniel's fingers flexed on the pistol grip, his arm shaking.

"Hurry up. We're all armed, and someone's going to get hurt." There was a taunt in the robber's tone.

One of the men holding a candelabra swung his pistol, picking out a target.

Agatha.

Her face went pale, and her eyes welled. Viscount Coatsworth bravely stepped in front of her.

"Gentlemen," Duke Heinrich said, "take what you came for. No one will try to stop you. But leave the Fraulein here."

"The boss said it was to be her and no one else. She's our insurance against someone doing something stupid. Now move or I'll shoot. An old lady or a young one? And old man? Who do you think will volunteer?" He glared at the guests.

Juliette started forward, but Daniel grabbed her arm. "No."

"There's no choice here." She stared hard first at Daniel and then at Uncle Bertie. "You had better find me quickly."

Daniel's face hardened. She could see he had no real option. If he fired, he might kill one of the intruders, but then the other three would fire as well. How many would be wounded or killed? She watched the thoughts roll through his eyes as he looked from one man to the next. He made one last frustrated gesture before leaning to drop his gun into the punch. With a soggy plop, the weapon became useless.

The robber grabbed her upper arm, and keeping his pistol firmly against the base of her neck, he turned her around to back out of the room. His compatriots covered the crowd, carrying the candelabra. She passed the doorway, and Mr. Beck looked bleak. When the thief covering him pulled his pistol away from Mr. Beck's temple, a round, red circle remained behind.

The thieves gave her no chance to grab a cloak, rushing her down the stairs and into a waiting carriage.

Daniel waited mere seconds before heading after them, with Sir Bertrand on his heels. They stormed through the entrance hall, Ed joining them, and burst through the front doors.

"You're not going." Daniel pushed Sir Bertrand away as they descended the stairs.

"You cannot stop me." Dodging, Sir Bertrand eluded another shove and bounded down the steps. "You're wasting time."

Cadogan's hack stood at the curb, and they leapt aboard. "Follow the carriage that just left."

Half hanging out the door, Daniel tried to see ahead, but fog had unspooled skeins in thick ribbons, and the nearest streetlamp was muted by mist. At the crossroad, carriages bowled along flashing in and out of the pools of light.

"What's going on, guv?" Cadogan shouted as he slapped the reins. "Get up there, girls!"

"Crime in progress!" he shouted back and ducked inside the carriage.

"Who are they?" Ed asked Sir Bertrand.

"I have no idea. I don't associate with random thugs." Sir Bertrand's breath hung in the air, a reminder that none of them, Lady Juliette included, were wearing a cloak.

"Where would they take her?" Daniel asked.

"Again, you are asking the wrong individual. I have no idea those men's identities, nor who hired them. How did you determine the house was in need of guarding tonight? And how did you fail so spectacularly?"

Daniel glared at the aristocrat. How dare he, when he was clearly up to no good himself, blame Daniel and Ed for not stopping mischief they could not have anticipated?

The carriage slowed, and before it stopped, Daniel was once more standing in the open door. "What are you doing? Get after them."

"Guv, they've disappeared." Cadogan waved to the Oxford Road. Carriages bundled by in both directions. "Opera must have finished, and the theaters, not to mention the doings in Vauxhall and Covent Garden. It's the time of night when the roads are the busiest. How can I follow anyone in all this?"

Daniel's stomach plummeted. They'd lost their quarry.

"Guv, we're being followed ourselves." Cadogan pointed his whip behind them.

Another carriage pulled up, and the door opened. The woman in the yellow dress and one of the footmen from the Barrington house sat inside.

Daniel's mouth dropped open as both the footman and the woman removed wigs and false teeth.

"Hello, brother," the footman said. "Seems we cannot leave you for even a fortnight without you getting into trouble."

"Tristan. Melisande." Sir Bertrand shot his cuffs. "Where have you been?"

"Time for all that later. Juliette is in danger. We should convene in the War Room."

Juliette shivered from more than cold. She had no idea where they were. Once the robbers had shoved her into the carriage, they dropped a sack over her head and told her to remain quiet or else.

She could only imagine what "or else" meant.

How had it come to this? Her simple plan to be reunited with her parents, to have a debut season of making friends and enjoying entertainments, of fulfilling all the hopes her long years of schooling had promised, was now dashed to bits, embroiled with espionage, thievery, lies, and now abduction. Her parents, wherever they were, clearly had other priorities than protecting and helping their daughter. She was as alone as she had ever been. *God, are You there? Are You even aware of what is happening to me? Do You care? Can You not be bothered either, to worry about me?*

The sack over her head was full of stale odors, and it trapped her exhalations against her face until she feared she might smother. *Think, girl. Do something to help yourself. There is no one else to aid you.* How long had she been in the carriage? Could she approximate at least a radius from the Barrington house? They hadn't crossed a bridge, and there was other traffic around them.

But she'd been so confused and shocked when they had shoved her into the carriage, she hadn't thought to keep track of time from the beginning of the journey. She had no idea where in London they were. Her hands grew numb, and she crossed her arms, trying to keep warm. The bulk of the men squeezing her between them actually helped, but she was repulsed all the same. She tried to catalog what she knew—their voices, their mannerisms in the Barrington dining room, their movements and speech patterns. Anything that might help her identify them or their destination.

After many turns and changes of pace, the carriage halted, and she was dragged out. Blinded by the sack and gripped hard on her upper arms by two of her captors, she tripped on a step she couldn't see. They hauled her between them, bumping her along. Her feet hit wooden floor, and a door closed behind her.

No light had penetrated the thick sack, and she blinked in the glare of a lamp when the cloth was yanked off her head.

"Sit." One of the men pushed her into a chair while another turned a lamp with a reflector so that the light shone into her eyes. Squinting, she tried to make sense of where she was. To her left was the door they'd come through, flanked by windows on either side, windows with heavy shades pulled. As the men moved about the room, something crunched beneath their feet. Broken glass? Gravel?

"Got what you wanted. Now we want paid."

"You are working to my timetable. You'll get paid when I decide."
A voice came from the shadows behind the light. "Put the candelabras
on the table with the other things."

Boots scraped, and she heard the heavy sound of quality silver hitting a wooden surface. The lamp jumped and flickered.

Odd shapes created dark places on the walls, like paintings, but as
if they were dripping out of the frames. One captor stood behind her,
close enough she could smell the odor of stale sweat and tobacco on
his clothes.

"Lady Juliette, or should I call you Agent Juliette?" His voice was
like silk-wrapped steel, and it cut through the fog in her brain.

"Pardon?"

"Don't play the innocent with me. I'm not stupid. You're the one
behind the thefts. Or rather, your family is. You've beaten me to several pieces, but I managed to procure a few of my own. Did you know
it was your parents' names on the tapestries? I was able to find the code
before it was obliterated."

Juliette thought she might be sick. Who was this man? For whom
did he work? He sounded English.

"I have been thwarted many times, first by Fournier, who coded the
list instead of just giving it to me as he was supposed to do. Then that
British agent who was trailing Fournier tried to stop me. He didn't
manage it, and he died for his trouble. But he did delay me so I wasn't
able to travel with the artwork. Before I could get to London, that idiot
Selby, who wouldn't know a crime if it formed a fist and punched him
in the face, scattered the pieces all over the city. He finally tumbled to
the fact that something illicit was going on, so I had to dispatch him.
But most infuriating were you and your uncle, always a step or two
ahead, stealing things before I could get them. I didn't realize who was
nicking the pieces until the auction house. You made a mistake there,
buying the dragon out in the open like that. Once I had your parents'
names off the tapestry and you buying the dragon, it was plain to see
you and I were after the same thing. The list of spies." He remained

in the shadows, but the whites of his eyes glittered. "My buyer grows impatient. He needs the list before his envoy leaves England, and the day is quickly approaching."

An English traitor to the Crown and a foreign agent colluding.

She wrapped her arms around her middle. The short cap sleeves on her evening dress did little to warm her. At least they hadn't tied her hands.

"You, Reece, deliver the message to the Thorndike home and get back here."

The man he called Reece stepped toward her, grabbed her hand, and wrenched the garnet ring from her finger. She cried out, not from pain but from the loss of her most precious possession.

"Quit bleating," the man in the shadows said. "It's so they will know we're serious and do, in fact, have you in our possession. While Reece is on his little errand, you're going to work."

Reece left through the back. The man standing behind her put his hands on her shoulders, and she flinched. He pressed his icy fingers into her collarbones.

"You are going to decipher the bits of code I managed to get my hands on while we wait for the rest to be delivered." A gloved hand reached out of the darkness and handed her a scrap of dark-brown paper pressed between two sheets of glass. "Here's the first one."

"What makes you think I can decode them? I'm barely out of the schoolroom."

"Don't play games with me. Did you know your friend Miss Montgomery is a fount of information? I put one of my men into her house as a servant, and he listened each afternoon as she took callers. She talked of how your father used to write you letters in code and what fun you had trying to decipher them."

Agatha, what have you done? Juliette hadn't kept her father's letters a secret. Agatha had helped unravel them occasionally.

"If you've already decoded what was on the tapestry, what's stopping you from unraveling this bit yourself? If you found my parents' names, surely you can translate these."

A disturbing chuckle whispered from his lips. "I never said I had decoded what was on the tapestry. I tortured it out of the man who wove it in there. And thank you for confirming what he told me before I sent him into eternity, that your parents are spies for the Crown. Perhaps the other information I got out of him will prove to be true also."

She clamped her teeth shut, pressing her lips firmly. What had Uncle Bertie said? Trust no one. She had trusted that her captor was telling her the truth, but he had been fishing.

He was not only a traitor, thief, and kidnapper, he was also an admitted murderer. The body count was rising. Fournier, Leonidas, and Mr. Selby that he'd admitted to.

"I'll need paper and pen and ink." She must appear to be working, but she must stall as long as possible.

The man behind her let go of her neck and picked up a candle. He lit it from the bright lamp and carried it through a curtained doorway. As he passed, she saw the shapes on the walls. Paintings, but with the canvases shredded and dangling. At her feet, shards of porcelain and glass and chips of stone. Plinths knocked over, a chair that was now nothing more than kindling.

What was this place? And how would Uncle Bertie and Daniel Swann ever find her?

Did God Himself even know where she was?

Daniel's mother opened the front door and stepped back. She stiffened when he followed the earl and countess into the hall. Her split lip had begun to heal, and the bruise along her jaw had turned a pale yellow.

Bertie joined them. "I sent Cadogan to fetch Haverly. We're going to need him."

"What about Mr. Beck? Where is he?" Daniel asked.

"He's keeping watch outside."

"Now see here." Daniel fisted his hands, gripping his truncheon.

"This is a robbery, and what's more, it's a kidnapping. We need to alert the entire police force, every night watchman, every beadle, and every observant street urchin if necessary. None of you seem fazed that Lady Juliette was taken at gunpoint. You're all under arrest for your part in this, and I want to know what is going on here. Who are you people?"

The man dressed as a servant removed his white gloves. "I am the Earl of Thorndike, and this is my countess." He indicated the woman in the bright-yellow food-spattered dress. "This is our home, and it is our daughter who has been taken."

Daniel realized his mouth had fallen open. He strove to gain command of the situation once more. "Sir, you and your wife need to step aside. Sir Bertrand Thorndike, you are under arrest."

The countess stepped forward. "Gentlemen, let's go upstairs and get to work. Mrs. Dunstan, please watch for His Grace and bring him to us the minute he arrives. Young sir, I promise all will be revealed momentarily." She shrugged at her husband and brother-in-law and mounted the stairs.

Who were these people? Why had they appeared in costume? Had Lady Juliette recognized them? Had they been working together from the beginning? Daniel hurried after them, determined not to let Sir Bertrand out of his sight.

He looked back over his shoulder at his mother, standing by the front window so dutifully, and tamped down his frustration. He would get to the bottom of this and find out what role she played in all of it soon. And if speaking with her violated his patron's wishes, so be it. He would have his explanations, especially if it helped rescue a kidnapped noblewoman, even if that noblewoman was a thief and a liar.

At the end of a long, dark hallway, Sir Bertrand pulled on a wall sconce and opened a hidden door. No one else seemed surprised, so Daniel hid his own astonishment. This was a house full of secrets. In single file they mounted a narrow staircase. When they reached the top, Daniel stood on the threshold, unable to conceal his bewilderment.

A vast room that must encompass the entire attic of the mansion opened before him. He could barely take in the contents, but immediately his gaze fell on the Lotto painting standing proudly on an easel.

"I knew it. You're all under arrest." He closed the door and leaned against it, keeping them all in view.

"Stand down, young man. No one is under arrest." The earl stripped off his footman's coat and loosened his cravat. "We're on the same side. We work for His Majesty's government."

"Why are we telling him this? Why did we bring him here?" Sir Bertrand raised his hands. "If we're going to tell all and sundry, we might as well post it in the dailies and be done with it."

"Marcus has had his eye on Mr. Swann for some time, and Mr. Swann is already heavily involved in this case. We had no choice but to bring him in, or else we would have had to disappear him onto a ship bound for Botany Bay." The countess removed her glittering necklace. "Tristan, I'm going to change. This gown is foul. There I was creating the distraction you would need to spirit away the silverware, and it all went for naught. I'm disappointed with you, Bertie."

She went round a corner, and Daniel heard rustling and bumping, as if cupboards were being opened as he tried to digest that the countess had intended to make a diversion at the party. They were all in on the conspiracy together.

"What attire do you think we'll need, and start mapping out where our quarry may have taken Juliette." Her voice sounded muffled. She was remarkably calm for a woman whose daughter had been kidnapped.

Daniel approached the Lotto. Next to it on the table stood the maquette, which he'd never seen but which had been described to him in great detail by its deprived owner, and the jade dragon, which he had seen in Lady Juliette's own hands. And on a square of velvet lay a collection of green and diamond jewelry. The missing parure.

"I assume you didn't need to steal the tapestries and the folio? What about the papyrus and the eagle? Where are those? They, along with the candelabra, fill out the list of items stolen from Turner and Rathbone."

The earl and his brother went still. "How did you get your hands on the list?" the earl asked. "Bertie stole the only known copy the same night he stole the Lotto."

"The question is, how do you know about the inventory list? Did you have to kill Mr. Selby to get your hands on it?"

He hated that his suspicions had come to fruition. Lady Juliette and her family were all thieves and killers. He could only imagine what Sir Michael would say when he brought them into Bow Street in irons. Though how he would accomplish that by himself eluded him for the time being.

"You weren't listening." Sir Bertrand picked up a glass paperweight and tossed it into the air, catching it lightly. "We're agents for His Majesty, not thieves and killers. I did break into Turner and Rathbone and steal their paperwork, but I deny killing Mr. Selby. We've had to acquire the items in that particular shipment, but only temporarily. I assure you that once this is over, all these valuables will be returned to their owners as mysteriously as they were taken. But I am curious how *you* got the contents of the list. I took everything in that office that could pertain to it. Did I miss something?"

"No. You were quite thorough. Please set that paperweight down. I'd not like you to brain me with it." This room was full of potential weapons, and he would have to be on his guard. "My copy was provided to me by the man who purchased the items on the Continent, an assistant at the art dealer's shop. It took him a few days to gather his wits enough to write it out, and it contained dozens of items, but each of the stolen pieces was somewhere on his list."

"You are talking about a list of artwork, but the list we're after is much more important," the earl said. "A French agent named Fournier spent a lifetime compiling a list of spies from various countries. He was growing old, and he wanted to sell the list to finance his retirement. He had a buyer who would be in England for a period of time, and he partnered with a courier to secret the list into the country. He grew to distrust his courier, however, and he encoded the list, concealing it onto pieces of artwork being shipped aboard the *Adventuress*. We sent an agent, code-named Leonidas, to intercept either Fournier or the list, but while he got close, he was unsuccessful. The courier managed to kill both Fournier and Leonidas. What he couldn't do, however, is obtain the coded names from the artwork before it shipped out. Both the courier and ourselves have been in a race to find the pieces."

Sir Bertrand yanked out a letter opener pinning a paper to the wall. "We can only assume that when the courier arrived at the gallery and found the items had already been dispersed to their owners and the inventory lists with those owners' names stolen, he fell into a rage and killed the dealer."

The earl removed his shoes, tossing them aside. "I befriended Mr. Selby when we received a communication from Leonidas that it was his dealership through which the pieces would pass. Fortunately, Selby's skill and enthusiasm for his job coupled with his punctuality in sending out the pieces saved our operation, but it cost him his life. Are you almost finished back there, my love? I'd like to get out of this ridiculous livery."

The countess emerged dressed in black. Her hair was plaited into a thick rope down her back, and she buckled a belt that held a knife.

Daniel began to believe they might be telling him the truth.

"And this man who killed Selby knows about this list of spies, has Lady Juliette and some of the artwork, therefore some of the pieces to the puzzle?" He tried to put it together with what he had worked out about the thefts.

"Yes. We watched his henchmen leave with two of the pieces tonight. There was code embedded on those candelabra, thus our interest in obtaining them. They have four or five bits of the code, but we cannot yet tell if they've deciphered any of them. That must be why they took Juliette. They think she can give them the codes we have here and possibly help them work out the solutions." Sir Bertrand set the letter opener on the desk.

"Who is he?" Daniel asked. "And how do we find him?"

"That's the question, isn't it? We've no idea at this point."

Chapter 16

JULIETTE WAS GIVEN A LAMP, paper, and quill and moved into a small office of some sort. One of the kidnappers put a bottle of ink on the table, and another put the scrap of ancient script and the alabaster eagle in front of her.

The mysterious man, who remained in the shadows of the front room, said, "You've got two hours, maybe three, until my contact arrives. He . . . and I . . . will expect answers by then."

"That's ridiculous. I've been trying to break this code for more than a fortnight, and have only managed—" She broke off, remembering she wasn't going to speak.

"Managed what?"

"To get nowhere," she mumbled.

"Somehow I don't believe that. What names have you found?"

She said nothing, holding her fingers out to the candle flame to try to warm them enough to hold the quill. Mere hours to get the answers to questions she'd been asking herself for weeks?

"The clock is ticking. I suggest you get to work."

Examining the papyrus fragment was difficult in such low light, but she eventually found the code, written in the same brownish black ink as the hieroglyphs. It was minute, and she wished she had a quizzing glass and bright sunlight. The glare off the sheets of glass had her double-checking that she had it right. What good would it do her to copy the code if she couldn't see it clearly?

The same style of groupings of five characters, letters, numbers, and symbols intermingled.

The eagle revealed another string of characters, etched along the underside of one wing, barely visible and found only because she ran her fingertips lightly over every surface.

She copied the code, in the groups of five, and then as two lines with no breaks.

"Don't forget the candelabras." His voice slithered through the doorway, and one of his henchmen brought them to her.

They were as heavy as she'd feared, and she doubted she would have been able to remove even one of them from the Barringtons' dining room by herself. Perhaps it was providential that she hadn't been forced to try.

Examining them required her to stand, but the moment she moved, the heavy hand slammed down on her shoulder and pinned her in the chair. Her teeth rattled, and her backside stung.

"Don't move."

"I merely wanted to inspect them." She indicated the delicate silver arms ending in rounded cups that extended above her head when she sat. "I can't see in this low light. Give me more lamps, and let me stand up to look these over, or I cannot do what you want." She tried to sound reasonable, but fear thinned her voice.

"Let her look, but keep an eye on her." The leader moved away from the doorway and farther into the front room. What was he doing out there? Was his vigilance in not letting her see his face a good sign? If she couldn't identify him, perhaps he would release her when he got what he wanted.

If she could deliver it to him. If she failed, she had a feeling he wouldn't take that kindly. She concentrated on the task. Yet if she gave him the names, she would be betraying those agents.

God, tell me what to do. Help me. At least help me find what I'm looking for here.

Within seconds, her fingertips brushed the code, etched into the undersides of the fluted edges of the cups.

Had God just answered her prayers, or was it a coincidence? Perhaps He hadn't abandoned her after all.

―――――※―――――

Footsteps thudded on the stairs and Daniel stiffened, gripping his truncheon and moving to stand behind the door.

Tense as bowstrings, they waited, and when the door opened, the earl lowered his pistol.

The Duke of Haverly walked in, his cloak—a disreputable thing no aristocrat would willingly wear—swinging about him. He carried a stone in one palm. "Special delivery."

A blonde woman followed him into the room, and the countess held out her hands. "Charlotte, I'm so glad you're here."

"Marcus said Juliette was in trouble. Of course I had to come. He also mentioned a bit of code-breaking to be done."

"And that's all you'll be doing, my dear. You'll stay here and work on the code." The duke's expression forbade argument.

This must be his duchess. Who else would he address so? And just how many people were in this ring of spies?

Where had he seen that cloak before? He walked back through his memories and went still. He'd seen that cloak in The Hog's Head. The dangerous man seated in the corner. Could it have been? Surely not . . .

The duchess rolled her eyes and looked to the countess. "I've only just informed him that we will be adding a much-anticipated 'spare' to our 'heir,' and he's broken out in overprotective chivalry."

"Congratulations, and in that case, I agree. You will remain here." The countess gave her a quick hug.

The duke noticed Daniel, and his brows rose. "It appears we have a visitor." He slanted a glance at Sir Bertrand and Earl Thorndike, who had just rounded the dressing screen, attired in dark clothing and tucking a pistol into his waistband.

"And a welcome one. I knew you'd had your eye on him, especially given his relationship to our housekeeper. It seemed a prudent time to bring him into the fold." The earl stamped his feet into boots and shrugged into a coat.

Daniel sagged against a table. They knew? About his mother? What else did they know?

Was it possible that one of them was his mysterious patron? Was that how his mother, a country housemaid, had ended up employed here? He looked from one face to another, but no one gave anything away.

"We'll go into all that later." The duke held up the rock. "This crashed through your front window moments ago, along with a note. And a token."

Instinctively, Daniel reached for it first and then stayed his hand as the earl took the paper and read aloud.

"Bring the artifacts and shed the Bow Street men. Put the crate on a wagon and leave both behind the German embassy in Knightsbridge within two hours, or the lady gets a quick trip to the bottom of the river. If we get the artwork and the rest of the codes, and she unlocks the names, we'll turn her loose. If not, goodbye lady." He held up Juliette's garnet ring.

The countess showed the first bit of emotion, blinking quickly as she took the ring from her husband's hand and slipped it on her finger.

"Well, that's unacceptable." Haverly reached up and untied the queue of hair at the nape of his neck and shook out the brown locks, totally transforming his appearance.

"Is Juliette being held in the German embassy?" the duchess asked.

"Doubtful." The duke studied the note. "I propose we go down and interrogate the messenger."

"You have him?" Daniel asked.

"It was his misfortune to arrive nearly at the same time as I, and that we had a Bow Street constable watching the house. Mr. Beck is holding our rock-throwing vandal in the study as we speak."

In the study, Ed stood near a man trussed to a chair. The room had been returned to order after the break-in, but the door to the hidden safe hung open, broken beyond repair, awaiting replacement.

The earl eyed it as he took up a position across from the messenger. "Constable Beck, nice to see you again." The duke nodded.

How well did Ed know the duke? Did he know they were all spies? Surely not, else he would have told Daniel or turned the investigation away from the agents.

Daniel focused on the prisoner. "He was at Barringtons'. He's one of the men who took Lady Juliette." Daniel reached out with his truncheon and lifted the man's chin with the brass knobbed end. "He held the pistol on Ed."

"So he did." Ed rubbed his temple.

"Ladies, I would prefer if you went back upstairs." Sir Bertrand nodded toward the door. "This man is about to disgrace himself, and I'm sure it would be an added blow to his pride to do so in front of you."

Daniel held the door for them, nodding a bow as they swept past into the foyer.

"Don't make a mess, darling," the countess called back over her shoulder. "But get what you need. Juliette awaits us."

As it turned out, they needn't have sent the women away. The miscreant took one look at the five men ranged against him and burst like an overstuffed sausage. Within ten minutes, Daniel sent Ed to Bow Street with the prisoner, and the rest made preparations to leave for Clerkenwell.

To the gallery of Turner and Rathbone. Daniel felt as if he had come full circle.

They left the Duchess of Haverly busy with pen and ink and the code words Lady Juliette had worked on for the past fortnight. The earl had lingered a long moment, staring at the written code, his eyes narrowed, before his wife's touch on his arm turned him away.

Daniel now hunched over on the wagon seat. He was the decoy, tasked with getting close without drawing suspicion. Dressed as a laborer, with tools and boards rattling in the wagon bed, he was supposed to drive up and make a considerable racket, allowing the others to sneak into the Turner and Rathbone shop the back way. Sir Bertrand had firsthand knowledge of the layout of the building, and he would lead the charge.

The carriage with the four others left first, and Daniel urged the horses to hurry. Clerkenwell was a fair distance, especially on a foggy night. Traffic had lessened to the point of disappearing, but he would still be on the outer edge of the time allowed. Hopefully, Juliette was stalling and the kidnappers wouldn't act precipitously.

He considered all the new information he'd had thrown at him in the last few hours. The Duke of Haverly knew who his mother was. And she knew . . . what? That the people she worked for were Crown spies? What was her status? Was she a spy? Was that why she'd abandoned him to someone else's remote care? To work for the government?

The countess had said the duke had long had an eye on Daniel. For what purpose? Was the Duke of Haverly his mysterious patron? Doing sums, he thought not. The duke would have been twenty-three or twenty-four when Daniel was sent away from his home. And he had been a second son, not the duke at that time. Had he served in the military, as so many second sons did? He would have been on the Continent when Daniel went to school. That would take him out of the running to be the patron, wouldn't it?

What about the earl? He was old enough to have taken on the care of a young boy thirteen years ago, however unorthodox the fashion, and it was his house in which Daniel's mother was employed.

Had his mother known the earl before she was hired? Was it possible the earl could be his father?

Daniel rejected that notion so hard it made him sit upright on the wagon seat. No. He refused to believe it.

And yet someone, somewhere had fathered him. And his patron was someone of means and influence. He'd gone to the best schools, and he'd been given the best clothes, and he'd been given the job of his choice over the smarting body of his boss.

If the earl was his father, that would make Lady Juliette his . . . half sister?

No. He didn't want the Earl of Thorndike to be his father.

Why did he continue to wonder? His mother had refused to answer his little-boy questions, and when he saw how much his asking hurt her, he had ceased. But he never stopped wondering.

God, You say You are the Father to the fatherless, but I feel You are just as unknown and unknowable as the man who sired me. If You are truly capable of interceding on behalf of men here on earth, please, help me rescue Lady Juliette and return her safely home.

As he reached the street where Turner and Rathbone was situated, he slowed. It was well past midnight, and even the pub was closed tight. No light shone from any window, and he kept his head down and his shoulders hunched. He eyed the central door between the two windows—shades pulled and no light around the edges.

A heap of darkness crouched in the angle of the steps of the neighboring shop.

It was barely over a fortnight since he and Ed had entered Turner and Rathbone Dealers in Fine Arts through the back door to find Mr. Selby murdered and the place ransacked. What would he find when he entered this time?

He pulled the horses up and leapt to the ground, his boots skidding on the frost-rimed cobbles. Picking up a toolbox from the wagon bed, he strode to the door. Selecting a large mallet, he pounded on the face frame beside the glass.

The noise was tremendous, and he accompanied it with some truly terrible singing.

The door wrenched open, as he had known it would. And he stared at the barrel of a pistol. He could see no face, only the sinister round opening. A feeling of familiarity swept over him. Not three hours ago, he'd been in this same position in a well-lit reception room.

"Get out of here," the voice hissed.

"I'm working!" he bawled. "Hired to fix this place up so the owner can rent it out."

"It's the middle of the night, you fool. Get away!"

Bending to the box at his feet, he threw the mallet, as if disgusted. And when he stood, he held his own pistol. "Drop it."

The hand jerked, and he flattened to the ground. The blast of the gun ricocheted through the street, and the smell of gunpowder filled the air.

To his side, the duke unfolded from the darkness and barged through the doorway, his gun out. Daniel followed him, low and quick.

Their feet crunched on the broken glass and stone, but with their eyes well adjusted to the dark, they saw their quarry slip through the open doorway that led to the office. Through the doorway, Daniel glimpsed Juliette at a table, her hand poised, holding a quill, and her eyes luminous.

A large man stood behind her, and in a flash he assessed the situation and hauled her up before him. The man who had fired at Daniel ran for the storage area, but he skidded to a halt when the earl and Sir Bertrand blocked his way.

"There's no way out. Keep your hands where I can see them." Sir Bertrand was as cool as a February morning.

Lady Juliette struggled in the grasp of her captor, but he held firm. "Father!"

"Jules-girl. Are you unharmed?" He kept his eyes on the man before him. "Turn around," the earl ordered.

Shock hit Daniel square in the chest.

Mr. Rickets.

The nervous, shattered assistant who had just returned from his first buying expedition to the Continent.

His eyes blazed, no longer the frail man on the verge of tears at the loss of his employer. His lips a rictus of anger.

"Is Mother all right?" Juliette asked.

Daniel took a step back to keep both Rickets and the man holding Juliette in clear view. He forced down his anger at the man's hands on her. He must remain calm. Though he held his pistol up, he kept it aimed just to the left. He daren't shoot, for fear of hitting Juliette.

"Your mother's fine, lass. She'll join us shortly." The earl used his knife point to urge Mr. Rickets farther into the office.

"Where are the other two?" Daniel asked.

"Let's just say that when they wake up, they'll have massive head-aches," Sir Bertrand said dryly. "We had the lock picked in the back door before you pounded on the front. Excellent job creating a diver-sion, by the way. Both those gentlemen tried to escape into the mews, but by now they're trussed up like Christmas pudding in the storage room. A specialty of my sister-in-law's." He actually chuckled. "Tying up bad men, not making Christmas pudding."

Lady Thorndike came into the room, surveying the tableau. "I'm a fair hand at Christmas pudding too. Those men won't be bothering anyone for some time." She put her hands on her hips. "Well, why hasn't someone done something about him?" She indicated the large man using her daughter as a shield.

"I'm getting out of here. I'll turn her loose when I'm away."

"Don't be a fool. There's no way out. We've caught your compatri-ots, and you'll be in Newgate before the sun rises. Unless you'd rather visit the morgue." Again Sir Bertrand's voice was cool, almost as if he were disinterested.

A long look passed between Sir Bertrand and Lady Juliette, and he winked.

How could he wink at such a time? Didn't he realize the peril his niece was in?

So quickly that Daniel barely tracked the movement, Lady Juliette struck with the quill she held, slamming the nib into the man's thigh and twisting away as his howl filled the small space.

Sir Bertrand's boot flashed out, kicking the gun, and he whirled in the same motion and sank his elbow into the man's midsection. A gust of air shot out, and the kidnapper dropped to his knees, one hand on his gut and one hand gripping the quill embedded in his leg.

The earl took a length of rope from his pocket and handed it to his brother. While the earl continued to hold his pistol on Rickets, Sir Bertrand tied the art buyer's hands behind his back and pushed him into a kneeling position. Next he tied the wounded man in a similar fashion.

"Cease your yowling, man. It's unseemly in front of the women." He nudged the man, leaned over, and yanked the quill from the wound.

Lady Juliette was in her mother's embrace, and Daniel couldn't tell if she was laughing or crying. The earl joined his family, wrapping them both in his arms.

Family. Clearly they had a close bond. Daniel felt a jealous pang that he thrust away as unworthy of the moment. But he couldn't deny that he would like to have felt the loving embrace of a parent sometime in the last decade or so.

He noted that Lady Juliette avoided looking at the injured man. There was blood enough to make Daniel wince. He couldn't imagine what Lady Juliette would do if she looked at it.

The Duke of Haverly stuck his pistol into his belt and slid his watch into his hand, holding the face toward the lamplight. "I would suggest we load this flotsam into the wagon and remove ourselves from the premises. We've made a fair bit of noise, and though London residents are famous for not wanting to investigate suspicious actions in the dead of night, the watchman will no doubt be making his rounds soon."

Lady Juliette raised her head from her father's shoulder.

"Uncle Bertie, you were right. Anything *can* be a weapon."

———

While the rest went back to their homes to get some sleep, Daniel went to Bow Street with his prisoners. Tired but on edge, he allowed Owen and Ed to help him get the men into a holding room as the sun rose, glittering off the fog. The prisoners would make an appearance in front of the magistrate before being toted off to Newgate to await trial.

Despite the early hour, the office was stirring to life with detectives arriving and clerks and court employees milling about. When Daniel walked four suspects into the room, heads turned and conversations ceased.

Sir Michael, informed that arrests had been made, waited for Daniel and Ed in his office.

"Gentlemen. It would appear you've had a busy night. I trust the case has been cleared up?" Sir Michael lowered himself into his chair and steepled his fingers.

"We caught the thieves in the act. They had several of the stolen items in their possession, as well as holding Lady Juliette Thorndike captive. They were apprehended at the Turner and Rathbone gallery. We do not believe there are any more accomplices at large." Daniel held his truncheon behind his back crossways, gripping either end.

"Sir Michael." Ed took the chair their boss indicated. "The lad handled himself well throughout the investigation, and it's due to his actions that the men were apprehended and the lady rescued. Her parents and uncle are most appreciative."

Not squirming required concentration. The Duke of Haverly had impressed upon Daniel that he must take the credit and that the case must be viewed as a simple crime solved by the police. The criminals had stolen the artwork and had murdered Mr. Selby to cover their crimes. He must keep the spy element out of the proceedings, especially from Mr. Beck and Sir Michael. Mr. Rickets would certainly not brag about being a traitor to the Crown.

Though Daniel had protested that it wasn't right to take credit that wasn't his, the duke insisted, and the Thorndikes supported him.

"I must say . . ." Sir Michael jarred Daniel's thoughts back to the present. "Though it took you longer than I initially hoped, and the case was more complex and extended further than anticipated, you've done well." He nodded grudgingly. "I've heard from my superiors that you are to be commended. Instructions have also come down that the trials for these gentlemen will be swift and private. They are undoubtedly guilty. If the thieves plead to the charges, they will be deported to Australia rather than executed." He checked a paper on his desk. "The leader, Mr. Rickets, will be tried and executed for the murder he confessed to committing. Both of you may be required to testify tomorrow. Until then, deliver the prisoners to Newgate. The trial will be held at the prison tomorrow morning at ten."

Swift justice indeed.

As Ed rose to leave, Sir Michael said, "Mr. Swann, please remain."

Ed clapped Daniel on the shoulder and closed the door on his way out.

The morning sun slanted in the windows behind Sir Michael, putting him somewhat in shadow, and Daniel waited, hearing the tick of the clock and the underlying hum of people in the building. Somewhere a door slammed.

"Solving this case has garnered the attention of my superiors right up the chain. The note I received this morning about the case and your involvement came from the Home Secretary Viscount Sidmouth himself, though how he came to know of the events so quickly is beyond me. He congratulates me on employing such fine and clever officers, but most of the praise is heaped in your direction. I assume the Thorndikes showed their appreciation? How much did they give you?"

It was not uncommon for those aided by a Bow Street officer to show their gratitude with monetary gifts, but Daniel had never shared the amount he'd received before. None of the officers did. It was an unwritten rule that went a long way toward quelling jealousy in the detectives' room. Not that Daniel had ever received enough to brag about.

"Sir, they have not given remuneration, nor did I ask."

"Matter of time, I suppose. Not to mention all the stolen goods you'll be returning today. I imagine there will be a tidy sum when it's all said and done. Enough to support you in the interim if you should seek another line of work?"

A laugh tried to emerge, but Daniel throttled it. So that was what this was all about. Sir Michael could hardly terminate his employment now, not when his higher ups had praised them both. But if Daniel were to voluntarily quit Bow Street . . .

"Sir, I cannot imagine a job I would enjoy more. I look forward to working with you for years to come."

He let a broad smile take over his face as he closed the door, whistling as he went down the hall, twirling his truncheon on its loop.

Chapter 17

Juliette pushed a strand of hair off her face and sat back, pressing her hands into her lower spine. "I've become as limber as an axe handle sitting here for so long."

"But we've done it. We cracked the encoded names, and now we have the entire list. Thanks to you and Charlotte." Her father nodded his thanks to his helpers.

The door opened, and Mother stepped inside the War Room. She looked as fresh and beautiful as always. Uncle Bertie, the Duke of Haverly, and Mr. Swann followed her.

"I believe we've done it. We've transcribed the list of international agents." Father presented the list to Marcus with a flourish. "Agent Leonidas did not die in vain. We have recovered the names."

Marcus took the paper, his face sober as he read. "We would all have been at great risk if Rickets had managed to complete his mission." He folded the page and tucked it inside his coat. "Mr. Rickets surrendered the name of the man to whom he had promised the list. A Russian diplomat who was not on anyone's watch list but who will be leaving the country with all haste."

"The trial was short, and they only called one witness, our Mr. Swann here." Uncle Bertie smoothed his hair back, breathing deeply. "We did not stay for the execution."

"You've removed the codes from the pieces?" Marcus asked.

"Those we have access to at the moment. Someone will have to tend to the folio." Father began cleaning their work area, tapping papers together and stoppering ink bottles.

"I suppose that falls to me. It should be simple enough." Uncle Bertie perched on a stool, his feet on the stretchers, elegant in spite of his casual pose. "A single night."

"I could join you again," Juliette suggested with a grin.

"No, thank you. Now that your parents are home, you can undergo proper training. The emergency has passed, and you will not be doing any fieldwork for some time." He leaned over and tweaked her nose.

She swatted his hand away.

Now that her parents were here. She could still barely believe it. "I keep pinching myself. I was so devastated when you weren't here to meet my ship. I thought you didn't care enough. That you were putting the needs of the estate before me. I'm sorry I doubted you." *And I'm sorry I doubted You, too, God. I can see I have some way to grow in both my spycraft and my faith.*

"We were sorry not to be able to greet you, but we were never far away, my dear." Her father smiled. "Your mother makes a very good Russian aristocrat with a penchant for Borzoi dogs. And she's adept with a shillelagh as an Irish peasant. And an Austrian woman in bright yellow who trips and falls to create a diversion."

Juliette straightened. "You what?"

"Ah yes." Mother laughed. "And your father is skilled at tossing cats into ballrooms where I happen to be holding onto a brace of hounds, as well as portraying dark strangers in the rookeries to direct you toward the correct receiver's shop. And he's an excellent footman, whether at Mr. Montgomery's for your debut or the Barringtons' for what turned out to be a really dreadful concert. It's all a matter of clothing and wigs and makeup, but beyond that, accents, movements, mannerisms." She shrugged. "People see what they expect to see and rarely look below the surface."

Juliette felt warmed and a bit frustrated. If she had known, it would have saved her a lot of heartache and doubt, and yet she had been under her parents' care the entire time. A small nudge at her heart reminded her—she had been under God's care the entire time as well. Now that she knew and was part of their secret world, she could see how her dream of getting to know them as their adult daughter would take on whole new realms. And not only them, but her heavenly Father as well.

"Detective Swann here will return the stolen items to their owners today as the conclusion to a successful investigation by the Bow Street detectives." Marcus nodded to him. "The newspapers will report that Mr. Swann and Mr. Beck have solved the case of the thefts and the murder, and we will return to normal. Now, I believe we should disperse. It's time you, Lord and Lady Thorndike, resumed ushering your daughter through her debut season. According to my mother, who stood in as her chaperone, there's a certain German duke who is showing quite the interest in Lady Juliette."

Heads turned, and Juliette's skin heated. She had no interest in the duke. Or anyone really. Her life had changed in unexpected ways over the last month, and she wanted time to adapt to those changes.

But her glance landed on Daniel Swann, and their eyes locked. For a long moment, no one said a word, and then he turned away, pushing himself to his feet.

Would she see him again?

She couldn't deny her interest in him, but should she? He was handsome, intelligent, capable, and brave. With him she felt valuable and protected. He had come after her, aided in her rescue, and the duke seemed to hold him in high regard.

She shrugged. They had known each other for less than a month, and he'd tried to arrest her for theft. It would be foolish to think a deeper relationship could grow out of such a rocky beginning. She would do well to remember that.

Yet she couldn't help but feel that future adventures awaited them . . . possibly together?

Epilogue

DANIEL WISHED HE COULD SHED his feeling of heaviness. He'd delivered the stolen goods to their grateful owners, and he'd even managed to remove the coded bit from the folio box before Sir Bertrand needed to break into the house once again, because of course Lord Gravesend had shown him the Shakespeare book when he'd returned the parure.

And as Sir Michael had predicted, the victims of the crimes had rewarded him handsomely and would not take seriously his protests that they owed him nothing. His bank balance was very tidy at the moment.

Rickets had been executed for murder and treason by His Majesty's government.

As Sir Michael had also predicted, the accomplices had pled guilty and would be leaving on the next ship bound for the Antipodes.

Daniel strode down Piccadilly toward an address given to him by the Duke of Haverly as he'd left the Thorndike house two days ago. There had been the location and a time and nothing else.

As he neared the middle of the block, he discovered that the address was for a bookshop. Hatchards. Dark-green paint, gilded lettering, and a royal coat of arms over the door.

Puzzled, he stepped inside and inhaled the scent of knowledge and adventure. It took him back to his days at Oxford, of practically living in The Bodleian as he completed his studies.

The shopkeeper looked up from his desk. "Help you, sir?"

"I'll just take a look about, if you don't mind?"

"By all means."

He wandered down a row of shelves, touching a spine here or there, seeing some old friends from his student days, but far more strangers he'd love to explore. Perhaps he would use some of his reward money to begin his library.

Reaching the end of a row, he paused. Was he supposed to wait for the duke here? Or someone else? The reading room, perhaps? He was on time for the appointment, whatever it was.

The bell over the door jangled, and he turned. The duke had arrived, his black cloak swinging about him and his boots gleaming against his white breeches. He nodded to the clerk, removed his hat, and started down the aisle. As he approached, he put his finger to his lips for silence.

Daniel nodded.

Reaching above Daniel's head, he took a book from the shelf and laid it flat on the top, the spine showing. Wollstonecraft.

Checking first one way, then the other, the duke withdrew a key and put it into the lock on a door that said "Employees Only" in bold letters. They entered a narrow hallway that led immediately to a set of stairs. Daniel followed slowly. With the door to the bookshop closed, the steps were in utter darkness.

A feeling of uneasiness crept over him, and he reached for his truncheon. Did every spy for the Crown have a secret lair? He felt his way up the stairs behind the duke.

The duke's hand came out to stop him. "Wait here."

He heard keys again, and another door opened. The low glow of a banked fire in a fireplace cast the room with a faint orange glow. He sniffed. Stale coffee and old smoke.

The duke lit a taper from the coals and used it to light several lamps. As he moved about the room, Daniel took note of the details. Paneled walls, muted carpet, a large desk, and two well-worn chairs.

File cabinets stood like soldiers along one wall, and no windows let in light. A grate high on the wall brought in fresh air.

"Sit."

"Your Grace, what is this about?"

"A few matters I wish to discuss with you in private." He flipped the tails on his coat and sat behind the desk.

Daniel perched on the edge of the soft chair.

"You've a quick mind, good skills, and bravery. I would like to utilize them. I want you to work for me."

He studied his hands, playing for time. Give up Bow Street? After he'd fought so hard to earn his place there? "In what capacity, milord?"

The duke smiled and leaned back, his fingers running along his watch chain. "Did you imagine I was interviewing you to be my new valet? As an agent for the Crown, of course."

"I already have a job. One not easy to procure." Or to hold onto, if Sir Michael ever got his way.

"I know of Sir Michael's vagaries. He's a prickly employer, but you manage him well. I don't want you to quit your work at Bow Street. It's the perfect cover actually. You have contacts throughout London, and you are privy to information that flows through the magistrate's court daily. Information is the coin of the realm in spy work. We can hone your skills, train you where you are in need. You will continue to act as a detective, and you will also be available to work for me when needed."

Daniel considered the offer. It seemed the best of both worlds. He would continue to serve the people of London and the surrounding areas, but he could also serve his country in a bigger way.

"You're soon to be twenty-five, are you not?"

"Yes. In about a month. March 20."

"And your status will change. You will no longer be supported by your patron."

How do you know that?

"Once that change occurs, you will be free to converse with your mother. I was never in favor of that particular clause in the bargain. Most cruel to both of you, but there you are. Your patron was adamant, I understand."

"Do you know who he is?"

"I am not at liberty to say. After your birthday, will you meet with your mother?"

He sat still, his muscles tense. "I don't know. She abandoned me, turned me away without a backward glance, and in all the years we've been apart, she's never once tried to contact me." Though he longed for a repaired relationship, would he ever be able to trust her again? If it suited her, would she again drop him like a hot rock? Surely he was better off on his own, not putting his trust in anyone fully.

"That would have violated the agreement, and you would no longer have been cared for in such a comfortable manner."

"Perhaps it was not so comfortable. It was lonely and confusing and hurtful to know that my mother couldn't wait to be shed of me." In his mind he saw that scared little boy, stifling his tears in a pillow lest the other boys in the dormitory overhear and torture him with it. He saw that lonely boy staying at the school when all the other students went home for holidays.

"See it from her side. You were an illegitimate child of a barely paid servant girl. She could hardly afford to feed and clothe you. She felt she was giving you a better life."

"She was giving herself a better life." He clung stubbornly to what he knew to be true.

"Just talk to her. If there's anything I've learned from being a married man, it's that there is always more than one side of a story."

"You have a child, correct?"

"Yes, a son."

"Could you ever imagine sending him away? Giving him over to strangers? What if he said he would rather be poor and feel loved than rich and alone?"

"I will acknowledge it was difficult for you, but if you think it wasn't difficult for her, you would be naïve. Give it some thought. Both talking to your mother and coming to work for me."

Daniel knew he'd been dismissed, and he stood, bowed, and went to the door. As he exited the bookstore, he noticed Cadogan at the curb. He began to suspect that the driver might also be an employee of the Crown, with all his tidy appearances. Either that or he followed Daniel for reasons of his own.

"Need a ride?"

"Bow Street. No rush." Daniel climbed inside, too tired to care about the jarvey for the moment.

If he did sign on to work for Haverly, he might see Lady Juliette from time to time.

That might be all the incentive he needed to take the duke up on his offer.

Perhaps he and Juliette had a future together after all, even if it was one of protecting England and her secrets.

He could live with that.

For now.

Acknowledgments

SPECIAL THANKS TO JOE AMBROSE, mathematician and nephew extraordinaire.

Thank you to my fabulous editors, Janyre Tromp and Dori Harrell, who with patience and great skill have helped me wrestle this manuscript into something hopefully worth reading.

Thanks must also go to my writing sisters at Seekerville, and to Gabrielle Meyer, who encourage, cheer, and occasionally just tell me to get on with it!

And many thanks to my patient husband, Peter, who was with me every step of the way as I struggled to write when the world seemed upside down. He encouraged me to keep my eyes on Jesus and my nose to the grindstone, and for that I am so grateful.

Author's Note

DEAR READER,

Plumbing the historical riches of the Regency era is an unending adventure. The more I read, the more I discover in this fascinating period. The world of Regency spies, intrigue, and espionage is fertile ground for the imagination. I beg the reader's indulgence as pertains to my depiction of the Bow Street Magistrate's Court and its famous detectives. The police force in London was in its infancy during the Regency period, and I've accelerated some of the abilities of the Bow Street detectives for the sake of the story. *Mea culpa.*

The art and artifacts portrayed in the book mostly have their origins in reality.

- The Lorenzo Lotto painting *Messer Marsilio Cassotti and his Wife Faustina* hangs in The Museo del Prado in Madrid, Spain. https://en.wikipedia.org/wiki/Portrait_of_Marsilio_Cassotti_and_His_Bride_Faustina.
- Donatello's *Saint Mark* is a marble statue now found in the museum of the Orsanmichele church, in Florence, Italy. A copy is located on the exterior of the building where the original once stood. The maquette in this story is fictional. https://en.wikipedia.org/wiki/Saint_Mark_(Donatello).
- The Brussels tapestries are based upon several examples from

the times, including the Medieval Brussels Tapestry in the Louvre, Paris, France. https://www.louvre.fr/en/oeuvre-notices /hunts-maximilian-month-september.

- The jade dragon is based upon an object sold by Morgan and Beeston Antiques and Fine Art in the UK. http://www.antiques -atlas.com/morganbeestonantiques/browse.php?code=as593a003.
- Egyptian papyri were sold frequently as souvenirs of trips to Egypt. With the discovery of the Rosetta Stone in 1799, one of the great mysteries of the ancient world was unlocked. You can learn more about papyrus as art at https://www.metmuseum.org /art/collection/search/544773.
- The alabaster eagle was created in my mind from the carved feathers on the *Winged Victory of Samothrace*. It's a favorite statue of mine but much too large to include in the Thorndike's stolen artwork collection. You can learn more about the *Winged Victory* at https://en.wikipedia.org/wiki/Winged_Victory_of_Samothrace.
- The Shakespearian folio is based upon the 1623 edition, which resides in The Bodleian Library in Oxford, UK. You can learn more about the folio and view the digital copy at The Bodleian First Folio, a digital facsimile of the First Folio of Shakespeare's plays, Bodleian Arch. G c.7. Title: First Folio home page. https:// firstfolio.bodleian.ox.ac.uk/.
- The peridot parure was included in the story because I love learning new words, and *parure* was a new one to me a few years ago. I made the set peridot and diamond in honor of my mother, Esther, whose birthstone is peridot. You can view an example of a peridot parure in this article from *The Daily Mail*: https:// www.dailymail.co.uk/news/article-2231487/Fetching-princely -sum-Auction-stunning-jewellery-owned-English-royalty-help -monks-raise-30-000-pay-monastery-repairs.html.
- The silver candelabra are fashioned after a pair I saw at the James J. Hill house in St. Paul, Minnesota. You can view the candelabra at the Hill House, or see them online here: https://www .mnhs.org/preserve/conservation/candelabras.php.

Other tidbits:

- I own a letter opener like Bertie Thorndike's, fashioned like a medieval sword (in my case, the famed Excalibur). I've not yet tried to hurl it at the wall like a dagger, but you never know.
- *The Complete Body of Heraldry* by Joseph Edmonson is a real book with stunning illuminations.
- Fore-Edge painting on books is a beautiful art. There are many fine examples online, and you can learn about the technique from a fore-edge painting artist here: https://www.foredgefrost.co.uk/.

REGENCY MYSTERIES

DON'T MISS BOOK TWO . . .

Millstone of Doubt

A body is discovered in the rubble after a mill explosion . . . but it may have been murder, not tragic accident, which took his life. Can Thorndike and Swann find the killer—or will their own pasts get in the way of solving this mystery?

Return to Regency England with Erica Vetsch and the Serendipity & Secrets series

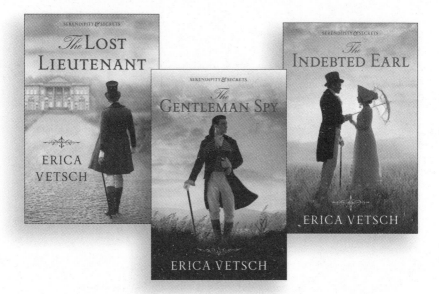

"Vetsch's impeccable research and compelling Regency voice have made Serendipity and Secrets one of the strongest offerings in inspirational historical romance in years."

—Rachel McMillan, author of *The London Restoration* and *The Mozart Code*

"I love the way Erica Vetsch creates characters I care about. Get them deep into trouble, and in the end, loyalty, bravery, love, and faith save the day."

—Mary Connealy, author of *Braced for Love*

"Vetsch's rich writing and carefully crafted stories sweep the reader into Regency England with all the delights of this fascinating genre."

—Jan Drexler, award-winning author of *Softly Blows the Bugle*